SCARY OUT THERE

SCARY OUT THERE

EDITED BY

Jonathan Maberry

STORIES BY

Linda Addison • Ilsa J. Bick • Kendare Blake

Zac Brewer • Rachel Caine • Christopher Golden

Nancy Holder • Ellen Hopkins • Josh Malerman

Cherie Priest • Madeleine Roux • Carrie Ryan

Jade Shames • Neal & Brendan Shusterman

Marge Simon • Lucy A. Snyder • R. L. Stine

Rachel Tafoya • Steve Rasnic Tem

Tim Waggoner • Brenna Yovanoff

SIMON & SCHUSTER BFYR

NEW YORK   LONDON   TORONTO   SYDNEY   NEW DELHI

SIMON & SCHUSTER BFYR

An imprint of Simon & Schuster Children's Publishing Division
1230 Avenue of the Americas, New York, New York 10020

Library of Congress Cataloging-in-Publication Data
Names: Maberry, Jonathan, editor of compilation. | Addison, Linda (Poet), author.
Title: Scary out there / edited by Jonathan Maberry ; stories by Linda Addison [and 21 others].
Description: First edition. | New York, New York : SSBFYR, [2016] |
Summary: "Multiple Bram Stoker Award–winning author Jonathan Maberry compiles more
than twenty stories and poems—written by members of the Horror Writers Association—in
this terrifying collection about worst fears"—Provided by publisher.
Identifiers: LCCN 2015044921| ISBN 9781481450706 (hardback) | ISBN 9781481450720 (eBook)
Subjects: LCSH: Horror tales, American. | Horror poetry, American. | Short stories,
American. | Poetry, American. | CYAC: Horror stories. | Short stories. | American poetry. |
BISAC: JUVENILE FICTION / Short Stories. |
JUVENILE FICTION / Horror & Ghost Stories. | JUVENILE FICTION / Monsters.
Classification: LCC PZ5 .S325 2016 | DDC [Fic]—dc23
LC record available at https://lccn.loc.gov/2015044921

To the memory of Rocky Wood (1959–2014)—former
president of the Horror Writers Association,
Bram Stoker Award–winning author, and a great friend.
We love you and miss you.
And we wonder what strange adventures you're having now!

And, as always, to Sara Jo.

ACKNOWLEDGMENTS

This project would not have been possible without the help of the Horror Writers Association (www.horror.org) and its members: President Lisa Morton, Leslie S. Klinger, Kate Jonez, and Catherine Scully.

Thanks to our agent, Sara Crowe of Harvey Klinger, Inc.; and thanks to David Gale, Liz Kossnar, Laurent Linn, and all of the folks at Simon & Schuster Books for Young Readers. And a particular thanks to the teachers and librarians out there who have been tireless in their efforts to open the hearts and minds of young readers by exposing them to books.

CONTENTS

Introduction by *Jonathan Maberry*   1

Brenna Yovanoff "The Doomsday Glass"   7

Carrie Ryan "What Happens to Girls Who Disappear"   39

Cherie Priest "The Mermaid Aquarium: Weeki Wachee
    Springs, 1951"   65

Ellen Hopkins "As Good as Your Word" (Poems)   88

Rachel Tafoya "The Invisible Girl"   149

Zac Brewer "Death and Twinkies"   170

Linda Addison "Secret Things" (Poems)   195

Josh Malerman "Danny"   201

Madeleine Roux "Make It Right"   233

Lucy A. Snyder "Shadowtown Blues" (Poems)   258

Nancy Holder "Beyond the Sea"   263

Tim Waggoner "The Whisper-Whisper Men"   285

Neal & Brendan Shusterman "Non-player Character"   313

Marge Simon "Falling into Darkness" (Poems)   327

Christopher Golden "What Happens When the Heart
    Just Stops"   335

Kendare Blake "Chlorine-Damaged Hair,
    and Other Pool Hazards"   365

R. L. Stine "The Old Radio"   385

Jade Shames "Rites of Passage" (Poems)   406

Rachel Caine "Corazón Oscuro"   413

Steve Rasnic Tem "The Boyfriend"   445

Ilsa J. Bick "Bearwalker"   464

SCARY OUT THERE

It's Scary Out There:
An Introduction

JONATHAN MABERRY

What scares you?

I bet it's not the same thing that scares me. Or the thing that scares your best friend. Or anyone else you know. Even if it's similar, it won't be the same thing. It can't be. Fear is too personal. Our fears are our own. We know our fears and they certainly know us.

When I was little, I remember being afraid of the darkness at the top of the stairs.

Truly afraid. Terrified.

There was something in it—I was sure of that. Something with claws. Something that crouched out of sight and panted like a dog. Something hungry. I knew that unless I came up the stairs with my back pressed against the far wall, that a hairy arm would reach out between the slats in the second floor rail and slash me. I knew it. Absolutely knew it.

That was when I was eight.

I'm not sure when I stopped believing that there was a werewolf on the second floor landing. Maybe it was around the time my best friend got sick with leukemia and wasted

away over the course of a long, bad summer. Or, maybe it was
when my father started hitting us kids. Or, maybe it was when
the gang of kids in the park threw rocks at a group of African
American girls who'd come to the local skating rink, killing
one of them and sparking a race riot.

Maybe it was any one of a dozen other things. We
lived in an old row home in a low income neighborhood in
Philadelphia. It was a very rough place to grow up. Poverty,
violence, crime, racism, hatred. There seemed to be a lot of
darkness, even on sunny days. Or . . . maybe I just noticed
the shadows when the sun was shining. The contrast between
dark and light was easier to spot.

Or, maybe what happened was that the things that scared
me changed entirely. I stopped being afraid of werewolves
and zombies when I realized how absolutely terrifying it
was to just say "Hi" to a girl. Or, when I walked into a new
school, and I was absolutely convinced that I was too weird,
too poorly dressed, too geeky, too bookish, too whatever to
make friends with any of the kids I saw. They all looked happy.
They all seemed to know one another. I was sure they each had
terrific families, got great grades, could afford nicer clothes,
never doubted themselves, were loved, were funny, were cool,
belonged. . . .

My fear changed, but my capacity for being afraid did not.
Fear, I realized, it changed, it evolved like some kind of twisted
chameleon. It raced ahead of us to make sure that we never

completely outgrew it. Fear peered into our thoughts and made adjustments, picked new weapons, mapped out fresh strategies so that it could set traps along our path.

I'm older now, and tougher. When I was a kid and afraid of even walking down my own block, I began studying martial arts; now I'm an eighth-degree black belt. Very tough. You'd think that would make me crush my fear and toss it over my shoulder.

Yeah, that would be great.

Fear is too sly for that. Too slippery and smart. Now that I'm older, I have a whole new set of fears. Tough as I am, there's no way for me to be there to protect everyone I love all the time. And there are new monsters: wars, political unrest that seems to be tearing the country apart, intolerance directed at those I love, new diseases. . . .

Well, you get the idea. Fear is always there. And it is so personal a thing. Some of the things that scare me don't make my best friend twitch. He's not afraid of those things. But I know for sure there are things in his life that scare him green. Things that don't make *me* twitch.

Maybe that's why I read horror stories. I want to understand my own fears, and I want to understand what's happening in the heads and hearts of my friends. I mean . . . how can you be there for your friends if you can't sympathize or empathize?

When I was a kid, I devoured every horror story I could get

my hands on. The darker, the better. Why? Because it helped to know that I wasn't the only one who was afraid of the dark. And it helped even more to know that I wasn't the only one who was afraid of the darkness inside my own head and heart. I read it all, in print and in comics. Horror poetry, too, because sometimes a poet can stab right to the heart of the darkness.

That's when I began writing horror stories too. To defeat monsters? Sure, that was part of it. Not all, though. I wrote horror stories so I could understand the shadows in my head. Sounds crazy, but it's not.

I bet you understand that. You're reading this book. It doesn't matter if you want to write horror. What matters is that you're willing to read it. Something about this book touched a nerve. Maybe it was the title, maybe the cover, maybe the text on the flap. Maybe it's one or more of the contributors.

Or maybe it's that you want to understand darkness too. The darkness around you in your life, and the shadows inside.

That's probably it. To one degree or another.

You're like me. You're like the amazing lineup of contributors in this book. Some of them you'll already know (who hasn't read a *Goosebumps* book?), while others will be new to you. And I've included poets along with the writers of prose stories.

Scary Out There is a project of love—admittedly of the dark kind—I edited for the Horror Writers Association. The HWA is the home of horror writing in long and short fiction, poetry, drama, and nonfiction. They recognize the very best in horror writing with their annual Bram Stoker Award, named for the author of *Dracula*. The contributors whose strange imaginings you'll find here are all members of that august body, and the variety you'll discover in these works suggests how long and how subtle the reach of horror can be. Like many works that we in the HWA consider horror, this is not a book dedicated to supernatural horrors. Sure, there are monsters here, but fear comes in all shapes and sizes, all frequencies and flavors. Being alone, being ignored, not fitting in, peer pressure . . . man, there are so many kinds of fear out there.

So . . . yeah . . . it's scary out there.

It's scary in here, too.

Take a deep breath and turn the page. . . .

Jonathan Maberry is a *New York Times* bestselling novelist, five-time Bram Stoker Award winner, and comic book writer. He writes the Joe Ledger thrillers, the Rot & Ruin series, the Nightsiders series, and the Dead of Night series, as well as stand-alone novels in multiple genres. His comic book works include, among others, *Captain America, Bad Blood, Rot & Ruin, V-Wars,* and others. He is the editor of many anthologies, including *The X-Files, Out of Tune,* and *V-Wars.* His book *V-Wars* is in development for TV, and *Extinction Machine* and *Rot & Ruin* are in development for film. *V-Wars* was also released as a tabletop board game. He is the founder of the Writers Coffeehouse and the cofounder of The Liars Club. Prior to becoming a full-time novelist, Jonathan spent twenty-five years as a magazine feature writer, martial arts instructor, and playwright. He was a featured expert on the History channel programs *Zombies: A Living History* and *True Monsters.* Jonathan lives in Del Mar, California, with his wife, Sara Jo.

   Website: jonathanmaberry.com
   Twitter: @JonathanMaberry
   Facebook: facebook.com/jonathanmaberry

The Doomsday Glass

BRENNA YOVANOFF

There were rats in the subway.

Or maybe not rats, but small, scurrying things that moved like rats. They had a dark, mangy texture that made it hard to tell if they were supposed to be mammals or reptiles. You couldn't kill them, because they weren't really enemies, but Nim liked to watch them anyway. She promised herself a closer look the next time she came through.

Currently though, she was on a mission, standing on a pile of scrap metal and broken tile under a dim, flickering light. The painted ceiling was crumbling now, but in a former life—some glorious, fictitious past—it must have been spectacular.

As game levels went, Subway Run was ridiculously straightforward, but the layout was designed to lure you into a false sense of security. There were hardly any health packs or checkpoints, and there were lots of places for things to hide.

Around her the tunnel buzzed with activity as other players passed through on their own private missions.

Nim noticed the boy at about the same time the first skin thief came slinking out from under a subway car, but only because she had a tendency to notice things. He was standing on the other side of the subway tracks, near one of the service alcoves. Staring at her. She did not like how he stared at her.

Her awareness of him was just an observation, though. The thief was closer.

It crept along the oily ground—ugly and hairless, with veins that crawled over its body like lines on a road map. She paged through her weapons and picked out a knife. The tiny one, which was hard to use and had an incredibly short range, but took up almost no space in her inventory.

Predictably, the thief plunged at her, all ooky and rotten, with its back hunched and its barbed tongue hanging out. As it clattered over the rubble, its claws made a sound like breaking plates.

Nim stood with her arms at her sides, waiting for it to complete its charge. As it reached her, she cut the barbed tongue out of its mouth and spun in a wobbly half circle, teetering on the launchpad.

She'd never been the most coordinated when it came to sports, but in Vertigo, it didn't matter if she wobbled on her actual feet—the game had gyroscopic stabilizers. Her headset was calibrated to the exact center of the launchpad though, and when she listed, the goggles glitched a little, creating a weird doubling effect—a blurry overlay that emphasized the line between the fake, virtual world and her own messy bedroom.

She caught her balance and the world righted itself. The severed tongue completed its arc and landed on the ground at her feet with a sloppy, squelching noise.

"Nim," said her best friend, Margaret, who was farther along the tunnel, slicing through a pack of limbo demons in easy strokes. "I know you know this, but that knife is ridiculous."

In the world of Vertigo, Margaret was nearly seven feet tall and mostly muscle and carried a machete made of fire and colloidal sulfur. It was surreal to watch this scarred giant brutalize her way through the game while Margaret-Margaret, *real* Margaret, was down in her basement wearing a USC T-shirt and a pair of boys' boxer shorts, listening to the Pixies with her headset on and her contacts out. She'd picked the biggest, baddest woman the character shop offered, but Nim suspected Margaret would have been just as happy as a man or a monster. Anyone but a short, grouchy Chinese girl with double-jointed fingers and a messy bob that was starting to grow out. People didn't bother you much when you were seven feet tall.

During the day they were . . . nobody, resigned to beigeness and boredom and tenth grade at Slope Hill, but when they logged on to Vertigo, they were magical. *Exceptional.*

There was something so gratifying about spending every day in ordinary-world, where people teased you or ignored you or called you fire-crotch (Nim) or flat (Margaret)—where they talked over you every time you answered in class, going out of their way to make sure you knew exactly how little you mattered. There was something about sitting through all that and then leaving it, happily, voluntarily, for the scariest place on the network.

In Vertigo, it didn't matter who you were. While Margaret smashed her way through the darkest corners, challenging herself to gruesome, manic speed runs, Nim survived by being clever. She was patient and tidy—deviser of traps and torture devices and massive explosions that could take out fourteen enemies at once. Her favorite weapon was the game itself.

There were a lot of rules and limitations, of course—a physics engine that tended to overcorrect every little gesture, and a pretty nonsensical magic system—but there were ways of exploiting them.

"You want the rest of these limbos over here, or should I?" said Margaret, her voice buzzing brightly in Nim's ear. "You can have them. I just maxed out my bank."

Nim stomped hard on the skin thief, then flicked the blood off her tiny knife and shook her head. Today, she was on a mission to figure out what to do with the dogs.

Vertigo had a roster of eighty-seven basic monsters. Most were sort of humanoid, with hypnotic lantern eyes or poison claws and only one or two basic attacks. The dogs were interesting. They were a problem, because no matter what, they could always hear you.

There were repellent sprays you could buy in the shop and a special bait you could make if you'd collected enough ugly, goopy mushrooms from a certain maintenance room down in the sewers that was really hard to find, but mostly you just snuck past them and tried not to make any noise.

Now Nim was on the hunt, cruising the derelict subway with a tiny knife and nothing else. The shadows felt warm and thick around her, almost like a solid thing. This was the magic of the headset—as soon as you put it on, every surface and texture was like life, only better. The world exploded into vivid clarity, and when a skin thief ran into the point of your knife and bled all over, it looked slick. Every sound and movement was amplified, translated through the headset with nightmare clarity.

Nim whistled softly, a long, low trill, and called under her breath, "Heeeere, puppy-puppy-puppy . . ."

The boy was standing in the open now, gazing at her across the tracks. Nim realized he was wearing a mask, but it was stupidly plain. The mask of a blank face. Of no one.

Even his outfit was nondescript—chinos and a polo shirt. He had no weapons that Nim could see. She wondered if maybe he had some kind of bonus that made him unattractive to basic enemies. It certainly wasn't impossible.

Vertigo was a strange and generous place. As long as you paid attention, there was treasure everywhere. A few months ago Nim had found a message on the wall of an abandoned house that you could see only when the moon was up. She'd followed the clues to a cove on Dreadnought Island and was rewarded with a spell that made you disappear completely as long as you stood in a shadow.

She had a hat that stopped time, but only in a certain room in the basement of Noble Hospital, and a talisman that worked a little differently on every kind of demon.

She'd puzzled over riddles, investigated every mysterious door—performed every tedious, cumulative task the game presented her with.

Her newest acquisition was something called a Doomsday Glass. It didn't look like much—a silver disc that fit in the palm of your hand—but when you stuck it to the wall, it spread to the size of a doormat and hypnotized anything that came bopping along.

It struck Nim as severely limited. She didn't *want* to make monsters stare at themselves. It seemed too simple, and Nim's gaze narrowed to razor sharpness whenever Vertigo seemed simple. Now she was on a personal mission to find the place where the simple got complicated.

She'd positioned the glass on the ground between the subway tracks, and now it glittered faintly in the cool light while she prowled the tunnel for the dogs.

As she moved through the rubble—which actually meant doing a kind of little dance, scuffing the launchpad with her feet—she was pretty sure that one had spotted her. She could hear the *tap-tap* of its claws, see the tendrils of smoke that drifted from between its teeth.

The problem of the dogs had a lot of variables. They were demonically fast when they wanted to be and could burn through most kinds of armor. She'd nearly died twice and wasted a lot of health packs before realizing something important. A dog could make a mess of you in about three seconds, but they never attacked until you looked at them straight-on.

This one was keeping pace. From the corner of her eye, she could see the glow of the coals burning way down in its throat. Picturing it made her think of fairy tales. She was a princess, small and innocent and attended by monsters.

Already, she heard the scrabble of the skin thieves. They respawned at a ridiculous rate—it was part of why Margaret liked to come down here.

The boy was closer too, watching as she wound through the rubble with the dog. And, yes, what she was up to probably looked weird, but the only thing that felt dangerous was the way he stared at her. He was using a newer character model— with dark, shaggy hair and a shambling walk—called James. His only defining features were the unremarkable chinos and, of course, the mask.

Nim stopped in the shadow of an overturned train car to wait for the dog, and when it caught up, she stepped across the subway rail and onto the Doomsday Glass. She did it slowly, carefully. The dog followed her.

The second its feet touched the glass, it seemed to tremble and grow bigger. She wondered if it would die. Explode. Attack. But it only shimmered slightly, then stayed where it was.

The boy was still standing on the tracks. As soon as he caught Nim's eye, she looked away. She felt dumb, but not dumb enough to stare him down. Sometimes boys could be weird about her and Margaret when it came to the game.

Case in point: There was a club that met after school to trade tactics and sell each other mods. Nim had gone once, thinking it might be fun—she could share her talent for finding secret items or at least be in a room with people who liked the same things she did. She and Margaret had been the only girls. Alex Ford's girlfriend was apparently a member, but she was at volleyball practice.

Almost immediately Nim had caused a stir by voicing her thoughts on how there were thirty costumes for her avatar, and every single one of them was a dress.

"Look, I *like* the game," she'd said. It was an understatement that felt more like a cinder block. "I just think it would be neat for everyone to not see my underwear—okay?"

This spawned a philosophical discussion on whether the digital panties of an avatar were really even *her* underwear.

When Nim had tried to offer an olive branch—a really premium piece of intel about a Spirit Lamp that was somewhere in the Iron Wood—no one seemed to care much, and

Austin Bauer, who'd been in all her math classes since the eighth grade and was usually not a total dickbag, had actually told her it didn't exist.

After that, the meeting had mostly consisted of making fun of Nim for anything that seemed remotely girly. For giving her avatar a pretty hat. For caring about things like basic human decency and pants. For decorating her screen name with little demon-runes when they all passed around a sign-up sheet to share their launch codes in case anyone wanted to meet up on a particular board. Surprise—in the three weeks since they'd attended the meeting, no one had expressed any interest in meeting up with Nim or Margaret.

The whole thing had turned into one big, stupid obstacle course where the obstacle was always to prove that she knew what she was talking about. And every time she did, her proof was deemed insufficient and she was given another test, and another, just for committing the grievous offense of wishing her character could wear pants.

The next weekend Nim had been poking around in the Iron Wood and seen the supposedly nonexistent Spirit Lamp glittering beneath the roots of a thorn tree. She'd snagged the lamp, gotten the trophy, and—only partially out of spite— posted her triumph to the achievements board. She hadn't gone back to the games club.

The skin thieves were closer now, clattering through the rubble. They were coming for her. She backed away, trading her knife for a scythe. She was efficient and precise, but not stupid. They might be weak alone, but they could still be dangerous in packs.

And then, as the thieves came slobbering at her around the Doomsday Glass, the dog did something quite surprising. It lunged from the glass and began to savage them.

So. Nim had found the place where the simple collided with the ingenious. Everything made sense again, and everything was even better than she'd thought. It was a good day.

Later though, when she logged out of Subway Run, there was a new message blinking on her dashboard. It was short and strange. It said:

From: jkx0x0

Hey Sugar,

You're not as good as you think you are.

It was signed *Mr. No One*

Nim looked at it a long time. Then she hit the button and deleted it.

"Report him," Margaret said at lunch, peeling back the top of her sandwich and picking through its guts with a plastic fork.

Nim flopped forward in her chair and put her head on her arms. "They'd just say how it isn't a terms violation and if it happens again maybe I should change my screen name to something more neutral and use a different avatar so I don't look so obviously . . ."

"Like you have *girl* parts?" Margaret said, rolling a lump of white bread into a ball and shoving it in her mouth.

The observation was built on a foundation of experience. Nim's first avatar had been a hyperfeminine model called Sugar, with a tiny waist and a cloud of red hair so voluminous and bright it nearly matched Nim's real-life color. She had *liked* the Sugar. It was curvy and pretty. It had looked like her, but better.

She'd regretted it almost immediately.

In Vertigo, the biological condition of being a girl meant a lot of attention, and not the good kind—in Nim's case, an impressive and never ending flood of messages about the carpet and drapes.

She stuck it out for a month, then traded in the orange haired Sugar for a model called Lola. It meant losing all her progress on Dreadnought Island, but she sucked it up and played the board again. She caught up to herself in a weekend.

The Lola was a hipless pixie with slender arms and basically no chest. She was about as asexual as you could get, with tiny hands and feet and hair so blond it was almost white. It was nothing like Nim's real-life hair, and that was kind of the point. Now, when she signed into Vertigo, she looked fragile, like she'd been through something mysterious and traumatic and had survived it. Her only act of rebellion had been to download a mod to put her Lola in pants.

It annoyed her that she was the only person who seemed

to care about this. When she'd broached it at the ill-fated
games club meeting, the rest of them had looked at her like
she was out of her mind.

Even Margaret didn't bother with mods—especially cos-
metic ones. The homegrown stuff tended to be janky, and
there were rumors that black-hat hackers built in all kinds of
spyware and sketchy back doors to monitor your activity or
highjack your machine. As far as Nim could tell, it was paranoid gossip. Most of the time the worst that happened was the
homemade mods didn't work, or they sort of worked, and you
wound up with your torso square with your headset and your
hips somewhere off to the left, getting stuck against the wall
when you tried to go through a door.

Anyway, it was a small price to pay to address the little
issue that anytime the Lola climbed a staircase or a ladder,
anyone behind her could look up her dress.

"Maybe it's someone on your launch list," Margaret said,
trying to sound helpful.

But that was worse, somehow. Nim would have to wipe
her whole list and add them all back one by one, and even that
wouldn't help, since if Margaret was right, Mr. No One would
still be some mysterious jerk who had her launch code.

In physics, Mr. Howard was drawing vectors on the board,
explaining their project for the quarter, which was a complicated telescope involving angles and mirrors and refracted light.

Nim sat at her desk, thinking about Vertigo and the Doomsday Glass, how she'd figured out its point. It was a tiny vacuum from which nothing could escape. A black hole. An event horizon full of monsters. Her favorite thing in the world was just knowing how something worked.

Mr. Howard eyed the class, gesturing with his dry-erase marker. "Can anybody give us a real-life example of a parabolic lens?"

Nim stared at her work sheet. When she closed her eyes, all she saw was the difference between lush, vibrant Vertigo-world and sad, flat ordinary-world.

Mr. Howard stood with his hands behind his back. The question still hung in the room. Next to her, Jake Sieverson, who had a mouth as pink as a girl's and very blond, very curly hair, was waving a hand, but Mr. Howard's eyes swept over him.

"Naomi," he said in a warm, hearty way that was supposed to make her want to share her ideas and opinions. "*You* look like you've got something on your mind."

Nim glanced down and shook her head. She did have things on her mind, but she was pretty sure no one wanted to hear about whether or not in-game physics resembled real-world physics, and no, she did not want to tell the class.

Jake Sieverson made an impatient barking noise and shouted, "Satellite dish!"

It was totally against the rules on the class conduct sheet, but Mr. Howard didn't get after him for not waiting to be called on, just nodded and then put them in their lab groups.

There was chaos as everyone bolted for the back of the room, elbowing one another out of the way. Lenses and mirrors sat in eight identical piles on the back counter. After a minute Nim straggled over to hover around the edges.

In Vertigo, she'd already be sorting through the lenses, figuring out how to turn the curves and angles into some overpowered ultramagnified death ray. The person with the power was the one who knew the secrets, and in Vertigo, she always knew the secrets.

She went home without her French book or her favorite hoodie, without thinking about the blank faced boy who'd stood across the tracks in Subway Run and watched her set up her experimental dog trap.

The only thing on her mind was the way the Doomsday Glass had revealed its purpose. She'd held the dog in place and made it hers. She'd figured out how to own the very monsters that populated the game. The message from Mr. No One was just some jerk screwing around. It wasn't that big of a deal. He hadn't even *done* anything.

She saw him again two days later.

Margaret was at pre-regionals for science olympiad, talking with her fellow aeronautics nerds about gliders, so Nim was by herself. She was hunting wraiths in the Dollhouse, which was widely understood to be the creepiest, most difficult board in all of Vertigo. Nim and Margaret called it the Escher House because of how the floor plan seemed to twist and fold in on itself, all secret trapdoors and staircases to nowhere and doors that opened on unkillable monsters or portals that plunged you into thorny mazes that were nearly impossible to get out of and sucked your health meter down to nothing.

It was a baffling death trap, and Nim adored it there.

Inside, it was ludicrously big—with echoing ceilings and miles of spiral corridors—and home to a pair of ravenous nightmares with tangled black hair and red dresses, who were always stalking you. She and Margaret called them the sisters. They prowled the halls, invisible until they were right next to you, but Nim had figured out a long time ago that—like everything else in Vertigo—there were ways of exploiting the rules.

Right before the sisters showed up, your vision would flicker blue, a little. It was hard to see if you weren't looking for it. Nim was always looking. You could see them in reflective surfaces sometimes, and if you hid or ran, they never chased you very far. If you made the mistake of letting them touch you though, they immediately spawned more. It had taken Nim three encounters to figure out that no matter how aggressively they multiplied, there were really only two of them.

The house itself held just an incredible amount of junk, like a lunatic museum full of tiny, precious artifacts. There was a vast, labyrinthine basement and, under that, a subbasement full of moldering catacombs and torture devices. There were libraries and ballrooms and a wood paneled study with the taxidermied head of a goblin in a bell jar on the mantelpiece.

It was one big archive of secrets, and Nim reveled in it.

Today, she was thinking she'd like to try the Doomsday Glass on the sisters. Most special items didn't work on them, or else they didn't work the way they were supposed to, but Nim was always up for a good experiment. Now she was waiting around in one of the ballrooms with her demon talisman equipped. Like a lot of items, the talisman had a backward effect on the sisters. If you carried it, they were impressively more likely to be interested in you.

She took out the glass and stuck it to the front of a low wooden cabinet. There was always the chance that it would make them turn on her, but she didn't think so. She just hadn't been able to get them to walk over it. If she could find the right spot though, maybe they'd move into range without seeing it.

The boy was in the corner of the ballroom, lounging in a huge, high-backed chair. He was sitting so still that Nim didn't notice him at first.

"Hey, Sugar," he said, and the sound of his voice made her skin crawl.

He'd painted the mask since last time. Now the bland, even features were orange and red and black, covered in spirals and jagged slashing lines.

He sat under a giant oil painting, by the trapdoor to the

torture chamber, watching. Nim knew the house was full of other players, but apart from the two of them, the room was strangely vacant.

The James didn't seem to mind the silence. He didn't seem to have any agenda besides *her*.

"Cheating," he said, nodding toward the glass. His voice was hoarse, like he was deliberately trying to make it deeper.

Nim didn't answer.

"Aw, come on." He sounded hearty. Fake friendly. "I'm just saying."

"Leave me alone," she said, snatching the glass off the cabinet and shoving it back in her pocket. "And stop talking like Batman."

He pushed himself up from the chair and padded across the carpet. "Don't be like that. Isn't this what you want—everyone paying attention to you?"

"What is your *problem*?"

Suddenly, the James's whole posture changed. He loomed over her. The way he stared out at her from perfectly symmetrical eyeholes was horrific. "*My* problem? Like you don't go around begging everyone to tell you how great you are? You think this is some special thing, built for you, but you don't even *belong* here!"

His voice was like a slap. She knew there were guys who thought that—that she was a fake and a poser, intruding on some private club. She wasn't stupid. She'd seen the Internet.

And still his viciousness stunned her. No one had ever just come out and said it.

Nim stared back at him. The talisman in her pocket was beginning to hiss, glowing faintly through her modded pants, but the James didn't notice. To him she was nothing. Just the tiny, wafty Lola. "Maybe you're the one who shouldn't be here."

He stood over her, taking up so much space he seemed to fill the room, and she heard his breath catch before he answered. She was pretty sure he wanted to call her a bitch, but he didn't say it. Vertigo had very strict profanity policies.

"Like you'd last twenty minutes without all your little cheats and tricks." His voice had risen an octave. He no longer sounded like a superhero with a head cold. He sounded petulant. Not the Dark Knight, but the Joker. "You'd end up in pieces, then cry about how it's *not fair*."

In the shadows wraiths were gathering, creeping around the edges of Nim's vision. "You don't know what I'd do."

The James was much too close now, pressing up against the field of the launchpad, making an optical illusion. He was in her room, and not in her room. It was disorienting, how his voice could be so hard and hateful when his face had no expression at all. "You just think you're *so good* at this."

"I am."

For a second the two of them stood toe-to-toe, nearly touching.

Then the light in Nim's headset went cold—a cloud pass-ing over a winter sun. "The sisters are coming."

"What are you talking about? Those freaks are invisible."

Nim shrugged—the creepy little girl in the horror movie. Her hair drifted around her in a white corona. "Stay and wait if you don't believe me."

For one impossible moment the James seemed to consider it. Then he turned and dove for the door in the floor.

She saw him the next night, in the funhouse at Dark Amusements. And again in Subway Run. And every time, she tried to restart someplace else, and every time, he appeared out of the shadows five minutes later like a boogeyman in accountant's clothing. Every time she blocked him, he made a new screen name composed of new gibberish.

In Vertigo the other players couldn't kill you, but they could definitely make everything harder. When he stood in her way long enough to keep her from opening the door to the operating theater in Noble Hospital, she lost her temper.

She held down the button on her headset until the help-line display came up, overlaying the hospital corridor with a tidy digital menu.

"I want to report a user," she said, staring past the translu-cent screen—right at the James, with his weird, painted face.

The voice in the headset was businesslike. "Name and complaint?"

The James stood in front of her, so close that if this were real, she'd be able to feel his breath. She made herself bigger, throwing her shoulders back. "jkx0x0, nth8383, others. A sustained pattern of harassment."

There was a pause, then the helpline rep said, "And have you tried moving boards?"

"I *can't*." She hated that her voice shook. "He shows up wherever I am. He *finds* me."

The headset showed a little animation of zombies marching to indicate the rep was typing, bringing up her account. "Are you using any unauthorized mods? If you've altered your account code, Vertigo takes no responsibility for malfunction."

So they knew about the wardrobe mod, *obviously*. Nim wanted to scream, but in the back of her mind there was a tiny voice that whispered this was what she deserved; it probably *was* her fault. She'd compromised her account for something so minor—not like the grinders, who modified their weapons to autoload or fire faster so they could cheat their way up the leaderboards and were total douchebags. All she wanted was just to wear some goddamned *pants*.

She took a deep breath and made fists. "Who is it though? At least tell me their launch code so I can block them permanently!"

The rep made a fake-sympathy noise. "I'm sorry, we can't give out personal information."

Nim had expected that, but still, it felt like getting punched.

The terms of service relieved Vertigo of any responsibility for anything. For instance, their policy that you should never give out your launch code—soundly and universally ignored. Right. In a game that basically *forced* you to cooperate in order to get anywhere.

The James was circling now, closer, closer. Their bodies weren't real, but she felt him in her nerve endings anyway. He bumped against the virtual bubble of the launchpad, but could not actually step inside.

His voice when he spoke was a soft, ugly monotone. "See? Even the help desk isn't falling for your little victim bit."

Nim stumbled away, nearly pitching off the launchpad and into her basket of unfolded laundry, and called him something really obscene.

Immediately, her headset blinked red and her bank dwindled by a hefty chunk. "Shit," she whispered, then winced as more credits vanished.

The James was directly behind her now. She knew that, under the mask, he was smirking.

"Fiery," he said. His mouth was virtual, but it felt very close to her ear. When she stared across the corridor at the darkened window of the operating theater, she saw a tiny white haired pixie, standing in a derelict hospital with a monster behind her. She could see the cold, digital gleam of his eyes in the glass.

He held her gaze. The word was a coincidence, a fluke. He wasn't talking about her real hair color. That wasn't possible.

Nim's resolve broke. She twisted away and ripped her headset off.

Vertigo was supposed to be hers. The safest place on earth. And when the monsters touched you, they were never really touching you.

"Plausible deniability," Margaret said, slipping a balsa glider wing into a precut slot and making a note on the width and the angle. "He can mess with you a billion ways and still not actually violate any terms."

It surprised Nim, how relieved she was that Margaret knew the words for what had happened—it had a name. She hated that it had a name.

Margaret scowled at her glider. "What did you even *do*? Like, to attract his attention?"

"I don't know," Nim said, rolling backward in Margaret's desk chair, twirling in a circle. "Why does it have to be something I did? I didn't *do* anything. He's the one who's a creep!"

For the first time, Vertigo felt unfamiliar. It felt scary.

"It's not like it's real, though," Margaret said. "Right? I mean, it's a *game*—it's not like it matters."

It did, though. Nim closed her eyes, struggling against how unbelievably much it mattered. There was no way to say this thing, a thing so huge and offensive it hurt—that someone could do absolutely nothing to you, and it could still feel like everything.

"He's *ruining* it," she blurted out. "It's mine, and he's trying to take it!"

"Well then, we should probably show him what's up already," Margaret said.

Her matter-of-factness made something glow in Nim's chest. "How?"

But in Nim's head a plan was already taking shape. The thing games taught you, more than strategy, more than problem solving or spatial reasoning, was how to play until you won. She already knew *exactly* what she'd do.

Margaret shrugged and reached for the glue. "I don't know. Like, trap him in the Bone Swamp until he loses all his bank?"

Nim sat up straighter. "I'm going to kill him."

For a second neither of them spoke.

"I'm going to do it in the Escher House. And I'm going to use the monsters."

"Nim," said Margaret.

"It's the most obvious place. He'll follow me—the sisters will do the rest. Maybe *I* can't kill him personally, but I'm pretty sure they can."

"*Nim*," said Margaret.

"*Listen.* The only reason they aren't fully bosses is because they lose interest in like two seconds if you outrun them or hide. What if they didn't? Even fully leveled, you wouldn't survive both of them at once."

For a long time Margaret seemed wholly intent on her

glider, but Nim knew she was thinking hard. "And how are you planning on holding their interest?"

Nim was ready for this. She was becoming something of an authority on the sisters. "I haven't been able to trick them onto the Doomsday Glass yet—they're too smart—but I have an idea. You know where they don't ever look? Up. I'm going to put the glass on the ceiling."

"That's ridiculous," said Margaret. "Anyway, they are way too strong. The glass will blow out in like two seconds—it's not meant for real monsters."

Nim shrugged, trying to look more casual than she felt. "So, timing will be a factor."

"You actually think you can reach the ceiling?"

Vertigo was ridiculously open, with tunnels and doors to everywhere, but there were still a few places you couldn't get to. For the first time, Nim smiled. "Most of the time you can't. But you know that one place in the library with all the ladders? If you go all the way up, you can get on top of those big shelves. I did it once."

For a second she thought Margaret was going to argue, to explain the mechanics of why Nim was stupid for even thinking this, why it couldn't work. Why they had to just let it go and accept that this was how Vertigo was now, forever and ever.

But all Margaret said was, "If we're going to be building an entire suicide mission around handling the sisters, I think I'm going to need to upgrade my machete."

* * *

Margaret volunteered to camp at the entrance to the east wing of the Escher House and keep any randoms from wandering in and accidentally distracting the sisters. It involved a certain amount of risk—wraiths tended to congregate in the halls—but, as Margaret pointed out, that really just made her job easier, since no one wanted to hang out there.

Nim armed herself with the scythe, but that was mostly academic. For one thing, it was impossible to kill the sisters, but for another, Nim didn't want to kill them, just lure them down to the farthest end of the library and keep them there long enough to do their job. For the first time since she'd switched avatars, she put the Lola in a dress. For old times' sake.

She was relatively sure her plan would work, but she was taking no chances. She picked her time and day carefully, based on what she knew. The James was almost always around on weeknights after eight thirty. Once the glass was in place, she equipped her talisman and prowled the Dollhouse.

As she wandered, little doubts began to gnaw. Maybe he wasn't coming. Maybe this was stupid. Maybe it was all a misunderstanding and she needed to relax. Maybe, after all this, he really was smarter than her.

It was with a sharp thrill that she finally caught sight of his chinos down the end of the hall. She dawdled, trying to appear vague and helpless. She made sure he got a good look before whisking off to the library.

There she waited, touching the shelves, running her fingers over rows of books. She could feel her pulse in her ears. The whole place was heavy with silence and dust. Night was falling now, the shadows growing long. Time passed in Vertigo in huge swaths. The sun plunged below the horizon, and in an instant the library windows darkened. The glass was a black mirror now, reflecting the room. For a second she saw one of the sisters standing right behind her, red clad, black haired. Ghostly, then gone.

The talisman was hissing softly in the pocket of her dress.

When the James spoke out of the shadows, his voice was sly. "I thought you were too good for cute little dresses, but you look hot. You should wear that all the time."

Nothing about it sounded like a compliment.

Nim was surprised at how sad she felt suddenly. "I'm tired of this now, okay?"

"If you can't deal with it, get out. I don't give a shit if you don't like it."

She turned slowly from the window—so eerie, so delicate. She was the girl in the horror movie. "You will."

Her headset flickered blue, just barely, just for a millisecond. If he ever just paid *attention*, he would know that. Over in the corner by the door, there was a sound like breaking dishes. The sisters had materialized, side by side. They were standing directly under the Doomsday Glass.

The James whipped around. "What the—"

His voice cracked and Nim guessed he'd never seen both sisters at once before. She had a feeling there were a lot of things she knew about Vertigo that he didn't.

She stepped toward him. Beyond him, the sisters shuddered but stayed where they were. They stood shoulder to shoulder beneath the mirror. Their hair seemed to drip around them like something liquid, devouring the light. Nim took another step, fingering the talisman in her pocket, challenging the James to a game of chicken he could never win. She was smiling.

The sisters were trembling harder now. She could feel them humming like power lines and wondered if she'd overestimated the strength of the glass. She took another step.

"Are you crazy?" the James said. "What are you doing?" He really still didn't understand that she owned them.

Their hands were outstretched now, as if to tell her they understood. They saw. She threw the talisman down at his feet and, for one perfect instant, everything froze. The light was so blue it was nearly purple. Nim was small and strange and utterly exalted.

Then the sisters fell on him—a storm of teeth and claws— already multiplying at his touch. They crouched in the vast, soundless library, ripping him apart. Above them the Doomsday Glass glowed white and hot and blinding like a dying star.

The whole room was filling up with black haired girls in

red dresses, false, but proliferating. Nim had never seen more than eight at once—they always disappeared as soon as the real ones started to drift away, but now they were multiplying exponentially, crowding in around the James.

Nim's headset crackled, flashing bluer and bluer. Belatedly, she understood that it was glitching. The game was cutting out. Parts of the mansion stuttered and froze. With a start she recognized one of the carnival rides from Dark Amusements, looming behind all of the books. Then the ceiling began to melt. Her world was coming down around her.

With a tremendous crash the Doomsday Glass exploded and the library with it, collapsing in a storm of dust and static.

Nim stood in the middle of her own messy bedroom. The headset had shut itself off. Her last glimpse of the Escher House had been the James in pieces, strewn across a bloodred floor.

At school Nim smiled. A lot. She couldn't help it.

She kept her triumph to herself though. Instead, she dove into the physics project. She didn't even argue when Matt Avery volunteered her to take the notes for their group. As a reward she was grudgingly allowed to help Austin Bauer with the math.

They spent three days figuring out the inside of their telescope, taking turns measuring the angles and tweaking the lenses. It wasn't exhilarating or dire, but it was still pretty interesting.

"Hey, Oz, you like that Vertigo game, right?" said Jake Sieverson on Thursday, flopping down next to Austin. "Did you hear someone crashed it? Like, the whole thing."

Austin made an ambiguous noise and didn't look up. "Don't call me that."

Nim turned away to hide her smile, fidgeting with the corner of her lab book. "I was playing when it happened," she mumbled.

"Dude, for real?" Jake was leaning on the table, looking right at her for probably the first time ever. "How was it? I heard a server failed or something."

Nim shrugged, trying to look casual, remembering all the times she'd been excited about something and immediately gotten shut down as soon as she tried to talk about it. "I think it must have been a design flaw. Maybe someone exploited a bug."

Jake was still watching her. He started to say something else, but Austin cut him off. "Why do you care? You don't even play."

Later, after Jake had gone loping back to his group, Nim turned to Austin. "He's not allowed to ask about it?"

"Screw that guy. He's such a tool—he never shuts up."

"Yeah, sure," Nim said, but it seemed kind of uncalled for to get mad at Jake, who was only making conversation. He was one of those people who'd talk to anyone about anything.

She flipped back through her notes, humming quietly, just

thinking about her triumph. "Pretty crazy about the server though, right?"

"Can't you talk about anything else?"

"Fine," she said, even though she was pretty sure she'd been talking about nothing but Cassegrain reflectors all week. He was being way crankier than normal. Maybe he still hadn't forgiven her for proving him wrong about the Spirit Lamp.

They worked in silence, adjusting the tension on their springs. As Nim was calculating ratios, Austin came around the table and leaned on the back of her chair. If he wanted to check her work then go right ahead, but he wasn't going to find anything wrong with it. She hunched over the mirror mount, measuring the angle. She'd forgotten her protractor and was using the hands on her watch as a sort of rough guide.

"Cheating," Austin said, nodding at the watch. In the glass, she could see the reflection of one hazel eye as he gazed down at her.

She sat very still.

His voice was low and oddly satisfied. He didn't really sound that much like Batman after all.

"Leave me alone," she said, even though he wasn't touching her.

She'd spent so long solving mysteries, but now and for the first time, she actually understood. Everything. To be a girl in a place boys thought they owned meant you never got to own it too. They wanted you modest. Grateful. Helpless, even when the truth was, she was better than him. *Would* always be better than him. It didn't matter.

The war between them was over, but that was a lie. She'd defeated him with the equivalent of an atom bomb, and in the real world, he had simply reset. It was never over, and she would be forced to prove herself—always—again and again. Nothing was ever better.

"What?" he said. "I'm just saying."

Brenna Yovanoff was raised in a barn, a tent, and a tepee, and was homeschooled until high school. She spent her formative years in Arkansas, in a town heavily populated by snakes, where sometimes turkeys would drop out of the sky. When she was five, she moved to Colorado, where it snows on a regular basis but never snows turkeys. She is the author of a number of novels, including the *New York Times* bestseller *The Replacement*. Her most recent book is *Places No One Knows*.

Website: brennayovanoff.com

Twitter: @brennayovanoff

Facebook: facebook.com/brennayovanoff

What Happens to Girls Who Disappear

CARRIE RYAN

She'd read the novels and seen the movies. She knew the popular guy just didn't suddenly decide to fall for the class outcast. And Cynthia knew she filled that role at her small parochial high school: her interest in European board games, her collection of vintage hair accessories, her odd hobby of amateur taxidermy. They marked her as *other*.

Except that Cynthia was beyond *other*. She was practically nonexistent. A ghost in her own hallways.

Her problem was that she *wanted* to believe. Because, in the movies the hot guy may only ask the weirdo out because of a dare, but eventually he always sees who she really is and falls in love.

In the movies he makes her beautiful. Wanted. He makes her matter, and everyone else sees it too.

Well, other than that one movie with the pig's blood, but there's always an exception to every rule.

And the rule for Cynthia was that she was nothing, and she'd stay that way until graduation. But in her heart, in the place of her most secret dreams, she craved to be the exception.

That was her downfall.

And like any good downfall it started innocuously enough. When the first text came in, Cynthia's phone vibrated against the hard plastic desk chair, rattling loudly in the silence of the math test. She jumped from the surprise of it, her hand reaching back to slap against her pocket. This caused a sea of snickers to ripple around her. Cheeks already flaming, she tried to slump out of existence, but it was too late.

With a beleaguered sigh Mr. Banks held out his hand, not even bothering to look up from the stack of papers he'd been grading at his desk. "No phones in class," he droned. It was the same message he gave day after day but the first time Cynthia had ever received it.

Because Cynthia never got texts.

Shoulders slumped, she slipped from her desk and shuffled to the front of the room. Every whisper, every giggle, was a needle scraped across her skin, giving off a sound like fingernails down a chalkboard.

She glanced at the screen before handing it over. The text stood out against the background picture of a blurry selfie taken at camp last summer.

HEY BEAUTIFUL.

One of her feet refused to move, staying rooted a split second longer than expected, and she pitched forward before regaining her balance. The wash of murmurs behind her notched higher. She tried to clear the lock screen, intent on erasing the words but her fingers were too clumsy, and Mr. Banks plucked the phone from her before she could finish.

The words still blazed on the screen. Of course Mr. Banks read them. His eyebrows twitched. The corners of his mouth tightened. Not in a frown, but a smirk. He glanced at her, and she read it all in his expression. In the way he shook his head once before dropping the phone in a drawer.

That he'd known instantly what she'd already figured out: It was a mistake. Those words hadn't been meant for her.

For a moment she was afraid he'd actually laugh. Or worse, read the text out loud, demanding to know who'd sent it. Instead, he slid the drawer closed and hunched back over his stack of papers. "You can pick it up at the end of school."

She turned back to her desk, eyes firmly glued to the ground. Every inch of exposed skin burned so hot she was sure those around her could feel the heat of her. For the rest of class she strained, trying to find words in the whispers. Trying to discern the tone of laughter. Feeling eyes on her, their judgment an iron casket closing tight.

That afternoon she hovered in the hallway, tucked between two banks of lockers, and waited for Mr. Banks to step out of his room. When he did, she darted in, yanked open his desk drawer, and fumbled for her phone. It was tangled among a nest of paper clips and old rubber bands. Capless pens and staples that had broken ranks from their glued brethren.

Sweat beaded on her neck. Though there was nothing

personal in the desk, it still felt like a violation to dig through it. An inviolate rule broken. But she couldn't face him. Couldn't risk him asking about the message. Phone in hand, she ran-walked to the door, the relief of near success practically choking her.

Mr. Banks was halfway down the hallway, headed her way. There was no way he missed her hasty retreat. But he said nothing as she scuttled past him with arms crossed and shoulders hunched. Eyes to the ground at all costs.

In her car she let the heat-soaked interior flush over her as she cupped the phone in hands shaky with adrenaline.

HEY BEAUTIFUL.

She didn't have the sender's number in her contacts, but that wasn't surprising. She had only three contacts beyond those of her family: a friend from camp, the owner of a local gaming shop, and a popular boy she'd overheard giving out his number at lunch one day. The area code was local, but running a reverse phone lookup yielded nothing.

She allowed a moment of unrestrained imagination. What it would be like if she *had* been the intended recipient. If she perhaps had some secret admirer. At first she pictured the boys in her class at school, but they all felt too familiar—too childish and immature.

They didn't feel *enough* for her.

No, she wanted someone sophisticated. Someone worldly who could pull her from her dull existence and introduce her to bolder and brighter worlds. He'd be older, much older, with the beginning edges of salt threading otherwise pepper hair. His skin would be dark, his lips lush, and his accent lilting as his tongue curled around poetry in her ear.

He'd be like the heroes in books and movies. The kind who could offer forever and not just right now.

Her problem was that she wanted it so much that even the fantasy of it turned her stomach sour. With a tight shake of her head, she wiped the screen and dropped the phone onto the passenger seat. Her car started with a coughing wheeze, and she drove home with every sense trained on her phone, willing it to buzz again.

It did, later that night.

The screen blazed bright in her bedroom, illuminating her desk. She fumbled from the sheets, reaching for it. Keenly aware of how her heart tripped over itself with surprise and anticipation.

YOU AWAKE?

She tucked one leg beneath her and sat. "Yes," she whispered. Because she'd never have the guts to actually write back. After a while the screen dimmed before going dark. But Cynthia just sat there in her empty room, thinking about how somewhere out there someone else stared at his phone, waiting for a response. For now, they shared this moment.

There was something a little beautiful and tragic in that, she thought.

• • •

The next day Cynthia checked her phone between every class, but there was nothing. The same that night and every other day that week. She guessed whoever was on the other end had realized his mistake and rectified it. She wondered if he now stayed up late texting with some other girl.

A girl nothing like Cynthia. Someone fun. Pretty. Interesting. Graceful.

She went back to tucking her phone in her back pocket again. No reason not to. So when it buzzed again during math that Friday, she jolted, knocking her book to the floor. It landed with a loud *thwap* that elicited several giggles. Mr. Banks raised his eyebrows in her direction, but she used the distraction of scrambling for her book to pull her phone free and slip it between her thighs, pressing them tight together to muffle any additional texts.

He continued lecturing about the difference between parabolas and hyperbolas but Cynthia no longer paid any attention. Every molecule of her being focused on the plastic case between her knees. Her breath shallower as she tried to figure out which she wanted more: another text or for the phone to remain silent.

At the end of class her thumb slid over the sweat dampened screen.

ARE YOU MAD AT ME?

She almost laughed. Had even begun to shake her head

in an answer. Before she remembered that the text wasn't meant for her.

The brief moment of elation crumbled. She turned the phone off and shoved it in her purse.

The next text came after Saturday night had tipped well into Sunday. She lay in the darkness, waiting. Trying to keep her courage up.

Because tonight she intended to respond.

YOU DIDN'T RESPOND.

She pushed herself up, tucking her hair behind her ears. Her fingers actually trembled as she clutched the phone. There was so much she'd imagined saying, so much she wanted to know about the person at the other end of the line.

Most important, she wanted to know what he expected. What he wanted. *Who* he wanted her to be.

But instead of asking any of that, she carefully typed out: *I'm sorry, I'm not who you're looking for.*

Then she reconsidered, deleted the last bit, and replaced it with: *you have the wrong number.*

She pressed send with a sigh.

Bubbles appeared on the screen, indicating that the sender was typing. Cynthia bit her lip, waiting, running the likely responses through her mind. *So sorry. My bad. D'oh.*

What she didn't expect was: *NO I DON'T.*

Her eyes widened. *I'm not who you're looking for.*

HOW DO YOU KNOW?

It was a valid question when she thought about it. The answer was remarkably easy: because no one was looking for her. No one even knew her number. But she wasn't about to tell him that.

He didn't have to know she was a loser. She certainly wasn't going to tell him if he hadn't figured it out already.

I don't know who you are, she sent him.

His answer took a while to type, Cynthia's heart pounding harder with each flash of the bubble on her screen. Until finally: *IF YOU DON'T KNOW WHO I AM THEN YOU CAN'T POSSIBLY KNOW WHO I'M LOOKING FOR.*

She actually let out a laugh at that, though it was a little more high pitched than usual. For a moment she wondered if this was what flirting felt like. Curling her toes against the mattress she leaned back, smiling. *Who is this?*

Those bubbles again, seeming to last forever. *THAT WOULD GIVE AWAY THE PUNCH LINE.*

She stared at the response, the tip of her thumb running across the edge of her phone case. Snapping it off and back on again. What if this was a joke. Or a trick. What if out there a group of guys from school—from her math class, perhaps— were sitting around laughing at her?

Making her want just to expose how pathetic she was.

And why was it pathetic to want, anyway? Wasn't that what life was about? Every action humans take is born of want:

wanting to eat, wanting money, wanting friends and love and warmth and meaning.

To just not be alone. Or invisible.

Or *other.*

HEY, YOU OKAY?

Her thumbs hovered. The problem was, she didn't know the answer.

Ten minutes later, the screen an uninterrupted dark, she set the phone on her bedside table and lay down, staring at it. Her mind played an endless loop of all the ways the conversation could have gone, but there were too many possibilities and so many of them ended wrong.

Better to be safe, she figured, than wrong.

She spent the week with her eyes up, watching those around her. Wondering which of her fellow students was the one who'd been texting her. She hovered by lockers and half-filled lunch tables whenever she saw the flash of a phone, hoping to catch a glimpse of its screen.

Even though she knew it was ridiculous.

But she'd heard nothing more, a fact that had caused her mouth to turn dry with a sort of desperate regret twined through with longing.

Her imagination concocted more and more elaborate fantasies that sprouted like weeds in her mind. No matter how hard she tried to yank them out, they only spread wider, growing wilder.

So that when Thursday morning's chapel service rolled around, she was ready to try something more forceful. In the quiet of Communion, as students shuffled up the aisle toward the altar, Cynthia slipped her phone free and thumbed a text.

You still there?

Perched on the edge of her seat, she pressed send and scanned the auditorium. Waiting for a head to shift, a shoulder to drop as someone reached for their pocket. She held her breath, straining for the vibration in the silence.

But there was nothing.

Until.

YES.

Her heart quickened. She whipped her eyes across the other students. Of course several had phones hidden in their laps, but they all appeared bored. None of them with that sense of anticipation or expectation.

Just to be sure she thumbed out *Good* and pressed send.

None of them reacted.

She turned back in her chair. A smile began threatening her face, but then she noticed the priest frowning at her and she forced her expression into something more neutral.

But that didn't stop her pulse from singing.

That night she waited. Expecting that since she'd reestablished contact, she'd hear from him at any moment. But the evening passed. Then the early night. Then the late night. Then the first of the morning. She considered texting him first, but that somehow felt too desperate.

He'd been the one pursuing her, after all. What did it mean if he'd given up? Perhaps he'd moved on to other prey. She'd known it would only be a matter of time.

Or maybe he'd realized she was the wrong number after all.

Either way, when she fell asleep just before sunrise, something inside of her felt newly hollow and fragile, and she didn't know how to handle it without breaking it.

It was early Sunday and of course Cynthia was awake. She didn't sleep. Couldn't sleep because of the waiting.

The waiting and the dreaming.

DON'T BE MAD AT ME.

The text lit up her room. The corner of her lip twitched with satisfaction. He recognized she had a right to be upset.

It made her feel a bit powerful. And so she flexed it, waiting before responding.

It worked. He bit first.

ARE YOU AWAKE?

She smiled and leaned back against her headboard. *So if you won't tell me your name, then tell me something else about you.*

There was a part of her that couldn't believe what she was doing. Pushing. Engaging. Asking.

Flirting.

I LIKE MUSIC.

Music wasn't really her thing. But it could be. *What kind.*

OLDER STUFF. CLASSIC ROCK KIND OF STUFF. DYLAN. KING.

She frowned, a soft alarm buzzing in the back of her head. *How old are you?*

The answer came fast. *YOUR AGE.*

Cynthia picked at the corner of her phone case with her thumb. *What school do you go to?*

There was a long pause. The bubbles of him typing didn't even appear for several minutes. Enough so that Cynthia had already swung her legs off the side of the bed and begun to pace.

IS THAT REALLY WHAT YOU WANT TO KNOW?

She let out a breath and sank into her desk chair.

ASK ME WHAT YOU REALLY WANT.

Heat washed over her. The problem was that there were so many things she wanted to know, but she couldn't decide which were more important. She wanted to know how he found her number. How he knew who she was. Why he'd texted her. If he liked her. Who he was. What he wanted.

It all came so fast in her mind it made her dizzy.

But there was the one question that had been the drumbeat underlying everything from the beginning. *Is this a joke?*

NO.

Of course he would say that. Even if it was an elaborate prank, he'd never admit it. *How can I trust you?*

BECAUSE I'M A FRIEND.

This gave her pause. She thought back to the students at the chapel service she'd seen with their phones out. *Do I know you?*

YOU DO NOW.

That wasn't an answer at all. If anything, it made this all feel like even more of a trick. *But before now. Have we met?*

A pause. Then bubbles. Then: *YES.*

It was as though the air around her had come alive. *When?*

Minutes passed. So many that Cynthia almost panicked that she'd somehow driven him away. A half-dozen times she typed out some sort of apology and then deleted it. Afraid to press send because then he'd never answer.

WHY DOES THIS MATTER TO YOU?

Inside, she warred, because it didn't actually matter to her if they'd met. What mattered was the assurance this wasn't all a practical joke. But his refusal to answer—to tell her his name, to explain how they knew each other—that's what scared her.

I just . . . don't know if I should be talking to you.

WHY NOT?

Frustration buzzed along her arms. It was so obvious, she felt stupid having to type it out. *Because. What if you're not who you say you are?*

A FRIEND?

She rolled her eyes. Heat flushed her cheeks, the back of her neck, dampening the nightgown at the base of her spine.

You could be someone from school playing a joke. A serial killer.
A pervert. A monster. Insane.

OR A FRIEND, LIKE I SAID.

But the reality was, she didn't believe that. Because she
didn't have any friends. So, why would one suddenly appear?
So out of the blue? There had to be a reason. Some sort of
ulterior motive. She shook her head, trying to find the words
to explain.

He responded before she could even type her reply. *WHY*
DO YOU BELIEVE THE WORST ABOUT PEOPLE?

She didn't know how this had turned around on her, but
she felt judged. As though he found her somehow lacking.
Not good enough. She wanted to prove herself to him. *I don't*
believe the worst about people.

YOU BELIEVE THE WORST ABOUT YOURSELF.

At this she choked on a laugh born of outrage and leaped
to her feet. She quivered with anger, knuckles white from gripping the phone. She started her response a dozen times and a
dozen times she deleted it.

Because maybe he was right.

It was so much easier to blame her loneliness on herself.
That she wasn't interesting or smart or pretty or fun or cool
enough to attract friends. Because, somehow it would be
worse if she was all of those things—brilliant and beautiful
and witty and vivacious—and folks still rejected her.

She didn't believe that it was better to have loved and

lost than to have never loved at all. Loss meant you somehow failed. That you couldn't hold on tight enough.

Defeated, she stood in front of the window, shoulders slumped. The phone buzzed in her hand.

WHY CAN'T I JUST BE SOMEONE WHO WANTS TO BE FRIENDS WITH YOU?

Her first thought was: What if I want something more? But she shook it loose before it could sink hooks into her mind. She couldn't help but wonder what kind of a loser took a string of texts from an anonymous stranger and spun them into such a far-fetched fantasy.

It was absurd. And yet . . . she couldn't stop.

She didn't know how to answer his questions. She couldn't just tell him that it was an empirical fact that no one wanted to be her friend. Then the real question came. The one thing she'd really wanted to know. *But how can I know for sure?*

LIFE DOESN'T COME WITH GUARANTEES.

Her answer was simple and raw and honest. *It would be so much easier if it did.*

There was a long break, enough so that Cynthia had settled back into bed and allowed her eyes to start drifting shut. The familiar hum lit the room.

SWEET DREAMS.

She wanted to feel disappointed, and, to be fair, she did. But that didn't stop the smile from spreading in the darkness.

• • •

The next morning Cynthia downloaded every Bob Dylan song she could find, playing them on an endless repeat. She wore earbuds to school so she could listen between classes. It made the waiting between texts easier.

Because, even given their lengthy conversation over the weekend, the texts were as sporadic as ever. Cynthia began to wonder about his life. When he texted her in math class on Wednesday that he was thinking of her, had he also been in school? Perhaps snuck away to the bathroom so he wouldn't get caught with his phone?

And late at night, when her eyes burned with the need for sleep, was he maybe just getting off work somewhere? Did he race home, thinking of her? Slip into bed, a smile on his face, and pull up her number?

Or maybe she was just one of a dozen. A hundred or a thousand girls, and maybe even boys, he rotated through.

All of these questions and doubts would crush into the silence. They'd fill the empty screen as she waited for him.

It became too much. The edge she sat on too razor sharp. So that when her phone buzzed late on Friday, she didn't even stop to think. She flicked the button to call him. Holding her breath during the long pause before it began to ring.

Panic ran through her, sending her heart thundering. Her brain screamed at her to hang up hang up hang up, but she pushed the phone tighter to her ear. He'd just texted. Which meant he'd been holding his phone.

Which meant there was no way he didn't see her call coming through.

Yet he wasn't answering.

She wanted to picture him sitting somewhere, staring at her name on his screen. But she couldn't, because in her mind he was only a shadow.

She closed her eyes. Not wanting to accept what was obvious.

It rolled over to his voice mail, and for a moment she thought that at least she'd be able to construct an image of him from the scaffolding of his voice. But she was met with only the robotic recitation of his number and the offer to leave a message.

She hung up without saying anything. Waited for him to text some sort of excuse or apology. He did neither, and she worried she'd broken an unspoken rule. Pushed too hard or too far.

Her fingers trembled as she typed out: *Why didn't you answer?*

She watched the bubbles of his response. *YOU DIDN'T WANT ME TO.*

The sound she let escape was a cry of frustrated desperation wrapped in a laugh. And then Cynthia did something she never thought she'd do. She turned off her phone. Then she rolled over in bed and cried.

. . .

That week his texts stacked up on her screen. All left unanswered.

HEY.

YOU THERE?

EVERYTHING OK?

TALK TO ME.

It was the last one that broke her. It said simply: *CYNTHIA.* And it came in late Saturday night as she lay in the darkness of her room.

She couldn't quite figure out why it brought tears to her eyes. Perhaps because it was the first time he'd used her name. Or perhaps it was confirmation that none of this had been a mistake—a wrong number.

It had been about her the entire time.

It's not fair that you know my name and I don't know yours, she finally wrote to him.

She should have expected the answer. It was the same as before: *IS THAT WHAT YOU REALLY WANT TO KNOW?*

No. She typed quickly. *Where did we meet?*

And then she wrote: *Wait. Not that.*

Why me?

WHY NOT YOU?

It was an unsatisfying answer. Flippant in its own way. As though there was nothing particularly interesting about her that stood out—separated her from the herd. She set the phone down, thinking that perhaps she should be done with this. Maybe even block his number.

But when it buzzed again, she couldn't resist.

I'VE NEVER SEEN SOMEONE WHO WANTED OUT OF HER LIFE AS MUCH AS YOU DO.

Heat flushed up the back of her legs.

He kept going. As her breath came faster and her knees grew weaker.

EVERYTHING ABOUT YOU IS A GIFT.

CAN'T YOU SEE THAT, CYNTHIA?

YOU MEAN SOMETHING.

She felt spent, emptied but in a way that seemed somehow delicious. She pushed herself deeper into the mattress, skin humming, as she let that last phrase repeat endlessly through her head.

Except she added "to me" at the end. Because it was clear that's what he'd meant. *You mean something to me.*

YOU STILL THERE? I CAN SEE YOUR LIGHT ON.

Cynthia frowned. *My light isn't on.*

There was a long pause. *AH, MUST BE YOUR FATHER'S THEN.*

She stared at the words before pushing from the bed. The long hallway outside her room was dark except for the wash of light sweeping underneath her father's bedroom door. She swallowed. Her flushed skin turned cold, clammy.

Quietly, slowly, she tiptoed back into her room and over to her window. A few doors down a car idled in the street, tucked in the black shadow of a thick tree. A weak glow lit the driver's side, only enough to give her a vague outline of the figure inside.

He was tall. Skinny. His elbow rested on the edge of the open window as he typed something out.

A moment later her phone pulsed against her fingertips. *YOU COULD INVITE ME IN.*

But she knew that could never happen. That somehow him stepping into her house would be wrong. Would break whatever it was between them.

She had to go to him. *I'll come out.*

She glanced down at her nightgown—white lawn cotton grown thin from hundreds of washes. It ended with a ruffle below her knees, and pink bows decorated the hem, most of them missing after so many years.

She suddenly realized how much it made her look like a little girl. That's not how she wanted him to think of her. *Just let me change first.*

His response was swift, lighting the room before she'd even reached for a pair of jeans. *NO. AS YOU ARE.*

Something inside of her squeezed in a way she'd never felt before. She couldn't decide if it was from fear or anticipation or both mixed together. But she thought she might like it.

Her breath came shorter. *Okay.*

But she didn't move. She just stood, staring out her bedroom window at the car idling in the darkness.

And she realized how ridiculous this all was. She knew nothing about this man. Not even his name.

Not even the sound of his voice.

She thought that if she could just have that, she'd know. Whether to trust him. To go to him. To believe in him.

She pressed the call button, holding the phone to her ear as she watched him. Waiting for the flash of light from his phone to illuminate his face. She thought she saw him shake his head, and a profound sense of disappointment weighed on her muscles.

Not for him. But for herself. Because she felt she'd somehow let him down.

She was about to hang up when she saw him lift his hand. The ringing ended with a *click*. And then she heard breathing. That's all there was. Him breathing, her watching him. Neither saying anything.

"Tell me I'll be okay," she finally whispered. "That you won't hurt me."

"You already know I can't promise you that, Cynthia." His voice was more sense than sound, as though the words somehow bypassed her ear and lodged directly in her thoughts. Each time she heard the roll and timbre of him it was a surprise, like discovering the sound of him over and over again.

She wanted more of it. "Then, tell me something about yourself. Something true."

There was his breathing again, an even rhythm that she unconsciously matched. "You already know it all."

"Tell me anyway," she whispered.

"I'm no good for you."

And he was right. She did know this.

"But it won't stop you," he added.

She pretended to think about those words, because she felt that somehow they should be important to her. But they weren't. Because she already knew the answer. "You're right. It won't stop me."

"It never does." He sounded tired.

She heard something in the background, a change in the tenor of the engine as though he'd shifted out of park. Outside she watched as his car began to ease from its place by the curb.

He was leaving. Without her. "Wait!" she called, starting for the stairs. When she pushed through the screen door and started across her lawn, he was already pulling down the road. Almost to her house. She sprinted, not caring about her nightgown or bare feet, to the middle of the street and stood with one hand raised.

For the barest hint of a moment she wondered if he'd just keep going. Plow through and over her. She thought she heard the cycle of his engine rev. But still she stood her ground.

He braked, his bumper coming to a stop inches away from her thighs. She was afraid to move, thinking that if she stepped aside, he would drive away. So she stayed in the wash of his headlights, their brightness throwing everything behind into darkness.

Something buzzed in her hand, and she realized she no

longer pressed the phone to her ear. She looked down to find a text. *YOU SHOULD GO BACK TO BED.*

She squinted, trying to see him past the glare of his headlights. But, as before, he was nothing but a vague outline filled by shadow. She shook her head.

YOU KNOW THIS STORY.

Her heart pounded harder, as though her chest had tightened around it. She nodded.

YOU KNOW HOW IT ENDS.

She hammered out her response. *Why will it have to end?*

EVERYTHING ENDS EVENTUALLY.

Cynthia stepped forward, placing her fingertips against the hood of the car. The metal scorched her skin, but she didn't care. She remembered, now, that his window was rolled down, so she let her phone fall to her side. "You have to know you can't tell someone they matter to you and expect them to walk away," she said aloud.

She thought she heard him sigh. And she knew then that he wouldn't leave her. Slowly, she eased her way around to the passenger side and leaned through the open window.

The interior was lit only by the shadows of night and the soft glow of his phone, but it was enough for her to realize she recognized him in a vague way she couldn't place. He wasn't from school, of that she was sure. The angles of his face were sharper than the boys she knew, his hair shaggier. He looked to be out of his teens, but how far out she couldn't quite figure.

His jeans were well worn, his leather jacket even more so. His glasses seemed to almost have a tint to them, causing what little light existed in the car to glance off them so that she couldn't see his eyes.

Looking at him made her stomach clench, but whether it was with unease or excitement, she wasn't sure. And she knew, then, that he'd been telling the truth when he'd told her he was an old friend—not in any way that was easy to explain or understand, but in a way that felt like some deeper truth.

She pressed her hand against her chest, reassuring herself of her thundering heart. "I know the question I want you to answer."

He didn't turn to look at her but continued staring forward, into the illuminated night. But she could feel the tension in him. The set of his shoulders and the grip of his hands around the wheel.

"Where are we going?"

He reached forward and flicked on the radio. It started scratchy before music filled the car. "Does it matter?"

She thought about that a moment, watching the way his fingers drummed against the steering wheel to the beat of the familiar song. She knew what the right answer should be: Yes. That it was stupid to climb into a car with a stranger. It was even more stupid to care what a stranger thought of her. To trust the words of someone she didn't know.

To believe them more than you believe yourself.

But none of that mattered to her. Because he'd come for her. He'd been the only one. Would probably ever be the only one. It was like in the movies, where suddenly someone had *seen* her.

All Cynthia had ever wanted was to matter to someone. And now she did.

She knew how this story ended—she'd read it before. He would take her to a wide field and hold her tight, and she would go willingly because she so badly wanted out of her life.

What did it matter if she was perhaps trading one hell for another?

She opened the door and slid into the car. "No," she told him. "I don't care where we're going."

He nodded once, but there was no smile, no semblance of victory for him. As though this was a game he was tired of winning. He flicked the sound of the radio up, and Cynthia sat back, enjoying the way the car's acceleration pushed against her. For once the world was open and wide and unknown before her, even if she knew it wouldn't last.

Carrie Ryan is the *New York Times* bestselling author of the Forest of Hands and Teeth series, *Daughter of Deep Silence*, and *Infinity Ring: Divide and Conquer* as well as the editor of *Foretold: 14 Stories of Prophecy and Prediction*. With her husband, John Parke Davis, Carrie writes the The Map to Everywhere middle grade series. Her books have sold in over twenty-two territories, and her first book is in development as a major motion picture. A former litigator, Carrie now lives in Charlotte, North Carolina, with her husband and various pets.

Website: carrieryan.com

Twitter: @carrieryan

Facebook: facebook.com/AuthorCarrieRyan

The Mermaid Aquarium: Weeki Wachee Springs, 1951

CHERIE PRIEST

B ut you never know!" Tammy plunged one hand into the trunk of mismatched shoes and felt around with her fingertips. "We could find buried treasure in here. You can't beat buried treasure for . . . what does the sign say, a nickel?"

Her sister reread the hand scrawled note taped inside the trunk's open lid. "A nickel," she confirmed with a shake of her head. "Honestly. Who pays a nickel apiece for mismatched shoes?"

"A pirate. One with a peg."

Elaine picked a blue leather sandal out of the pile and spun it around on her pinky finger. "I'd love to meet the pirate who'd wear one of *these*. Peg or no peg. Hey, speaking of pirates—I hear we get to do *battle* with pirates."

"Battle? With pirates?"

"That's what Mr. Newton said."

Once again elbow deep in stale footwear, Tammy laughed. "Mermaids versus pirates. That's going to be *amazing*. Ooh, what's this?" Her hand hooked something down at the bottom. She yanked it up and out—a shiny silver crown with big, fake-looking gemstones.

"What on earth is that?"

"Buried treasure. I told you we'd find some!" She held it up to the sky and let the afternoon sun beam through it, casting choppy rainbows across the lawn. "This will be perfect for my outfit—look, it's got little clips on it and everything. It'll stay on my head underwater, right?" Without waiting for an answer, she said to herself, "I bet it will. Anyhow, it's worth a nickel to find out.

"Excuse me, ma'am?" She waved her hands and held up the silly tiara. "I found this in the shoe bin."

The old lady on the porch squinted down at the yard sale and at Tammy with her treasure. "I forgot that was in there. It's part of an old Halloween costume."

"Great! Now I can wear it with *my* costume." Tammy grinned big. "We're going to be mermaids. It's our job, starting tomorrow."

"Oh." The old lady's face went tight and sour. She put one hand on the porch rail and one on her hip. "Over at the springs, you mean. At Weeki Wachee."

Elaine nodded and stepped up to stand beside her sister. "Yes, ma'am. We've joined the mermaid show. We got hired yesterday, and we start tomorrow. Mr. Newton's going to teach us how to breathe through the air tubes and everything."

The woman on the porch sniffed, like whatever the girls were talking about didn't smell very good. "That's not a decent job."

"Have you ever *seen* the mermaid show?" Tammy asked, still holding the tiara aloft.

"Of course not."

"Then, how do you know it isn't decent?"

She crinkled the edge of her nose and frowned harder. "I've seen those girls, running around in their bikinis, flagging down cars to bring people into the springs. I remember when it didn't used to be that way."

Tammy rubbed her foot into the grass and rolled her eyes. "Ma'am, can I buy the tiara or not?"

"For a dime."

"But the sign on the trunk said—"

"That was for the shoes. It says the shoes are a nickel, and it doesn't say anything about costume trinkets."

Tammy gave Elaine a look that asked what she thought about the deal.

Elaine shrugged. "It'll look good with a fish tail. I say you should buy it."

"All right. Asking a whole dime for this thing is practically highway robbery, but I'll pay it."

"We don't have no highway here." One pointed foot at a time, the woman tiptoed down the wood porch steps.

"I guess 19 don't count," Tammy said of the nearest proper road, wiggling her fingers around in her pocket. She pulled out a dime and made a show of presenting it.

"I guess it don't." The woman took the coin and pushed it into her purse. "Is that all, then? Y'all don't want anything else?"

"No, ma'am," the girls said together. "Thank you," Tammy added.

The old lady nodded and turned her back to them. She went up the porch stairs again, returning to her post, where she could oversee the sale on her broad, green lawn.

Tammy toyed with the tiara as they left, wandering back down into the dirt road and toward U.S. 19, the only paved strip in that part of Florida—a two lane road that ran along the Gulf Coast past all the little towns, joints, and junctures . . . including the springs at Weeki Wachee.

But Weeki Wachee wasn't a proper town; it was just a freshwater pool that a sharp ex-navy man had turned into a roadside attraction. How Frank Newton got the idea to dig an underwater auditorium and fill it with mermaids, no one knew—but word sure did get around about the show. People came from all over the country to see the aquatic acrobatics, and girls came from miles away, hoping to make the cut and wear the fins.

The yard sale lady was right about the bikinis, too. And maybe she was right that it wasn't decent to go running around half-naked all the time, but in 1951 there weren't many visitors passing through that part of Florida. People brought in tourist money however they could, and teenage girls in bikinis brought in a *lot* of tourists.

Besides, neither Tammy nor Elaine had any problem with the skimpy uniform, and if Frank wanted girls to dress that way and chase down cars, that was all right with them.

At least he wasn't weird about it.

Frank was a big guy, wide in the shoulders, with thighs like tree trunks, and the sort of chest where a big tattoo would look right at home. The way he talked—the way he handed out orders and suggestions, the way he taught them how to use the equipment—you could tell he'd been a military man. He wasn't unkind, but he was direct. He wasn't unreasonable, but he was demanding.

Tammy and Elaine caught on quick, and Frank approved.

He liked them not just because they were pretty red-haired sisters, but because they were sturdy farm girls who'd grown up in orchards, climbing orange trees and working hard for a living. Swimming around in the tank was tough, especially with legs bound together in phony fins and only a set of skinny, hidden tubes to breathe from. It didn't matter how pretty a girl was, because if she wasn't hardy enough to swim and smile without much air, she wasn't ready to join the show.

Tammy was all set to swim within one week, and her older sister joined the next.

For their first show together Frank dressed them up the same—passing them off as twins for the sake of the underwater play they were performing.

It worked out well. The girls were only a year apart—"Irish

twins" their mother called them—and with enough of the right greasepaint glitter makeup, at a distance, inside the tank, nobody knew the difference.

The tiara Tammy picked up at the yard sale helped. It gave the audience a way to tell them apart. She twisted the hairpiece into her curls as tight as she could, pushing the metal bobby pins up against her scalp to keep it secure through all the swirling, diving, and splashing. With the tiara perched on her head, that little coronet with the tacky stones, Tammy was the one to watch.

She was the girl with the silver crown.

The shows took on a comfortable, familiar pattern.

Sometimes, the themes were different—pirates, or police, or shipwrecks—but the daily routine was usually the same. Every day, there was practice and training, with Frank barking the story along through a megaphone. Every day, there was time spent sipping from the tiny air hoses and learning to breathe without gasping in front of the audience.

Breathe and smile. Drink a bottle of fizzy Grapette underwater while the kids clapped and their parents wondered *How on earth do they do that?*

But they weren't on earth.

They performed beneath it, under the blue skin of the pooled spring and down in front of the enormous, underground window—they frolicked like polar bears in a zoo, with only the thick and tinted fishbowl glass between them and the wide-eyed watchers.

And all the people in the auditorium sat and shivered, cool as almost ice in the orange-hot heat of a Florida afternoon. Openmouthed, they watched the women in bright bathing suits from a fairy tale—they saw how their fins twisted in the current, how their smiles stayed in place because people had paid good money to see them.

It was magic, and it hid out in the open. The rules were different, there.

"Car!" Frank bellowed through his megaphone. *"Car!"*

All the girls knew what to do. The mermaids rallied from the tank with a flurry of flinging water. Wet hair went tied up in scarves or combs, and fins were quickly, carefully stripped. Pruney feet with painted toenails felt about for sandals, and, finding them, they pattered away from the spring.

"Hurry up!" Frank hollered. He pulled a short-sleeved, button-up shirt over his wet chest and retreated toward the ticket office. "Go get 'em, ladies!"

All eight of the mermaids on duty charged out of the dirt and gravel parking lot and over to U.S. 19. And, yes, a brand new '51 Chevrolet was coming in from the north. It was black with chrome and fins shining like silver, and inside it must have been hot as an oven, come noon in July.

The car slowed for the swarm of girls and stopped on the

side of the road. All of the windows were down, so within seconds, each one framed at least two grinning young women wearing not very much in the way of clothes.

The driver grinned back from beneath a gleaming mop of slick black hair and matching eyebrows. If it weren't for the pink haze of sunburn across his nose, he would've looked like a happy vampire.

Elaine spoke first, leaning into the car. "Hey there, mister."

"Hey there, sweetheart," he replied, and his voice was shiny too. Oil on aluminum. "To what do I owe this pleasure?"

One of the other girls spoke next. She batted her eyelashes and hung her boobs over the passenger side window. "We're the girls of Weeki Wachee—a little place you can find right over there, through the trees. We put on a mean show, if you'd like to make a little room for us in your wallet."

"What kind of show?"

"Mermaids!" several of them said at once.

He laughed, and the sound shimmered around the edges. "All right. You've got me now. Let's see what you little sirens can do."

The girls chased his car into the lot and vanished in a trickle, one or two returning to the tank or to the concession and ticketing area. The rest swarmed into the locker room and began dressing up. It could be quick, and it didn't have to be perfect. It was just one guy, not a family or a group to fill the eighteen-seat auditorium.

But the week had been slow, and Frank was a big believer in word of mouth. He said it was always worth putting on the show for the occasional individual, because that one guy might go home and tell his friends.

So Tammy slid over the side of the tank with one practiced, slippery motion.

She imagined she was a seal, a sea lion, or a penguin— something with rounded edges and a shape meant to move through water. Once she was in the aquarium, it was all too easy to sink like a stone. It was hard to remember not to paddle and kick, to pretend she was born with the aqua-blue fin. It was hard to swim by flexing her waist and snapping her ankles.

She did it beautifully, and down into the spring she tumbled.

The water was too cold at first. She closed her eyes, then opened them. She found the rubber breathing tube and remembered how to swim, and breathe, and smile. She tucked the tube away behind an ornamental rock, so the man in the auditorium couldn't see it.

Two other mermaids joined her, and then her sister did too. They moved together; they found their tubes and discreetly sipped enough oxygen to writhe their swimming selves into position. They were sea lions and sirens, every last one of them.

Tammy waved at the man—he'd said his name was Ed— standing all alone in the auditorium. He didn't take a seat. He stood at the glass and he waved back. The gesture was filtered through the window, and the sparkling clear water, and through the bubbles of the breathing tubes behind the rocks. But Tammy saw it, and she smiled at him because that was her job now.

But suddenly, she didn't mean it.

Her smile froze where it was, and it did not melt.

It unnerved her, the way Ed stood there in the empty room with the tiny tile mosaics in blue, pink, and gold. It cast a chill through the window and into the spring water to see him there, arms folded after he finished waving at them.

Through the glass with the soft green tint she saw him differently, standing alone in the empty room with the folding seats like a movie theater. He did not look like the same man who drove the black Chevy down U.S. 19. He looked colder and sharper. The pink was gone from his skin and the blue was brighter in his hair through the lens of the window glass—and through the heavy, cool weight of a million gallons between them.

Elaine swam up to Tammy's side and handed her a new bottle of Grapette. Startled out of the spell Tammy took it and popped the bottle cap. In sync, she and her sister drank together, and the man clapped to see the little red-haired sirens take their sodas underwater.

Such a precious trick. Such a pretty thing to watch.

And maybe that was what it came down to, when Tammy later tried to think of what had bothered her so much about

Ed and his blue-black eyes, his blue-black hair. Through the whole story—even when Frank joined in as the pirate king and the funny fake cannon sent explosions of bubbles and waves through the water—Ed was never watching anything or anyone except for Tammy. And he never looked her in the eyes, but he stared somewhere higher, above her forehead. He was looking at the cheap, pretty tiara fixed to her head with bobby pins and skill.

When the show was over, Ed went on his way, and Frank called Tammy aside as she toweled herself dry.

"That guy, Ed. Did you know him?" He looked worried, but he was trying to hide it.

Tammy shook her head. "Never saw him before."

"Huh." Frank twiddled absently with the end of a cracked breathing tube, one he was repairing or replacing from a compressed air tank. "I wondered, that's all. He talked about you like he knew you, but he didn't know your name."

"What'd he say?"

Frank tossed the tube aside, into the trash. He shrugged his big shoulders with the tight-looking muscles underneath them and leaned back against the doorframe. "He said he liked the show. And he especially liked the girl with the silver crown."

"Oh. I guess that's me, then."

"I guess it is, but I don't like how he said it. Where did you get that little crown anyway? I've noticed it before. It looks nice with the fins, but maybe you shouldn't wear it any-more."

"I found it at a yard sale in New Port Richey. Why shouldn't I wear it? Because some creepy guy pointed it out on a lark?" She was nervous again, not because of Frank, who made the same concerned face her dad used to make when he smelled trouble, but because she couldn't stand the thought of taking off the tiara. She'd been wearing it more lately, even without the costume. Even for fun, down at the movies or at the beach. It belonged one of two places: in the locker at the ladies' rooms or on her head.

Preferably, on her head.

"Look," he added, still in father mode, "I didn't like that guy, that's all I'm saying. I didn't like the way he looked at you. Nice guys don't stare like that. If you see him around, or if he comes around again . . . I want you to tell me about it. And next show, maybe you can leave off the hairpiece. We'll find something else to match your costume."

"Okay," she told him. She knew he was right, but he was a little bit wrong, too.

It wasn't weird, the way Ed had looked at her. It was weird how he'd looked at the tiara, like he'd seen it before. Like it meant something to him. Well, it meant something to Tammy, too.

Two days later Frank was sick—or that's what he said. There was a sign up at the entrance to the concessions and ticket area, where the doors were locked and there weren't any lights turned on inside.

BAD CASE OF THE FLU.

TAKE THE DAY OFF.

BACK AT THE REGULAR TIME TOMORROW.

Tammy and Elaine were early for work, and they were the first to see the sign. They puzzled over it.

"But Frank's *never* sick," Tammy complained. "He's practically invincible."

"I hope he's all right."

"He will be. He's practically—"

"Invincible. Yeah. I heard you." Elaine picked at the tape on the sign and leaned her head close to the door. Somewhere in the distance, down a floor or two below—she thought she heard something. But it was faint. There was nothing certain, nothing she could point to and say, *Listen. What's that?*

So she didn't say anything about it, and the pair of them walked back to U.S. 19 to walk or hitchhike home, like they did most days. It was better to do it while the morning was still new and before the sun got too high.

One by one the other girls arrived and read the sign, and one by one they turned and went back home with a grumble.

But not a single girl listened as hard as Elaine did, with her ear right next to the concession room door. None of them heard the splashing, the soft rubbing coming from down below in the auditorium. None of them pulled at the door or fought the lock.

A day off was easier than chasing phantom sounds.

But Frank was not home in bed with the flu. He was there at Weeki Wachee, downstairs in the auditorium where the eighteen cinema seats lined up like soldiers facing the aquarium window. He was standing on a stool, wearing a grim expression and a pair of shorts, but nothing else. He held a rag and a sponge—the big kind, the kind they used for washing cars.

Beside him was a bucket, and inside the bucket was soapy water that had turned almost purple.

He wrung out the sponge and the rag and pulled them back and forth over the wide underground window that was bigger than a movie screen: wiping, smoothing, cleaning. Erasing the message he'd found there, first thing that morning—a message which was so much worse than the one he'd left to protect his girls.

If they saw this one, they'd only be afraid. There was no need to involve the police, no reason to let the authorities wander around asking questions and issuing warnings. Cops would be in the way. They'd be bad for business.

And there was nothing to be afraid of, anyway.

Or that's what he told himself, same as he told the mermaids. But all the same he'd be on the lookout for a dark eyed man with hair blacker than the ace of spades. He'd keep his eyes peeled for that fellow who called himself Ed.

With runny, tinted water staining his hands, he kept on

working—wearing away the series of letters that stood as tall as his arms were long. By suppertime not a trace would be left, and it was better that way.

But for now, the window still read: IT BELONGS TO ME AND YOU MUST GIVE IT BACK.

Frank didn't know how he knew it was Ed, but he did. And somehow, he knew precisely what Ed wanted back. It was that stupid crown, the one Tammy wore in the show. There was something uncanny about it—something that made you want to touch it, hold it. Even wear it, not that Frank would ever do such a thing.

That ridiculous bauble wasn't normal—and neither was Ed.

Somehow, they belonged together. He wondered how they'd ever gotten separated in the first place.

Maybe he could retrieve it when the girls had all gone home. Maybe he could throw it away himself—or leave it out for Ed to find. Frank didn't like a bully, and he didn't like following orders from random vandals. But maybe if he did what the message said, Ed would go away.

"You shouldn't be the last to leave."

"What?" Tammy asked. She wrapped her towel quickly around the tiara and pulled it out of the locker, hiding it against her stomach.

Frank closed his arms over his chest. "We talked about this. Where was your sister today? And what have you got there? Is that that hair doodad? I thought we talked about this—I don't want to see it anymore, not in the show."

"I *know*, and that's why I'm taking it home. What are you doing in the *ladies'* room?" She felt guilty and nervous, and she knew it was dumb. The tiara was hers. She could take it home with her if she wanted to. Frank should be the one feeling guilty and nervous. *He* was the one sneaking up on her in the bathroom.

"I thought everyone was gone," he told her. "I was going to check in here for . . . um . . . toilet paper. I was going to take out the trash."

"You should've knocked."

"I *did* knock. Didn't you hear me?"

"No." But when she said it out loud and thought about it, yes, maybe. Maybe she *had* heard him. She clutched the towel bundle and retreated, pushing her back against the locker door to shut it.

He stepped back too—almost sitting on the edge of the sink, he leaned so hard against it. Maybe he felt guilty and nervous after all. "How're you getting home today?"

"Hitch or walk, same as always."

"By yourself? No, I don't like that. Let me give you a lift."

Outside, the sun burned down hot and steady, even though it was almost seven o'clock. Tammy thought about it for a second, but only a second. She trusted Frank. Everyone did—you pretty much had to . . . and it was amazingly, blindingly hot outside. She didn't really want to walk. "All right. Yeah, I'll ride with you."

"Good. Let me lock up around here, and we'll head out."

She nodded and held the tiara tighter, as if she were afraid he might try to take it away from her. He almost looked like he wanted to.

He didn't try it. He only stomped away in his brown sandals and tan shorts. Over his shoulder he said, "Five minutes. Meet me at the spring."

"Five minutes," she echoed.

And she wandered down to the spring's edge to stare down into the human sized aquarium filled with tubes and props. The sky gleamed in ribbons, and the sunlight on the waves threw stripes of white to cut up the blue surface.

Behind her, against the sky, there was a flash of some other color.

Dark and also blue—a navy blue that shined nearly black, or was it the other way around?

Tammy froze, squinting at the reflection. Just past her head, it was there—the pale silver face with cruel, small eyes as bitter as coffee beans. And above the eyes, that shock of hair—so dark, and blue, yes, blue. Blue in the reflection, with the sky behind it. How had it ever looked black?

She turned around fast, throwing up an arm—throwing up a defense against nothing at all. He wasn't there.

And then, with a quick cuff of his fist against her chest,

just beneath her throat, she fell backward—towel and tiara and dry clothes and all.

Back and down.

And as she fell her eyes met his, and they were the same ones from the Chevy, from the shiny black car that no one ought to drive in Florida, not in the dead of summer. The reflection and the man didn't match—they couldn't match.

But there he was, where the silver-faced man had loomed behind her. No, not a man. A fey thing, dark and terrible. Something that belonged in the dark, in the water of a swamp. Not in the sun, not in a spring.

As she fell, she thought—in that half second before she hit the water and closed her eyes from pure reflex—that there was distortion around him like a halo, like the way hot air rises from asphalt, or the way gasoline fumes twist outside a car's tank while the pump fills it up.

And in that split instant when she hit the water and her eyelids were dropping down hard, she saw Frank, too. Coming up behind Ed with a look on his face like murder.

Tammy slapped into the water backside first, and it stung when her shoulders smacked down. The weeks of training held her gasp in check, and when she broke the surface she took a deep breath, then sank. She let the water close over her before opening her eyes again.

It was strange and hard to watch from underneath, but there they were—Frank and Ed, tussling in a hard way, a jerky way, a rough way that made her glad she was in the water and not up there with *them*.

Her stomach tied itself tight into a knot, and she wasn't sure why. She shouldn't be worried for Frank. She should stay there, in the water, in the spring where she was safe and where she knew how to reach the air tubes. Frank was practically invincible. Navy veteran. Solid as a side of beef. Tough and quick.

But he was not *different*. Not unreal, not like Ed—if that was even his name.

(It probably wasn't. Silver-skinned things with black-blue hair don't have names like "Ed.")

Tammy pushed the towel with the tiara up under her armpit and kicked herself down and away from the surface. Let Frank throw the bum out. Of course he would. He *had* to. Because if he didn't . . . *then* what?

A pulse of water answered her, close to her legs. (Or was she wearing the tail? Was it right beside her fins? Suddenly, she wasn't sure.) A hand grabbed her foot and pulled her through the water. It tugged her like a fish on a line; it reeled her close with silver-spider hands.

She forgot. Ed *made* her forget.

She forgot all the training and the tubes, and she cried out a burp of surprise. And then there was no more air. Ed's hands—both hands, then—clamped around her foot. Her ankle. Her leg. Up around her knee, and reaching higher.

Give it back. His lips didn't move. He didn't speak, but she heard him anyway.

Tammy flailed, almost dropping the towel but catching it at the last second with two fingers. It sank slow, unraveling from its balled-up twist in slow motion. Unraveling but not untying, not undoing completely. Not letting the treasured tiara fall free.

Tammy reached, elbows thrusting in every direction for the nearest hose. There were *always* hoses, hidden here and there. Always hoses for breathing, for refreshing, for shaking off the sparkles that crept up behind her eyes when it'd been too long since she'd had a breath; and the fizz was coming up now, and so were the silver-spider hands, curling like an octopus up her thigh.

Another splash, and something hit hard against her head.

(It was Frank. That part was an accident.)

When he joined them, he turned the water pink, a little bit, in a curly cloud there by his side. He took Ed by the hair, right by that billowing head that looked for all the world like a poisoned anemone. He yanked Ed hard, snapping his neck back, and up.

The octopus, silver-spider hand seized, and struck, and let go.

It went, sucked into a flurry of frothy spring water and violent rich foam, a curtain and a tower of bubbles.

And the static.

There was a dazzling flash, and there was Frank—turning the water all pink but not giving up. Frank, with his sun-brown arms and legs as strong as chains, the big ones that hold ships to docks—the big ones that hold anchors on ocean liners . . . and Frank was holding on, but the thing called Ed was spinning—trying to cast him off like the alligators people wrestled for tourists.

And Tammy was spinning too.

There wasn't any air, and there weren't any hoses. Did Frank pull them all up when the day was out and over? Did he put them all away? Of course, when no one needed them. Of course, when the mermaid aquarium was empty, in the auditorium with eighteen seats, lined up like soldiers in a row, lined up like lines on a page, in a story, in a fairy tale where something had gone terribly, terribly wrong. Of course there wasn't any air.

Tammy let go of the towel. It dropped away with its strange little prize, a glimmering cheap hairpiece with gems made of sea glass.

She didn't know how she knew about the sea glass, but she would've bet her life on it. Maybe she *was* betting her life on it. No, that couldn't be right.

She wasn't even sinking anymore—but rising, slow and unafraid. Her back breached the surface; she could feel the late day sun warm against the wet shirt there, and warm against her skin. She wasn't a real mermaid. This wasn't a real aquarium, but that tiara was real, and its sea glass gemstones were magic of a glorious kind. And Ed was real, and he was magic of a terrible kind. The two went together, somehow.

She felt . . .

She heard . . .

She saw . . .

Below her the crumpled towel stopped atop a rock. It teetered, toppled against another boulder, into a plant. Onto a compressor, and down again, another step or two to the spring bottom, where it came to rest in the soft, white silt. It came unfolded, unwound, and from beneath one waving corner of terry cloth, there sparkled something bright and cheap and priceless.

A deadly lure, glittering with enchanted glass.

Cherie Priest is the author of twenty novels and novellas, most recently *The Family Plot, I Am Princess X, Chapelwood*, and the Philip K. Dick Award nominee *Maplecroft*; but she is perhaps best known for the steampunk pulp adventures of the Clockwork Century, beginning with *Boneshaker*. Her works have been nominated for the Hugo and Nebula awards for science fiction, and have won the Locus Award (among others)—and over the years they've been translated into nine languages in eleven countries. Cherie lives in Chattanooga, Tennessee, with her husband and a small menagerie of exceedingly photogenic pets.

Website: cheriepriest.com

Twitter: @cmpriest

Facebook: facebook.com/cmpriest

As Good as Your Word

ELLEN HOPKINS

Fine Day

Early spring, the ground velvet
brown just beyond April thaw.
Robins comb the earth, hungrily
plucking foolhardy worms,
as overhead cottonwoods shake
crowns of near-fluorescent green.

From a safe distance, I watch
a motorcade in serpentine form
slither along creviced asphalt,
through wrought iron gates.
None of the passengers know
I'm here. None know me at all.

But I know the boy who rides
in the place of honor inside
the long black Cadillac

hearse. We were more than
friends. We took a vow
and this is his promise, kept.

Yes, it's a fine, fine day
for Cameron Voss's burial.

More Cars

Than I expected to see pull one by
one to the side of the road. Cameron
is—I mean was—a strange boy.
(No stranger than I, of course.)

I'm surprised so many people
have turned out to say goodbye.
Far fewer, I have little doubt,
would do the same for me.

I'm sitting on a hillside grave,
shaded by an elderly oak, cool
grass licking my skin. This is
the oldest part of the cemetery,

and I'm pretty sure whoever I'm
sitting on doesn't mind. Laura

Simpson is her name. She died in
1802. Her spirit must be long gone.

A breeze rises warm, lifts
my hair, puffs a kiss on my neck,
and I remember Cam's words:

> The flesh disintegrates to reveal the spirit,
> initiate its journey. The spirit may
> wander or stay bound to those it loves.

Who did Laura Simpson love? Are
they here? Is she? And where is Cam?

The Flesh Part of Cam

Is, I assume, in the shiny, copper
casket levitating over the freshly
dug hole in the ground. I know
there are straps holding it there,
but from here it seems suspended
in mid-air, a product of magic.

> Cam's family gathers to witness
> the lowering. I've never met them,
> but I've seen their photos on his

Instagram. His mother sobs
loudly. *Why? Why?* His father
slides an arm around her shoulder.

I could tell them why. But they
wouldn't want to hear it. Couldn't
understand why their son chose
to put an end to his life. He was
only seventeen. Just like me.
Suddenly the breeze turns chill.

It whispers through the greening
leaves, *Seventeen. Seventeen.*
Goosebumps rise up like ghosts
from their graves. It's time to go.
I take a deep breath. "Goodbye Cam.
"Sleep well. I'll see you one day."

I Start Across

A long stretch of lawn, beaded
     with headstones. My VW waits
on the far side, staring at me
     with mournful eyes. Cam told

me once that before he died

he wanted to take a cross country
ride in a car just like mine. "Why
        were you in such a hurry to go, then?"

I whisper the words into the sky.
        They are answered there by the hideous
cry of a crow. *Chloe!* It screams
        and I start to run. How can this evil

tongued bird know my name?
        Winter's littered branches snatch
at my feet as I stumble toward
        the harbor of the street. *Chloe!*

I look over my shoulder, and see
        the black feathered dagger perched
on a wire, staring curiously. It
        never wanted me at all. "Stop it!"

I command myself out loud and slow
        my pace to a measured walk. Why
am I so spooked, anyway?
        Maybe coming to pay my respects

wasn't the best idea. But I wanted
        to say goodbye to Cam, since, despite

many long conversations, we never
    managed an in-the-flesh hello.

Safe in My Bug

My hand trembles as I turn
the key. How absurd. Ghosts
only go a-haunting at night,
and if I imagine contempt
in the eyes of a bird, it is only
the manifestation of my own guilt.

The car knows the way home,
lets me think about how Cam
and I met that day, in a chat room
named "Contemplating Death."
I had recently lost my best friend
to leukemia, and as her short life

neared its end, I kept promising
to go visit. But watching her waste
away creeped me out and she died
before I ran out of excuses. It wasn't
my own death I was considering
that afternoon. It was Erica's, and

for some reason, it didn't occur to me
that dreams of suicide had drawn
most everyone into that cyber crypt.

 Hi. I'm Barry and I want to kill
 myself. Sounded like SA—Suicides
 Anonymous. Whatever. Anything

was more entertaining than thinking
about what a poor excuse for a friend
I was. I didn't care one bit about Barry,
though. "Hello. I'm Chloe and I want
to know what happens after the light
sputters out." Nobody had an answer.

I Lurked for a While

Strangely fascinated by the (all
things considered) rather trivial
reasons people gave for wanting
to exterminate themselves.

 My boyfriend walked out on me.
I flunked out of chemistry.
  I had sex with my brother.
  My sister is really my mother.
I sat at the keyboard, fingers

itching to write, "What the hell
is wrong with you? These things
aren't worth dying for."

And then, like he could read
my fingers' minds or something,
up pops Cam's instant message:

What would you die for, Chloe?

That Was the Beginning

Of our beautiful, but totally odd,
relationship.

Odd, because, though we lived
on opposite far edges of the same
city, we never hooked up for real.
Introverts to the point of pain,
we kept waiting for the right time.

Time ran out.

Odd, because though we never
hooked up in real time, we fell as far
in love as two people who've never

met in the flesh can. Most people
probably believe actual skin-to-skin
contact is a requisite for romance,
but it wasn't Cam's touch I tumbled for.

It was his incredible quirky brain.

Odd, because falling in love led
us to make a suicide pact. Before
I met Cam, I'd never seriously
considered snuffing the flicker
of my lousy life, which proved
so much richer with him in it.

Despite his need for control.

Odd, because that promise to die
in tandem is what made us beautiful.
We were Romeo and Juliet, except
without the duels, balcony
confessions, kissing and sex.

Zero sex, although we did talk about it.

We talked about what we liked.
(I made everything up. All the sex

I've ever had was in my imagination.)
We teased each other with fictional
scenarios of what we'd do to each
other when we finally met.

On this side of death, anyway.

We Also Talked

Often late, often long, about
the other side of corporeal death.
I asked if he was certain about
an afterlife. He didn't hesitate.

> *How could you doubt it? The body*
> *is a vessel, and inside it, the essence*
> *of existence. Some call it the soul,*
> *and it can't be extinguished.*

I'd only recently considered it,
had no clear sense of a hereafter.
"But what comes next? Heaven?
Hell? Something else completely?"

> He paused, and I could almost
> hear him shrug. *We can't be*

certain 'til it happens, and that's
half the fun of it, you know?

Uncertainty never sounds like fun
to me. I was more confused than
ever. I asked if he thought people
had sex after they died. He answered

with a question, *Why would*
the spirit rely on the physical
for pleasure? I figured it was
rhetorical. But then he continued,

Without the constraints of flesh,
energy is free to do what it will.
Imagine the rush when separate
energies collide. Totally orgasmic!

I Thought He Was Enlightened

So when we started talking
about being together forever,
sans flesh, I wasn't scared
at all. I was intrigued.
Anyway, what did I really
have to lose? Not like this life

was taking me anywhere special.

Not like this life had brought
me anything but massive clouds
of sorrow, from my father's death
when I was twelve to my best
friend's, not so long ago.

Cam took charge of planning how
we would do it. He wanted to go
out in style—via bullet or rope,
so people would remember.

I preferred something a little less
dramatic, not to mention painful.
Pills for me. There are plenty in
the medicine cabinets—Mom's,
and mine. The one thing Cam
was adamant about was going at
the same time, so the exact same
door in the continuum would open
for both of us simultaneously.

I believed him in a way. But,
personally, I was discussing
abstractions. Anyway, my M.O.

has always been more talk
than action. Did I swear I'd do
the deed at the precise moment
he did? Yes. When he asked,

   Do you give me your solemn word?

I vowed that I would swallow
those pills right before he stepped
off the desk in his room, noose
around his neck jerking tight.
I swore I would, but when Cam
jumped feet first into the forever
night, I had only taken two
Valium with a tumbler of Wild
Turkey. I got buzzed. Cam died.

It Is Late Afternoon

By the time I get home, shadows
deepening toward evening. Silence
swallows the house, and I'm grateful
for my mother's usual Saturday

afternoon bowling. I go into
my room, drop the blinds, hang
a sign on the outside of my door:

Taking a nap. DND.

She knows the code: Do Not
Disturb. She's seen it hundreds
of times, and unless I'm already
waist-high in manure,

she respects my right to be weird
in private. In semi-darkness,
I flop down on my bed, close
my eyes, consciously relax

every muscle, begin to drift
toward a gentle rose-colored glow.
Closer. Closer. The light grows
brighter. Darker. Red. Blood

scarlet. I jump back into awareness.
I'm in my room, and it's black
in here, except for . . . a red light.
Flashing. Flashing. Flashing on

my computer screen. No, not just a light.
Words. Hard to read from here.
I get up, cross the floor. Five words.
Flashing, red: *What would you die for?*

My Entire Body

Goes rigid, morgue cold.
    "Turn it off!" screams my brain,

and I lean toward the computer,
    but suddenly I don't want to

touch it. Mustn't touch.
    Mustn't look. I turn away,

flip on the lamp. Soft copper
    light scatters the darkness.

      Chloe! I jump at the sound,
        but the voice that falls heavy

      in the hallway belongs to
        my mother. *Dinner's ready.*

Dinner? Yeah, I'm starving.
    But I answer, "Be right there."

Some masochistic sliver
    of my psyche makes me

turn back toward my desk.
 The monitor no longer blinks.

A single word remains,
 a steady crimson glow:
  die.

Every Molecule

Of air is sucked
 from the room. Run.

 Run or follow through.
  Follow through and die.

  Run. Try. Can't. Stuck.
  Rooted to the rug. Move!

  I move. Stumble. Fight
  to reach the door. Breathe.

   Can't. No oxygen. Vacuum.
   Door. Almost there. Reach.

    Something. Pulling. Tugging
    me backward. Scream! Can't.

No air. Need air. Hands. Clawing.

Hands? Can't be. There's no one here

but me. Knob. Reach. Turn the knob . . .

The Hands

Let go suddenly, and when the door
jerks open, I almost fall, face forward
against the far wall. "Goddamn it!"
A brew of emotions
simmers inside.

     Fear.

        Anger.

     Curiosity.

Hands? (Claws.) No
way. My room is empty,
right? The words on my computer,
written by a dream. Right?
Spooked or not, I turn around,
suck in breath.

Two steps, I'm at my door.
I switch on the overhead
light. It floods

the room with stark
white and nothing
is amiss. No hands.

No red glow. No
words. Just a blank
black screen. I reach
for the power button, erupt
a cold sweat beneath the hair,
lifting on the back
of my neck.
    The computer
        is already off.

Mom Screams

From the kitchen,
    Chloe! Damn it! Dinner!

"I'm coming!" I insist
loudly, but have to take
several deep breaths and
dig my fingers painfully
into the opposite biceps

so I can try to quit shaking.

Mom would want to know
what's wrong, and what could
I tell her? That my Mac seems
to have a mind of its own?

Okay, none of that crap
happened. It all rolled straight
out of my burial-fueled
nightmares. I stuff it inside,
go to share Mom's table

and make her happy,
though I'm not sure why.
She should feel as miserable
as I do. But no. She's humming.
Singing some old eighties

crap under her breath.
When she hears my footsteps
scratching the floor,
she turns, grinning
like some demonic clown.

> *Hope you're hungry.*
> *I bought too much Chinese.*

The sweet and sour is gag me
sweet, and the chow mein
noodles remind me of worms,
but I stuff them into my mouth,
try not to choke when they squiggle

down, and hope Mom's post
bowling, carb craving appetite
keeps her swallowing
instead of talking. Right.
Like that's going to happen.

Blah, blah, blah. Blah, blah,
blah. What did you do today?

I could give her my usual,
"Nothing much," but then
she'd feel the need to pry
information from me. I
shove another forkful

into my mouth, chew slowly
while I consider a lie.
Screw that. Too much
work. I shrug. "Went to
a funeral. Burial, actually."

She cocks her head, curious.
You don't say. Like, whose?

"Just this boy I know—knew.
And to save you the trouble
of asking, he committed
suicide. Hung himself
until dead." Shock value.

    All she says is, *Oh.* Then, after
    some thought, *Are you okay?*

My shoulders jerk up and down
again. "Sure. I didn't know him
all that well. Just weird. One
second he's here. The next,
poof. Wonder where he went."

    *If he took his own life, he went
    to Hell. You should know that.*

I'm sure that's what her pastor
would say, but Cam pretty much
convinced me there's no such
place as Hell, or Heaven, either.
"You really believe that, huh?"

Well, of course. Don't you?
She stares like I'm a stranger.

"I don't know. I just wish
I could be sure that there really
is something more." I think
for a minute. "Hey, if I died,
where do you think I'd go?"

Zero hesitation. *You're a good*
girl. Good girls go to Heaven.

Am I good? I suppose for
the most part I am. I don't
cause a whole lot of trouble.
Treat my mom okay, go to
church with her on Sunday.

But sometimes I think dark
thoughts, and that was especially
true when I connected with Cam.
Does simply discussing suicide
lock you out of the Pearly Gates?

I wish the definitive afterworld
manual wasn't written thousands

of years ago. Surely the rules
have changed by now. Or maybe,
like Cam said, all that garbage

was made up by men thirsty
for power. Mom offers two
fortune cookies, allows me to
choose first. As I unwrap mine,
she opens hers and reads,

>   *You will receive good news*
>   *from a long distance.*

"Hope it's money," I joke,
then immediately turn serious
when I crack open my cookie.
A broken promise leads
to an unexpected encounter.

Goose Bumps Erupt

"I've got a headache,"
I claim, and it's the truth.
"I'd better go lie down."

>   *Take an ibuprofen right away.*

You don't want that to turn
into one of your nasty migraines.

I get them sometimes, usually
induced by stress. "Will do."
But there's something better

than ibuprofen stashed
in my underwear drawer.
I return to my room, where

Valium, Percocet, and Wild
Turkey lay in wait. I saved
them up for over a month,

sneaking Mom's painkillers
here and there to augment
my personal collection—

some bought at school, some
traded for, some prescribed
by my personal therapist, Paula.

Okay, I have a few issues,
including anxiety and panic
attacks, as well as intermittent

insomnia. I do want to sleep
tonight, so I pop a single Valium,
plus a Percocet, wash them down

with a small glass of whiskey.
I don't want to get sick, just
messed up enough to tumble

straight down into a darkness
dreams dare not invade.
It doesn't take long. I'm sinking . . .

I Hear

The door knob turn, lift my eyelids
as far as they'll go, try to discern

who has crossed the threshold and
owns the footsteps creaking the floor.

I see nothing. I try to sit up, but have sunk
so low into my bed that it holds me

in place. "Who's there?" It's a lame
attempt to exhale words. They lodge

in my throat, a huge wad of fear-flavored
gum. Closer. Whoever it is has almost

reached my side. Still, I can't see him.
I've no clue how I know the intruder

is male, but I sense he has something
unsavory in mind as he moves into place,

and now the mattress depresses beside
me. He wants me. Wants to touch

my nakedness, sleep-warm beneath
the covers. "N-n-no." It's a soundless

stutter, and the invisible he is weighting
me, pushing down on my body. I know

what he wants and try to scream, "Help,"
but all that escapes is a breathy hiss.

He buzzes in my ear, *Don't fight.*
It won't hurt. Imagine the rush

when our energies collide. You broke
your promise, but I'm patient, and

since you wouldn't come with me,
I decided to visit you. Just relax.

Cam. No, impossible. But the sheet
lifts, the pressure shifts, an icy hot

wave splashes against my skin, and
still I'm deep-mired in quicksand.

Our joining has no single entry
point. It's like every pore opens

up, inviting the tiny electric pricks
that sizzle, close to pain, and tingle,

arousing the private places no one
but I have touched. Though it only

lasts a moment or two (who could
take more?), the apex is spectacular.

And with it, the weight disappears.
I'm alone in my bed, the force field

has disintegrated, and I can move
again. Breathe again. Talk again.

"Cam? Was that you? Where are you?
Please tell me where you've gone."

I lie still for a moment, hoping to hear
his voice, but the answer does not

come as a whisper. It's a single word,
lettered red, on the screen of my computer.

Correction. My powered-down computer:

   Paradise.

I Slap Myself

Into the present.
Sit up to watch *Paradise*
fade into the ether.
            Letter by letter.

I take deep breaths
to counter the anxious
tremors. It was a dream.
            Not.

It was a hallucination

care of last night's
self-indulgence.
            Not.

It was a product
of my overactive
subconscious brain.
            Maybe.

As my heart rate slows
from wind sprint to crawl,
a phrase surfaces.
            Sleep paralysis.

According to Paula,
it's when you wake up
while your brain's caught.
            Mid-REM sleep.

Mid-dream. So you're half
here, half wherever, and
your nightmare visitor
            isn't real at all.

The Experience

Isn't completely foreign.
Something similar happened
not very long after Daddy drowned,
trying to save a toddler from a car
overturned in a swollen stream.

When I heard the door open,
I thought it was he, come to say
goodbye. That time, though,
I viewed the scene as if looking
up through water, and there was

no voiced communication,
nor low voltage electricity.
Still, some unidentified weight
did land heavily on top of me,
crushing every emotion but terror.

When I confessed this to Paula,
she gave me the lowdown on
sleep paralysis. "But it seemed
so real," I argued, half disbelieving
her and half relieved it probably

wasn't Daddy's ghost after all.
Of course it seemed real. Many
people think they're being attacked
by an evil spirit. But surely your dad
wouldn't want to scare you like that?

"I don't know," I admitted.
"Sometimes he was really mean.
Sometimes I thought he liked
to be mean, like it helped him
forget the bad stuff at work."

Paula nodded. *A cop sees a lot*
of terrible things. Makes sense
he might take it out on his family.
But I'm betting he was a good man
at heart and that he loved you a lot.

She Convinced Me

It was all in my head—
a byproduct of my twelve-
year-old psyche trying
to process my father's death.

I haven't had another episode

since. Not until this morning,
that is. Yes, they were akin.
But the differences were notable.

I pull myself out from under
the covers, into morning cool.
Mom will come knocking
soon, insisting I go to services.

Funny, because she was not
a believer until after Daddy died.
It didn't take sleep paralysis
to send her looking for answers.

Too bad she found them where
she did, because her so-called
church seems more like a den
of thieves to me. It's cultish—

all about hellfire, brimstone,
and speaking in tongues, as if
anyone could actually decipher
exactly what such babble means.

But it brings Mom comfort,
so who am I to tell her I think

Pastor Smyth is full of crap
and living large off the generous

gifts of his faithful followers?
Regardless, I exit my bed,
reach into my closet for a skirt
(women in this congregation

do not wear pants), head
for the shower. I pause at
the mirror, startled by what's
reflected there. Head to toe,

my skin is red, as if sunburned.
It wasn't that way last night.
I remember the electric sizzling
and know they must be related.

Now, as I stand here staring,
a series of small bruises
shaped like fingerprints
appear all over my body,

most concentrated on
my inner thighs, breasts,
and circling my neck.

I blink disbelief. Once.

Twice. They've disappeared.
I hear Mom in the hallway,
lock the door, hide behind
the shower curtain, adjust

the water temp to cool.
By the time I finish and
towel dry, my skin has
faded from red to pink.

I cover it all anyway, with
a demure baby blue blouse
and floral patterned skirt
that stretches to my ankles.

Plus I keep my makeup
barely there, nothing
dramatic to disturb Pastor
Smyth or draw his attention.

Nope. Please, just let me
sit in the back, tuning out,
trying not to think about
what yesterday might mean.

Somehow I Manage

To mostly do exactly that.
Good thing. Pastor Smyth
is wordy today. A few key
phrases do not escape

    my attention, however:
    darkness wrestles light
    key to the kingdom
    doorway to everlasting life.

My own thoughts turn
to Cam, of course, but also
to Erica and Daddy, all three
moldering in the ground.

Did any of them discover
the doorway, let alone the key
to some Disneyland in the sky?
The question has barely coalesced

inside my head when I notice
the vibration of my cell, which
is sleeping in my bag. I reach
for it with a trembling hand,

extract it stealthily so no one—
especially not Mom—notices.
I move it carefully into my lap
and words swim out of the dark

screen. *Paradise is better*
than Disneyland. No tickets
required, and no key, either.
Your friend's here. Your daddy, too.

I close my eyes. (Why did I
look, anyway?) When I reopen
them, the text has faded away,
away and the screen is black

again. Black, because I turned
off my phone before services,
like I always do. "Please leave
me alone," I beg silently,

just as Pastor Smyth winds up
the benediction and everyone
rises for the coffee hour. My heart
races, but Mom doesn't notice

that either as she goes to talk

to Daddy's old patrol car partner,
Mark. She stands very close—
maybe too close for church—and

as always when I see them
together, a hot shot of anger zaps
my nerves. Yes, it's been five
years since Daddy died. Plenty

of time for Mom to hook up
with another guy. But why Mark?
That feels totally wrong, and it's
becoming ever more obvious

that they've bonded, both here
and well beyond church, which
is probably where it started.
Mark, in fact, was the one who

convinced Mom that this peculiar
brand of born-again believing
is her entry code to the Pearly
Gates. Arm in arm, they approach

Pastor Smyth, who grins broadly
at their news. Now all three turn to

stare at me. Whatever they're selling,
I damn sure don't want any.

As If I Have a Choice

Mom kisses Mark softly
on the cheek and as she starts

in my direction, my phone
vibrates. Like an idiot moth,

    drawn to a smoking lantern,
    I peek at the text. *Snake oil.*

My ghost has a sense of humor.
Wait. My. Ghost. I just thought

that. Does that make him real?
I suspect my cell holds an answer

to the unvoiced question, but I
don't try to look because Mom

    is standing in front of me. *Mark*
    is coming over to watch the game,

and he's bringing pizza for dinner.
Hope you don't mind. We've got

something kind of important
we want to discuss with you.

"Game?" Mom watches games?
What kind, and since when?

The baseball game? It is April,
you know. Mark's a Yankees fan.

Oh, of course. And it *is* April.
Like that's ever meant anything

before. What the hell's going on?
"I don't care if he comes over."

Actually, I do, but whatever.
She turns and gives Mark a thumbs-up,

and I follow her to her car, wishing
I'd driven my Bug so I could skip out

on whatever it is they're determined
to tell me. It can't be anything good.

On the way home I sit in quiet
anticipation of a Valium cocktail.

That's what I need. Deep silent
space and zero communication

with the living or the dead, whether
or not it's all in my messed up head.

I consider the text I might or might
not have received in church. *Paradise.*

Is that the same place as Heaven?
If it exists, Erica would be there.

But what about Cam? Or Daddy?
Not only was he mean, but despite

the noble way he died, he did plenty
of dirty cop things. Makes me wonder

out loud, "Hey, Mom. Think Daddy
ever found the key to the kingdom?"

> *If you mean do I think he's with our*
> *Heavenly Father, of course I do.*

"But what about . . . ? He did
some shitty stuff, you know."

> She actually lets the S-word slide.
> *He was a good man who behaved*
>
> *badly sometimes. God understands*
> *human frailty and forgives our sins.*

Every sin except suicide, apparently.
But I keep that nugget to myself.

By the Time

Mark arrives, extra large meat
lovers' pizza in hand, the game
is underway, the Yankees ahead
by one run in the second inning.

And I am one Valium toward calm
acceptance of the approaching
storm. I didn't want to get too
buzzed until *after* the thunder

rumbled. But I'm not going to
wait seven more innings before

liftoff. I don't watch baseball,
but I do know there are a minimum

nine to suffer through. Mom
must really have a thing for this
guy. But I don't, so as I pick
pepperoni and sausage off

my pizza in protest of eating
in front of the television, I forge
ahead and ask, "What is this big
news you want to share?"

I expect maybe they'll finally
fess up and tell me they're dating
or even that they're taking a trip
together, implying they're having

sex. But when Mom mutes the TV
and they both turn away from
the game and toward me, I know
suddenly and without a doubt

there's more. Mom clears
her throat. *Ahem. Mark and I
have tried to keep our relationship*

private, and away from here,

because I realized it might upset
you. But we've been seeing each
other for almost two years, and,
well . . . The truth is, we're in love.

We think it's time to take a big
step forward and sanctify our union
in the eyes of God. We want
to get married, Chloe. And soon.

Glad I didn't eat any greasy
meat. But I wish I'd popped
a couple extra pills, and I'll need
to score hella more. This won't be

easy to live with. I feel like
someone just sledgehammered
me in the gut. "Know what?
You suck. Why weren't you

straight up with me? You can't
just drop something like this
in my lap. 'Come have some pizza
and, oh, by the way, we're getting

married soon.' What does that
even mean? Like, when?" I try
not to look at Mark, but fail.
Smirk. Is that a word? Yeah,

it is, and that's what he's doing.
Calm down, honey, says Mom.
*You're right. I should've been
honest with you, but I didn't*

*want to take a chance on hurting
you before I was sure this was
love. We're talking about a June
wedding. Kind of corny, I know.*

Now she looks at him with this
weird adoration in her eyes.
It totally creeps me out and I try
to remember ever seeing her

look at Daddy that way. Nope.
"Well, obviously I can't stop you.
But don't ask me to be a bridesmaid
because I sure as hell won't be there."

I Stand to Leave

Mark gets to his feet too,
puts a hand on my arm
to halt forward progress.

> *You go right ahead and*
> *be angry. But don't you*
> *dare talk disrespectfully*

> *to your mother again*
> *because I sure as shit*
> *won't stand for it. You*

> *don't have to like me.*
> *But you do have to accept*
> *that I'll be living here,*

> *and that means if you want*
> *to keep living here too,*
> *it will be by my rules. Get it?*

I jerk away, sheer hatred
foaming at the corners
of my mouth. I glance

at Mom, whose eyes stay
fixed on the muted TV.
I really want to spew a stream

of obscenities, but know
it will only make me feel better
for the shortest of moments

before the crap pile hits
the fan. So I fall back on
my usual, "Whatever,"

turn on one heel and stalk
from the room. This will be
a two Valium night.

Tumbling Early

Toward abysmal
sleep, I know morning
will still arrive too
soon to vanquish
the pills' shadow.

I stumble to my desk,
find my phone in

the depths of my purse,
struggle to set the alarm
that will send me off

toward school on time.
My sight blurs and
my head spins, but I
manage (I think)
the necessary task.

Now I wrangle myself
out of my clothes,
slip naked between
the sheets, set my cell
on the nightstand.

I turn off the lamp,
inviting night's envelope,
and just before I close
my eyes, notice the text,
highlighted in red.

No rules here.

If Sunday Was Awful

Monday is worse, starting
with the alarm dragging me
into the mist-shuttered morning.
I'm a crawling, voiceless zombie.
I skip breakfast and manage
to escape out the door without

having to talk to Mom. Screw
her. And Mark. And Pastor Smyth
and anyone else involved in
the upcoming farce. I get to school
just as the first bell rings, which
makes me tardy to first period.

And from there it's all downhill.
My chemistry test comes back marked
F, with the cheerful comment:
If this represents your cumulative
knowledge to date, be prepared
to repeat this class next year.

In the hall on the way to English,
Taryn Murphy elbows me into
a locker. *Get out of my way, freak.*

Who taught you how to put makeup
on, anyway? Considering I'm not
wearing any, what the hell?

PE brings the ultimate nightmare
cliché—starting one's period right
before changing into white shorts.
Not going to happen. I go ahead
and ditch, ducking around the gym
to hang out in smoker's alley.

I'd probably bum a cigarette,
except there's no one here but me,
so I settle, back against a building
wall, on a thin strip of cement.
Face turned into the weak sun, I close
my eyes, feel the cloud appear.

It Arrives

On wing, chill and
menacing, accompanied
by a trio of squawks.

Chloe.
Chloe.

Chloe.

Not one crow this
time, but three, as alike
as single-egg triplets.

    Black feathers.
    Black talons.
    Black pearl eyes.

I should be scared.
So why does crazy laughter
spill from my mouth?

    They circle.
    They caw.
    They perch on a wire overhead.

"Screw you," I say out
loud. "What you gonna do,
peck me to death?"

    Black feathers ruffle.
    Black talons stretch.
    Black pearl eyes stare.

"Screw this," I echo,
getting to my feet,
hoping the crows

don't smell blood.

The Day Doesn't Improve

In Government, I sit in back, staring
out the window, watching a murder
descend, a black feathered storm
cloud, over the branches of a big oak.

The crows must've smelled blood
after all. Mr. Webb notices my inattention,
calls me out on it, initiating a chorus
of snickers. I freaking hate school.

I do manage to meet up with my pill
connection in the parking lot right
after the last bell. Two good minutes
out of four hundred eighty or so.

I've got a mountain of homework,
but I'm still not ready to go head
to head with Mom about her totally

selfish decision to marry another cop.

So, rather than turn toward home,
I detour across the city, to the cemetery
I visited just a couple of days ago.
This time I go ahead and travel the road

Cam's funerary entourage parked
along. I've only got an approximate
location for where his grave should be,
but it doesn't take long to find the spot

where the grass was recently peeled
back like skin to let the backhoe dig
a casket-sized hole, drop a Cam-filled
coffin in, then close it all back up again.

Sprays of wilting chrysanthemums
and lilies leak their dying perfumes
into air richly scented with damp earth.
"Is this what Paradise smells like?"

I lie on top of Cam Voss's fresh grave,
back against the thick peel of grass,
pretending I can't hear bones rattle,
until I'm chilled all the way through.

I'm Shivering

When my cell buzzes in my pocket.
My stomach knots dread, but I can't

not look. Will I learn how Paradise
smells? But no. It's a text from Mom.

Went out with Mark after work. Ring
shopping. There's pizza in the fridge.

Rings. Awesome. What's next?
A white freaking dress? Oh, well.

At least I won't have to go head
to head with her tonight about

the insane decision to commit
her life—and mine—to a cop again.

A dark form appears suddenly
in the sky, circling. Circling.

Closer. Closer. It's black, but
too big for a crow. A buzzard,

that's what it is, circling to take
a peek at the quiet form lying

here like a headstone. I jump
to my feet. "I'm not dead yet!"

I yell. Still the ugly bird makes
long, slow loops above my head.

I hurry to my car, drive surface
streets home to avoid evening

traffic. Mom is still gone
when I walk through the door,

and that's just fine with me. I go
into my room, toss my backpack

on the floor, remove the textbooks
I'm supposed to read. Thirty pages

in one, twenty in another. Not to
mention the essay due tomorrow

that I haven't even started. Nope.
Not going to happen. I reach

into my pocket for my phone.
Not sure why. No one ever calls

and, other than the odd one from
my mom, the only texts I get anymore

come from my demented psyche.
Hey. Where is it? Not in either

pocket. I check my bag, dump it,
in fact. All that falls out is my wallet,

two pens, a half pack of gum,
and enough pills to put me in

the proper place for several days.
Anxiety nibbles, a caterpillar

chewing into my brain. I go ahead
and down a Valium, pray the worm

turns into a butterfly. Just in case,
I search my backpack. Nothing

but homework. I must've dropped
my phone somewhere between

grave and VW. I could drive back,
but it's a long way, I'm starting

to get buzzed, and I don't really
want to wander around a cemetery

at night. I'll go tomorrow and hope
no grave robber finds it first.

I Head to the Kitchen

For a drink and a cold slice.
I'm reaching into the fridge
when I hear a familiar ringtone.

My phone is on the counter.
No. Impossible. I didn't take my phone
into the kitchen earlier. My heart

flails, but I push back total
panic, will myself to move closer.
And, of course, there's a message.

> *I brought your cell. Didn't*
> *want grave robbers to have*
> *it. You owe me. Big time.*

I feel sick. I grab my phone and
a glass of water, hurry back
to my room and gulp another pill.

I close my eyes, wait for the kick.
When I open them again, I find words
floating on my computer's black screen.

>   *Come to me, Chloe. I've waited*
>   *too long. You're overdue here*
>   *and have nothing to live for there.*

This isn't happening. So why
do I talk to an empty room?
"You're wrong. I have Mom."

>   *Not true. She belongs to him*
>   *now. Do you really want*
>   *to belong to him too?*

Good point. What do I have
to live for, really? But . . .
"What's it like in Paradise?"

>   *Remember when I came to you*
>   *in bed the other morning?*

It's like that whenever you want.

The memory makes me tremble.
"Sounds nice." My voice is Valium
thick. "But I'm afraid to die."

   Death is an open door—easy
   to walk through. What's hard
   is living. Take another pill.

Another pill. Yes. I down two,
for good measure. He's right.
Living is hard. I'm tired of it.

I should tell Mom goodbye,
but first I swallow a couple
more tickets to Paradise.

   That's it. Hurry, Chloe.
   I'm standing right on the far
   side of the threshold. Come to me.

One Valium. Two. Three. Toss in
a couple of Percocets. How many
is that now? Can't remember.

Enough? Maybe not. I finish
my stash, one by one. Anticipation
shimmers. "I'm on my way, Cam."

Sleepy. Getting sleepy. I crash
on my bed, reach for my cell
to call in my final farewell.

There's a text. *No, Chloe!*
Turn back. It's horrible here.
Paradise smells like brimstone.

Turn Back?

Too late.
Much too late.
Brimstone?
Paradise.
Lost.

No. "But . . . but . . .
I can't come to you.
I'm good.
Mom says.
Good girls go
to Heaven."

Across the room,
the computer screen
lights, bloodred.

White letters
lift and throb.
Throb
like
my slowing
heart.

Don't be absurd.
You're a liar, Chloe.
You made a pact
and broke it.

Don't you understand?
Haven't you heard?
You're only as good
as your word.

Ellen Hopkins is the award-winning author of thirteen *New York Times* bestselling young adult novels in verse, plus four novels for adult readers. She lives near Carson City, Nevada, where she has founded Ventana Sierra Youth Housing & Resource Initiative, a nonprofit helping youth at risk into safe housing and working toward career goals through higher education. She is both blessed and cursed to care for three generations of children (including her husband), all living under one roof, with two dogs, a rescue cat, and two ponds of koi.

Website: ellenhopkins.com
Twitter: @EllenHopkinsLit
Facebook: facebook.com/ellenhopkinsauthor

The Invisible Girl

RACHEL TAFOYA

I t started with my toes.

When I woke up on Thursday, I didn't have any toes. I felt my stomach drop out of my body, and I tasted my heart, all bloody and beating. My feet came to an end at a rounded stump. My toes had been surgically removed in the night. That was the only explanation.

I reached out to touch them. Why wasn't there blood everywhere? My fingers met skin, but I saw nothing. My toes were still there, just . . .

Invisible.

I heaved but nothing came up. I put on two pairs of socks. My toes still filled up the ends, and I traced their outline. One two three four five, one two three four five. Toes. I just painted them black. They matched my fingernails. My toes themselves were pretty long, and I never liked looking at them, but it's not like I wanted them to disappear.

I'd never spent so much time thinking about my toes.

Was I dreaming?

I took my socks off. My toes were still gone. My thumb

and forefinger squeezed my big toe, hard, and I could feel the pressure, feel the hard surface of my nail and the fleshy pad at the bottom. But I could see both of my fingers where my toe should have been. My stomach clenched again, wanting to vomit but nothing came up.

Next, I put on a pair of tights and watched the fabric stretch out over the surface of my nonexistent toes. I did it three or four times, just covering my feet and uncovering them, feeling the fabric against my skin, revealing the blank space where my toes once were.

I took off all my clothes and looked for other gaps in my anatomy, but there were none. It was only my toes. So I began pinching myself all over, hoping to wake up. There was a wake of little crescent moons from my nails trailing across my body.

Something was wrong with me. And I had to get to school.

My mom put eggs in front of me. I pushed the plate away.

"You need protein." She sighed, not looking at me.

"Gordy gets pancakes."

My little brother scraped his fork across his plate, trying to shovel the carbs into his body.

"Gordon is five," my mother said. "He eats well at school. You are seventeen and apparently need to be told what to eat."

I managed two bites and then grabbed my keys. My feet felt swollen with both tights and a pair of socks shoved into my boots.

My mother glanced at me before I left. "I didn't know you had tights."

"I don't wear them a lot," I muttered. "I have to go."

She stalked over, grabbed my backpack, and shoved something inside. "A protein bar. Eat it."

"Mom." I swallowed. "I think there's something wrong with my feet."

She gave me a look like I was crazy, because clearly I was.

"I'll show you," I said, taking her hand and leading her away from Gordon. I removed my shoe and started peeling off my tights.

"Casey." She sounded disappointed, and I was hopeful for a second that she recognized what was happening. She leaned down and touched my thigh. The lines on them. I jumped back. "I thought you stopped all this."

"They're old . . ."

Mom looked me dead in the eyes. The ones on my thigh were old. I quickly put my tights back on. She wasn't going to see past those stupid scars.

She let me go. I ran for my car. I felt every single step.

No one said anything at school, of course. No one can see through me. Well . . .

At lunch I had fries, a slice of pizza, and a Coke. Mila offered me her bag of chips, so I had half of those before excusing myself. When I went to the bathroom, the door was

closed, so I leaned on the wall to wait my turn, but two minutes went by in silence, so I opened the door.

"Hey!" a girl snapped. "Can't you hear?"

She was sitting on the counter, smoking.

"You weren't making any noise."

"Fine. You can stay," she said, waving me in.

"I don't . . . need to that bad."

She laughed and it sounded cruel. I realized I'd never seen
her before. She looked kind of old-school with her combat
boots and denim overalls. A flannel shirt was tied at her waist.
She looked out of place. Then I saw the scar across her neck.

"Whatever. I won't tell about your puking." She took a
drag. "Not like anyone would hear me."

"What are you talking about?" I asked. I scrunched up my
toes in my boots. I wondered if they'd come back. I wanted to
check.

"I sort of lost my voice a while back." She dragged her finger across her throat, where there was an awful-looking gorge
in her neck, one that looked far too fresh to be real, all red and
angry. I could almost feel it burning across my own skin.

I started to close the door. "I'm sorry to bother you."

She rolled her eyes. "You're just like everyone else."

Not everyone else's toes are disappearing. Unless that's a
part of puberty they never explained.

"Who are you?"

Her gaze zeroed in on me. Her lips began to turn purple.

Her whole face was turning purple, like she was holding her breath too long. Then she blew smoke in my face. It didn't sting. It didn't even smell bad.

"I have to get to class." I stepped back.

"Whatever." She sighed, and crossed her legs, ashing her cigarette into the sink.

My window of opportunity was gone so I had to digest my food all day. My stomach felt like a volcano.

"I'll see you tomorrow," Mila said as I headed toward my car after class.

"Bye." I waved, but she was already turned toward Noah. Everyone was waiting for them to start dating. She liked him so much. Everyone knew. I knew.

Noah knew.

I unlocked my car and sped home. Mom and Gordy were at the doctor's. I went straight for the bathroom, but instead of kneeling, I ripped my tights off.

My toes were still gone.

Weirdly enough I couldn't throw up after that. Instead, I got into my car and drove to the nearest clothing store. With sweaty hands and the change I scraped up from my purse and the car I bought a pair of tights. Then I curled up in my bed and tried to cry, but couldn't. I put on YouTube videos of much prettier girls putting on their makeup. I brought out my one brush and mimicked their perfect strokes and pretended that I could pull that off too. I knew they didn't think they were lying when they said *Anyone can wear this*. I didn't do my homework. I massaged my see-through toes until my mom came home, and then I shoved my socks on.

I should have made her look again.

But I knew she wouldn't see.

"Dinner!"

Fruit salad, biscuits, and meat. Every single night here was a plate full of fruits or veggies and a plate full of meat. I shouldn't complain. It was a balanced meal. It tasted fine. But it didn't taste good. Mom just wanted Gordy to eat what he needed. If he ate balanced, he stayed healthy. If he stayed healthy, then his anemia wouldn't come back.

But his sickle cell would always be there.

It wasn't that bad, as far as genetic disorders were concerned. Recently there had been more treatments. It wasn't a death sentence. But I knew it killed my mom that I wasn't a bone marrow match.

"How was school?"

I flinched, but she was talking to Gordy.

"We watched a movie about talking to strangers. It was stupid." He laughed at his own review.

She smiled at him. "It's important to know how to stay safe."

"But they tell us we're safe at school."

"It's a worst case scenario kinda thing," I said to him. "Don't worry about it."

Gordy reached over and took my biscuit. "What does 'scenario' mean?"

"It's a situation," I said.

"What's a situation?"

Mom rolled her eyes. "You're confusing him."

"A situation is a thing. You know 'thing,' right?"

He smiled at me. Mom did not smile. (Did she ever?)

"Honestly, Casey."

I stopped talking.

I woke up in the middle of the night, freezing cold. The covers were up over my feet, and my socks were off. Panic struck my heart and I shot up to cover my feet.

My right foot was gone. My breath whooshed out of my lungs, and I clutched my foot, rubbing it haplessly, as if to put feeling back into it, but I could feel it just fine. No, that wasn't the problem. Clearly, the problem was in my head. A wire had shredded in my brain, and now I was imagining things.

Then I saw the girl.

The girl from the bathroom was standing against the wall of my room, hands behind her back. She stared at me, like I had scared her.

"How did you get here?" I whispered.

She said nothing, stayed still. Something about the dark of the room almost made her look sick. Her skin was ashen and her face hollow.

"Who are you?"

She remained still as a board.

"Get out of my house!"

The girl just stood there. I was too scared to move. If I moved, then she would move and then it would be real. But there was a chance that I could still be dreaming right now, as long as I remained perfectly still.

The girl let out a long, aching breath.

I threw a pillow as hard as I could. When it came to land, I was alone again. I stayed sitting up for as long as I could until my eyes started getting heavy. Then I built a small fortress of pillows to keep me propped up and continued staring at the wall until I fell asleep with my head lolled to the side.

When I woke up, both my feet were gone.

The party was at Mila's. She wanted so badly to impress Noah, and her parents had tons of alcohol.

I stayed away from it. I didn't need any more hallucinations.

A few people nodded at me when I came into the house and then went back to their conversations. I checked the basement and saw a game of spin the bottle. I quickly left. The living room had music blasting and people dancing. Well, not dancing so much as rubbing together, as if they wanted to start a fire. All the people who wished they were dating but didn't for some reason. What were they waiting for?

Mila was hiding with Jordan and Kylie. They were giggling and slightly buzzed. I started toward them. I wanted to pull Mila aside and tell her everything. I wanted to start with my toes. But as I drew closer, I heard their conversation.

"He said I looked nice today," Mila squealed.

"I bet he's going to kiss you tonight," Kylie said.

"You're so lucky"—Jordan tossed her hair—"Noah is so cute."

Noah was the nice kid in school, the one whom everybody knew, whom teachers asked for favors, who played on sports teams, but wasn't the star player. He didn't steal attention from the real overachievers, but he was on the radar. He was practically a model student. Practically.

Almost.

(Not at all.)

Why did I come to this party?

I was wandering the upstairs when he showed up. He grabbed my arm and pulled me past everyone, toward Mila's parents' room, into the walk-in closet. He pinned me against the dresser, and I let him. His lips pressed into mine. I let him. He tasted like beer. He put his knee between my legs. Maybe it was my fault. Maybe I should tell him to stop. His hands held my face. But if not him, then who on earth would touch me?

After a few minutes Noah pulled away, breathing heavily. He pulled the door open and vanished. Oh right, this is why I came here.

To be noticed.

And yet, standing in Mila's parents' closet, alone, with Noah's breath on my lips, I didn't feel any more visible.

I dreamt that night of the girl leaning over me. I dreamt of her slowly opening her mouth to reveal a row of jagged, pointed teeth. I felt her pull the covers off my feet, and a searing pain burned through my ankle.

When I awoke on Saturday morning, part of my leg had disappeared as well. Chunks had been gouged out of my flesh. But it didn't hurt. It was just invisible, like before. I traced the lines of my still there skin and bit my lip until it was okay to cry.

I did homework in the living room with the TV on. Then my eyes began to slide shut, so I grabbed my jacket and stepped outside. I walked through my neighborhood, hoping to wake myself up. I could walk to a café and get coffee. I could walk to the library. I could walk to Noah's house and demand that we stop. That if he wanted to kiss me, he had to do it publicly. And not when he's drunk.

In the end I went with coffee. As I waited for my drink, I noticed a boy in the corner of the room. He was staring at me. I didn't want to stare back, but I was curious. He was tall, lanky, and pale. Baggy jeans with chains on the front, long, dyed black hair hanging in front of his eyes. As I watched him, he pulled his sleeve up from his arm, and I saw blood pouring out of his wrist. He smiled at me.

Then some other customer walked right through him, and he vanished.

Just like the girl in my room.

I left my coffee and hurried home.

Monday. I walked through school with tights and thigh high socks on over them. I wore boots. I had long sleeves under a sweater. I was a cocoon, and not a single person said anything.

In the night my wrists had disappeared. There was a gap between my hands and my elbows. Just where the boy had bled in the café. He was in my dream last night too, with the girl. They fed on me with gnashing teeth.

I didn't fight back. There was no point in a dream.

The bell rang and the halls emptied. I took my time. I went to the bathroom and purged my breakfast. My throat stung from the bile, and I stood up on shaking legs. I had not returned to the bathroom where I'd met the girl. I ignored it dutifully. But as I walked back toward class, I noticed something.

A locker, with paper hearts taped on to it, a candle on the floor in front, Sharpie on the door, and a flower in the vent. Sam. The girl who committed suicide at the beginning of the year. The girl who was weird enough to get talked about, but not enough to have friends. The one who dressed like she was in the '90s and who went to a senior's party and everyone said she was a slut who did drugs. Sam.

I forgot about her. She didn't forget us.

. . .

Gordon was in the hospital again. He was in pain throughout his whole body, they said. He can't take much more, they said. We have to be careful.

Gordy looked at his toes. His perfectly visible toes. I touched them, and he giggled.

"Casey, stop it," Mom snapped.

We remained quiet as the doctor calmly took my mother's abuse. Finally, when she quieted down, he took her by the shoulder.

"We may have found a donor, Jen, but it's dangerous to get your hopes up right now. It's early in the process."

First she covered her mouth with her hands. Then she hugged the doctor, and she hugged Gordy, and that was that.

I vanished from the room.

Tuesday was nothing. Tuesday was quiet in the house and homework and my mother cleaning everything she could find. She bustled into my room without asking and ripped the sheets off my bed. Meanwhile, I thanked the Lord that I had my sleeves rolled down.

Noah called me at dinnertime.

"Can you come over?"

"Why?"

He sighed. "I need help with my math homework."

"And?"

Another pause. "And my parents are out to dinner for at least two hours."

So, I went to Noah's house. There was no homework. He pulled me inside and pushed me against the door without saying hello.

"Why are you doing this?" I breathed at him.

He rolled his eyes. "Come on, Casey, let's just enjoy the time we have."

I used to enjoy this. I used to think it was secret and kind of sexy, and I was into it. But Mila kept talking about Noah, and she would report every interaction they had at lunch, and everyone followed their story with rapt attention, and I was supposed to follow along.

The first time he kissed me, I wanted to tell Mila first. I actually went up to her and said, "Mila, I have to tell you something." And she responded, like a glowing mother, "Me too! I totally have a crush on Noah. It just, like, hit me. I think he's wonderful."

Suddenly, I had betrayed her, and I hadn't even known.

"You know how much Mila likes you," I said to Noah as he led me up into his room.

"I don't really care," he said. "I don't want to date. Dating is pointless. I'm a senior in high school. I'm going to go to California next year."

Pointless. Yeah.

"So, what are we doing?"

He let go of my arm. He turned slowly. "If you want to stop, just say so."

How could I explain? That I hated him and loved him? That I knew it wasn't actually love, but my brain knew nothing else but this. That I wanted to be touched, that I used to think this was fun, that I wished I knew how to say no, even though I didn't want to stop forever, I just wanted to be in control.

I didn't say any of this. He kissed me again and erased my thoughts, and it seemed like maybe it was going to be okay until he went for my shirt and I forgot, I forgot, because it was Noah, because maybe I wanted him to see.

"What the hell?"

He stared at my wrists. Stared through my wrists.

We locked eyes. Fear permeated his gaze. He looked at me and he was disgusted.

I grabbed my shirt and ran.

Stupid stupid stupid.

As soon as I walked into school on Wednesday (my left calf was gone gone gone), Mila was waiting for me.

"You bitch," she spat, and turned on her heel.

"Mila!" I shouted and ran after her. There was only one explanation. Noah had told someone that I'm some kind of circus freak. "I wanted to tell you!"

"Screw you, Casey," she said as I jogged beside her. "I guess Noah probably already did, huh?"

"It's not like that. Mila, please!" I grabbed her arm. I pulled up my sleeve. "Look at me!"

She met my gaze, and she rolled her eyes and pulled out of my grasp. She didn't even glance at my arms.

I didn't eat lunch. I hid in the library; hid from the dirty looks everyone gave me. I threw up the protein bar that my mother made me eat this morning. Guess what happened this weekend? Crazy Casey went to Perfect Noah's and kissed him. Crazy Casey said she didn't care about her best friend Mila. (What a bitch.) She seduced Noah and they slept together, but it didn't mean anything to him, even though she was clearly obsessed with him and had been for months.

Nothing about her invisible limbs.

I went into the private study room in the back of the library. There was a girl in there, overweight with clothes stretched so tight, they looked like they were going to pop off at any minute. I was about to step back and apologize when she stood to face me. Her skin was tinged blue, almost like Sam's. Water dripped off her. Her hair was plastered to her face. And she was getting bigger, as if she were absorbing water.

She was sobbing. "Why can't I be pretty?"

Puffed up and waterlogged, like she'd thrown herself into a river and no one had found her.

I slowly slid my backpack around to throw at her, to make her go away like the others.

She bared her pointed teeth. "Like you!"

Then she rushed at me, hands going for my throat. I ran for the bathroom and locked the door. It wasn't real.

She banged on the door.

I slid down to the floor. It wasn't real.

"Give me your body," she hissed. "Give me your pretty little head."

"I'm not pretty." I wrapped my hands around my face.

"Give it to me." She gave a strangled scream.

"I'm not pretty!" I yelled into my knees. My nails bit into my tights, pinching my skin. "I'm nothing! Nothingnothing-nothing!"

Silence crept up and rang in my ears. I was alone. I decided to stay in the bathroom for a while, except sitting there next to the toilet was making me feel sick. When I finally pushed up onto my feet, wobbling a few times, my vision spun. I grabbed the handicapped rail and pushed my hand against my eyes. My shirt had ridden up. I caught a glimpse of something.

I went to the mirror and lifted my shirt. There, across my stomach, as if someone had raked their hands across my navel, five long, see-through lines appeared. Like an animal had torn at me, but instead of blood and guts, there was nothing.

Someone knocked on the door. I tucked my shirt into my pants, stuffed my jacket on, and pushed out into the library again. There were kids peppered throughout the stacks, and I just kept thinking, someone heard me, someone *must* have heard me. But I was wrong. Either no one heard, or no one listened.

• • •

When I drove home, there was a second car in the driveway. It took me a solid minute to realize whose car it was. Dad's.

Gordon must be getting a transplant. Or he was dying. It was the only reason Dad would show up.

I walked into the house and smelled dinner. Transplant.

Macaroni and cheese. Gordon laughed. Dad waved at me. My breath whooshed out of me, and I had to steady myself for a second.

"Hey, Case Face."

Definitely a transplant.

"Did we find someone?" The words rushed out of me.

"Yes, the doctor's found someone," my mom said. "Now, sit down. It's Gordon's big night. Tomorrow will be a long day."

I stared at Gordon all evening. I watched his little body moving, pictured his little bones beneath and the bullets in his blood that were tearing him apart. I watched him smile and tried to smile back, even when my family sat on the couch and my dad and mom plucked at Gordy's toes and counted them and laughed (one two three four five little piggies), just like they used to do with me. He was too old for it, but no one seemed to care.

(It's nothing.)

Ten times I tried to say, *Something is terribly wrong with me*, once for every missing toe.

• • •

I called Noah that night.

He answered but didn't speak. I could practically feel his breath on my neck as we sat silently.

"Why did you do it?" I said. My eyes burned.

"I got freaked, okay? I keep thinking about it. I'm sorry. I didn't want to do that to you. I really didn't. It just happened, and I thought if I pushed you away, then you would get help. Clearly, I'm not good for you. We're not good for each other anymore. But I could try to be better. I don't know anymore. But, Casey . . . you need hel—"

I hung up.

I awoke in a sweat with three pairs of eyes and three sets of broken teeth on me.

My hand was in the boy's mouth. I saw my flesh disappear between the yellow-white knives of enamel. It didn't hurt. It just was.

My skin was there and then it was not.

"Please don't," I whispered.

The boy gave a smile, but it ripped right past where his lips should have been.

"Please don't," he mocked.

All three of them chanted the words. The girl from the library fell on me and held my arms against my chest. The weight was crushing. The boy grabbed my legs. They still laughed and pretended to plead.

Sam walked up to me. She knelt down by my head. I could see her neck, still raw and burned. "You need help," she said.

Stupid.

Her jaw opened wide, unhinged, like a snake.

"You're nothing."

"You're ugly."

"You bitch."

She descended toward my throat, to shut me up forever, I hoped. I could finally stop hurting people, stop hurting myself. I could join Sam and the other kids who lost themselves, and then none of this would matter. I could finally stop pretending.

A knock sounded on the door.

The ghosts vanished.

I made sure all of me was covered before I peered into the hall. Gordy stared up at me. He was crying. He put his hand on his lips, to shush me. Dad was on the couch downstairs, so we had to be quiet. I opened my door wider for him.

He crawled into my bed and shook. Slowly, I wrapped my arms around him.

"Casey."

"Yeah, Gord?"

He kept his eyes shut tight. "I'm scared."

I pet his head. "About the transplant?"

He nodded.

"I'm scared too."

He took my hand, the one that had just been bitten off, but his eyes were still closed.

"Why do Mom and Dad sleep in different rooms?"

"Sometimes people stop loving each other." The words felt thick in my mouth. Surely they had said as much to him? I couldn't be the first one explaining divorce to Gordon.

"Do you not love me anymore?"

I didn't know what to say to that.

"I want to see you."

I squeezed his hand. He burrowed into me.

"I miss you."

I looked up from Gordon and saw the ghosts standing against the wall. Waiting their turn. They wanted to finish me off, and I almost let them. (I let them in.)

"I'm sorry, Gordy. I'm so sorry."

I felt something in my toes, in my stomach, in my wrists. When I looked down, I could see them again. I could see the scabs. I could feel the burn from the cuts.

Gordon put his hands around my scars.

Rachel Tafoya is an author, a teacher, a huge nerd, and a bookseller. She is a graduate of the Experimental Writing for Teens class, which she now teaches at the Doylestown Bookshop. She also works at that bookstore and crams in as much writing time as possible between those two jobs. She is the author of *The Night House*, and has been published in *Radius Magazine*. She is the daughter of author Dennis Tafoya. She and her adorable dog make their home in Bucks County, Pennsylvania.

Website: todaysemotions.tumblr.com

Twitter: @RachelTafoya

Facebook: facebook.com/RachelTafoya

Death and Twinkies

ZAC BREWER

Jeremy Grainger had nothing to lose. His mom was never home, off spending her hard earned, bar-waitress cash on bingo and booze instead of groceries or rent. His dad had split before the words "I'm pregnant" could cross his mom's lips. The three assholes since who'd tried to take his place had been of a similar, slimy sort. Apparently mom had a type. All three had been unemployed in the legal sense, but sold drugs out the back of their piece of crap trailer. Only one had ever hit Jeremy. One had hugged him a little too long, a little too tightly. The other one just yelled. The best of the bunch was the yeller, Jeremy supposed. So what did he have to lose? The torn clothes he was embarrassed to wear, which he washed out in the kitchen sink with dish soap every night? The friends he didn't have? A shred of dignity, or even a splinter of hope? Neither of which he'd ever experienced. No. Nothing. Jeremy Grainger had nothing to lose.

Nothing at all but the pulse in his veins.

As he made his way down the dirt road that led out of the trailer park, he passed Bernie's truck and caught a glimpse of his reflection. Bernie was a mean guy. He managed the trailer park, but made most of his money cashing in his elderly mother's social security checks. He was fat and smelled faintly of spoiled tapioca. But he was always smiling. Maybe because he knew what he was—a no-good piece of crap—and he was just fine with that. It must be nice, Jeremy thought, to know what you are and to be okay with that. For the most part Jeremy had no idea who he was. Unless you counted the passing thought that his own reflection whispered into his mind. *I'm a loser*, he thought. *A worthless loser.*

And he was a loser. Born from a long line of losers. The furthest any of his relatives had gotten in school was his uncle who lived states away in Cincinnati, working as a mechanic. Everyone else made it to high school, but dropped out. Many of his relatives couldn't even read by that time. And the sad thing was that none of them seemed to care.

Jeremy had cared at first, but he learned quickly to give that all up. If he got good grades, he'd be accused of thinking he was better than them. If he interjected something he'd learned in school that day, mockery followed instead of praise. So Jeremy stopped caring and accepted his fate. He was a loser, and no one would give a crap if he threw himself off the Johnson Street bridge.

Inside his right front jeans pocket was a bus ticket to Saint Louis that he'd swiped from the purse of Mrs. Stevens, his English teacher. Sticking out of his left pocket was a flask filled with something that smelled like his mom's breath whenever she "worked late." He hadn't yet decided if he was getting on a bus or jumping off a bridge, but he was hoping the stuff inside the flask would help him make up his mind. Because Jeremy was done accepting the hand that fate had dealt him. He was going to take responsibility for his own life, no matter how little of it might be left. It was now or never. If he was going to die, he'd better get moving. The bus was leaving the station at five past midnight.

He didn't even know why he had the ticket with him. No bus could take him away from his problems, away from his pain. They would follow him around like a morbid shadow, always licking at his heels. But something made him take it, and that same something made him put it in his pocket right before he walked out the front door. Either way, he wasn't going back. Not to that trailer. Not to that life.

He moved out of the trailer park gate, and as he spat on the rusty sign that read WELCOME TO SUNNYVALE MOBILE HOME COMMUNITY, a strange question slipped into his thoughts. Had he said good-bye to everyone? To everything?

It was strange, only because Jeremy had no one and nothing. No pets, no family who cared, no friends. He was all alone in the world, so who would he say good-bye to?

The sky above was as clear as it could be, a blanket of stars above him. The air was warm enough to skip wearing a jacket, but cool enough to warrant a hoodie. Large oak trees lined the two lane road outside the trailer park, casting huge black shapes against the backdrop of perfect stars. Jeremy shoved his thumbs in his front pockets and walked down the road, glimpsing up every now and then to admire the stars. He'd always liked nighttime.

The Johnson Street bridge was about a mile from the trailer park. It was a train bridge, but as far as he had ever seen, no trains ever used it. The metal was rusty, and weeds grew up along each end, poking through the cracked pavement where the tracks of the bridge met the tracks embedded in cement on either side. Like everything else in this town, it was used up and forgotten.

He stepped onto the rails and balanced his way to the center of the bridge before moving to the side that faced away from town—the side that showed nothing but trees and the river and the calm serenity of night. Ducking under, he made his way to the edge, holding on to the bridge with his hands, his feet poised on his toes. He leaned over a bit, just wanting a moment to look and to think before he jumped. But no thoughts came. He'd been expecting a crashing wave of doubt or a bright reasoning of why he should live. But there was nothing. Nothing but him and the bridge and his ripped up sneakers. Nothing but the night and a light breeze in his hair and the smell of goddamn dish soap on his clothes. There was nothing.

Nothing.

He leaned farther forward, relaxing his grip on the metal rails. This was it. He was going to let go. No more pain. No more loneliness. Just the emptiness of what comes with death. He was ready.

Out of the corner of his eye something moved. Instinctually, he tightened his grip on the cool metal once again, leaning back and turning his head toward it. Sitting on the bar to his right was a boy about his age, with shaggy black hair and skin so pale that it almost glowed. He was dressed in black slacks in need of ironing, a black sports coat with the rolled sleeves pushed up to his elbows and patches all up and down the sleeves, a T-shirt from some band called The Smiths, and on his feet purple Chucks that had seen better days. He didn't speak. Just sat there, looking down at the water, as if he were contemplating something deep and meaningful. Or waiting. Jeremy couldn't tell which.

For a long time Jeremy didn't speak. For one, he didn't really want to engage in conversation with anyone. Anything he'd had to say, he'd already said. For two, he didn't really want to leave. This was it. The bridge. Him. The end.

So he stood there, occasionally glancing at the boy, wondering what he was doing there, how he had gotten over the rail and stood beside Jeremy without him noticing, and what the odds might be that they were both there for the same reason. He didn't think he could go through with it with an audience, and certainly not with another participant. But he wasn't exactly sure what to do. There was no going back to the trailer, and the bus ticket wouldn't get him anywhere but onto another bridge, in another town. It had to be tonight. He needed peace. But he needed to acquire that peace alone.

He parted his lips and took in a breath, but before he could speak, the boy said, "It's a long way down, isn't it?"

Jeremy nodded and practically breathed out his response. "Four hundred twenty-seven feet to the surface. And the water's sixty feet deep."

"The surface is pretty still for a river. Almost looks like a reflecting pool on a night like this." He inhaled on his cigarette and blew a faint haze of smoke out into the night air. His eyes remained focused on the water below. "A good night for reflecting."

Jeremy furrowed his brow. Who was this guy, anyway? He watched as the boy inhaled again, the paper of the cigarette burning away, the ember brightening before returning to its normal glow. Jeremy didn't smoke. He'd tried it a few times, but everyone around him smoked, and not smoking just felt like the right thing to do. He didn't want to be like them. He wanted to be different. And if he couldn't be that . . . then he didn't want to be, at all. "You shouldn't smoke, y'know."

"Why?" The boy took another drag and, as he exhaled, the corner of his mouth lifted in a small smile. He turned his head, meeting Jeremy's eyes for the first time. "Because it'll kill me?"

If it had been anyone else speaking those words, Jeremy

might have brushed them off. People said it all the time. Mostly because they heard it all the time. But this boy . . . something about him made the words seem more poignant, more immediate, more . . . real. "What are you doing out here?"

"Waiting."

Curiosity got the best of Jeremy. He looked at the boy and cocked his left eyebrow. "For what?"

"For the inevitable." He shrugged. Briefly, his eyes swept the shadowy treetops in appreciation. "It's kinda my thing. Waiting. For whatever's going to happen."

"Doesn't sound like much of a hobby." A cigarette was starting to sound like a good idea. Jeremy was wondering if the kid was ever going to leave.

"It's more of a job, really. So . . ." The boy reached inside his coat and pulled out an old pocket watch. After noting the time, he put it away again and looked at Jeremy. "It looks like we've got some time. You wanna tell me what you're going to do?"

"Do?" Jeremy blinked in confusion. "What do you mean?"

The boy watched him for a moment, as if waiting for an admission that would never come. When he spoke, his voice was low and almost gravelly. "Well, you walked out here all determined, but the bus ticket in your pocket makes me wonder if you're serious or not."

Jeremy's heart picked up its pace. No one could possibly know what he'd been planning. He'd been so careful. He hadn't told anyone or left any clues. There was no way this guy had any idea that he'd been planning to jump. No way. "Have you been following me? What are you, some kind of stalker or something?"

"Heh. Yeah. Because I have all the time and interest in the world to follow around some sixteen-year-old kid who can't even make up his mind about whether or not he's jumping or getting on a bus." The smirk on his mouth was sharp and meaningful.

Jeremy stood up straight. "Kid? You're what, sixteen, seventeen? I'm not a kid. Or if I am, so are you."

The smirk remained, untouched by Jeremy's words. "Let's just say I look younger than I am."

"So, how old are you?" He wasn't curious, and it wasn't like he wanted a conversation, exactly. But the kid was here, so . . .

The boy shook his head, a dark light crossing his eyes. "It doesn't matter. What matters is what's in your pocket."

Jeremy nodded, again wondering who this boy was and how he seemed to know so much about Jeremy's life. "The ticket."

"I was referring to the flask. Mind if I steal a drink?" The boy grinned, and Jeremy handed over the flask, his hand paling in the night. As he tried to work out what the deal was with this kid, the kid took a swig from the flask and made a face. "That tastes like shit. Man, I wish I could get drunk. Even a nice buzz, y'know?"

As Jeremy took the flask back, he said, "Wait. If you can't even get a buzz, why would you want a drink?"

The boy shrugged. Something about him seemed almost familiar to Jeremy, as if they had met before, if only briefly. "Don't we always want what we can't have?"

Jeremy thought about his family, the long line of losers. All his life he'd wanted them to be anything but what they were. But it didn't matter what he did. They would never change. "I guess."

"What about you? What do you want?"

Moonlight gleamed off the water below. A soft breeze rustled Jeremy's hair. He closed his eyes for a moment and whispered, "Peace."

"You just proved my point." He shook his head, gently biting his bottom lip for a moment. "Life is chaos. It's always been chaos from the first moment cells bumped into one another in that slimy cesspool and formed what we now call life. Even now, every cell in your body is bouncing around in existence. In chaos. You cannot achieve peace. It doesn't exist, yet you just said that's what you want."

Jeremy shrugged. "If life is chaos, then death is peace."

The boy looked at him, his dark eyes darkening further. He appeared both fascinated and repulsed by Jeremy. "You've got a lot to learn about the afterlife, my friend. But then . . . all of you do."

"All of us?" People. He meant people. But he'd separated himself from the group.

"All of you. Every one of you who takes a razor to your wrist or swallows too many pills. Every one of you who jumps in front of a bus. Every one of you who stands on a bridge and thinks about jumping." The boy shook his head again, his features filled with disgust. "You don't know shit about what's waiting at the bottom of that river. And if you think it means peace, then you know less than shit about it."

Jeremy pressed the opening of the flask to his mouth, tipping his head back. The crap inside tasted god-awful, but after a few more sips, his heart had settled into a calmer rhythm. The boy next to him finished his cigarette and flicked it over the edge. Jeremy watched the ember as it tumbled through the night air and was finally swallowed by the darkness below. He wondered if he would land the way he hoped, headfirst, knocking himself unconscious before the water consumed his body and filled his lungs. But even if he landed flat, it wouldn't take long for his airways to be filled with cool liquid and for the fuzzy feeling of drowning to take over his senses. He pictured himself tumbling like that cigarette through the air, his ember bright, then suddenly extinguished. It would be beautiful.

"Is that the best analogy you can come up with?" He locked eyes with Jeremy. "Seriously. Some crappy cigarette plunging into less than clean water—probably sewer runoff? That's what you imagine as a beautiful death? No offense, kid, but you suck at metaphors."

Jeremy's fingers trembled as he looked into the boy's eyes. He knew those eyes. But how? "How'd you know what I was thinking?"

The boy sighed. "C'mon, kid. Put it together. You know who I am. You know why I'm here. Don't make me say it."

And Jeremy did know. He supposed he'd known for several minutes that he'd been carrying on a conversation with Death himself. The thing that surprised him was that he'd always thought of death as an act, a state of being. Not a person. Certainly not a teenager.

"Not what you pictured, eh? Were you expecting a long black cloak with a hood? Maybe a sickle in my skeleton hand?" Death chuckled under his breath. "I'm that way for some people. I sprout feathery wings and appear in a basking glow of light for others. For you, I'm just a kid. Somebody easily disregarded. Somebody nobody would believe is Death."

"Bullshit." It wasn't bullshit and he knew it, but he didn't exactly know what to say. So instead, he took a cue from Death and waited.

Below, on the banks of the river, frogs were singing. It was faint and so distant, but if Jeremy listened close, he could hear them.

Death sighed, pinching the bridge of his nose for a moment. He squeezed his eyes tight, like he was just trying to get through another day at work—which, when Jeremy thought about it, he was. "If you're hoping I'll go on and prove it to you, you're sorely mistaken, kid. It's not my job to convince you who or what I am. It's not my job to make you jump or to talk you out of doing so. I'm just here. Waiting. For you to make a decision."

"You're lying."

"And you're shaking." His tone shifted then, briefly. It was stern, serious. He meant business. Never call Death a liar. "No reason to shake. You're not afraid of me . . . remember? You sought me out. Well, here I am. So are you doing this or not?"

He looked down at the water. He was doing this. That much had been decided before he ever even reached the bridge. But that didn't mean he didn't have questions. "What's it like?"

"What is *what* like?"

"Death."

Death rolled his head to the left and looked at Jeremy with raised eyebrows. "Seriously? You're asking Death what death is like?"

Jeremy shrugged. "I guess so, yeah. I mean, who would know better than you? If you are who you say you are, I mean."

"You've got me there."

"So. What's death like?"

Death sighed into the night air, giving the impression that Jeremy was making this night a lot longer than it needed to be. "Well, I'm a Sagittarius. I like puppies and long walks on the beach. I prefer classical music, which surprises most people.

They seem to think I'd be into this so-called death-metal. But I can assure you that all that screaming and heavy drums do not carry my endorsement. But to each their own, I guess."

"Never mind."

"Well, what the hell did you want me to say, kid? I'm Death, remember?"

"That's not what I meant."

"I know that's not what you meant. You meant the afterlife." Death raised a sharp eyebrow at him. "I'm not explaining that."

The frogs below were still singing, but they paused for a moment before continuing their tune. "Why? Is there a rule or something? Or is it different for everyone?"

"I can't answer that because I've never experienced it. I don't know." He met Jeremy's eyes again, folding his arms in front of him.

Jeremy held his breath for a moment. If Death didn't know, then who did?

"I've heard things, have theories. But I am not the afterlife. I am Death. The moment when life ceases. It's not my job to guide you through the afterlife—if there is one. It's my job to wait for your brain functions to cease and then make note that you are no longer among the living." He leaned away from the railing, in much the same way as Jeremy had when Death had first arrived. He was so nonchalant about the whole notion, so casual and matter-of-fact. He didn't have any answers. Jeremy leaned back against the railing in shock. "I'm kinda like the midlevel filing clerk of existence. It's not really as exciting as you mortals think."

Jeremy watched the water below with great interest. He couldn't stop thinking about the cigarette. Tearing his gaze away, he looked at Death. "You won't . . . take my life?"

Death's dark eyes darkened even more, until all that Jeremy could see within them was black and empty. "Death doesn't come for anyone, Jeremy. It just waits for you. All of you. For as long as it's supposed to."

"How did you know I'd be here tonight?"

"Are you kidding me? You've been planning for months. I listen. Through the chatter of thoughts that humankind flings out into the universe, I can tell when a cancer patient is nearing their final days. I can tell when a war is about to take another soldier. I can tell when a potential suicide has reached the point where they mean business." Death smacked him on the shoulder. They were pals, he and Death. "You seem like you mean business tonight. Do you?"

Jeremy shook his head. "You can't talk me out of it."

"I'm not trying to. Like I said, I'm just waiting. That's all I do."

"I have a shit life, y'know." He spoke through clenched teeth. His eyes burned with angry tears.

"I know." Death's voice was soft and hushed.

"My mom didn't want a kid, but got stuck with me. Now she drinks and runs around and where does that leave me? Smelling like goddamn dish soap when I don't smell like dirt. No kids at school will talk to me, let alone sit by me at lunch. I've got no money, no nothing. I'm just a loser. And I think the world would be better off without me." Against his will a tear escaped his eye and rolled down his cheek. It hung on his chin for a moment before letting go and dropping down into the depths.

Death whispered, "Then why are you up here and not down there? If you're so worthless, why haven't you jumped yet?"

"Because I'm afraid." Jeremy's bottom lip trembled. The water below looked both terrifying and soothing. Confusion filled him. What was he doing out here? Was he really talking to Death about whether or not he'd jump? Maybe he was dreaming. Maybe he was still asleep.

"Trust me. You're awake." A small smile touched Death's lips. "What are you afraid of?"

Jeremy wiped his eyes with his hand. "Pain, mostly."

"But not just pain, am I right? It's never just a fear of pain that makes any of you hesitate."

Hot anger burned at Jeremy's core. "Stop lumping me in with other suicides. I'm not a number. I'm a person."

"Don't bullshit yourself, kid. You're a person if you don't jump. If you do, you're just a statistic." There was that tone again. Jeremy winced to hear it. But just as quickly as it had come, it was gone again. "So, what else is it, if not just pain that you're afraid of?"

Jeremy shook his head. "It's stupid."

"Try me. I bet I've heard worse." Death smiled a knowing smile.

Jeremy really wondered why Death ever bothered to ask anyone anything. "I'm afraid I'll miss out."

"On what?"

"That's exactly the problem. I don't know. Just . . . that I'll miss out. What if I'm wrong? What if I jump and then find out things would have changed, would have gotten better if I hadn't?" A sigh escaped him, warm breath on the cool night air.

"So do you want to die or not?"

"Yes."

"Then jump." Death leaned toward him and pointed down to the water, his voice filled with impatience. "Find your balls and step off the bridge. There's a big fire just outside of Spencer. I'm due to meet two people there."

Jeremy's fingers tightened on the rail, but he wasn't certain why. He was pretty sure that Death wasn't going to push him. "Will it hurt?"

Death shrugged. "Probably. Shit, I don't know. I've never died before."

To the left an owl hooted into the night. After it quieted, Jeremy said, "Y'know, for Death, you sure don't have many answers."

"Death never brings answers, kid. Only more questions." To that end, he pulled out his watch again, checked the time, and emitted a small groan before putting it away again. Right. He had a schedule to keep.

"Doesn't it bother you? Seeing so many people meet their end?"

"Of course it does. I'd be a heartless prick if it didn't. But mostly it sickens me. So many people just throw it away, toss their life in the trash in a desperate search for something else that probably isn't any better than this and might be a whole lot worse. People seem to think that answers will be given to them when Death comes. They don't get that, just as my job is to wait, their job is to search for their own purpose." He took a deep breath and blew it out. As if on command, the frogs below went completely silent. "It just pisses me off, is all."

Jeremy shook his head. "I don't have a purpose."

"So jump already. I've got places to be."

"Stop saying that!"

For a moment, Death grew quiet. It was almost as if he wasn't used to people standing up to him. After a while, he reached into Jeremy's pocket and withdrew the ticket. As he scanned the print, he said, "Why Saint Louis?"

"Because."

"You packed pretty light. I'm betting you'll jump." He withdrew a package of Twinkies and pulled open the cellophane on one end.

Busy day, Jeremy thought. Death had probably missed his

lunch hour. "Why would you bet that? I don't have anything to pack. So I didn't pack anything."

Death took a bite of one of the Twinkies, and without swallowing, said, "What would you do? In Saint Louis, I mean."

Jeremy didn't know. He didn't know anything anymore. "Probably kill myself."

"Long bus ride just to delay the inevitable, if you've made your mind up about that." Death shook his Twinkie at Jeremy the way someone else might wag their finger. "Or is that a hint of doubt I detect ebbing from you?"

Jeremy wished, not for the first time, that Death couldn't read his thoughts like pages out of some dirty magazine. "I just . . . wish I had a reason to live. Just one."

"Twinkies are pretty good." He shoved the rest of the Twinkie into his mouth. When Jeremy looked at him, his mouth was full of yellow spongy cake and cream. Without swallowing, Death said, "What? They are."

"You know what I mean. One person who cared about me. One small glimmer of possibility for a good future. Just something to hold on to." It was all Jeremy had ever wanted. Just one thing to hold on to.

Death swallowed the Twinkie in his mouth and started sucking the white filling from his fingertips. "Well, right now you're holding on to the bridge. That's something. You haven't jumped yet. Maybe you start with the bridge and then keep going, see what else there is to hold on to."

The metal of the bridge was growing warm in his hands. He'd been holding on to it a lot longer than he thought he would be. "And if there's nothing?"

Death shrugged, as if the answer was obvious. "Then Saint Louis has quite a few lovely bridges."

"Look. Could you just leave me alone for a while?"

"Afraid not, kid. I mean, I can become invisible, but I'm always here, and always waiting. Just the way it is." He held out the open cellophane package to Jeremy and said, "Twinkie?"

Jeremy stared at him in disbelief. He was standing on a bridge, and Death had just offered him a Twinkie.

Death moved his hand closer and said, "They're amazing. I promise."

What do you do when Death offers you a Twinkie? You take it.

Dumbfounded, Jeremy said, "Thank you."

As Death wiped his fingers on his jacket, he said, "So, what was the moment for you?"

"What you do mean?"

"Look, you suicides are all the same." He eyed the uneaten Twinkie in Jeremy's hand and said, "You piss and moan about how awful and tragic your life is and how no one understands you. And you each have a moment that pushes you over the edge. What was yours?"

Jeremy shook his head. It took him a moment to respond. "Some dick on a bridge gave me a Twinkie."

Death chuckled. "You're a funny guy. I like that."

Jeremy stood there for a long while, listening to the night. One hand holding a Twinkie. The other hand holding the rail. "It was the dish soap."

A silence fell between them. One that stretched on for several minutes. It was Death who broke that silence. "Wow, you have exceedingly low standards, kid. I was expecting something akin to Poe or Plath, and you give me a commercial that appears during soap operas."

"My mom doesn't buy laundry detergent. She says dish soap is cheaper and does double duty. Plus, I think she's screwing the guy who manages the dollar store, so she gets the dish soap at a discount or free or whatever." He went cold when he spoke of his mom. His heart felt hard at the very thought of her. There was a time when he'd actually punched a kid for insinuating she did certain things for financial benefit. But that was before he was willing to look at his mom with honest eyes. "That damn dish soap. I hate the way it smells. It's almost medicinal. I mean, it's better than having clothes that smell like BO all the time, but it so obviously smells like cheap-ass dish soap, y'know?"

He didn't know, or maybe he did. He nodded anyway.

"So, a few weeks ago, I reached under the kitchen sink to grab a bottle. I'm standing there in a towel, my dirty clothes soaking in hot water in the kitchen, and all I want is to scrub them with some goddam dish soap and hang them up to dry so I can go to bed already. Only when I reach under the cupboard, there wasn't any dish soap left." His jaw tightened as the anger he'd felt in that moment washed over him once again. "And I started crying. And I realized that I didn't give a crap about the stupid dish soap, but that was the only way for me to be just a little bit normal, and that I'd never really be normal. And that's when I decided I was sick of trying. I was just sick of trying to keep pushing forward when the best I could ever hope for would be that there would be some stinky-ass dish soap under the sink when I reached for it. And I knew right then that I wanted to die."

Death didn't speak. He merely stood there, watching Jeremy with intense interest.

Jeremy shook his head and took a bite out of the Twinkie in his hand. "That's pretty sad, right? You've seen starving kids and war and crap, and I'm whining about goddam dish soap. But . . . you asked, and that's my answer."

In the distance sirens blared. Fire trucks, Jeremy was almost certain.

Death remained very still. "Why'd you bring the ticket?"

"I don't know." The words rolled off Jeremy's tongue without thought, without care.

"Liar." A hint of admiration leaked through in his tone. Must take some big balls to lie to Death.

"I just thought . . . maybe if I chickened out . . ."

"You'd have another option."

"Yeah." But there was no other option now, was there?

What could he do? Walk back to the trailer park and lie on his filthy mattress, waiting for things to improve when he knew they wouldn't? No way.

Death climbed up onto the rail and sat on it. "What if I made you a deal?"

Suspicion filled Jeremy. He looked at Death warily. "What kind of deal?"

"Not one I've ever made before. But like I said, I like you."

Jeremy didn't understand. "Why?"

"Because you called me a dick." Death grinned.

Jeremy was starting to realize what a twisted sense of humor Death had. "What's the deal?"

"I'll jump for you. And when I do, it'll erase your past. It'll give you a new beginning. Then, when you get on that bus, you'll have no regrets. You can start over. A clean slate. No more trailer park. No more dish soap. No more Jeremy Grainger. You can be whoever, whatever, you decide to be."

"But you're Death. Death can't die." Jeremy furrowed his brow. "Can you?"

Death sighed. The sirens in the distance had already silenced. "You want the deal or not, kid?"

It was hard to resist. A new life? On his terms? It sounded exactly like what he needed. "What do you want in return?"

"That flask, for starters."

That was too easy. There had to be a catch. "What else?"

"A promise." Their eyes met and Death's tone grew serious

once again. "Never let the bastards get you down. Don't let anyone or anything dictate your joy or lack thereof. Get your shit together however you want it and live life on your terms."

"Okay." He pulled the flask out again and handed it over. As he did so, he noticed that Death was staring down into the water, just as he had been a moment ago. "What's the matter?"

"It's a long way down." Death leaned forward even farther, until his fingertips turned white from holding him on the bridge. He met Jeremy's eyes and said, "Don't ever forget that."

The boy that Jeremy had come to know as Death fell forward. His body tumbled only once in the air before it struck the surface of the water and plunged into the depths. Doubt filled Jeremy's heart just as the splashing sounds from below filled his ears. Had the boy really been Death? Or had he been just another suicidal teen, just another statistic? Had all the perceived knowledge about Jeremy and his intentions just been insightful guesses?

Or had he just been given a second chance at life? A new life. Far away from the problems of Jeremy Grainger.

His heart was racing in confusion and terror. It drummed louder inside his head as he heard the splashing below go quiet. Before he realized what he was doing, he was running. Down the tracks, off the bridge, onto the gravel beside the tracks. The air whipped his hair back from his eyes. His palm was sticky from the Twinkie, but he couldn't remember having dropped it. He had to find someone to help the boy who'd jumped into the river. But it was almost midnight in a small town. Who would even be awake at this hour? He strained his thoughts, but couldn't find an answer, no matter how hard he tried.

Then, on the horizon of the next hill, the soft glow of fluorescent lighting. The bus station. Parked outside was the 12:05 to Saint Louis. Inside Jeremy's pocket was the ticket, but inside his head were doubts. What if he just watched a boy die? What if he could still help him? What if . . . ?

But then he saw something through the window that eased his nerves and set his annoyance level on overdrive at the same time. He stepped onto the bus and dug the ticket out of his pocket, handing it to the driver. Then he made his way about halfway down the aisle and took a seat next to a boy in a rumpled, patched jacket, holding a flask in his hand. His clothes were completely dry, his hair, too. He looked, in fact, precisely the way that he had the first time that Jeremy had laid eyes on him.

As Jeremy sat hard in the seat next to him, he cracked a smile—the first he had in a long time. "You are such a dick."

It was a trick. There was no deal. The decision to live or die—to move on or dwell, had been up to Jeremy the entire time.

Death grinned and reached inside his pocket. "Twinkie?"

Zac Brewer grew up on a diet of *The Twilight Zone* and books by Stephen King. He chased them down with every drop of horror he could find—in books, movie theaters, on television. The most delicious parts of his banquet, however, he found lurking in the shadowed corners of his dark imagination. When he's not writing books, he's skittering down your wall and lurking underneath your bed. Zac doesn't believe in happy endings . . . unless they involve blood. He lives in Missouri with his husband and two children.

Website: zacbrewer.com

Twitter: @unclezacbrewer

Facebook: facebook.com/NYT-Bestselling-Author-Zac-Brewer-241859875932/

Secret Things

LINDA ADDISON

Demon Slayer

It builds in me again,
  swelling under thin scars
hidden by long sleeves,
burning for release.

It burns away my determination.
  I lock the door, pick up the
edged tool, relieve the pressure,
one more time.

Finally able to breathe again,
  I need a hero to slay
this myth buried in me,
disfiguring my future.

Maybe I can become a warrior,
  find one person who cares,

unveil the shadow of anger,
the shifting darkness.

Write a new story,
    when the pressure begins,
slay It, recognize my light,
and become Legend.

Don't Talk to Strangers

He waited for the young ones
    where shadows grow wild
and parents never go.

Their voices appeared first,
    giggling, crying, whispering,
teasing, loud then quiet.

Soon footsteps stumbled in
    running, skipping, stomping,
ashes, ashes, they all fall down.

Then came their hands.
    Tender fingers, brown, pale,
dirty nails, shiny clean nails.

After a while curls of hair
    floated by, tight, loose,
dark, light, purple and pink.

Saddened it would end soon,
    he held his breath
before their eyes arrived.

Convergence of Troubled Strands

I have been here before,
outside, always outside,
unseen, frozen in place.

Everything moves faster:
Mom, Dad, teachers,
Those-Who-Could-Be-Friends.

I try:
    wear the right clothes,
    get the right haircut,
    smile at the right time.
Still invisible.

I can't breathe in this
desert. The thought of

being a ghost suddenly
    tastes real, then I
    raise my eyes,
  see you standing still.

Another phantom, you
see me, nod, our shadows
meet, suddenly there is air.

#LoveLetter for @OverU

How do I #Trend thee?
Even as I #Like every update,
every /photo/
    you #BlockMe.

@OnceUponATime we were
#InARelationship before
I wasn't allowed to
    be a #Friend or #CloseFriend.

On #TBT I post pictures from
when we were #HappyInLove
but you don't #Like them,
    you #UnFollow me.

I #TotallyRegret hitting you
but you will not #ForgiveOrForget.
If only you #Loved me the same,
   but you never #Heart my posts.

It's not #MyFault, you #MadeMeDoIt.
@IHeartYou #Forever. We are #MeantToBe.
So I will #SeekOut and follow everyone
   you know until #YouHeartMe again.

Linda Addison is an award-winning author of four collections, including *How to Recognize a Demon Has Become Your Friend*. She is the first African American recipient of the HWA Bram Stoker Award. She has published over three hundred poems, stories, and articles and is a member of Circles in the Hair, the Horror Writers Association, Science Fiction & Fantasy Writers of America, and the Science Fiction Poetry Association.

Website: lindaaddisonpoet.com

Twitter: @nytebird45

Facebook: facebook.com/linda.d.addison

Danny

JOSH MALERMAN

"Ho w much does it pay?"

Dad's first question. Of course it was Dad's first question.

"Eight dollars an hour."

"Eight dollars?" Mom said, peering into the kitchen. "Kelly, that's gotta be twice what I made back when I did the same exact thing."

"You babysat?" Kelly asked, sticking a fork into a piece of pancake. Mom looked surprised that her daughter wouldn't have guessed this on her own.

"Well, of *course* I babysat. Everybody babysat in the nineties."

Kelly looked to Dad across the table. Dad shook his head.

"No, I did not babysit," he said. "And I think eight dollars is too little. It's less than minimum wage. And I don't love the idea that you'd be responsible for somebody else's kid. Not even for a night."

"Dick Herman"—Mom used his full name, entering the kitchen now, one hand on her hip—"you sound like you're a hundred-year-old man."

"Do I? So I do. I don't like it."

"Don't like what? We hired babysitters for Kelly all the time when she was a kid. She's fifteen. She's old enough." Mom looked directly at Kelly and winked. "She's *responsible* enough too."

Kelly tried to imagine Mom babysitting. But she couldn't see anything except the bespectacled woman in an ankle length dress, ready for work, standing before her. Kelly imagined Mom sitting prim on a couch in a silent house. No friends over. No phone calls. Babysitting, and nothing more.

"Where do they live?" Dad asked, shoveling pancake into his mouth. "Maybe we know them. Who are they?"

Kelly pulled the piece of paper from the pouch of her hoodie sweatshirt.

"The Donaldses."

"Donalds?" Dad turned toward Mom. She knew more people around town than he did. Mom shook her head no.

"Don't know them," she said. "But I'm sure they're very nice people. How old is their kid?"

"Could be ten kids," Dad said, shaking his head.

"One kid," Kelly said. "They didn't say how old."

Both parents frowned.

"Didn't say how old?" Dad shook his head again. "What if it's a baby? For Christ's sake, Sue, it's winter. What if there's an emergency? Can you imagine Kelly carrying a baby on foot through a snowstorm?"

Now Mom shook her head.

"That's enough, Dick. Seriously, do you have to imagine the *worst* thing possible?"

"It's got you thinking though, doesn't it?"

"No. It doesn't have me thinking. Kelly Herman, you're a fifteen-year-old, magnificent student, and a beautiful, intelligent woman. *And* if there's an emergency, you have a cell phone. If you want to dip your feet into the workforce, I'm one hundred percent behind you."

"Dad?"

Kelly had a special bond with Dad. The same sense of humor. A similar worldview. When he said no, she usually let it die.

"No," he said.

Not this time.

"But what percent are you behind me?"

"On this?"

"Yeah, on this."

Dad leaned back in his breakfast chair and mused on the numbers.

"Forty."

Kelly smiled.

"That's one-forty between the two of you. An average of seventy. I'm going to give them a call."

Dad looked to Mom. She was smiling.

"That's my girl," she said. "Using your brain. Let us know how it goes."

. . .

Kelly used the landline in the office. She liked sitting in the office chair, leaning back as far as she could, putting her socked feet up on the desk. It made her feel like she was in charge of a big company. If she was, she thought, she'd be a good boss. But the idea quickly scared her. People coming to her with questions. The responsibility of answering those questions. Employees. It was probably a lot different from piecing together the yearbook with the staff. But who knows?

"Hello?"

A man's voice. An adult. Weird feeling, calling a stranger.

"Hello, I read your ad and—"

"Are you a babysitter?"

Kelly blushed, despite being unseen.

"Um, yes. Sure."

"Sure? You said you're calling about the advertisement?"

"Yes." Kelly felt like she'd already botched it. "I'm a babysitter."

"And you can watch him tonight?"

Him. Good. A boy sounded easier somehow.

"Yes. I spoke with my parents. They're for it."

A pause on the line and Kelly thought it meant the man was considering what she'd just said. Maybe "they're for it" was a weird, young thing to say. Then she heard a muffled exchange between the man and a woman and understood the couple were talking it over.

"How old are you?" the man asked.

"I'm fifteen."

"Experience?"

"No. Not really. How old is your son?"

More of the muffled exchange. Kelly looked at herself in the mirror hanging on the back of the open office door.

You look old enough to do this, she thought, and made a face like her mom would.

"I'm sorry," the man returned. "What's your name?"

"Kelly Herman."

She thought she sounded too young. Like Kelly Herman was a kid's name.

"Well, Kelly Herman, we were hoping for somebody with at least *some* experience."

Kelly nodded at her reflection.

"I totally understand," she said.

"Do you?"

"Well, yeah. I mean, it's your kid. He means the world to you."

Kelly felt a small thrill. She'd expressed herself somehow in that moment.

"Hang on a second," the man said.

There was more of the muffled exchange, and Kelly stared at herself in the glass.

"Hello again," the man said. "I apologize if I sounded a bit worried. But you're absolutely right. He means the world to us. Can you be here at seven?"

Kelly's heart fluttered. She caught her reflection, a real reaction, wide-eyed and happy.

"Yes! Mom or Dad will drive me."

"Great. Let me give you directions to our home. Where do you live?"

Kelly told him and then began writing the directions on a small yellow sticky pad. She had to use two of the squares. When he was done, she thanked him.

"Wait," the man said. He paused. Then, "You don't know our names yet."

Kelly felt embarrassed for not having asked.

"Um . . . Mr. and Mrs. Donalds?"

The man laughed, deeply.

"No, no. That won't do. I'm Charles and my wife is Allison. And we're very excited to see you at seven."

Kelly, sensing an opportunity to make up for what felt like a blunder, asked, "Mr. Donalds, Charles, what's your son's name?"

A brief silence. A pause. A beat.

"Danny."

Danny Donalds, Kelly thought. About as childish as Kelly Herman.

"Awesome," she said. "Can't wait to meet him."

"Thank you, Kelly. Seven o'clock, then."

They hung up. Kelly scribbled the names on a third yellow square. She looked directly into the mirror and smiled.

"You got a job!" she exclaimed. Then she ran downstairs to

tell Mom and Dad and to make sure one of them was going to drive her there at seven after all.

"Dunkirk?" Dad said, arching an eyebrow. "Nice neighborhood."

"Perfect," Mom said. "Surprised we don't know them."

"Can one of you drive me?"

Mom and Dad looked to each other.

"I'll take you," Dad said. "I'd like to get a look at this place."

Kelly squealed and hugged Dad. Then she made for the stairs again.

"Kelly!" Mom called.

"What?"

"How old is the kid?"

Darn it. Kelly realized she hadn't found that out. If she told her parents that, they might not drive her there.

"Five!" she said.

"Five?" Dad called. "Isn't that a little young?"

"Oh, stop it," Mom said. "What do you want Kelly to do, babysit a twenty-year-old?"

Kelly vanished into her bedroom before her dad could change his mind.

School was a dull blur. Mr. Laurel went on and on about *great fiction*. Mrs. Cannes acted surprised when none of the students were prepared for the day's science experiment, then realized she was reading from a chapter ahead. Lunch was all right. Gym was a lot of standing around. And between classes Kelly's friends made little if anything of her new gig.

"I've been babysitting my brother for six years," Andrea said.

"You'll end up watching a lot of TV," Tonya said, pulling on the ends of her red hair. "Just don't let the kid wet himself and you'll be fine. How old is he?"

Kelly stammered a response before coming clean.

"I don't know, guys."

It felt like a confession. But her friends didn't care.

"Whatever," Tonya said. "Babies and kids. Kids and babies. All the same."

Andrea changed the subject and that was it. That was the big to-do about Kelly's first job.

And yet she still felt it meant something bigger.

At six fifteen Kelly was asking Dad if he was ready to go. He said they'd be fine if they left at twelve to. Kelly didn't want to be late. Dad understood. So they compromised and pulled out of the driveway at 6:44.

Kelly had been to Dunkirk before but she couldn't remember why or when. Did she have a childhood friend who lived here? Maybe she and her parents had gone to a party? A wake? Maybe they'd just watched a Lions game back when Kelly was still a little girl. It wasn't a big deal, and yet, the drive did feel profound.

The enormous evergreens lining the road caught early flakes of a bigger snowstorm on the way.

"Don't like the sight of that," Dad said, eyeing the white-tipped trees.

"Think of it this way," Kelly said. "Everybody has to drive slower when it snows. It's almost safer that way."

Dad frowned.

"Sure is a nice neighborhood though. Kills ours."

As if cued by his words, the trees split wider and seemed to vanish entirely, giving Kelly a view of large homes, brightly lit facades, nice cars in circle drives.

Kelly was a little awed. It added to her blossoming anxiety.

They probably know a good babysitter when they see one. But are you a good one, Kelly?

She tried to lean on Andrea's and Tonya's indifference at school. Who cared if the couple didn't like her on sight? She'd do a good job either way. And who knows? Maybe Kelly was embarking on a lifelong friendship. Maybe she'd sit for Danny more often. Maybe she'd watch him grow, eventually from afar, and run into him one day, on the street in a big city, where she'd hug him and tell him that she used to babysit him and holy cow how the world turns.

"Turn here!" Kelly said.

Dad made a right, probably too quickly, and the car slid, just a little bit.

"Gotta be careful out here tonight, Kelly. I hope the Donaldses know how to drive in bad weather."

"I'm sure they do, Dad. They're from Michigan too."

"Are they?"

The way Dad asked it (how did Kelly know where they were from?) gave her a sinking feeling, and all at once Kelly realized she didn't know a single thing about these people.

"There it is," Kelly said, pointing.

Dad slowed the car and rolled to the end of a long, dark drive. He eyed the house and eventually nodded his approval.

"Nice place," he said.

Kelly opened the passenger door. Before she got out, Dad gently took her arm.

"I'm gonna wait here till they greet you. Get a good look at them. Then I'll head home. You call us if you need anything. Even if you only need advice. Okay, Kelly?"

Kelly smiled and exited the car.

She walked up the driveway toward the house.

Kelly knocked and the door opened almost immediately. She was surprised to see a good-looking man, younger than Dad, wearing a pink button-down shirt. His short black hair had spots of gray but even the gray looked healthy.

"Kelly Herman," he said, and a smile exposed a good set of teeth. Behind him Kelly saw a woman standing with her arms crossed.

Kelly shook his extended hand with a gloved one of her own.

"Come on in," he said, eyeing the idling car at the end of the long drive. "Is that your father?"

Kelly looked over her shoulder.

"Yeah," she said, a little embarrassed. "Wanted to make sure I made it up the drive, I guess."

Mr. Donalds, Charles, nodded. Then he waved to Kelly's dad.

"Would you mind taking your boots off?" the woman, Allison, said.

Kelly stepped inside, took off her boots and coat. She set her boots neatly on the front rug and felt the cool tile beneath her socks. Charles closed the front door, took her coat, and hung it on a rack beside them.

"We're going to the cinema tonight," he said, heading toward what looked like the kitchen. Kelly marveled at how white it was in here. And how big! A wide, white staircase to her right ended in a dark hall above. With no sign of Danny around, she wondered if he wasn't up there, in his room.

"Dinner and a movie," Charles said, smiling over his shoulder as Kelly followed him into the kitchen. "Can you get more plain than that?"

"Well," Kelly said awkwardly, "you probably deserve a night out."

A moment of silence followed. Allison entered the kitchen quietly. Charles stood at an island with a marble top. Allison leaned against a matching marble counter, near him. They stared at her, and Kelly found herself wishing there was some kind of music playing.

"*Deserve*," Charles said, smiling. He looked like a politician when he smiled. And his clothes only added to the image. "Good choice of words. What are you going to school for?"

"She's fifteen, Charles," Allison said, not a little icily. "She doesn't choose yet."

Charles shook his head. He looked a little embarrassed. Kelly remembered something her dad told her a long, long time ago:

Sometimes, Kelly, you meet someone and it just feels plain . . . weird. And when that happens, when you get that feeling, remember that it's not you. It's them.

Them, Kelly thought, looking from one to the other.

"Uh, what movie are you going to see?"

Allison stepped forward.

"It doesn't matter. We'll figure it out when we get there. I'd like to talk about our son."

Kelly nodded.

"Okay."

Another beat. A brief silence.

"We'd like Danny to be in bed by nine o'clock," she said. "He likes to play games, likes to be around you. If you're watching television, he may curl up next to you on the couch."

Kelly nodded again. Beyond Allison's shoulder she saw a thermostat glowing a soft blue on the wall. She wondered how low it was turned.

"Danny's a good boy," Charles said.

Kelly nodded.

"You may not see much of him," Allison said. "Sometimes I have to call his name four, five times before he shows himself."

"Likes to peer around the corner of doorways," Charles said. "Make a face at you."

The couple laughed, quietly, but Kelly saw some strain there. Was it sadness? She wasn't sure. They looked into each other's eyes and Charles nodded. A silent communication. Charles turned to face her again, now more serious.

"Kelly," he said. "We have a confession to make."

To Kelly, the house felt very big. Very still.

"Yeah?"

Charles nodded again. He reached out his hand and Allison slowly took it. Kelly looked to their clasped hands, thought of her father, probably home by now, then looked to see Charles was staring deep into her eyes.

"We don't have a son," he said.

Allison allowed a muffled moan to escape her.

Kelly looked from one to the other.

"What do you mean?"

Another beat. A pause. Kelly looked over her shoulder to her boots on the rug by the front door.

They both started to speak at the same time, and Charles held out an open palm, suggesting Allison go ahead. She began, then stopped.

"Well, Kelly," Charles said, his eyes rippling with kindness, "we like to imagine that we do."

Kelly shifted from one socked foot to the other. She felt chilled.

"He's practically real," Allison suddenly said. "The way we love him."

She brought her eyes to Kelly's and Kelly saw conviction there.

"Um . . . okay," Kelly said. It was hard. Speaking at all.

Charles let go of Allison's hand and stepped out from behind the island.

"Humor us," he said, smiling, spreading his arms wide, suggesting everything was all right, there was nothing weird here. "Watch our boy while we go out to dinner and a movie."

Kelly looked from one then to the other, one then the other.

"What . . . what do you mean?"

"He means we'd like you to play along," Allison said. There was strange dignity in her voice. Kelly wondered if it was what madness sounded like.

The couple were clearly embarrassed. Kelly thought of her father again. She wished he was still idling at the end of the drive.

"Uh . . . I'm not sure I understand," she said at last, and the couple nodded along with her.

"Not much to understand," Charles said, smiling sheepishly.

"We don't have any kids. We'd like one." He spoke slowly, pain-fully. "So we pretend that we do. We call him Danny. If you can find it in your heart to watch him tonight, we'd feel very much obliged."

Kelly felt anxious. A little scared. Should she call Dad? But, on the other hand . . . weren't they just asking her to stay a few hours in an empty house?

"Um," Kelly said, "is the pay the same?"

Charles's eyes opened wide.

"Oh yes! Of course. Still eight dollars an hour. As adver-tised. We'll be gone for about four hours. Thirty-two bucks. Well, make it an even forty."

He reached across the island and gripped Allison's hand again. The two of them stared at Kelly, and Kelly saw despera-tion in their eyes.

"Sure," she said. "I'll . . . um . . . I'll watch Danny for you guys tonight."

Charles sighed. A tear trolled down Allison's face.

"Thank you," Charles said. He stepped to Allison and embraced her. He looked at Kelly over his wife's shoulder. "*Thank you*," he whispered again.

"He likes to eat cereal," Allison said as Charles helped her into a brown, elegant winter coat.

They were standing near the front door. There seemed to be a lot of space, a lot of house behind Kelly.

"But don't let him eat too much of it," Charles said, "or he'll be up all night."

Kelly thought she saw him wink. But then she wasn't sure.

Charles slipped on a pair of leather gloves.

He opened the front door and held it open for Allison. When he was halfway out himself, he turned and stuck his head back in, peering around the white wood.

"Remember! Make sure Danny's in bed by nine o'clock." Then, "Thank you, Kelly."

"Okay."

The front door closed, making something of a white wall before her.

Kelly turned slowly and looked to the stairs and the dark hallway at the top.

She looked down at her boots on the rug.

Then she went to the living room, planning to watch TV.

It was difficult, figuring out what to watch and at what volume to watch it. Scary movies were out of the question. So were most thrillers. But reality shows almost carried with them something worse. No ghost hunting shows. No way. At first Kelly had the volume loud, hoping to mask any sound the house might make. Then she turned it way down, worried she might miss a sound the house might make.

The couch faced the television, and directly behind it was the foyer where she'd seen the Donaldses off and the stairs just beyond it. Kelly sat at the very end of the white couch and turned, often, to look at the white, empty stairs.

Two men were boxing on TV. Kelly changed the channel. A man and woman were kissing, and she left it. Low volume.

Through a window to the right of the television she saw the snow was falling pretty hard. She thought of what her dad said. About how he hoped the Donaldses were good drivers.

Kelly looked once again to her boots on the rug by the front door.

She felt weird here. And a little scared.

There was really no reason to stay. Sure, forty dollars was a good thing, but maybe not good enough to keep her in this empty house. All she had to do was put her boots on and start walking home. She could call Dad. He'd come for her in a second. Or however long it took. Ten minutes? Fifteen? Kelly felt a twinge of panic. Fifteen minutes meant that, if she decided she wanted to leave this place, she'd have to stay for another fifteen minutes. That wasn't counting how long it might take Dad to get in the car and go. But, then again, she could put her boots on and begin walking. But why? And what would she tell Dad?

They don't have a kid, Dad. They pretend that they do.

That ought to get him moving quickly.

Kelly looked to the bottom of the stairs. Then up them.

She stared at where the white steps led to the darkness until she thought her eyes were going to play tricks on her. Then she turned away and forced herself to watch the TV.

Come on, she thought. *You're getting forty dollars to watch an empty house.* Then, *You're housesitting, not babysitting.*

This thought comforted her.

You're housesitting. Not babysitting.

Below the TV, as part of the white entertainment center, books were stacked on a shelf. Kelly looked to their spines, then back to the TV. She looked over her shoulder again, thought of the cold marble-topped island in the kitchen and the look on Allison's face when Charles told her that they liked to pretend. Kelly looked back to the spines under the TV.

A photo album caught her eye.

She shook her head no. She wasn't here to snoop. She was here to make forty dollars. Her first job. A real moment. Something Dad and Mom were probably very proud of.

On TV, the same couple that'd been kissing were now swimming in a lake. Kelly could hardly hear them, but she didn't want to turn up the TV. She set her phone beside her on the couch. Maybe Charles and Allison would call. Maybe they'd check up on Danny.

Danny.

Kelly shrugged off the idea and tried to smile. If ever there was weird, *this* was weird. She tried to understand where the Donaldses might be coming from. They didn't have any kids. They wanted one. So they made one up. It really wasn't a big deal. People made things up all the time. In a way, they were acting like kids themselves, playing pretend. If Kelly thought about it, in a certain way, it was okay. Not weird at all.

She shifted on the couch and heard a creaking come from upstairs. Possibly right above her.

Kelly looked up.

She turned quickly to face the stairs. Her body felt hot. She took the remote control and turned the volume of the TV down even more.

Her first instinct scared her. Her first instinct was to call out his name.

Danny?

But she didn't. She looked to the window by the TV and saw the snow was really coming down and she knew that a storm could cause a house to creak. She looked to the ceiling again, to where she thought she heard the sound. Then back to the stairs.

She took hold of her phone.

Call Dad.

But she didn't *want* to call Dad. She wanted to stay here (*housesit*) until the Donaldses got home. Then she wanted to put forty dollars into her pocket, get a ride home, and then maybe tell Mom and Dad all about the Donaldses and their . . . son.

No, she didn't want to call Dad.

She waited. Waited for another creaking.

The snowflakes outside the window were big, heavy-looking things, and Kelly imagined them covering her whole, hiding her.

She waited and she waited some more, trying not to look for too long into the darkness at the top of the stairs. Instead, she focused on the spine of the photo album.

Don't go looking through their things.

She rose from the couch, leaving her phone on the cushions.

She went to the shelf and knelt and pulled the white, puffy volume out. In cursive letters, the cover read:

Birthdays.

Kelly held the book a moment. The TV got brighter as characters walked down a sunny country road. Kelly wiped a thin layer of dust off the cover of the photo album and brought it with her back to the couch.

She set it next to the phone and pretended to watch TV.

But it didn't last long.

She opened the album.

Through the window, the snow fell, but *in* the window Kelly saw herself reflected, and she didn't like what she saw. She thought she looked guilty.

And yet she couldn't stop herself. She flipped to the first photograph.

Both Allison and Charles looked much younger. Allison wore light blue high-waisted jeans, and Charles, with no spot of gray in his hair, had a sweatshirt tied around his waist. They were standing on either side of an empty chair. Both had a hand on the back of the chair. Charles was pointing to the camera, as though guiding the wayward eyes of a child, telling him where to look. Before the empty seat, on the table, was a vanilla birthday cake with a single candle stuck into it.

One.

Kelly looked over her shoulder, to the entrance of the kitchen, where the Donaldses had "confessed" to her. She looked to the ceiling. Then back to the book.

She flipped the page.

They looked pretty much the same, though there were signs that the two were growing more conservative. Charles's hair was shorter, Allison wore more ladylike makeup, and between them, the chair was a nicer one. A higher back. And upon the back was Allison's hand, as Charles knelt beside the empty space and pointed, this time, to a white and blue cake on the table.

Two.

Kelly paused, looking up to the TV but not watching the TV. She felt like she shouldn't go on. She felt a tugging in her chest. A sadness for these two. And yet there was something so . . . *authentic* about their poses, the looks on their faces. Kelly wondered if this was what love was. Two people sharing such a thing.

She flipped the page.

A closer shot. The two of them framing the same empty chair from the last one.

Three.

She flipped the page.

A new house, it looked like. Maybe this one. Charles was dressed nicer. They both looked cleaner. Allison's eyes were half-closed. Kelly wondered if it was the only photo they took that day.

Four.

A light flashed below the TV, and Kelly looked to see it was eight o'clock. She flipped the page and saw Allison genuinely smiling. Charles leaning back, staring at the empty chair (a new one) as though their son had done something funny.

Five.

Kelly looked to the clock.

8:01.

Make sure Danny's in bed by nine!

Kelly looked over her shoulder, to the bottom of the stairs. Suddenly it felt like she couldn't look anywhere. If she looked to the kitchen, she thought of the thermostat and how cold it felt in there. The front door reminded her that she was alone. The bottom of the stairs led to the top of the stairs, and at the top of the stairs was that dark hallway.

She flipped a page, looked down.

Six.

She flipped another one.

Seven.

Another one.

Eight.

In this one Allison was clearly older. Charles still had his pretty smile, but the corners of his eyes were beginning to droop.

And in the chair between them . . . emptiness. Kelly stared into the emptiness for a long time. She was trying to make out a face. Make out a shoulder. She didn't like that she was doing that.

She flipped the page.

Nine.

Nine? Kelly thought. How old was he?

Breathing deeply, she turned the pages.

Ten.

Eleven.

Twelve.

Thirteen.

Fourteen.

Fifteen.

At fifteen, the Donaldses looked more like they did now than they did at the beginning of the book. Kelly felt a chill wash over her body. Fifteen was as old as she was.

She looked to the stairs and to the top of them, and she no longer imagined a little boy up there. Now she imagined something closer to a man.

She flipped the pages.

Sixteen.

Seventeen.

Eighteen.

Nineteen.

A man. In this house. A man. Not a boy.

Kelly flipped the page, wide-eyed, and saw the next one was blank. But the last one, the nineteenth, was definitely taken in this house. The child's birthday cake was on the marble-topped island in the kitchen.

Kelly looked to the entrance of the kitchen.

A man.

She imagined facial hair. A certain look in his eye.

But it's not a man. Look at the photos again. They were all children's birthday cakes. Not a man. Just the same imaginary child for nineteen years.

Kelly closed the book quickly and rose. She placed the album back where she'd found it and returned to the couch.

Forty dollars, she thought. Then she looked once more to the front door. To her boots on the rug. Just getting to them, the short way across the white tile, looked like a long way to walk.

And the rug was near the bottom of those stairs.

She told herself to calm down. Told herself she was just housesitting, but the word carried less steam than it did before.

The digital clock beneath the TV told her it was already 8:30, and Kelly thought that meant she had another two and a half hours here. In this house. She didn't want to stay that long. She got up. She turned to face her boots.

Sit down, she told herself. *Watch TV. Watch a movie. By the time it's over, they'll be home.*

This sounded reasonable. This sounded like a plan she could hang on to. This was her first job and she wanted to handle it well.

Kelly sat down on the couch again and intentionally turned her back on the front door, the stairs, and the rest of the white house. She flipped the channels, trying to find the beginning of a movie. Any movie. Anything that might give her two hours. Her eyes traveled down the length of the TV screen, to the shelf beneath the screen and to the spine, again, of the photo album.

Birthdays.

She recalled the way Allison and Charles aged in the pictures. How their features had hardened. How their eyes seem to turn a bit gray through the years.

Birthdays.

She looked back to the screen to find that she was at the beginning of a movie after all. It was the opening credits, though she'd missed the title. She turned the volume up, just a little bit, enough to make her feel like she wasn't so on edge.

It wasn't a comedy, but it wasn't scary either, and Kelly was fine with that. A drama, she understood, about a family (that was fine), though she didn't yet know where the story was going to go. That was okay too, as Kelly wanted to watch it, get into it, and find out where the story went.

She watched TV.

If you're watching television, he may curl up next to you on the couch.

Kelly tried to push this out of her mind. But the thought made her shiver, and Kelly couldn't help but look over her shoulder, quickly, once more to the foot of the stairs. She followed them up, how could she not, and stared into the darkness there. She imagined a child. Then a man. A child. Then a man. She saw the photos flash across her mind's eye and truly imagined the couple setting the photos up, setting the timers on the cameras, telling each other to get ready, telling their son to do the same.

Make sure Danny's in bed by nine!

Kelly looked to the clock.

9:07.

She looked back to the darkness at the top of the stairs. What could she do? Did they expect her to go upstairs? To enter that dark hallway and tuck him in?

She tried to shrug it off. She *did* shrug it off, enough so that she was able to watch the movie again, though she'd missed a bit. But what did it matter? Every minute that passed was a minute closer to the Donaldses coming home. And that moment, far away as it seemed, *was* getting closer.

Kelly watched TV.

The movie was dull, but it continued, and the minutes passed.

She sunk into the couch. She began to understand what was happening in the movie. She checked her phone. She looked to the window and the snowstorm outside. She thought of Dad. She thought of Mom.

And she heard a second creaking come from upstairs.

Kelly sat upright and looked to the ceiling. But the sound she'd heard hadn't come from directly above her like the other one had. This one had come from farther along the ceiling. Closer to the top of the stairs.

He likes to peer his head around the corner of doorways, make a face at you.

Kelly stared at the darkness at the top of the stairs. She looked to the entrance to the kitchen. She heard another creaking.

She almost stood up. She didn't know what else to do. Her phone was in her hand, and she didn't even remember picking it up. Maybe she was about to call Dad. She didn't know. Her boots lay waiting by the front door.

Kelly looked to the window and saw a blanket of white. It looked soft. Very soft. Like she could enter it and start walking and get home safely without a problem.

She heard a fourth creaking and this time believed it was coming from someplace closer.

On the stairs.

The three words came to her so naturally that, at first, she saw them only as a point of fact.

They have an imaginary child, she told herself. *They do it because they're sad. Please, Kelly, understand that. The Donaldses are sad. But you can't let their sadness scare you.*

This sounded right to her, and yet she stared at the stairs.

Not at the dark hallway where they led and not at the ceiling above her, but directly at the white stairs themselves.

She looked to the TV. She tried to settle into the couch again. She tried to get back into the movie. If she could just get into it, time would pass and the Donaldses would be home and then she would be home soon too.

She waited for another sound. She waited a long time.

None came.

Wind tickled the window by the TV and instead of frightening Kelly it calmed her down. A little. It reminded her that snowstorms make sounds. Snowstorms cause houses to creak.

Kelly reached for the controller, to turn the volume down, or up, it didn't matter. She tried both.

She turned once more, toward the stairs, then back to the TV and set the controller down next to her and felt someone's naked leg beside her.

Kelly leapt from the couch.

It was a body it wasn't a body it was a body it wasn't a body it was a body it wasn't.

She stared, trembling, at the open space on the couch.

If you're watching television, he may curl up next to you on the couch.

Danny likes to play games.

Sometimes I have to call him four, five times before he shows himself.

Kelly crossed the room, nearly running, and stumbled,

putting her boots on. She put her jacket on too and then opened the front door and exited the house and entered the snowstorm.

She checked her pockets. She had her phone. She looked back to the house and didn't care anymore about forty dollars, didn't care anymore what Dad or Mom might say. She was leaving, she'd *left*, and she'd call Dad from the road.

Then she stopped halfway down the long drive and looked back to the house. To the windows and the front door.

At the end of the long drive a pair of headlights popped up in the snowy distance, and Kelly quickly hid, kneeling half in a ditch that began behind a low row of white bushes.

She watched the car approaching and knew it was them before they reached her. They were home early. But they didn't see her, of this she was sure, as they turned slowly into the drive and the soft snow crunched beneath their tires as they rolled to the house, lighting up every window on the way.

Kelly knew she should go, should continue into the storm.

She watched as the Donaldses parked their car, then got out and walked through the snow to the front door. At the door Charles put his arm around Allison. He held the door open for her and they entered. The door closed behind them.

Kelly stared at the house. She waited. She stared.

She stomped quickly through the snow, back to the house. It took her forever, and it felt like the light above the front door exposed the entire world. But she made it to the side of the house quickly, ducking beneath low-hanging branches of frosted evergreens.

Light poured onto the snow through the window that she knew was the window next to the TV, and Kelly stepped into the light and up to the window and looked into the house.

She wanted to see them. Wanted to see how they'd react when they found out the babysitter had left their child . . . all alone.

She saw them. Saw a look of incredulity upon Allison's face, saw Charles trying to calm his wife down. *Where is she?* Kelly heard Allison say, desperation, horror in her voice. Neither had taken off their coat yet. Charles went to the foot of the stairs and began to ascend, but Allison stopped him with a sudden shriek.

Kelly watched as Allison took a step backward, closer to the window, and gestured toward the entrance of the kitchen.

"Danny," Kelly heard Allison say. "Why aren't you in bed? Where is your babysitter?"

Charles, with one foot still on the first white step, looked to his wife, then to the entrance of the kitchen. Kelly couldn't see into the entrance. Couldn't see what they were seeing. But she believed they were mad, in a way, pretending for so long, until it felt real.

"What did you say?" Charles said, and his voice was muffled by the glass. "She's where?"

"Right where?" Allison asked.

They turned their worried faces toward Kelly at the same time. As if someone had told them that the babysitter was outside, looking in through the window.

Kelly ran. Into the storm she ran. Down the long drive. When she got to the main road, she continued to run. She called Dad. He'd come for her. But until he got to her, she ran.

Josh Malerman is the author of the novel *Bird Box* and the novella *A House at the Bottom of the Lake.* Malerman is also the songwriter/guitarist for the Detroit rock band The High Strung, whose song "The Luck You Got" is the theme song for Showtime's hit show *Shameless.*

Twitter: @JoshMalerman

Facebook: facebook.com/JoshMalerman

Make It Right

MADELEINE ROUX

Right, um, I'd like to report a murder."

The cop was staring back at me like I'd just burst into the station doing a tap dancing routine. No jazz hands, I guess, but for my part I couldn't stop thinking about my hands. Hot, hot, too hot and needly, like someone was poking them over and over again or holding them over a range.

"Could you repeat that?" He was lumpy and short, like maybe he had to be standing on a box to see over the counter. Wasn't sure he was even a cop. No hat. Rumpled uniform. But there was a badge, yeah? So he had to count.

"I'd like to report a murder."

My voice came out less shaky and weird that time.

Skeptical. But of course. I hate that look. That look adults give you when they think you're full of shit for no other reason than they've seen a few more years than you. I made my face real hard. I know things, buddy, things that'd make your hair fall out.

"Start from the beginning," he said, finally maybe believing me just a bit. The station was dim and brown, used tea bag brown, a brick box with phones blaring off like a seagull screech every once in a while. Not all that many folks calling in at midday. More than you might think, though.

Area's gone to shit. That's what my uncle would say.

Anyway, the beginning. I'll go back and start from there for you, too. Hard to know where the beginning's at, looking at it here from now. But it starts round about when I moved to Bramhall to live with my uncle.

Uncle Sid is a twat. And yeah, that's the kind of rough language that got me sent there in the first place. The social services people, also a bunch of twats, thought I wasn't doing so well living with my dad. They got called a few times, like, because of drugs or whatever. Not mine, his. Or because I cut school a few days. But I didn't mind his rotating list of girl-friends, so give me points for that at least. Some of them were even sort of nice. One called Molly had big red blotches all over her tits and forearms, but she snuck me cigarettes once in a while, so she couldn't be all bad.

But the social workers weren't pleased, and when they ain't pleased, things go bad for you. Worse for my dad, sure, but bad for me, too, because they shipped me off to live with Uncle Sid in Bramhall—a "nice" town with "nice" people—to straighten out a girl like me.

"You should be happy," the lady social worker they sent over said. "Bramhall is lovely, so much nicer than Moss Side. You'll see, Lauren, this is a place where you can really flourish."

Right. I flourished on over to Uncle Sid's with all my shit, looking at how everything in the world I owned fit into, like, two squashed cardboard boxes. Depressing. I'm not a Make the Most of It kind of girl, but maybe, I thought, it could be better. Watching Dad waste away wasn't fun, sure, but he's my dad. You make it work.

I'd make it work with Sid, too. The social workers had to take me over to Bramhall because it was a drive, and they told my dad to get me over there, but then he never bothered, so they finally arranged for me to get picked up. Bramhall's not like Moss Side. Bramhall is green, lots of old, white cottagey buildings everywhere, like maybe Shakespeare wandered around here ages ago writing his things. That's what it made me think of when it went by out the window—posh idiots in wigs and funny outfits dancing about on the village green, holding hands and singing or whatever. But Sid didn't live in a nice cottagey place, his dump was farther outside town, a council block set a nice *appropriate* distance from the fancier housing. At least that made me feel a little more at home.

Sid's place is short and dumpy, like that cop at the station, but not lumpy, just a crumbling brick rectangle with the bare minimum effort put into the lawn. Weeds and crumpled up cans of lager and patches of dirt with yellowing cig butts stuck here and there like pimples. I remember the sky was cement gray that first day and that Sid wasn't anywhere to greet me.

Turns out he was inside on the fluffy chair with his feet

up on the table, watching whatever wasn't ads. I'm not sure
Sid ever saw a whole show, just clicked around to avoid the
adverts. The social worker lady with me made him look at
some paperwork and took my uncle's grunts for agreement.
Guardianship. What a laugh. Someone called a guardian
should be tall and strong, right? Sword, shield, bright, shiny
armor that can actually deflect a thing or two. Looked like anything you chucked at Sid would just sink right into his blobby
body and get absorbed, like one of them amoeba things I got
tested on in science.

The neighborhood seemed to go on forever in one direction, other brown, slumping buildings clustered on either side.
Right before the lady left, I heard a bunch of nasty idiots walk
by, cursing and laughing. Kids my age that thought they were
real tough, picking up whatever rubbish they had found on
the street and hurling it at neighboring houses. A can hit the
bricks on Sid's house, and I watched his face go splotchy and
red, all one color, so that his thin lips and stump of a nose disappeared into one spit-mad circle.

Sid's a builder, so his hands look like a boxer's. That's also
why he looked so incredibly stupid trying to scribble down
his name, the pen disappearing into his giant fist like it was a
toothpick.

"Bloody kids," he muttered, then he remembered the lady
was still there and signed his name on the papers she had
given him. He glanced at me, standing there like a total idiot

with nothing to do, two cardboard boxes stacked in front of me like a little wall. "Suppose you're not like that," he added. No telling if it was a question.

I didn't actually want the lady to go. I didn't know her, right, didn't *care* about her, but she at least felt safe and like something that might put a little fence between me and Sid. She smelled like the makeup corner at Boots, and men—my dad, Sid—got real quiet and weird when she was around, like a dog that's just done a piss in the corner and got caught.

When she went, though, Sid was different right away. He glared at me, pointed at the boxes and then to the stairway. Shit, but it was narrow. I wasn't even sure if my boxes would fit through. Couldn't even imagine Sid stuffing his whole lumpy bulk though it, cookie dough through a bendy straw.

"You're up there," he said, going back to his brownish, fluffy chair. "Second room. Don't go poking around in mine, yeah? Mind your business and we can be all right."

That was the most encouragement I was going to get, obviously. I went up, parked my things in the little empty room, and sat on the bed for a while. It had a mattress but no sheets and peeling wallpaper that looked damp and sad at the edges. I wondered if maybe the social worker lady was supposed to look in on all these things. Make sure Sid had blankets and food and the like, things a girl needs to live. Groaner—he probably had no idea that I'd need tampons. I'd stuffed a few at the bottom of my duffel, but that wouldn't last me even a month.

At least that gave me something to do. I didn't tell any of this to the pig, okay? Wasn't going to tell him about tampons or whatever, not "relevant," like they say on those crime shows, and anyway, adults get so weird whenever you talk about a period, like it's the worst thing you could do, like you got naked and waggled all your bits at them.

I had a little cash saved up from writing essays for the dumb shits in my class back in the old neighborhood. I had a way with words when I wanted to. Never told the twits I'd nicked most of the essays off other Internet people. Like it mattered. Everyone got what they wanted. I took the cash and went real quiet down the stairs—you learn to do that, tiptoe everywhere, when you don't know what you'll find in the next room. Maybe it's your dad passed out on the floor, maybe it's him and his latest girly slobbering all over each other.

Point is, you learn to get stealthy.

But Sid had only moved once, I think, to get up and grab a beer and then flop back down into his chair. There was a sofa on the bottom floor too, pushed up against the windows near the door. The walls were empty, a few nails here and there, like there had been posters or pictures put up and taken down. Carpeting, swirly and orange like a calico cat, had been worn down to prickly nubs. For some reason Sid parked the TV in the middle of the room, just an arm's length from the archway that led to the kitchen. Prat.

It was like he was floating out there in the sea of orange

carpet, away from the windows and away from the walls.

An old *Eurovision* tape was on, and he didn't take his eyes off the screen, probably because some Swedish girls were jiggling their tits all over the place and trying to sing. The VCR looked about as up to technological snuff as the miserable old television set.

"Going out," I said. "Need some things, toothpaste and whatever."

"You going to cause trouble for me?" He hadn't turned around, but I stopped anyway. "Place ain't what it used to be. Gangs of kids everywhere. Can't go anywhere in peace with those bastards just waiting to get in your face. You ain't one of them, eh? You best not be one of them."

I rolled my eyes at the back of his balding head. "I need *tampons*, like for my *monthly time*, all right?"

Worked like magic, like it always does.

"Go on, then."

It's weird how when you're in a place you don't like, you kind of shrivel up when you're there. You don't know until you're away from it and you feel your shoulders get loose and comfortable again. That's how it felt leaving Sid's, like he was that big eye thing in those shit nerd movies with all the elves and wizards, like he could see everything I was doing even when I was just sitting in my new room staring at the sad, molding wallpaper.

He was the eye thing, red and splotchy, but now he couldn't see me, so it felt much better.

Problem was, I didn't have any idea where to get anything in the new neighborhood. Sid's van with all his builder junk was parked by the curb. The sky was still gray, solid, unbroken gray, and every house in both directions looked more or less the same.

Except for one.

I'd pulled out my mobile, because that's what you do when you need to find a place. But I forgot all about searching. Suppose I must have been nervous pulling up to the house before, because I hadn't noticed that the house directly next door looked weird. Nobody lived there, and someone had made an attempt to board over the windows, only it looked like they'd given up halfway through. A real estate agent's sign stuck at a crooked angle out of the dirt patch near the sidewalk, but the phone number to ring had been graffitied over in black.

I couldn't help but think the house looked like a corpse, like what Sid's dump would look like if all the insides had been scooped out. Hollow. The door was dark, dark brown, and in this shit weather looked even darker—a big, open mouth, like the house was screaming or maybe trying to swallow someone whole.

"You're new, aren't you?"

His voice was odd. Nice odd. Much posher than me or Sid. I turned to find a kid maybe my age or a year older peering at me. He was darker than most of the people I'd seen on the ride in. I'd known plenty of Pakistani and black kids and all sorts else of mixed and Indian and Asian back in the old neighborhood. Here though I'd only seen white folks in their cars or on the sidewalk.

He was watching me close. Studying me sort of, from behind a thick fringe of black hair that he kept shaking out of his face and tucking behind his ears.

"Just moved in with my uncle," I said, shrugging. Cool, yeah. Whatever. He was nice to look at, but Jenny in the year above had taught me that you can't just come out and act like a boy is fit. You have to pretend you don't even notice. I shoved my hands in my pockets and kicked at nothing on the pavement. "I'm Lauren."

"Tash. Welcome to the madhouse."

"Madhouse?" I had to laugh and shake my head at this kid. "This is nothing, man."

He wouldn't last ten whole seconds in Moss Side, not if he was in the habit of just rolling up to randos on the street and making conversation.

"You just got here," he pointed out, pushing the dark hair back from his eyes again. "Give it time."

His eyes were dark, too, black but not *black* black, because you could see colors and shapes shifting inside. Maybe that was taking it a bit far, but look, most of the kids in Moss Side have gotten in so many fistfights they look like stomped lumps of clay.

"Suppose that house is a bit creepy," I said. *Well* creepy. Maybe he had a point. "And I am living with my uncle, and he's the worst, so."

"Sid Fry?" he asked. He was taller than me by a few inches, but that wasn't saying much. I wasn't growing up to be a super-model, that was for damn sure.

"Yeah, that's him. Fat, grunty bloke with the red face?"

"I know him."

"Yeah? Where do you live, then?" At some point we had started walking. Just seemed like the thing to do. Felt good to get away from the empty house and Sid's and just put some mileage on the shoes. I like the cold weather too. I hate feeling too hot and then getting sweaty.

"Better you not find out," Tash said with a sigh. He put his hands in his pockets too, but he walked with his head up and straight, his shoulders and all the rest of him tilted back, lead-ing with his belt buckle.

"How's that?"

"I don't think your uncle's too keen on immigrants."

I nodded. That sounded about right. Uncle Sid had stopped coming round for holidays ages ago, but I still have a vivid memory or two of him cursing at the dinner table (a half-broken card table, really, but Dad had gone to the effort to put real china plates down on it, so) about the *disgusting Pakis* that had moved in next door.

Area's gone to shit.

"Maybe I like the idea of hanging around you," I said, giving him a smile. "Maybe I like the idea of giving that old pillock an aneurysm."

Tash made a soft sound like a snort. "You and me both."

We walked and walked. No place in mind. Maybe a mile on I remembered my actual reason for going out and asked about the closest shop. There was one down the road a way, and the place next door did an okay kebab, so that became the plan.

The houses got nicer. Much nicer.

"Bit weird here," I said when the conversation dried up. Tash had finished telling me about what to expect at school, what teachers to avoid, what the general population was like. He wouldn't be there to help, since his mum paid for him to go to Cheadle Hulme, but other kids had told him the lay of things.

"Weird how?" he asked.

"Like, all the buildings in this part, right? They're all *Jane Eyre* and whatever," I said, taking out a smoke. Tash didn't want one. Didn't strike me as a smoker anyway. Nice boys with accents like his and ironed shirts didn't bum smokes off the social services girl. "I mean, we had a few of those with, like, the chapel and town hall, but everything here looks like it came out of a fairy tale."

Tash was quiet for a minute, and when I looked over, he was staring back, lips pursed like he was trying to hold in a fart.

"What?" I blew my smoke down and away from his face, even if he was being really irritating with that look.

"Have you read *Jane Eyre*?" he asked quietly.

"Obviously." He wouldn't give up the look, and it made me want to come clean. "Skimmed it."

"I don't blame you," he said with a laugh. "It's practically a million pages long. I think the Bible is more of a page-turner."

"You've read the Bible?" It was out of my mouth before I could really think about it. Shit.

"Well, yes."

Right, good job, you racist.

"I didn't mean it like that," I added real quickly, though I kind of did, I suppose. "I haven't read it. I've got a rude mouth on me sometimes. Sorry."

He wasn't frowning at me—in fact he seemed weirdly pleased with himself. An old lady with a tartan scarf wrapped around her head glanced at us as we went by. She squinted, staring like I had food stuck all over my face. I wiped at my chin and nose, just in case.

Tash waited outside while I went into the shop, which was all well and good because I didn't need him staring at me while I got my tampons sorted. On a whim I bought him a Kinder and one for myself. I'd half finished the chocolate by the time I was back on the pavement—and I *paid* for it all, okay, I know what you're thinking.

Anyway.

"Here," I said, holding out the candy for him. "Chocolate?"

"Not for me."

I shrugged. "More for me, then. Definitely not giving it to Sid. Wanker."

Tash laughed loudly, like, too loudly for in public. But that was a nice change. He didn't seem to care, I guess, so I tried not to care too. "If you hate him so much, why are you here?"

"No choice, really. Unhealthy family environment, I think that's what Lydia called it."

"Who's Lydia?"

"The child protection lady."

"Oh."

"Yeah, I'm one of them," I said, not like it took a mind reader. "Dad's a mess. Sid's worse, right? I can already tell he's going to be a pain. At least Dad didn't notice what I was up to." Sigh. Running my stupid, fat mouth. "Way too much information, I'm sure. This kebab place is all right?"

We were right outside it, and the spicy meat wind wafting out the doors was making my stomach rumble even after the chocolate.

"For around here, yeah."

I held the door and we went in, and weirdly, somehow, I'd managed to make a friend. Day one. Me. Fancy that.

Tash was waiting on the pavement for me after school hours were over, and he was ready with a sympathetic look.

First days are always trouble, especially when you're dropping in midsemester and everyone's already got their friends
and alliances and favorite spots to sneak a smoke. It was sorta
easier though, I guess, knowing I might see Tash when it was
all over and done with. And he was there, like *right* there, just
waiting for me, so that gave me a breather.

He was there the next day too, and the next, and by
Thursday I just expected to see him.

"Aren't you worried about Sid seeing you?" I asked. "Crusty
bastard's not exactly forward thinking when it comes to the
mingling of the races, yeah?"

Tash shrugged, a cute half smile making him look younger
and more dangerous at the same time. But he wasn't actually
dangerous, not to me, couldn't be. "I checked for his van."

"Clever."

"I do try."

It looked like he was trying to grow a mustache. He had
the shadow of one over his lip and some scruffy whiskers on
his chin. I wondered if maybe that made him a bad sort at his
posh private school. Ha. Him a bad boy. That was a laugh. But
I liked it, liked that I was the kind of girl he shouldn't be hanging around, but he did it anyway.

"Shops today?" I asked.

"I had something else in mind." His black eyes danced and
he looked over my shoulder to the corpse house next door.
Yes, I'd actually begun thinking of it as Corpse House. Not

very cheery, I know, but it fit, and it gave me something to spook the idiots at school with.

"We could go inside," he said, inching toward the wide steps leading from the sidewalk to the front door.

"What, now? Cheeky. It's midday. Someone will see us."

"Then we'll go in through the back. Come on . . ."

Right. So. First thing's first—I didn't *want* to do this. I didn't want to, but impressing this fit boy with pretty hair and an almost-mustache was getting high on my To Do list. In maths I'd been sleepy and let my brain and eyes go fuzzy, just dazing out, and *wham*—out of nowhere—I think of Tash putting his lips on mine. *Kissing.* That never happens and it probably should. I started to think I was maybe broken or something because I never really thought much about kissing boys. I was always in trouble for skipping class or smoking, not for sneaking off for a quick grope.

We go around to the back.

Like every day before this one, the sky is flat, sad gray and it's half dark even though it should still be light out. I've got my school bag and decent clothes on, not the type of getup you'd want for sneaking around. But Tash is in charge and I'm following, and the more I think about it, the more I wonder if he's trying to get me alone. Sneaking around is exciting. Gets your heart going.

And I get it now—he's, like, *seducing* me.

Holy. Tits.

The house is brick, like Sid's, and the real estate agent hasn't been by in ages to do the lawn. There's a tree in the back, just one, gone wild, branches thrusting over the privacy fence toward Sid's place, and toward the back, and every which way. A tire swing hangs lopsided from the lowest branch.

"Who lived here?" I whisper, keeping an eye out for anyone peeping at us.

"We'll find out, won't we?"

"But their stuff must be cleared out . . ."

There's a tiled overhang above the back door and a few windows with loose boarding that look prime for breaking in. So we do it. We break in. Really, I do it, prying a rotting board loose with my fingertips and then swearing when it clatters loudly to the ground at my feet.

A dog barks, but then the neighborhood is silent. The window doesn't put up much of a fight, the lock rusted and useless. It goes up with a sigh, and then I'm in, panting, holding the thing open for Tash to cram inside. Tougher for him, seeing as how he's a big wiry fellow, but he gets all his limbs in. We're in the kitchen, and it's . . . wrong.

The stuff's not cleared out, but it's not messy either. It's still. Calm. Like the family just picked up and left. A fine layer of dust has settled over everything, making the stacked china and cereal boxes and bread bin look fuzzy, like I'm looking at the world through a series of old photographs.

"Creepy," I mumble, turning a circle where I stand. My

shoes leave trails in the dust on the floor. "Why would they just *leave*?"

Tash is quiet, looking at me with these weird, intense eyes, and it makes me feel naked to the bones.

"Maybe they didn't."

"Maybe they didn't what? Leave? Then, where are they, genius?" I laugh, shaking my head. "Just nipped out for a drink? No one's been in this place for years."

I wander to the sink. A dirty mixing bowl is in the basin, furry with mold. I turn and go toward the refrigerator, but Tash calls my name—he's already gone down the hall and into the sitting room. That room's worse. Spookier. You always think a creepy old house will be cold inside, but it's warm, like bodies have only just been there, taking up room and sucking down air.

"All right," I say in a tiny, tiny voice. "I officially cannot stand it in here."

One of the chairs in here is knocked over. The coffee table is crooked. Something went wrong, and I don't know if Tash knows what it is, but I want to be out. Now.

"Hey." His eyes are normal again, not intense, and he starts back toward the kitchen. "We can go. Just thought it might be a laugh to explore."

"Maybe some other time, yeah? Just . . . need to get away from here is all."

• • •

We go back the next day.

It's partly Tash's fault, partly mine. I can't stop thinking about it. The dishes in the sink. The open cereal box on the countertop. The knocked over furniture. I might not be the cleverest girl around, but it feels like a mystery, like a story but all of the chapters are jumbled. I want to put it in order.

It even distracts me through Sid. Through the shouting. Through sitting at the dinner table with his bloody *Eurovision* tapes blaring in the background, eating crap bacon sandwiches he made with the single knife in the whole place, his on a normal plate, mine on paper, *and if I have to hear those minging Swedish tarts and their pop song one more time . . .*

So we go back. Tash doesn't even ask about the bruise on my cheek. I ain't exactly Houdini with makeup, but I think I covered it up all right. Still, I see his eyes catch on it, and the look I give back says: *Don't ask.*

And he doesn't.

Guess I shouldn't have complained about the perky Swedish girls and their stupid song.

We make it upstairs that time. I wander the bedrooms. This was a nice family, I think. The parents kept the little paintings and art projects their kids had done, didn't just toss them in the bin like my dad might. There were two kids, seems like, a girl and a boy. I stand in the boy's room for a long time while Tash rummages somewhere else. There are Manchester United pennants on the wall and shelves with DVDs, video games, poetry books, a Bible, Superman comic books. It gets too strange again and I have to go, right then, and that time I run down the stairs and hurl myself out the broken window.

I don't care if Tash thinks I'm lame over it—people lived there and now they don't, and while I can't stop thinking about it, I want to. God, I want to.

The next day we go back. It's like I can't stop myself—can't stop *him*. I've started doodling on my assignments in the margins, little theories, little stories. . . . What if they were witness protection? What if the mob put a hit out on them? Carbon monoxide poisoning? *What, what, what?*

That day Tash says we should check the basement. So we do, and I can tell the second the door opens and the cool underground cave air comes rushing up to meet us that this room is different. I go down, slowly, one awful step at a time. The threadbare lightbulb dangling above the stairs. When it clicks on, even the air in my lungs feels cold.

It's . . . empty.

Tash eases by me and goes to stand in the halo of pale white light pooling under the bulb. Just concrete. Smooth, very smooth cement, like glass.

"Something's weird," I tell him, afraid to put even one foot on the too smooth concrete.

He gives a single pained laugh. "Something's always been weird. You didn't just figure that out, did you?"

"Course not. But . . . Dunno. Thought maybe I could piece

it together. But there's nothing down here, just that old dryer."

In the far right corner was a single dryer unit, the matching washing machine nowhere to be found.

"Lauren," he said, and when I looked at him his black eyes had gone all electric and intense again. "There's something I want to show you."

"Go on."

He nodded toward the corner with the dryer. "Move it out from the wall."

"*You* move it. Lazy."

Tash snorted. "You move it, Lauren. I can't."

"Weaker than you look, mate," I joked, but like the empty basement, like the smooth concrete, it was all wrong. But I went anyway. Had to. What's that word? Compelled. It's like that, like I could feel his eyes moving me across the floor, lifting my hands and bracketing them around the dryer. Like it wasn't even me wiggling that heavy piece of shit out from the wall.

But I did. He didn't need to say what he wanted to show me. It was there, the only wonky bit of the concrete. Something stuck out, round, almost white, a knobby dark dent at the end reminding me right away of . . .

"Shit. Shit. *No.*"

I don't know what Tash did, but I ran. Not out of the house. Why not out of the house? Compelled. I just couldn't go, because the answer was right there. It was right there in the concrete or maybe in that look Tash kept giving me. When I looked up again, I was in the boy's room, sitting on the bed, trying to catch my breath.

Tash followed, quiet as you like, and leaned on the doorframe, waiting or, I don't know, watching.

"That was bones we saw," I muttered. Sweating. *Christ.* I was sweating like mad now. "Bones . . . Tash, what the *hell*, mate?"

He came and sat next to me on the bed and lifted his hand. I flinched. Sorry, but, instinct. Habit. But he wasn't taking a swing at me. His knuckles almost touched the patch job I'd done with Rimmel.

"He hit you," Tash says softly.

"Yeah."

Bones.

"He's *awful.*"

Actual human bones.

"Obviously."

Area's gone to shit.

"A monster."

At that, I go quiet for a long time. Tash stares at me, and it's not scary this time, just gentle. I finally look back, and it's like I can see in his brain. It's dark in there, terrifying, but I don't want to look away. He waits for me every day after school. For the first time in, like, *ever*, I want to touch another person, touch a *man.*

I lie down. I want to do it, and Christ I hope he lies down with me because otherwise I'm going to look stupid. But he does, and I can see how difficult it is for him to swallow normally. The same thing's happening to me. It's so, so quiet and for five minutes? Ten minutes? We just stare at each other, sometimes he smiles and I smile back, other times I don't know what my face is doing.

"Tash, what did I see down there?"

"You trust me, don't you, Lauren?" he asks, and I do, so I nod. "You had better, yeah? You're lying in my bed with me."

Even if I knew it deep in my chest, still stings to hear it. We laugh. You have to, right? You have to laugh when a thing like that is said, when a thing like that is the truth. I lean in to kiss him, and I lean right through his beautiful face. I'm shaking, Christ am I shaking, but he's still there, letting me do it, letting me have it all sink in.

"Your uncle's a builder," he murmurs, and it's like he's kissing my ear, my cheek, my lips . . . I can't move, I can only nod, only shake. "Lauren, he isn't a person. He's a monster, yeah? He's a monster."

It's like I'm suspended there, stuck, like the air has turned to ice around me, freezing me in place on my side. But time is moving, and I can hear everything Tash is saying. When I close my eyes, I see the white bump in the concrete. His hand moves over my shoulder, and it doesn't feel like anything but cool air, cool air turning colder, turning frozen. His hand is on my stomach, going lower. I'm going to let him. I would let him.

I *would* like him to.

"You have to make this right," he whispers, kissing me again.

"I have to make this right."

Tash touches his lips to the bruise on my cheek, and the little spark of cool feels nice. When I look again—really look— those two black coals for eyes of his are gone.

"Right, um, I'd like to report a murder."

So here we are, back at the beginning.

"Could you repeat that?"

It's easier to say the second time around. "I'd like to report a murder."

"Start from the beginning," he said, resting his elbows on the desk.

Christ, where to start? It was easier telling you lot. My hands are throbbing then, hot, hot, too hot and needly. Pricked all over. I hold my hands up for the cop and let him get a good look. I couldn't get all the blood off, or really I just gave up trying. That's probably what feels so weird and hot.

"There's only one knife in the house," I say, which is weird, because that's not a good place to start the story. But I'm laughing—it's funny, isn't it? It's all too unbelievably funny, when you think about it. "Left it on the table. Right in the open. Shouldn't be hard to find, and that's your job or whatever."

The cop's eyes are getting big now, and he's listening. He's
listening good and proper.

"I had to make it right, you see," I tell him, like I'm telling you. "The area had gone to shit. It really had. Sid made it
shit. He's a monster, yeah? I had to make it right." He's coming
around the counter now, eyes big and nervous, and he's putting his hand on his belt, like reaching maybe for a weapon,
something to subdue me. That's fine. I'd like to be subdued for
a while.

I don't put up a fuss. I don't fight back.

No, I just keep my hands up and smile, maybe laugh again.
Can Tash see this? He's probably laughing too.

"He was just a piece of shit," I tell the cop, and the word
"piece," the way it sounds, the way it slides out of my mouth,
makes me remember the knife going in, smooth as silk,
smooth as that perfect concrete, right into his lumpy belly. I
shiver, because putting the knife in didn't feel good, but it did
feel right.

"Just slow down, little miss," he says, hemming me in
against the counter.

"No, it's fine now," I tell him, like I'm telling you. "It's all
fine now. I made it right."

Madeleine Roux is the *New York Times* bestselling author of the Asylum series. She received her BA in creative writing and acting from Beloit College in 2008. In the spring of 2009 Madeleine completed an Honors Term at Beloit College, proposing, writing, and presenting a full-length historical fiction novel. Shortly after, she began the experimental fiction blog Allison Hewitt Is Trapped. Allison Hewitt Is Trapped quickly spread throughout the blogosphere, bringing a unique serial fiction experience to readers. Born in Minnesota, she lives and works in Seattle, Washington.

Website: madeleine-roux.com

Twitter: @Authoroux

Facebook: facebook.com/madeleinerouxauthor

Shadowtown Blues

LUCY A. SNYDER

Scary

There are a trillion things about being teen
to scare the devil out of you. Or maybe *in*.
It's basic: TV people say this must be your best
time ever, but these months are lumps of misery
in a gruel of boredom. And a queasy terror
that TV might be right: Life won't get better.

It's scary, so scary out there.

You can't stop puzzling grim possibilities,
turning the future over like a cube to solve:
What if all the tedious crap of adulthood
is a burden that breaks you like a straw?
What if you sprint to meet your dreams
but crash in a stinking welter of failure?
What if nobody ever really loves you
so you die alone, broke, old, forgotten?

It's scary, so scary out there.

It's more fun to fear fictional monsters:
possessive devils, snap-jawed aliens,
howling wolves, snarling madmen,
ravenous dead, tentacled abominations.
Cue up the movie, crack open the book
Gasp and shriek and forget the world.

It's scary, so scary out there.

Dangerous

"Oh, Johnny, it's dangerous outside," Mama cried
When good friends tried to take you caroling one December.
"Just stay in here where you'll be safe and dry."

You couldn't wait to ditch her drab little town when she died,
Tried to forget her in that coffin, but still you remembered:
"Oh, Johnny, it's dangerous outside," Mama cried.

Nobody in the city would hire a kid, no matter how you tried
Homeless, shamefaced, you panhandled, growing thinner
Hitched back to her old house; at least it seemed safe and dry.

The floor is warped, the windows crawling with flies
And their relentless buzz calls you a loser, a sinner.
"Oh, Johnny, it's dangerous outside," Mama cried.

You tried to visit your good friends but they'd always hide,
Whispering, pretending you were nothing but a ragged stranger.
You burned when you spied them at the prom, so safe and dry.

Dogs found their bones in the woods; you weren't tried.
You rock yourself in her rotting house, mind an ember.
"Oh, Johnny, it's dangerous outside," Mama cries.
"Just stay in here where you'll be safe and dry."

turnt

let's get turnt, says the heartbreaking boy
i wanna get crazy, lose my mind tonight
smile, girl, shake what ya mama gave ya

the stereo rattles his Kia's tinted windows
hungry, you shake your head, say it's late
but he grabs your wrist: just one drink?

his Marlboro's burnt down to the filter
he's sweating smoke and his whiskey
smells so sweet. you take a long draw

he says Whoa girl you got a hollow leg
and your heart is pounding skin itching
ancient genes singing pupils constricting

he says Hey that cost me twenty, ease up!
but you know drink's not your demon tonight
it's the only solution to snuff your appetite

but your cheap date's pulled the bottle away
you're still so famished you can't even think
and before you can say Stop you're turning

pulse hammering inside the secluded car
skin splitting over hairy muscle, scarlet claws
and he's screaming, wailing like he's burning

your mind is a feral void of rage and need
and this boy you hoped to please is meat
booming bass muffles the crack of bone

conscience returns; you see what you've done
stare at sticky hands, know you have to move
again. avoid boys, endure your life alone.

it's dark outside; the night's your mother
shielding you, soothing your shame
so you quietly walk yourself home.

Lucy A. Snyder is a four-time Bram Stoker Award–winning writer and the author of the novels *Spellbent*, *Shotgun Sorceress*, and *Switchblade Goddess*. She also wrote the nonfiction book *Shooting Yourself in the Head for Fun and Profit: A Writer's Survival Guide* and the story collections *While the Black Stars Burn*, *Soft Apocalypses*, *Orchid Carousals*, *Sparks and Shadows*, and *Installing Linux on a Dead Badger*. She lives in Columbus, Ohio, and is a mentor in Seton Hill University's MFA in Writing Popular Fiction program.

Website: lucysnyder.com
Twitter: @LucyASnyder
Facebook: facebook.com/LucyASnyder

Beyond the Sea

NANCY HOLDER

The sea has neither meaning nor pity.

—ANTON CHEKHOV

The sea. Vast and black, an open grave.

Where Marie died.

Where I left her to die.

It was chilly for a June night, especially in San Diego. Anya had on shorts, flip-flops, a T-shirt, and a hoodie; she had realized too late that she should have worn a lot of heavy clothes. She hadn't been thinking, but that was the point, wasn't it? To stop thinking. There was no fairness or logic. There was nothing. Nothing left.

The moon was full. A year ago, it had not been. Exactly three hundred and sixty-five nights ago a crescent moon had hung in the sky, dancing with bright stars. A gigantic bloodred bonfire had burned away whatever was left of Marie's inhibitions. In the scarlet light Anya's best friend's eyes had spun like soccer balls. Marie, a good girl gone very bad, very harsh, very crazy, whirling in a thong and a bikini top, head thrown back, while too many guys watched and hooted and cheered when she stumbled toward the fire. It was all guys, in fact, except for Anya and Marie. Those were not good odds, even if the guys hadn't been older unknowns. Anya was furious with Marie for luring her there with the promise of a party. This was just a drugfest and date rape waiting to happen.

"Let's leave, let's *go*," she had insisted. Ordered. Pleaded. The sea air reeked of weed. The guys were throwing half-full bottles of alcohol into the fire to see what would happen. Glass was exploding, comets of crystalline shards popping like fireworks. Marie kept dancing, not so much oblivious as lost. Utterly.

Drowning in misery.

Only, Anya hadn't known that then. She hadn't known what drowning looked like. Numb with anger, she had shifted her weight and watched her cell phone battery run out while Marie ignored her. She hadn't brought her car charger. She couldn't call anyone. Couldn't use her safety word to let her mother know she had an emergency. Marie hadn't even brought her phone. Marie had brought a little straw purse containing twenty dollars and her student ID. Bitch.

I was her ride. And I left her.

They had found Marie's purse on the beach ten hours before her body had washed up. Her eyes had shone like mirrors, and that was how they confirmed death by drowning. Marie's bloodstream had been filled with drugs and her lungs with seawater. How long had it taken? Had she suffered?

Hard to say.

Now, a year later, Anya's conscience pushed her to her knees. Water swirled inches below the rock shelf she perched on and splattered spray and salt on her face. Barnacles bit into her skin; the rock was gritty and wet. There were no tears. There had never been, not in the whole long year. She was as dry as a desert.

The cove was hard to find, though close to busy places: the Cabrillo lighthouse, now a museum, and Fort Rosecrans National Cemetery, where they buried people in the military. You had to leave your car in a hiking trail parking lot, walk down the trail, and then push through chest high clumps of white sage and deerweed bushes. The cove's seclusion had been part of the draw. You could do what you wanted and no one would be able to stop you. But Anya hadn't wanted to do any of it, and she couldn't stop Marie from doing it either.

Marie, her best friend for her entire life—preschool, Brownies, soccer, boys—had been out of control. Her parents' ongoing divorce had been hideous. In the middle of it Marie's stupid cheating boyfriend had dumped her. First came the cutting and then the partying, and Anya had *known* the cove was a mistake. But she couldn't deny Marie anything. They had once been so close that now saying yes to anything and everything Marie wanted felt like building a bridge over troubled water, a way to calm her friend down. Maybe even to save her.

Now, a year later, she stared into the water and faced the truth: by then Marie had scared her and hurt her, and their friendship had been all but dead. In the black glassy ocean, she couldn't see her reflection, but she couldn't face herself anyway. No one knew that she had left Marie here, no one in the world. Those guys that night had been so preoccupied with Marie that they had forgotten Anya had been there. Or if they remembered, they didn't know who she was. For months she had held her breath, bracing for trouble, or at least blame. Checking social media for someone to mention that Marie had been stuck there because her best friend had driven off. All night, every morning, at school, she braced for consequences. She began taking stuff to knock herself out, wake herself up. No one noticed that, either.

The realization that she was going to get away with it made it worse. Guilt weighed her down, gnawed on her bones, picked away at her heart. And it never got better. The months and weeks and days stretched into one silent scream. She couldn't live with herself any longer. Couldn't bear this horrible tension of waiting for it to be over. It was never going to be over.

Until she ended it.

"You're such a chickenshit," Marie had flung at her that night, when Anya had pulled on her hand and told her that they had to leave *now*. "A little goody-goody."

Anya was stung. "Who talks like that? Are we in a fifties sitcom?"

"Blow me," Marie sniped.

"You're such a bitch. I'm going to leave you here."

"Yo, I'll drive you wherever you want," one of the boys had called, and Marie had smirked at Anya. Then she had wordlessly turned her back on Anya and taken a swig from the bottle of tequila the same boy held out to her.

By then Anya had been so furious that she had driven straight home. Her parents were doing something, she didn't remember what, and they registered that she had beaten her curfew, but that was all. Maybe if they'd asked her how her evening was, shown some *interest*—but no, that wasn't fair. She hadn't asked them how their evening was, either.

After Marie's body was found, Anya still didn't tell anyone that she'd been there, didn't come forward as a witness. She kept her grades up and still played soccer and didn't drink or cut like Marie had. Marie had sent out calls for help. Anya didn't deserve help. To ask, she would have had to say what she needed help for. She was the most functional suicidal person in the world.

She read obsessively about drowning. What it felt like, what you looked like. Often, you didn't realize that you were in trouble. Maybe you'd tumbled out of a boat or you had gotten too far from shore or you were drunk in a pool. You could drown in six inches of water. For a while you tried to keep your head above water. Most people didn't think of flipping onto their back and floating, which could save you.

If you didn't think of floating, you dog-paddled and called for help, and then you bobbed down, came back up. You kept sinking and forcing your way to the surface. Each time you went deeper. You started to get confused. You couldn't remember how to get to the surface. You couldn't make it anyway. Panicking led to big mistakes, like opening your mouth and sucking in water, maybe seaweed, maybe a tiny fish. It was choking to death anyway.

If the water was rough and the beginning struggles were worse, then it all happened quicker, down to the suffocating. That was why Anya had thought about trying to drown herself in the pool at school. To prolong her own agony. But it had to be here, the scene of her crime.

Marie had been so out of it that she might not have ever realized she was drowning. She might never have struggled. But Anya had been drowning for a year. Tonight, she was going to let herself open her mouth. It had been closed for far too long.

I killed her. I knew I shouldn't leave her here. I was so petty.

She couldn't make up for it. She never could do that. But she could end it. She wanted to. She was ready. She had rehearsed this moment so many times that part of her felt as if it had already happened, and right now she was just watching a rerun.

Feeling in the pocket of her sweatshirt, she got out her flashlight and smeared watery yellow over the crashing waves.

The swells raised forward, then trailed back out like someone hurriedly unrolling a carpet. Or like a group of dancers. Everything about the ocean was rhythm, a gigantic heartbeat. She was sick of listening to her heartbeat. She wanted to make sure she did it right. She didn't want to jump in too close to shore, in case she lost her nerve and swam back in. She didn't want to fall against the rocks and break something, because Marie hadn't broken anything. She wanted to die like Marie, only not drugged up, because she needed to make sure she wasn't rescued.

Moonbeams sparkled on the vast black expanse, silver mingling with the gold of her flashlight's circle. She started timing the rushing of the waves.

Then a seal darted in and out of the light, as if chasing it. It made no noise, just wriggled across the blackness, and she pondered the likelihood that she might hurt it when she jumped. Narrowing her eyes, she tried to figure out if it might swim away anytime soon. But it continued to laze back and forth.

And then she realized that what she was looking at was not a seal. It was a human floating facedown in the water, arms out to the side, head invisible. A swimmer? The ocean swept it forward, back, forward, forward forward forward. Then a giant wave rose up and crested over it, churning it under the dark surface.

"No!" Anya shouted, and without another thought she jumped in.

The water was cold; it was a shock. She went under and immediately plummeted; holding her breath, she struggled to peel off her sweatshirt. Her flip-flops were already gone, and as she sank, her bare foot hit something hard. It was a rock. She pushed down on it, propelling herself back toward the glimmering silvery moon.

With a gasp she broke the surface and flailed and wheezed for a few seconds, then pulled herself together. As she scanned for the other person, a rolling wave dragged her away from the cove. The dark, churning water was brushed with patches of moonlight that rippled like neon as she reached for the sand and saw it recede from her grasp.

"Hey!" she shouted, treading water in a circle, spewing out saltwater. "Hey, where are you?"

No answer.

Coughing, she kept treading water, ears cocked, scanning. Facts about surviving in water scrolled through her mind like a science fiction data stream. *I'll stay alive just until I find this person*, she promised herself.

She spied a dark shape about thirty yards to her right, which was even farther away from the cove. Wishing so very much for her flashlight, she stroked through the water toward the black blob. Then something physically grabbed her leg. Yanked. When she opened her mouth in surprise, her assailant hauled her an inch or two below the waterline and dragged her along so fast she was almost hydroplaning. It didn't hurt. There were no teeth. Or else she was going numb.

She fought, trying to kick, but all her attention was focused on not choking. Her back arched as she tried—and failed—to lift her face out of the water. Whatever had hold of her kept hold. All she could do was keep her mouth closed.

But she was running out of air.

This was the turning point, when people's lungs burned and the impulse to expel the old air and suck in new was nearly irresistible. She went limp, losing focus. Her arms trailed over her head. Classic instinctive drowning response.

Don't open your mouth. Don't do it.

Her lungs were about to explode. Blurring, she tried to figure out what was gripping her, how she could force it to let her go. Gathering every last ounce of her strength and concentration, she crunched her body sideways and snaked her right arm down her body, then shot it out at a forty-five-degree angle from her waist.

She made contact with nothing. Then, as quickly as it had started, the dragging ceased. The sensation of being restrained was gone.

She bobbed to the surface and sucked in oxygen in huge, starving gulps. A hoarse, near soundless scream tore out of her constricted lungs, then another, and although she told herself that her chances were better if she stayed on her back, she popped up to a vertical position, pumping her legs to stay in place, and examined her surroundings.

The cove was a lot farther away. A *lot*.

And then she realized that she had been caught in an undertow. A riptide. It had dragged her out to sea.

Oh my God, my God, I really am going to die.

But the peace she had been seeking did not come with that realization. Because of the figure, she told herself. The one she had jumped in to save. That was why she was freaking out.

But *had* there been a figure? Had she imagined it?

No. She knew it had been there. But by now whoever it was had to be dead, right?

Except that *she* wasn't. One of the ways to prolong your life if you were stuck in water was to do the dead man's float to rest, then flip over onto your back to breathe. Maybe that's what that person had been doing. Was doing right now.

She felt another tug. Tingles of fear prickled like gooseflesh. She was back in the undertow, then. She remembered what to do: swim parallel to the land rather than toward it. That way you didn't fight the riptide, didn't waste valuable energy.

But the cove was so far distant. Too distant. It was rapidly becoming a black dot.

As she stared at it, something to the left caught her attention. She turned her head; beneath the moonlight she saw the shape again. Her heart caught.

"Hey!" she yelled, or tried to—the saltwater had made her hoarse. She rasped out another cry and then splashed the water hard. She was moving; she could feel it.

Moving farther off.

Then the figure raised its head. She couldn't make out any features, or if it was a man or a woman, but it was alive. And it seemed to be looking at her.

Then it swam toward her.

"No, stay back, I'm caught in the undertow," she said, or rather, planned to say, but what she actually said was, "Help. Oh God, please help." She detested herself for her whining, pleading whimper, but there really wasn't anything this person could do about it, unless they were wearing a life jacket or had a flare gun or had planned a meet up with a lifeboat. They wouldn't be able to save her any more than she could save them.

Weariness prevented her from waving her hands to warn them off. The person kept swimming toward her. She burst into tears and rode the swells, passively waiting, barely able to keep herself upright because she was so exhausted.

Maybe it's a hallucination, she thought, and then: *Maybe it's Marie. Her ghost, coming for me.*

A thin thread of horror wove through her tiredness. The figure moved into and away from the moonlight, still too far away to make out any features; Anya wasn't sure she would still be above the waterline by the time it reached her. Her teeth were chattering and her muscles were locking up. Treading water then was as difficult as pedaling a bicycle up the steepest mountain in the world, at the highest gear.

The swimmer neared. Its right arm rose out of the water and the moonlight glinted off it. It was pure white, and Anya tried to make sense of that. Was it wearing a white wetsuit? A jacket?

Then she saw its face. Or rather, where its face should have been.

It was a skull, smooth and white and skinless.

Its arms were bone.

It was swimming toward her.

She shrieked, dunked below the water, and nearly strangled, then tried to kick herself out of reach as the thing gathered her up in its arms and lofted her back to the surface. Anya wanted to struggle, but she was limp in its embrace. Her head lolled backward and she drew in air, staring up into empty eye sockets.

There was no face, no expression, unless you counted the macabre smile of its lipless mouth. Without eyebrows or facial muscles, it still seemed to glare at her with demonic glee. Its jaw dropped open, and its teeth clacked.

Her shout of terror was more of a sigh, her struggle, a spasmodic twitch. Now, when it counted, when she was in imminent danger, she was too worn out from her other struggles to fight.

"Help," she whispered. Or thought she did. She couldn't hear herself. Was this the thing she had jumped in to save? "Marie?"

It laced its bony fingers around her neck and pushed her head under the water. Anya's back arched; she tried to raise her arms to save herself, but it was like being paralyzed. She couldn't move.

It's killing me.

She needed air; she was going to inhale and that *would* kill her—

Don't do it don't do it oh God I have to

The bones around her neck tightened their grip. Her thoughts dissolved and floated away. She lost all sense of who she was, what was happening. There was only blackness. There was no sound. Everything was about air.

Her lips parted from the strain. Her nostrils flared.

Just as she started to draw in a greedy gulp, her head shot out of the water into the night. She coughed and gasped crazily, wildly, and then something grabbed her under her arm and around her chest and hauled ass. Swimming hard, fast, life or death; churning the water with powerful, awkward strokes.

"Help me!" the something bellowed.

And it sounded like Marie.

Anya didn't know if it was, couldn't puzzle out what was happening. She didn't know if the thing that had her now was the same thing that had captured her; if it was rescuing her or making sure she died. But she helped as she had been ordered, using every last ounce of strength to kick her legs. The effect was futile, maybe an inch back and forth, but it was all she had left, and she gave it.

"Shit, shit, shit!"

It was Marie's voice.

A hand seized Anya's right ankle and tugged. Marie screamed. Water splashed all around and she kicked harder. The hand tugged again, prying her slowly out of her rescuer's grasp. As Marie's fingers slid downward, Anya glommed onto them.

"Get away, damn you!" Marie yelled. The water churned and frothed and someone else shouted, but Anya couldn't make out the words. They were swimming again, she and maybe-Marie, and she found new reserves inside herself. Kicking now, paddling, getting away

—from it—

—with it—

She was hyperventilating, gasping, eyes rolling, plunging one arm into the water, saving her savior, saving herself. They were moving in concert now, and as more oxygen hit her brain, she looked back over her shoulder to see the skeleton swimming after them. Its teeth were clacking and its eye sockets were full now, of . . .

Oh God, what is that?

Death.

Dead things.

Death was slimy and gross and not looking peaceful. Death was rot. Its eyes brimmed with rot. She could smell it, almost taste it. And why not? It was the thing she had craved for a year, wasn't it? To rot?

"Go faster, Marie!" she yelled.

Then she was rolling in the white water, thrown around like a dead body, forehead smacking the sand, seeing gray and yellow bubbles. She heard the clacking, and Marie's screaming, and got onto her back through a supreme effort of will. The angle of the breakwater afforded her a view downward; in the surf Marie was on her back too. She looked exactly as she had the last time Anya had seen her, from her bikini top to her long, black hair. The skeleton was looming over her, then crouching low, grabbing her, picking her up.

Marie kicked and shrieked as it dangled her overhead, then threw her into the water. She went under.

Anya pushed herself upright. She tried to stand but succeeded only in falling back down on her hands. The skeleton stood waist-high in the water, bones clicking, no skin or flesh anywhere. All bone; and on some of that bone, barnacles grew, and there were snails. Seaweed dangled from its mouth and in its right hand, oh God, in its hand—

A frisson of horror rooted Anya to the spot.

Marie's head was dangling from its fist. Marie's eyes bulged, but Anya couldn't tell if Marie saw her. Marie's mouth opened and shut as if she were trying to speak, but there was no sound. Seawater streamed from her lips.

The monster advanced, lurching from the sea on skeleton legs, moonlight sparkling on its smooth ivory and in Marie's eyes. Anya scrabbled backward as waves raced through its leg bones and frothed around her on the beach. She could hear herself whimpering.

Marie's head swung from side to side as Death shambled out of the water; Anya kept scooting away on her butt. The overhang she had knelt on stretched above her head, and she realized that she was literally backing herself into a corner. It was too late; if it came after her, she was trapped.

"Marie," she said, steeling herself to look at the head, "help me."

The head swayed; the eyes stared sightlessly.

Then the skeleton raced up to Anya and thrust its skull at her. Fish swam in its sockets, and moonlight danced. Its jaw dropped down and a voice slashed at her:

"It's not your time."

Then its jaw unhinged and it became a maw, swooping Anya's head into it. And she saw—

Oh, she saw . . .

Dawn.

And Anya was bobbing in the water, her shoulder rhythmically tapping a large rock rising about ten feet above her. She grabbed at it with bloody fingers. Her nails had torn away.

Something in the swirls and eddies bobbed against her, and then fingers quite distinctly gripped her arm. She screamed. The grip tightened, and attached to it was dead weight. A figure popped to the surface beside her, black hair waving like seaweed.

She took a deep breath, then gently poked at the body. It made a half turn, the hair draping the face as if determined to conceal its features. Her insides churned. She sucked in a shuddery breath, then determinedly smoothed the hair away.

Marie's face. Smooth and beautiful, *normal*, attached to her body. Anya jerked her hand just as Marie's eyes popped open. Glassy, unfocused, light bouncing off them; Marie's hand clamped on to her. Marie looked not at Anya but through her. Her fingers were squeezing Anya's arm so hard that it felt as if her fingernails would slice right into Anya's flesh. Then a long, low sigh pushed out of her mouth as if she were deflating.

Anya's heart was beating so hard she was afraid it would pop. She glanced shoreward, astonished to find that she was maybe forty yards from the cove. She looked down at Marie. At her *ghost*.

She remembered the skeleton and scrabbling beneath the overhang and what it had said to her. That it was not her time. She hoped so very much that that was true.

Then Marie sucked in air and consciousness blazed in her expression; she smiled very faintly at her once best friend.

"Anya." Her voice was a thready whisper.

Anya's skin crawled. She clung to the rock and drew back a leg to kick at the ghost. At *her*. But she remembered that Marie had tried to save her.

Marie's smile faded. "You need to get out of the water *now*."

"Because of the . . . the monster?" She didn't know what else to call it.

"Yes," Marie said. "Because of me."

Frozen with fear, Anya gripped the rock with both hands. Could she make it to land?

"You came because of me," Marie said. "And it nearly got you."

Anya swallowed. "It . . ."

"The thing that got me. Got *us*."

She gestured with her head toward the ocean beyond. Anya looked. Gasped.

The sea was littered with floating bodies, perhaps two dozen, facedown, arms outstretched. They rode the swells like pieces of debris. Anya found she couldn't scream; instead, she was overcome with a deep, burning pang of overwhelming grief. Something loosened inside her, but not too much. Everything inside her had been clamped down tight for way too long.

"I went swimming that night after the guys left me, and it came after me," Marie said, and her voice shook. "It killed me."

"*I* left you," Anya said, and the something loosened a little more. She stiffened as a body rode the waves toward her. But as it bobbled closer, the figure sank and disappeared. "I was scared—" Her throat tightened. She couldn't breathe.

Marie shook her head and took her hand. She did a breaststroke with her free arm toward the cove, bringing Anya with her. A chorus like one long wail rose from the ocean, keening, mourning. The sound became the tolling of a bell; she and Marie were passing a red metal buoy about six feet tall bobbing on a rubbery platform. The top of the buoy was a bell; on the center of the buoy was a sign that read DANGER. NO SWIM-MING. RIPTIDE. NO LIFEGUARD ON DUTY.

"I didn't see that sign," Anya said.

"If you had stayed, it would have gotten you, too," Marie told her.

"You wouldn't have gone swimming. I wouldn't have let you," Anya said.

Marie turned her head. "You think you could have stopped me? I *did* see the sign. And I went in anyway." She started to cry. "That was my life then. I went in anyway."

"No," Anya insisted. "No, Marie." And then she said in a flood, "I've been holding my breath for a year. Ever since you . . . ever since. I never confessed. No one knew."

"There was nothing *to* know," Marie said.

Night.

The cove, the full moon, and the bonfire.

Marie was belly dancing. The guys were leering and hooting, throwing alcohol bottles into the bonfire to make them explode. Comets of glass shards sprayed the night sky with new stars. Beyond, the ocean rolled black and silver beneath the moon.

Anya gaped and made a little circle of her own. Had it been a dream? A hallucination brought on by a contact high with all the weed? Anya touched her face, her hair, her arms. All dry. She looked out at the ocean.

And saw the floating bodies listing over the waves like

body surfers in slow motion. Into and out of the light. And among them, something white swimming from one to the other like a sheepdog checking on its lambs.

Her blood froze. Then clouds swallowed up the moon and swathed the ocean in inky black. Opening the coffin lid.

"We have to go," she half shouted at Marie. Marie raised her brows, turned around, and shook her ass at Anya. The guys cheered, and one of them struggled to his feet, aided and abetted by his friends. He staggered toward Marie with his arms opened wide. With a triumphant grin, she shimmied toward him. As Anya watched, the white skull glowed through his skin. Evil blazed in the empty eye sockets where bloodshot brown eyes had been.

Then it was gone, and he was just a slightly too old guy who was way too drunk. Maybe he had killed Marie that other night. Maybe that was what Anya was seeing. Maybe the entire year had not happened, and her suicide attempt—

—I never got that far; I jumped in to save someone. . . .

—Didn't I?

"Marie, we have to leave," she said, crossing over to Marie and planting herself between her best friend and the drunk guy.

Sparks flew as Marie shook her head, black hair a nimbus, soft and floating in the night breeze. "No way. I'm having too much fun."

Anya reached out and grabbed Marie's hand. "I am taking you home *now.*"

Marie staggered a little as she glared at her and tried to shake her off. "Who are you, my mother?"

This time Anya knew not to lose her temper. But she was so far from that. So far.

Very soberly she said, "Who am I? I'm someone in desperate need of a do-over."

Marie blinked and shook her head. She pawed at Anya's fingers. "No such thing."

"There is. There really is. Now, come on."

"Hey," said the big, drunk guy. "Let her party."

"Come on," Anya said more quietly. "Marie."

There was a beat. Another. Marie stared hard into Anya's eyes, and her own eyes welled. Her hand in Anya's went limp.

She said under her breath, "But it's scary out there." Then her face crumpled and she touched her head. "And even scarier in here." Tears rolled down her cheeks. She began to cry, great rolling sobs that shook her entire body.

Oh, thank you, universe, Anya thought. *Whatever god or fate or fairy godmother has given this to us, thank you.*

She drew her weeping best friend into her arms and held her tightly. Felt her own tears, held in check for a year, held so long, held taut, streaming down her face. Tasted the salt. Felt the struggle drain out of her. And out of Marie. Even in the darkest place, there is hope.

"Breathe," she told Marie. "Just breathe."

Nancy Holder is a *New York Times* bestselling author
of over ninety books and two hundred short stories,
essays, and articles. She has received five Bram Stoker
Awards, a Scribe, and a Young Adult Pioneer Award.
Her series, Wicked, was optioned by DreamWorks, and
her fiction has appeared on recommended lists from
the American Library Association and the New York
Public Library Stuff for the Teen Age. She coedited
Futuredaze 2: Reprise, featuring science fiction short
stories from authors such as Neil Gaiman and Cassandra
Clare. She is a trustee of the Horror Writers Association
and the director of ceremonies for StokerCon. Her most
recent YA novel is a thriller titled *The Rules* (Delacorte).

Website: nancyholder.com

Twitter: @nancyholder

Facebook: facebook.com/nancyholderfans

The Whisper-Whisper Men

TIM WAGGONER

S he runs down the street, shouting at the top of her
lungs.

"Hello? Can anyone hear me? Is there anyone
there?"

The only sounds are her voice, her ragged, panicked
breathing, and her sneakers pounding on asphalt. No cars,
no barking dogs, no chirping birds, no *anything*. It's a beautiful day in late April—cloudless blue sky, sun bright overhead,
warm but not too warm. People should be out doing yard
work, washing cars in their driveways, or walking their dogs.
Kids should be playing in their backyards or on sidewalks,
riding bikes or skateboards. There should be joggers running
by, couples walking hand in hand, cars cruising up and down
the street, people on their way to the park, the movies, the
mall . . . going *anywhere*, doing *anything*, just getting outside
to enjoy the day.

But there's no one. No one but her.

She doesn't know how long she runs, how many times she
shouts without getting any response. She's not even sure what

neighborhood she's in anymore. The houses here look the same as on her family's street: ranch style houses with small yards, an occasional two story home here and there to break the monotony. But she doesn't recognize any of the street names.

Lungs burning, throat sore, feet and knees aching, she slows to a walk and then finally stops. She doubles over, puts her hands on her knees, and spends the next several moments gulping air, sweat pouring off her. As her heart rate begins to slow, she thinks back to when she started running. Or rather, she tries to. But no matter how hard she tries, the memory won't come.

Her breathing eases, becoming almost silent, and she finally hears something beside the noises she's made herself. She straightens, listens.

It's a soft sound, one that reminds her of a rushing river or distant highway traffic. But it's not either of these. There's no river or highway close by. Wind rustling tree leaves? No. The air is still, and she can see that the leaves aren't moving. She holds her breath, listens harder. It's a *shhh-shhh-shhh* sound, but it's not regular. Sometimes its rhythm is faster, sometimes slower, the volume louder or softer. Almost like people talking. No . . . *whispering.*

The sound should fill her with relief. It means she's not alone. But there's something strange about it—sinister, unsettling—and it provides no comfort. Just the opposite. It fills her with dread.

She catches a glimpse of movement out of the corner of her eye then, and her head snaps around in that direction. She has the impression of someone dressed in black from head to toe disappearing behind a large oak tree. But the figure moves so fast, she's not sure she didn't imagine it. She sees another flash of darkness, this one on the other side of the street, and she turns that way. She's faster this time, and she sees this figure more clearly. It moves with a silent gliding motion, like the shadow it resembles. She can't make out any features, for the thing is nothing but a dark silhouette, a human shape cut from black construction paper. It too quickly vanishes, ducking behind a car parked in a driveway. But she knows it's still there. She can feel its presence, feel it watching her. Just like the one hiding behind the oak tree. And they aren't the only two. She can sense that, too. They lurk behind trees, the sides of houses, inside drainage openings, and their whispering grows louder, becomes harder edged, until it resembles the ratcheting thrum of cicadas. Fear cuts through her like a blade of ice, and she has to get off the street, find someplace safe where she can hide from the shadow-things.

She doesn't think. She picks a house at random and runs toward it. It's another ranch home, one that doesn't look all that different from hers, really—although she barely has time to register that fact, terrified as she is. She races across the neatly trimmed lawn, bounds up the concrete steps to the porch, and begins pounding on the front door with her fists.

"Help me! Please! They're after me!"

She feels a tingling sensation on the back of her neck, and she knows the shadow-things have left their hiding places and are moving toward her, silent and swift.

"Please!" she shouts one more time. But the door doesn't open. If there's anyone inside, they're not going to answer. Maybe she sounds crazy, and they're afraid to let her in. Or maybe they've peeked out the window and have seen the dark creatures approaching the house. Or maybe this house—like the rest of the neighborhood—truly is deserted, and there's no one to help her.

The whispering grows louder still as they draw near, and she thinks she can almost make out words, but she can't quite. She presses against the door, eyes closed, praying that they'll go away, knowing they won't.

The air becomes colder as they approach, and she feels frigid breath on the back of her neck. She squeezes her eyes shut even tighter, as if that will help somehow, and she tenses her body in anticipation of shadowy hands reaching out to touch her. She feels the sensation of fingers brushing the skin on her neck, their touch so cold it feels as if they draw all the warmth from her body.

She sucks in a breath and starts to scream—

Alex sat up in bed, drenched with sweat, heart pounding, breath coming in ragged gasps. Dim light came through the crack between her window curtains, and she knew it was close to dawn. She sat unmoving until her pulse and breathing slowed and some measure of calm returned to her. Only then did she take her phone off the nightstand and check the time. 5:17. She sighed. Her alarm was set for 6:30, but she knew there was no way she'd be able to fall back to sleep, not after that dream. Might as well get up and get ready for the day.

She drew the covers off her, swung her legs over the side of the bed, and stood. As she left her room and headed for the bathroom, she felt a cold sensation on the back of her neck. She told herself it was only her imagination, but she didn't believe it.

Alex dragged through her first couple classes, and by the time she got to Ms. DiPietro's psychology class, it was all she could do to keep her eyes open.

"You look worse than you did yesterday."

Alex turned to Jackie and gave her a withering smile. "Thanks a lot."

"She's not wrong," Kerri said. "Seriously, how *are* you?"

Jackie Kingston and Kerri Howell were two of Alex's best friends. They'd been close since the beginning of middle school, and now in their second year of high school they did their best to take their classes together. It didn't always work out, though, and this semester psych was the only class they shared. Jackie sat to Alex's right, while Kerri sat behind her.

"I'm okay," Alex said. She thought her voice sounded weak, too soft. Entirely unconvincing.

Jackie wore her blond hair in a ponytail, had large owl-like glasses, and wore shirts that displayed her favorite obsessions—usually singers. Today she had on a Taylor Swift shirt. Kerri, on the other hand, enjoyed looking her best. She was a beautiful African American girl, and her hair, nails, and makeup were always perfect. She wore dresses most of the time, even in winter. Fashionwise, Alex normally fell somewhere between her two friends, but lately she'd taken to wearing a pullover hoodie and jeans every day. As tired as she was in the mornings, it was simpler to grab the hoodie and leave the house. No makeup, either. She just didn't feel like bothering with it.

"You had that dream again," Jackie said. It wasn't a question.

"Yeah. Same as always."

"Have you talked to your parents about it?" Kerri asked.

"No, I haven't said anything to my dad and *stepmother*," Alex said. Then she sighed. "Sorry. I didn't mean to snap. Just tired, you know?"

Ms. DiPietro usually stood in the hallway chatting with the teacher next door until it was time for class to begin. She always walked in right before the bell rang, and she came into the room right then.

"Maybe you should talk to Ms. DiPietro," Jackie said, grinning. "She *does* teach psych."

"Funny," Alex said in a tone that indicated she thought the opposite.

The bell rang the moment Ms. DiPietro reached her desk. Alex wondered how the woman was always able to time it so precisely. It was like she was a robot or something.

"Good morning, class. Today we're going to talk about fear."

Ms. DiPietro wasn't very old, late twenties, maybe early thirties. Alex wasn't good at guessing the ages of adults. She was a tall, slender woman who dressed more like a business-woman than a high school teacher. Today she wore a sharp gray business suit and killer black heels. She had long, glossy black hair that she wore loose. Alex envied the woman's hair. Her own brown hair was short and curly, and no matter how she tried to style it, it always stayed that way.

Kerri leaned forward and whispered close to Alex's ear.

"This is your lucky day. Maybe you'll pick up a few tips about dealing with nightmares."

Alex knew her friend was only teasing, but hearing her whisper like that made her feel instantly sick to her stomach. She thought about raising her hand and asking if she could be excused to go see the school nurse. But she didn't. She didn't want the other kids—especially Jackie and Kerri—to think something really *was* wrong with her. Besides, she couldn't stand the thought of lying on the cot in the nurse's sick room all by herself while the nurse tended to other students. The last thing she wanted right now was to be alone. So she remained in her seat and gripped the edge of her desk to steady herself and keep from trembling.

"Fear is a natural, inevitable part of the human condition," Ms. DiPietro began. "No matter how hard we try, none of us will ever be free of it. Because of this, it's important we learn to do more than just live with our fears. We need to *embrace* them."

Alex liked Ms. DiPietro and thought she was a good teacher, but half the time she had no idea what the woman was talking about. This was definitely one of those times.

Ms. DiPietro lectured a while longer, and then she told the class to get out their notebooks and pens.

"I want you to take the next ten minutes and write about something you fear. And not something unimportant like spiders. Something deeper, more personal. Don't worry. You're not going to have to share this with anyone in the class. I just want to give you—in one small way—the opportunity to confront your fears. Go ahead and get started."

Like the other students, Alex had taken a notebook and pen from her backpack, and now she stared at the blank page in front of her. Most of the other students, including Jackie and Kerri, were already writing. But Alex had no idea what to put down. The easiest thing to do would be to write about her recurring dream of the shadow-things she'd come to think of as the Whisper-Whisper Men. But not only didn't she want to revisit that dream, if only in her memory, she didn't think it would fit the assignment. The dream was scary, sure, and she *hated* it, but she didn't think it counted as a fear she had. Not the way Ms. DiPietro meant the word, anyway.

What was the worst thing she could imagine? That was an easy one. The death of her mother. Her *real* mother. Alex had been six, and her brother, Steve, almost eight and a half when their mother had been driving home from the airport late at night after getting home from a business trip. It had been raining, and her car had been struck head-on by a drunk driver in a pickup. She'd died that morning in the hospital. Their dad had thrown himself into his work after the funeral, and Alex and Steve didn't see much of him after that. They were stuck in after-school care and dropped off at relatives' houses on the weekends. Even after their dad remarried, Alex and Steve kept going to after-school care until they were old enough to stay home and take care of themselves. But as bad as all that was, did any of it count as a *fear?* She was a little nervous about taking driver's ed over the summer, but mostly she was excited.

She thought back to her nightmare. The Whisper-Whisper Men, whatever they were, were scary, no doubt. But they weren't the worst part of the dream. Not by a long shot.

Ms. DiPietro had stood by her desk the whole time, watching them write. Now she glanced at the clock on the wall.

"You have one more minute to finish up," she said.

Alex's paper was still blank. Without thinking about it too much, she scrawled a short sentence.

I'm afraid of being alone.

She looked at it for a moment, then added two more words.

Like Mom.

It wasn't much, but at least it was something. She put down her pen and turned to Jackie. She saw her friend had covered two and a half pages. She turned around to see how Kerri had done, but her seat was empty.

As first Alex thought that maybe Kerri had gotten up to use the restroom without her noticing. But her backpack wasn't there either.

She turned to Jackie and in a low voice asked, "What happened to Kerri?"

Jackie frowned.

"Who?"

Alex thought it was a weird joke and refused to talk to Jackie throughout the remainder of the class. They had different lunch periods, so Alex wouldn't have to sit with Jackie, and that was fine with her. It was almost as if Jackie and Kerri had read what she'd written and decided to use it as the basis for a practical joke. Kerri had disappeared and left her "alone." Except there was no way they could've pulled it off, even if they'd wanted to be that cruel—which, she had to admit, was out of character for both of them. Alex hadn't written down her response until the last minute. There hadn't been enough time for Jackie and Kerri to read the words and cook up their scheme—all without saying a word to each other. And Ms.

DiPietro didn't allow students to use their phones in class, so they couldn't have texted back and forth. And no matter how deep in thought Alex had been, she didn't think there was any way Kerri could've gotten up from her seat and left the room without Alex seeing her.

But it *had* to be a joke. What else could it be?

As she walked through the hallway to the cafeteria, she noticed that it didn't seem as crowded as usual. Normally, she had to push and shove to make her way to the caff, but not today. Was some kind of cold or flu going around? Had a lot of people stayed home sick? Maybe that's what had happened with Kerri. Maybe she'd started to feel sick and had left class and gone home. But if that was the case, why had Jackie pretended she didn't know who Kerri was?

Alex wasn't hungry, so all she bought for lunch was an apple and a bottle of water. She picked a seat at an empty table, sat down, sipped the water, and ignored the apple. The cafeteria was usually full of students, and finding a seat could be problematic—especially if you wanted to sit next to your friends and avoid certain other people. You could never guarantee where you were going to sit. But not today. Not only did she have an entire table to herself, about a third of the seats in the cafeteria were empty. Maybe more. The caff was normally a noisy, bustling place, but today it was quiet, the atmosphere subdued. As near as she could tell, no one seemed to notice the change or be particularly worried about it. No one acted weird or anything. There were just a lot fewer people here than usual, that was all.

But then a thought occurred to her. A terrible, awful thought.

Your dream's coming true. People are starting to disappear, and it's going to keep happening until no one is left but you.

It was a ridiculous thought, but no less frightening for it. And then she noticed that the soft murmur of conversation around her had taken on an ominous aspect. The voices had grown softer, sibilant, sounding more like whispers than people speaking out loud. As in her nightmare, she couldn't make out the words, wasn't even certain the language she was hearing was even English. The other students continued to act as if nothing was wrong, chatting and laughing, but in feather-soft whispery voices. As she watched, it became more difficult to make out individual facial features, almost as if the cafeteria's lights were dimming. But she realized the lights overhead were as bright as always. It was the *people* who were growing dimmer, as if they were becoming cloaked in shadow.

Alex put down her water bottle, picked up her backpack, and left without bothering to throw away her water or her untouched apple. She walked toward the exit, telling herself not to run. *If you run, they'll chase you*, she thought. She looked straight ahead, and as the whispering continued—in fact, seemed to grow louder—she felt the weight of dozens of eyes upon her. When she reached the door, she was tempted to glance behind her and see if everyone *was* looking at her, but she feared if she did, she'd see dark figures sitting where boys and girls had been only moments before. Still, she almost did it, but then the whispering stopped and silence filled the room. If she turned back, would she discover that the shadow-things had gotten out of their seats and were coming for her? Or would she discover that the caff was now entirely empty? She didn't know which she'd find more terrifying, and in the end she pushed open the door and rushed into the hallway— the virtually *empty* hallway—without looking back.

The dismissal bell came as a huge relief to Alex. Her last class of the day was modern American history with Mr. Robertson. Except he wasn't there—and when she said something about his absence to one of the six other students who showed up, they all looked at her like she was crazy. The other kids took out notebooks and textbooks and acted as if they were in an unsupervised study hall. It was majorly bizarre.

She lived only a few blocks from the school, and she always walked—unless the weather was *really* bad, and then Steve drove her. Even though he was a senior and had a car, he usually walked too. Their school was a large one, and walking saved him the hassle of dealing with the traffic caused by all the other kids with cars trying to leave at the same time. None of Alex's friends lived close enough to walk, so she always waited on her brother. They weren't besties or anything, but they got along okay. And she didn't want to walk home alone, especially after the strange day she'd been through.

She waited for Steve outside the main entrance, as she always did. Far fewer kids came out the doors than usual, and there seemed to be fewer buses in the parking lot. She continued waiting for Steve until the buses were all gone and only a few of the teachers' cars remained in the front lot. That's when she finally gave up and started walking home. She told herself that Steve had probably gone out with friends after school and forgotten to text her about it. Or maybe some kind of flu epidemic really *had* hit the school, and he'd gone home sick earlier in the day.

As she walked, she wished she hadn't waited so long for Steve. The sidewalks were empty now, and she was forced to walk alone. There was usually a good amount of traffic on the streets near the school, especially this time of day, but hardly any vehicles passed by. *The flu*, she thought. *It's hit the whole town.* But she hadn't heard a single person coughing or sneezing at school, hadn't heard anyone complaining of a sore throat, aches, or chills. She hadn't even seen anyone who'd looked sick.

She kept looking around as she walked, expecting to see dark figures peeking out from behind trees and parked cars, and around the sides of houses. But she didn't. She expected to hear the *shhh-shhh-shhh* of sinister whispering, but there was nothing. There were still traffic noises and birdsong, too. Just not as much as usual.

She checked her phone several times as she walked to see if Steve had texted her yet, but he hadn't. Neither had anyone else, which was weird. Usually she heard from Jackie and Kerri by now. They both rode the bus home, and the three of them texted back and forth during the ride. Kerri *might* have gone home sick and wasn't feeling up to texting right now, but Jackie was fine. As far as Alex knew, anyway. Alex wasn't upset with Jackie anymore. The day had been filled with too much strangeness for her to hold a grudge against Jackie for pretending she didn't know who Kerri was. Besides, she wanted to know if her friends were okay. She *needed* to hear from them, to make contact. She sent both of them a quick *Hi, what's up?* text and then, after considering for a moment, she sent a similar message to Steve. She kept walking then, but she held her phone in her hand instead of putting it back in her pants pocket. She wanted to feel it vibrate the instant someone texted her back. And the weight of it in her hand reassured her, made her feel connected, less alone.

She thought back to what she'd written in her notebook during Ms. DiPietro's class. *I'm afraid of being alone. Like Mom.* She also thought about some of the things Ms. DiPietro had said during her lecture before the exercise.

Our fears are always with us, whispering in our ears. Telling us we're not smart enough, that no one likes us, that no matter the circumstances, we will never truly be good enough. They also tell us we're physically in danger, of course. They warn

*about injury, illness, and death, but they speak of other dan-
gers too. Being laughed at. Ignored. Disliked. Rejected. And no
matter how hard you try to run from your fears, you can never
escape them. They're inside you. Part of you. And you take them
with you wherever you go. That's why I say you have to embrace
your fears. You have to get to know them, truly understand
them. You need to get to the root of a fear, the place where it all
started. Only then will you be able to truly face it.*

Even though Ms. DiPietro hadn't looked at her directly
while saying all this, Alex had nevertheless felt as if the woman
had been speaking directly to her. She only wished she understood what it all meant.

By the time she reached home, she still hadn't received a
reply text from anyone, and she was actually hoping her stepmother was there. Renee was a Realtor, and while she worked
odd hours, depending on when someone wanted to see a house,
more often than not she was there when Alex and Steve got
home from school. Alex wasn't sure why. Maybe she thought
she was doing the mother thing. Renee wasn't an overly warm
person—not when it came to kids, anyway—but she did make
an effort, and Alex supposed that counted for something. But
even though they weren't close, it would be a relief to see her,
to see *anyone*, and the moment she opened the front door and
stepped inside she called out, "Hey, Renee! I'm home!"

She disliked the pleading, almost desperate edge to her
voice, but she couldn't help it.

No answer came.

"Hello?" she called out again. "Renee? Steve?" Her brother's car was parked on the street outside, so it was possible he was here too. Although why he would've ditched her to walk home on his own, she couldn't say.

Still no answer.

She felt a cold stab of panic. She shut the door, shrugged off her backpack, and ran into the living room, unable to stop herself. When she found no one there, she continued running through the house, checking the kitchen, the dining room, the bedrooms, even the basement. She saved the garage for last, afraid to look inside. What if Renee's car was there, but she wasn't here? What would that mean? She forced herself to look and was relieved to find the garage empty. Renee was out showing a house or maybe just running some errands, that was all. But then Alex remembered the nearly empty teacher's lot at school, the missing buses, the light traffic on the way home, and she no longer felt so relieved. Maybe more than people were disappearing.

Alex closed the door to the garage and headed back into the kitchen, on the verge of full-fledged panic. Her mouth was so dry, and she wanted to get a bottle of water from the fridge. That's when she noticed the note held to the refrigerator door by a pair of small magnets.

I have to work for a bit this afternoon. I'll pick up something for dinner on the way home. Do your homework! ☺ *—Renee.*

Alex's stepmother wasn't the type of person to write the word "love" before signing her name. A smiley face was as far as she went. But right then that was okay with Alex. In fact, it was wonderful.

She checked her phone. Still nothing.

She returned to the front hall, grabbed her backpack, and headed down to her bedroom to get started on her homework. She passed Steve's bedroom along the way. The door was closed, and on impulse she stopped and knocked. When there was no answer, she hesitated a moment and then grasped the doorknob. As she turned the knob and started to push the door open, she thought, wouldn't it be strange if the room were entirely empty, as if Steve didn't live here? As if he'd never existed.

She stopped, the door halfway open. Without looking, she turned her head and slowly closed the door.

Alex liked to lie on her bedroom floor—sometimes on her stomach, sometimes on her side—while she did homework. Today was a stomach day. But she'd managed to get only half-way through her math before putting her work aside. She'd been listening to music on her phone, and she turned it off and removed her earbuds. She still hadn't gotten so much as a single text from her friends, so she'd decided to give them a call. Steve, too, maybe, although if he was out somewhere having fun with his friends, he'd probably ignore her call and let it go to voice mail.

She opened up her contacts list and stared at the screen in shock. It was empty. She checked her saved texts only to find there were none. Same for her e-mail archive. She used her phone's Facebook app to access the site and discovered she had no friends there. She checked Twitter, Instagram, Pinterest, and Tumblr, but it was the same everywhere. No saved messages or images, no contacts or friends.

"Something's wrong with my phone," she said aloud, more to break the silence than anything else. Or maybe all her accounts had been hacked somehow. It was possible, right? With a trembling hand she placed her phone on the carpet and left it there. She stared at it for a moment, unsure what, if anything, she should—or *could*—do next. And then she heard the sound of the garage door opening, and the relief that hit her was so strong, so overwhelming, that for an instant she couldn't move. But then she was on her feet and running down the hall.

She was standing in front of the door to the garage when it opened and Renee walked in, carrying a plastic bag from a fast-food fried chicken restaurant. Alex was so happy to see her stepmother that she threw her arms around her neck and gave her a massive hug, almost knocking her down in the process.

Renee laughed in surprise and gently pushed Alex away with her free hand.

"What in the world did I do to deserve that?"

Renee was a petite woman, shorter than Alex by a couple

inches. She had a round face and short, black hair that always looked perfect, even when she first got up in the morning. She wore a white blouse, black skirt, and black flats. She'd once told Alex that she'd rather wear prettier shoes, but given how much walking she did on her job, flats were a smarter choice.

"I'm just glad to see you," Alex said. "Is that all right?"

Renee narrowed her eyes, as if she was suspicious—or more likely, just confused. But she said, "Of course it is." Then she smiled. "It's nice to be welcomed home like that."

Alex eyed the plastic bag. She hadn't noticed before, but it wasn't very large.

She frowned. "Is there more chicken in the car? Do you want me to go get it?"

Now it was Renee's turn to frown. "I don't understand."

Alex pointed at the bag. "It doesn't look like there's enough in there to feed all of us."

Renee gave her a puzzled look. "All?"

Alex's voice froze, and for a long moment she couldn't say anything. When she was able to speak again, her words came out sounding like a desperate plea.

"You know . . . you, me, Dad, and Steve."

Renee cocked her head slightly to the side.

"Who?"

Alex didn't eat much, and after a while she asked Renee if she could be excused from the table.

"I don't feel all that well, and I still have a lot of homework to finish."

"Of course. What is it? Your head? Your stomach? Do you want some medicine?"

"No, I'll be okay. I just want to get my work done and go to bed."

Renee looked concerned, but she said, "Sure. Let me know if you need anything, okay?"

Alex nodded. She picked up the paper plate with the remains of the chicken leg she'd nibbled on, threw it in the trash, and then headed down the hall toward her room.

She didn't bother finishing her homework. What was the point when there was a good chance none of her teachers would be there tomorrow to accept it?

She changed her clothes, turned off the light, and crawled into bed. She had her phone with her, but she didn't check for texts, e-mails, or missed calls. She knew there would be none.

She had no idea if she was going crazy or if what seemed to be happening was real. And if it *was* real, was it happening everywhere? If she used her phone to access the Internet and check out a news site, would she see a headline about thousands, maybe millions of people mysteriously disappearing? If she looked up the number of people living on earth, what would it be? If she remembered right, it should be something like six or seven billion. What would it be right now? Three billion? One? Even less?

She decided against looking. Whatever she found, she knew she wouldn't like it. Instead, she plugged her earbuds into her phone, put the sound receivers into her ears, and put on some music. At least she tried to. But instead of music, she heard whispering. She tore her earbuds from her ears, threw her phone across the room, and wept.

Alex remained awake long after her tears dried. She lay in bed and stared up at the ceiling—or rather, the darkness where the ceiling should have been. Her room was across the hall from Renee and her dad's room. It was just Renee's room now, she supposed. She listened to Renee getting ready for bed, and then, later, to her stepmother's soft snoring. Renee refused to believe she snored, even though everyone in the family told her that she did. It wasn't a big deal though. She didn't snore that loud, and tonight Alex found the noise comforting.

She wasn't sure how long she lay awake listening to it, but sometime during the night it abruptly ceased, and Alex knew that in the morning she'd find herself alone in the house.

Alex stepped out into bright morning sunshine. She didn't have her backpack. No reason to go to school if no one else was there. Before leaving the house, she'd worked up the courage to check on Renee. She hadn't been surprised to find her bed empty.

The weather was exactly the same as in her dreams, and

she wondered if she'd somehow found a way to cross from one world to another, from reality to nightmare. Or maybe there never had been a difference between the two, and only now she was aware of it. And of course, there was always the chance she was insane, that she was only imagining all this. That seemed a surer bet than the entire world changing around her. But whatever was happening, she knew she wouldn't find any answers staying inside.

She walked out into the street, picked a direction at random, and kept going.

She had no idea if she'd managed to get any sleep last night. If she had dozed off, she hadn't stayed asleep long enough to dream. That was one thing to be thankful for, she supposed. As in her dreams, the world was silent. It was weird, but she had dreamed of being here so many times that, in a way, it almost felt comfortable.

She'd had a lot of time to think last night, and she'd decided to do what Ms. DiPietro had talked about. She had to come to terms with her fear. Understand it. *Embrace* it. So, instead of running from the Whisper-Whisper Men, today she intended to seek them out. She was scared at the prospect, downright terrified, in fact. But she could think of no other way out of the living nightmare she'd found herself trapped in. So, as she walked, she listened closely for soft whispers, kept a sharp eye out for quick, shadowy movements. But she heard and saw nothing. Had the shadow-things abandoned her too? Yesterday, she would've felt relieved to find herself free of them. But today? Without them she was truly, utterly alone.

Tears came then. Tears of anger and frustration. And despite her earlier determination not to run, she found herself walking faster, then jogging, then finally running all out. Somewhere in the back of her mind, she thought that maybe if she re-created the circumstances of her dream, the Whisper-Whisper Men would come. Maybe they were like cats, attracted to an object if it moved like prey. But still she detected no movement, heard not a single whisper.

She released a loud cry of anguish, slowed, stumbled, and went down on her hands and knees. She remained that way for several moments, gulping air in between sobs, but eventually she looked up and realized where she was. She'd stopped directly in front of the house she always ran to for help when the Whisper-Whisper Men began to approach her. There was still no sign of the shadow-things, but Alex rose to her feet and started toward the house anyway. This time when she reached the front door, she didn't bother knocking. Instead, she tried the knob and found it unlocked. She took a deep breath, then opened the door and stepped inside.

It was dark, and when she closed the door behind her, it became pitch-black, like the inside of a deep subterranean cave, a place where light could never reach. It had been warm outside, but in here it was cold, so much so that she immediately began to shiver. She stood there, shaking, heart pounding in her ears, trying to decide what she should do next.

"Hello? Is anyone here?"

At first there was only silence, and then she heard it: the whispering. Dozens of voices surrounded her, all speaking at once. And this time she thought she could make out what they were saying. Part of it, at least.

Alone . . . alone . . . alone . . . alone . . .

Is that what the Whisper-Whisper Men were? Her greatest fear brought to shadowy life? But then the whispers became louder, more distinct, and she realized they were actually saying two words.

She's alone, she's alone, she's alone. . . .

The words struck Alex like a punch to the stomach. She knew what they meant, and she understood that her greatest fear wasn't for herself, but for someone else. Someone very important to her.

I'm afraid of being alone. Like Mom.

You need to get to the root of a fear, the place where it all started.

In the darkness she spread her arms wide, and the Whisper-Whisper Men glided forward to embrace her.

Alex's vision cleared, and she found herself looking at a rain streaked windshield, wipers swishing rapidly back and forth, making a sound like whispering. It was night, and the headlights from oncoming traffic were bright distortions viewed through running, rippling water. Their light threw shadows onto the side of the road that looked remarkably human shaped. The car was moving, not all that fast from what Alex could tell, but there was a strong wind outside, and it pushed against the car, making it hydroplane from time to time.

Alex turned to look at the driver. The woman behind the wheel appeared to be in her thirties, and she had curly brown hair, just like Alex's. She wore a dark jacket—Alex couldn't make out the color—and she gripped the steering wheel tight, hunched forward as if it would help her see better.

"Mom! It's me! Alex!"

Her mother frowned, but she didn't turn to look at Alex.

She can't see or hear me, Alex thought. No, that wasn't entirely true. She'd frowned when Alex had spoken. She reached out and tentatively touched her mother's elbow. Her mother reacted with a start, causing the car to swerve. She got control of the vehicle, and then turned to look at the passenger seat. She squinted, as if trying very hard to make out something that she couldn't quite see. After a moment she shook her head and faced forward once more.

So Alex *was* here. Kind of.

She next tried to touch the steering wheel. If she could grab hold of it just before the accident, maybe . . . But her hand passed through it as if it weren't there. She tried to grab her mother's arm, and the same thing happened. Gentle touches she could manage, but that was it. There was nothing she could do to change things. Her mother was still going to die. But then Alex realized there was one thing she *could* do.

She scooted close to her mother and gently laid a hand atop one of hers. Her mother stiffened for a moment, and then relaxed, a small smile on her face.

"I have no idea how I got here. But I *am* here, Mom. You're not alone. Neither of us is."

Alex increased the pressure on her mother's hand, smiled, and waited for what was to come next.

Tim Waggoner has published over thirty novels and three short story collections of dark fiction. He teaches creative writing at Sinclair Community College in Dayton, Ohio, and in Seton Hill University's MFA in Writing Popular Fiction program in Greensburg, Pennsylvania.

Website: timwaggoner.com

Twitter: @timwaggoner

Facebook: facebook.com/tim.waggoner.9

Non-player Character

NEAL & BRENDAN SHUSTERMAN

It was not an alarm, but the incessant beeping of a microwave that woke Darren up. He could sleep through the sounds of battle and the wails of the dying—but a relentless microwave was hard to ignore. It was still dark outside, and the faint smell of burned food filled the entire apartment. He looked around. His mattress, which sat like a beached whale in the center of the kitchen, had a green energy drink spill near his feet that looked like toxic sludge, and beside it the refrigerator door was ajar. From the other room came the sound of swarming zombies and the *rat-a-tat-tat* of gunfire.

"GET THE KIDS! SOMEBODY SAVE THE KIDS!" shouted a voice he didn't recognize.

He crawled up on his spindly legs, raising himself to his feet. There was no kitchen table, or at least, not anymore; what was left of it sat in a broken heap of tangled wood in a corner, a bed sheet draped over it as if it were a corpse. He carefully stepped across the floor, trying to avoid bugs of various species traveling from one Doritos bag shelter to the next. He kicked aside a half-eaten bowl of mac and cheese that had more larvae than mac or cheese, and made his way to the beeping microwave, which was smoking. Inside, Darren found an inedible mélange of blackened foodstuff. The kind that comes frozen—the kind any idiot can cook. His mother or his father must have set it for fifty minutes instead of five and had promptly forgotten about it. Eating, after all, was only secondary to them now. He pulled the corpse of the TV dinner from the microwave and threw it into the overflowing trash. What time was it? It was dark, and the clock on the microwave was no help; it blinked a perpetual midnight. In this house it was always the witching hour.

From the other room came more gunfire.

"OH GOD! SOMEONE HELP! THEY'RE EVERYWHERE!"

"TAKE COVER!"

He found his parents in their usual spots in the living room. The springs in the sofa had long since given up their battle against gravity, and the two of them sank into the cushions as if rooted there. His father held a weapon that wasn't there. His mother moved her arms as if directing airplanes on a runway. Both wore immersive headsets that put them into the world of the game, but it also played on a huge TV screen above the web filled fireplace and on smaller screens in every other room, so they wouldn't miss a thing, even when they took bathroom breaks.

Ever since *Mantra of Madness* was launched six months ago, it had consumed his parents like a stomach slowly digesting a heavy meal. The game's previous expansion packs had cost them their jobs, their friends, their bank accounts. This one had consumed what was left of their lives. The apartment was different before *Mantra*. Things were functional. Darren had a bedroom. But that bedroom had quickly become a storage space for all the stuff his parents didn't need anymore—which was everything. His parents had talked to him before. But now snarls and gunfire had replaced their conversations. Anything that didn't involve blowing away satanic alien zombies wasn't worthy of their attention. They treated Darren like an NPC in the real world. A non-player character. Computer generated, and soulless.

"Mom? Dad?" The first intrusion. He knew they wouldn't respond until the third or fourth.

"Mom? Dad? Can you hear me?" They shifted their shoulders uncomfortably, aware they were being summoned from somewhere outside of their current reality—but it probably only registered subconsciously.

"You burned your food, and you have to eat!"

"Did you wake him up?" his father said to his mother.

"No, another NPC must have woken the sleeper," his mother said. "Damn computer."

"That's why I hate this level. Too many civilians to protect," said his father.

Darren tried again. "Did you hear me? Your food is burned."

"There'll be rations at the next checkpoint," his father said.

And so Darren gave up. Only once their mission was complete, and they realized that virtual food could satisfy only virtual hunger, would they leave the game long enough to gorge themselves. Right now they would eat only if he cooked it and put it in front of them. And as much as he hated doing that, he knew he would, because the only thing worse than watching them play was watching them starve.

He wanted to scream, he wanted to cry, he wished he could just bawl his eyes out at what his life had become, but the tears just wouldn't come. How had their lives come to this? The change had been gradual and insidious, like the weeds that had strangled their yard. Suddenly, this was the new normal, and there was never a moment to cry. He figured someday he would, and it would feel good. It would make him feel better. He would cry himself to sleep and have dreams without the sounds of an apocalyptic war.

Darren shuffled back into the kitchen. He looked at the wall clock, which had fallen from the wall and was now a baseboard clock. Its plastic face was cracked, and the hour hand was stuck at five o'clock, although the minute hand still ticked around the dial, as if in denial that anything was wrong. It wasn't only the digital clocks in his home that had lost their sanity. He considered putting the broken clock back up on the wall, but then considered the rest of the mess and realized that any cleaning he could do would just be large quantities of zero. Best not to demoralize himself by trying. So, ignoring the squalor, he found a pan that was only slightly crusty, scraped it off, and cooked some larvae-free mac and cheese for his parents.

Back in the living room he gave them each the first forkful. Only after tasting it did they respond by taking the bowls from him. Then they would eat it in between the major action.

Before becoming entirely immersed in *Mantra*, his parents had gotten him his own headset. For his birthday. That's what they called it—a birthday present, even though his birthday had been two months prior. He had opened the box. He had looked at it. He had thanked them.

"Now you can play with your friends," his father had said—as if the only way to play with one's friends was in a virtual RPG.

They had seemed satisfied. But he had never put the headset on. Seeing a window into that world on the TV was more than enough. Why would anyone want to be immersed in a satanic alien zombie apocalypse?

"Aw crap! Holloway is down!" his father shouted, nearly dumping his bowl.

On the screen one of their teammates had been taken out by something unthinkably evil. Darren had no idea who Holloway was in real life—this online game was global. The players could be from down the street or halfway around the world.

"Damn good player," his mother lamented. "Gonna miss him."

"Maybe he'll find us in his next iteration."

Then on the TV, red eyed rats flooded from a sewer and chowed down on Holloway like piranha until there was nothing left of him but bones, armor, and weapons.

"Waste not, want not," his father said, and their characters scavenged Holloway's belongings. Such was the way of the game.

Darren was about to leave and fix his own dinner when he chanced to spot something in the corner of the screen. A girl. Pale blue shimmering hair. Almost silver. She was looking out of a broken window of what should have been an abandoned suburban home. The weird thing about it was that Darren could almost swear she was looking at him.

Darren went to school the next morning. Darren came home from school the next afternoon. Darren avoided his friends, because what would be the point? It would be too awkward. He had to take care of his parents. Keep them from starving, or setting the house on fire, or leaving the water on, flooding the house out. You can't have friends with those kinds of things on your mind.

"Hi, Mom. Hi, Dad," he said each time he returned home. It was more like a joke than an actual greeting, because they never responded unless they were on their way back from a bathroom run or had taken off their headsets for some other reason. Then they would look at him with bloodshot eyes and slur something like "OhHeyHowuzSchool."

"Good" was always his response.

On the TV was a long city avenue of high-rise apartment buildings. A different landscape from yesterday. Some sky-scrapers had toppled, others were leaning into one another. His parents had split off from their team, or the rest of the team had died. They now walked down the street precari-ously, because death and dismemberment could be around any corner.

And from distant places, civilians wailed for help, or just wailed.

"OH GOD, LET IT END!"

"PLEASE! PLEASE DON'T EAT MY BABY!"

All part of the ambience.

But then, as Darren watched the scene, he saw her again. The silver girl. How could she be in two different landscapes? This time she was peering out from behind a pillar. And she was beckoning to him. She wore a glistening gown that was tattered and shredded like everything else in that world.

"Mom, Dad—do you see that?"

"Keep your wits about you," his father said to his mother. "We could be walking into an S.A.Z. ambush."

"The girl—do you see her? There on the left with the silver-bluish hair."

"Huh? What? Just an NPC. Stop distracting me."

But still she beckoned. So Darren did something he had never dared to do before. He put on his headset and turned it on.

The effect was instantaneous. The retinal projector erased all visual cues from the outside world. He was immersed in the dark, fiery, terrifying world of *Mantra of Madness*. He felt dizzy and nauseated. He wanted out—but he fought the feeling. When he turned, he saw his parents. He had seen their avatars before, but had never really paid attention. Now, in three dimensions, they were impressive. They looked like his parents, and yet not. His mother had larger breasts, a slimmer waist, and her hair, which had gotten tatty and mousy, now bounced like a model's. His father looked like a steroid injected bodybuilder version of himself.

"Well, look who finally decided to join the party!" his father said proudly. "About time you checked out the character we made for you! I've been leveling him up for when you were finally ready to play."

"Stay behind us," his mother told him. "This place can be dangerous. We'll protect you."

It was the first time they had actually noticed him for weeks.

He looked around. The girl was still there. She had moved to a different pillar farther away, but she was still beckoning to him.

Darren willed himself forward. The game obeyed his mental commands.

"No!" his father shouted behind him. "Don't go after that! You can't get points for killing that!"

But Darren ignored him.

"If we have to come rescue you, I'll be really pissed off!" his mother said.

He rounded the corner to see the torn fringes of her gown slipping into a dark doorway. He followed. The doorway opened on a set of emergency stairs that led up and up and up, until finally he emerged on the top floor of a skyscraper. The view was startling. All around him a city was on fire. Non-player characters were hurling themselves from rooftops to keep from being torn apart by satanic alien zombies.

The girl stood at the edge, but there were no creatures on this roof, and she didn't look like she was jumping. She smiled at him.

"You came. I knew you would come."

"Who are you?"

"That doesn't matter. What matters is that you're finally here." She moved closer. He reached out to touch her face. Even though he knew she was just a projection on his retina, he could swear he could feel her skin. So soft, so warm.

"This is a horrible place," she said, a tear dripping down her cheek. "You can see that, can't you?"

"Yes. . . ."

"That's why I need you to save me."

Darren laughed. He was amazed they put this amount of programming into an NPC. Unless of course she was the kind of NPC around whom the plot turned. Not just an extra but a principal in the story. How ironic if he came across a key element of the game that his parents had missed!

"Save you how?" he asked, ready to play along.

She didn't answer him right away. Instead, she leaned close and kissed him.

He knew it was virtual. He knew it couldn't be happening, but it didn't stop him from reacting as if it were real. And he wanted more.

"I'll tell you a secret," she whispered in his ear, and he could feel her breath as she did. "Your mind wants to tell you that this is pretend . . . but you don't have to listen. And when you stop listening . . . that's when it really gets fun."

And what she did to him next . . . He knew it wasn't happening anywhere else but in his head, but that didn't matter. Because it was far more real than anything that had ever happened to him in his life.

He was hooked—but in a very different way from his parents. Day after day he would enter the game, leave his parents to fight monsters, and run off to find the silver girl. He would even kill monsters himself if he had to—but only to protect her. He had to admit, though, that the most satisfying thing was killing off other player characters. They would see him there, in his armor and with his laser cannon. They would think he was an ally, but then he would turn on them with a blast to the head. He would watch their digital brains explode and splatter the scenery. Their avatars would go down, and the rats would come. He wouldn't even take their belongings. He wasn't there to scavenge. His victory was in their fall. It could have gone on like that if the silver girl—whose name he still did not know—hadn't stopped it.

"They come back," she told him. "You can kill them, but they always come back. And every time they do, the game creates a hundred new monsters to kill those of us who can't get out."

Then, around a smoky corner of Armageddon, two players came. Darren recognized them right away.

"What the hell are you doing?" his father shouted at him. "Are you still wasting time with that NPC?"

"So what?" said his mother. "He's not in the way, and he's enjoying the game. Leave him alone."

"He's not playing right!" said his father.

But his father's attention turned to a gaggle of decomposing attackers. His parents began firing on them, shouting orders to each other—and just like the silver girl said, more kept coming and coming.

"You see how it is?" she said.

When Darren looked at her again, her eyes were now as bright silver-blue as her hair. There was an intensity in her that he could only guess at. He wanted some of that intensity for himself. He craved it. He'd do anything for it.

"Save me," she said, as she had on the first day. "You know what you have to do."

Yes, he did know.

When he removed the headset, it took a few moments to adjust to the "real" world. His parents were sitting there, immersed in their battle. He was almost startled to see how scrawny and malnourished they were. Without him feeding them, had they eaten at all?

He found what he was looking for in the kitchen and returned to the living room. He began with his father, figuring he might put up the biggest fight. But he didn't even gasp as the carving knife slipped between his ribs and into his heart. Neither of them saw it coming. How could they, when they were more interested in the zombie attack?

A minute later the zombies killed his parents' unmanned avatars, and they were being devoured by rats. But at least these players would not be returning to the game.

Darren reached for his headset, ready to return to the girl, but her voice called out from the TV. "No!"

He turned to see the silver girl peering out at him from the TV screen. She was only pixels now. He touched the screen but couldn't get through to her. This wouldn't do. He longed for her to be injected right into his optic nerves. Why couldn't he? Why would she say no?

"They're not the only ones," she told him. "As long as there are still player characters, I won't be safe."

"And when they're all gone?" Darren asked.

"Then it's just you and me."

He touched his fingers to the surface of the screen, and she raised her fingers to touch his. He could almost feel her fingertips. Almost. He looked at the headset in his other hand. If he put it on, he knew she would run from him. He'd spend a lifetime searching for her in that world. The only way to get her back was to take on this mission. He dropped the headset to the bloody floor. There was work to do.

The night was chilly, so Darren put on a jacket. He could hear the reports of machine guns, laser fire, and commands being shouted in more than one home on his street. Those noises, he knew, would lead him to where he needed to go. Not just tonight, but tomorrow and all the days beyond. Funny how his knife, still dripping blood, was a far more effective weapon than a laser cannon.

"PLEASE, FOR THE LOVE OF GOD, DON'T HURT US!"

"SOMEONE! ANYONE! HELP US!"

Tonight, in Darren's world, he'd be racking up the points.

And in the silver girl's world, the rats would be feasting.

Neal Shusterman is the *New York Times* bestsell-
ing author of over thirty novels for teens, including the
Unwind Dystology, the Skinjacker Trilogy, *The Schwa
Was Here*, and *Challenger Deep*, winner of the National
Book Award. He has collaborated with his son Brendan
Shusterman numerous times—including a story appear-
ing in Shaun Hutchinson's *Violent Ends* story collection,
as well as a novella in *UnBound*, a collection of tales in the
Unwind world. Brendan also created the illustrations for
Challenger Deep, and is hard at work on his debut novel.

Website: storyman.com

Twitter: @NealShusterman

Facebook: facebook.com/nealshusterman

Falling into Darkness

MARGE SIMON

The House of Night Hospital

Entry

where all is white
specters line the stairs—
those who gasped last their breath
on sweat damp sheets

Surgery

where knives slashed flesh
so many lives unsaved

Corridors

funeral wreaths hang on doors
nurses walk the hallways
knives tucked in belts

Chapel

milky eyed mourners
hands trembling
heads bowed in perpetual prayer
twining rosaries
in bony fingers

Morgue

Boxed cubicles like
office drawers,
cold as hell
can't tell one
from the other
without a
not-so-sexy
toe tag.

Exit

No way out
but down.

Silver Sandals

In October they disappear. . . .

pretty girls in silver sandals
skin tattooed with moon and stars
tattered clothes left by the highway
screams unheard

in the house far from the city
bodies strung across the ceiling
spirits trapped in bottles waiting
offerings for the souls unborn

crimson spatters on the flooring
grimoires line the crooked shelves
pretty girls with no release from
spells unknown

Hitchhiker's Home

Mirrors broken
in a storm of hate
shards glimmer
in a slate dark sky

innocence lost
when she left
laughter silenced

by a drifter's blade

narrow hallways
overseen by the eyes
of obscure relatives
in gilded frames

ghosts wander
upstairs and down
cries only their mothers
hear in nightmares

once she thumbed a ride
hoping for freedom
but they brought
her back home.

Zombie Symptoms

Suzanne didn't notice it coming on,
as indeed none of the infected do,
during the first eight hours.

It's a matter of incubation time,
for the virus to penetrate the system.
There's the headache, then fever,
an unaccustomed glow in the eyes.

She felt a bit flushed,
thought it might be her sinuses,
or perhaps a little cold, until she
realized her rings had fallen off
the bones of her left hand.

After that point, Suzanne forgot
about what she was wearing,
didn't mind the panic in the faces
of those she passed on the streets.

In her eyes, an ephemeral light,
and her stomach screamed for flesh.

Voodoo Queen

Blood colors her hat
of haute couture style,

you'll find her at market
wearing a smile.

She's shopping for charms
and desirable potions

all sorts of the nastiest,
smelliest lotions,

whether once human
but probably not.

She's frequently sought,
for she's one of the best,

so the zombies attest,
with conditions severe,

her wares give their skin
a healthy veneer.

Huffing

you can't jail a guy
for stealing a stack
of little brown sacks
from the jiffy store

he got his mother's can of
oven cleaner from that dark space

under the sink buried
inside that extra dishpan

she never saw him
stick it under his new leather jacket
& take it off down the street to
Joe-Bob's garage where

they pass the can around
but he can't stop huffing
until the shadow spiders came
not for any others just for him
bebopping swaydancing inside his eyes
nobody could reach him after that
& nobody wanted to

he just sits there
forever blown away
he can't remember
& he won't care

so report him for
copping a bunch of brown sacks
why don't you.

Marge Simon lives in Ocala, Florida, and is married to Bruce Boston. Her works appear in publications such as *Daily Science Fiction* magazine, *Pedestal*, and *Dreams & Nightmares*. She edits a column, "Blood & Spades: Poets of the Dark Side," for the HWA newsletter and serves as chair of the board of trustees. She won the Strange Horizons Readers' Choice Award, the Science Fiction Poetry Association's Dwarf Stars Award, and the Elgin Award for best poetry collection. She has won three Bram Stoker Awards for superior work in poetry, two first-place Rhysling Awards, and the Grand Master Award from the SFPA. In addition to her poetry she has published two prose collections: *Christina's World* and *Like Birds in the Rain*. Her poems appear in *Qualia Nous, A Darke Phantastique*, the *Spectral Realms*, and *Chiral Mad 3*.

Website: margesimon.com

Facebook: facebook.com/profile
.php?id=100000459397561

What Happens When the Heart Just Stops

CHRISTOPHER GOLDEN

Kayah Fallon stood in the doorway to her bedroom, eyes wide, frozen to the spot, afraid she was watching her mother die. Details whispered at the edges of her peripheral vision—the open dresser drawer, the tumble of half-folded laundry, the smell of vomit—but she could not tear her gaze away from the pain etched upon her mother's face.

"Kai?" her mother rasped, and the word snapped Kayah from her paralysis.

She rushed across the room and knelt beside her mother. Naira Fallon lay with one leg folded underneath her. Halfway to sitting, she clung tightly to the mess of bedclothes tangled at the foot of her daughter's bed, as though she'd been trying to rise but hadn't quite managed it. Some of the fresh laundry had spilled onto her lap, and the rest had tumbled to the floor with the basket.

Naira tried to speak again but managed only a wheeze.

"What happened?" Kayah asked, hating the fear in her own voice. "Come on, lay down." She took her mother's right arm—the one propped on the bed—and found that her fingers were fisted in a knot of blanket. "Let go, Mom. Lay down."

But Naira seemed unable to unclench her fist. She groaned and her breath came in quick, hitching gasps.

"It hurts to breathe," Naira said.

Kayah looked around the room as if some solution—some miracle balm—might suddenly present itself. It did not. The pitiful painkillers in the meds cabinet would do nothing for whatever the hell this was.

"Where does it hurt?" Kayah asked. Stupid question. Automatic.

"My back. My chest . . . feels like a bear hug that won't . . . let go."

Again, Kayah tried to get her to lie down. She couldn't think of anything else to do. Naira's skin was clammy with cold sweat, and Kayah's brain started to pull together pieces of a puzzle she hadn't realized needed solving until now. The last couple of afternoons, coming home from her job as a seamstress, Naira had complained about pain in her back and side. She had pulled muscles on the job before, and this had not seemed much different, though a little more painful. The discomfort had made Naira's sleep uneasy, and this morning she'd been short of breath. Kayah had demanded she stay home and rest, even if Naira missing work might mean a day or two when they wouldn't have enough to eat. The disagreement had turned to a squabble, and the last thing Kayah had said to her mother that morning had been curt and unkind. The memory weighed on her.

Now Kayah glared at the spilled laundry as if it were her enemy. Her mother had been restless. Washed both the city soot and the dirt and manure of the farm from her daughter's clothes. Tried to clean Kayah's room and get the laundry folded and put away. And she'd been struck down.

Heart attack, Kayah thought. *It has to be.*

Which meant there wasn't a damn thing she could do for her mother here in their apartment. Like some trigger had been pulled inside her, Kayah tore from her mother's side and raced from the room. The butchers at the Emergency sometimes did more harm than good; everyone knew that. But right now they were Naira's only hope.

The apartment consisted of five rooms—kitchen, common room, bathroom, and two bedrooms—on the fourth floor of a dingy, half-empty building. Once there had been an elevator, but it had rusted so badly the smell filled the corridors, and it hadn't run since some time before Kayah had been born. Now there were only the stairs, and there was no way that her mother would be able to descend on her own, nor could Kayah carry her. She stood in the common room, a moment of indecision halting her as she glanced at the door and tried to imagine some way to drag her mother down four flights.

Impossible.

Her little sister, Joli, was two floors up, being looked after by Mimi Cheney. The old woman loved taking care of the seven-year-old while Naira and Kayah were at work, and Joli often stayed with Mimi until dinner was ready. But there would be no dinner tonight.

Kayah darted to the corner of the living room, where cracked windows looked down on the street, long unrepaired. The late afternoon sun cast long shadows, throwing much of the road below into darkness. But she heard a whoop of amusement and then a low bark of derisive laughter, and she went to the west facing window.

In the alley below, half a dozen street kids were gathered around, encouraging the efforts of a seventh boy, who stood atop a small tower of rusty barrels, spray-painting a design that would've been lovely if the words hadn't been obscene. Even with the afternoon shadows Kayah recognized most of the kids. Ever since the Cloaks first appeared, people tended to stick to their own neighborhoods. She might not roam the streets with them, but she knew their names.

She had to bang the frame to get the window to give way, and the warped wood shrieked as she dragged it upward. The late summer afternoon had turned cool and the breeze chilled her, despite the blood rushing to her face and the way her heart hammered in her chest. She stuck her head out the window.

"Quinney!" she shouted.

They all turned to look, four boys and three girls, all of them skids. Street kids. Skid marks. The patch left on the ground when their parents tore out of town. Some of their parents had been taken rather than left, but the effect was the same. They were all orphans in one way or another.

Tynan, the boy atop the rusty barrels, twisted around to glance up at her, lost his balance, and fell back against the spray-painted wall before crashing down among the toppling barrels.

The rest of them fell about, laughing at Tynan. All except for Quinney, the tall, ghostly pale, ginger boy they all followed. In his tattered denim and a ragged brown canvas jacket that had once been waterproof, he looked every inch the scavenger and future thug. And maybe he was both, but right then Kayah needed him.

"What is it?" he asked, throwing the words at her as a challenge, even as the others kept laughing at Tynan, pointing at the paint smears on his clothes and arms.

"I need you up here, right now!" Kayah called.

The whoops were predictable. One boy patted Quinney on the back, and a dark skinned girl started to swear, obviously staking her claim on her boyfriend.

"Shut up and listen!" Kayah shouted. "I've gotta get my mom to the Emergency. I think she's having a heart attack, but I can't get her down the stairs by myself."

"And you expect us to carry her down?" one of the other boys sneered. "It's gonna be dark soon."

Quinney slapped the back of the boy's head hard enough that he went sprawling to the ground. Then Quinney looked up at Kayah again.

"You know I'm not your friend," he said, looking up at Kayah.

She wanted to scream. Her hands were shaking and the chill of fear made it feel like her blood had turned to ice in her veins. Was this death approaching? Did she even know if her mother was still alive, back in her bedroom?

"She made the blanket your mother wrapped you in when you were born," Kayah pleaded. "Without help—"

"Kid ain't wrong. Nightfall's coming. You want help, and I want a kiss," Quinney said.

No whooping accompanied the words this time. The girl who'd thought Quinney her boyfriend glared at him. The others grinned or stared in surprise. Tynan whistled in appreciation of the bold callousness of it.

"You son of a—" Kayah began.

"One kiss!" Quinney said, grinning, arms spread wide, as if she were the one being unreasonable.

Kayah glanced up at the eastern horizon, where the deep indigo of dusk had already begun to settle in.

"If she lives," she said.

"Done!" Quinney declared.

He turned and started barking orders, grabbed Tynan and practically flung him from the alley, and in moments, all but two of the skids—one boy and one girl—had vanished from sight. Kayah could hear them shouting at one another as they raced around the front of the building, could hear Quinney's voice as he instructed Tynan to find them a vehicle to beg, steal, or borrow.

A dreadful numbness had started to envelop Kayah. Help was coming, but somehow their imminent arrival made it all the more real. She ought to return to her mother's side; she knew that. But it terrified her to think what she might find. Her mother had been in so much pain that she had vomited next to the sprawl of clean laundry; this woman, always so proper, had lost control of her body. And it was killing her.

Kayah stared down at the boy and girl in the alley, him with curly hair and nearly black eyes, her with that dark skin and a knotted ponytail. Quinney's girlfriend. Kayah expected to see hate in her eyes, but instead she saw pity. Strange that with all of the assaults upon her emotions in the past handful of minutes, this would be what made her cry. But the tears started then.

Shaking, she turned back toward her bedroom, thinking, *Mom.* Thinking, *Don't go, please don't die.* Thinking, *She shouldn't be alone.* Then Quinney was banging on the apartment door. He'd made it up the stairs impossibly fast, or so it seemed. Suddenly time was playing tricks on Kayah.

Like ice shattering, she broke. The world sped up around her. She heard noises outside her apartment, the sounds of people hurrying to prepare for nightfall. She felt the cool breeze and heard her name called from out in the hall, and she moved. Her mother would not die tonight.

Kayah sprinted to the door, threw the lock, hauled it open.

Quinney's playful swagger had been replaced by an intensity she had never seen in him before, though they'd lived on the same apartment block all their lives.

"Where is she?" he demanded.

Kayah led the way, Quinney keeping pace with her. As she hurried into her bedroom, she saw that her mother had slid to the floor after all. Naira lay on her side, skin paled to gray, beads of sweat on her face. She still breathed in quick gasps, as though each sip of air pained her, and as Kayah knelt by her again, Naira shuddered in despair.

"Stavros, grab the blanket," Quinney said.

Kayah glanced up at the skids moving around her. She knew them all. Delmar lived on nine block, but had been hanging around with Quinney and the dark, silent Stavros for years. The scrawny, tattooed girl who'd come up with them was Priya, but she looked skittish, like she'd bolt the second something went wrong.

"Get it together, Kayah," Quinney said. "We've gotta move fast."

She nodded. Who the hell was he to tell her? It was her mother, gasping and shuddering on the floor. And night was coming.

"Give me that," she said, reaching for the blanket as Stavros tried to find its corner. Kayah snatched it from his hand, snapped it open, and spread it on the floor. "Delmar, take her arms."

The burly kid glanced at Quinney, uncomfortable with someone else giving him orders.

"Move it, Del," Quinney snapped. "Lady's dying."

Kayah gripped her mother's ankles, nodded to Delmar, and together she and the skids lifted her onto the blanket. The numbness inside Kayah echoed Quinney's words. *Lady's dying. Oh, spirits, no. The lady's dying.*

"Can I—" Priya began.

"Back up, Pri," Delmar said. "You ain't got the muscle."

The girl scooted backward, moving out of the way so Stavros could move in beside Kayah. Delmar and Quinney each grabbed a top corner while Kayah and Stavros took the bottom edges. At Quinney's signal they hoisted Naira off the floor. To Kayah, her mother felt impossibly, alarmingly light, as though her life had already begun to ebb, leaving her almost hollow.

"Priya," Kayah said. "My little sister's upstairs at Mimi's—"

"I'm gone," the girl snapped, and darted back the way she'd come, understanding immediately.

Joli would have to stay with Mimi for tonight. If they got to the hospital before the Cloaks came for them, they would be fools to do anything but spend the night there. In the morning, if all went well, Kayah would come back and take Joli off the old woman's hands.

If things went poorly . . . Mimi would be looking after Joli for a lot longer than one night.

"Quickly, now," Delmar said, and Kayah wanted to hit him. What a stupid thing to say. Did he honestly think she needed that prodding?

Quinney caught her eye, and Kayah saw that he understood. It stilled her frantic heart long enough for her to focus on the moment, and on her mother. Kayah stared down at Naira as they hustled her through the living room, maneuvered her through the apartment door, and started down the stairs. A hundred thoughts flitted through Kayah's mind like bits of shattered crystal, each one jagged with another facet of her fear. Was it too hot, wrapped in that blanket? Would it make it harder for her mother to breathe? Would the pain of being carried down the stairs worsen her condition?

She'd seen a body wrapped in a blanket before, an old man named Antonio from down the hall. His apartment had always reeked of garlic and sickness and the smoke from clove cigarettes. But by the time Antonio had come to be wrapped in a blanket, he'd been a corpse, slung over the shoulder of his huge, slow-witted grandson.

The grandson had left Antonio at the curb with an array of metal trash cans that lined the block on rubbish day, still wrapped in his blanket. The thought made fresh tears spring to Kayah's eyes, but she bit her lip and forced them to cease. Her mother was still alive, and Kayah would die herself before she would let Naira be tossed out and forgotten like garbage. Die . . . or kill, if she had to.

As horrible as that had been—that body left at the curb, rolled in a blanket—there were worse ways to die. She refused to think about that. Come nightfall, she would have no choice, but there was still light in the sky.

Soft grunts and whimpers issued from Naira's lips as they bundled her down the stairs, turning at the landings. Stavros seemed not to care, but Quinney and Delmar both wore deep frowns of concern, and more than once Kayah saw them wince when they thought they had hurt Naira.

"Watch it, Stavros," Quinney snapped as they reached the first floor and Stavros backed through the door into the building's dingy lobby.

"I can do fast or I can do gentle," Stavros muttered. "Kinda hard to do both."

Quinney shot him a hard look. "Try harder."

A wave of gratitude flooded through Kayah. It felt ridiculous—Quinney had stuck up for her mother, not saved her life; that was yet to come—but it was something. It said Quinney didn't think her death was a given, that he believed there was a chance to save her. That meant everything.

Priya came rushing down the stairs behind them. "Mimi's got your sister, but we're losing daylight fast!"

Down below, Tynan popped his head through the building's entrance.

"We've got a truck!" he shouted before turning to bolt out the door again. "Come on!"

A truck. Kayah burned with hope and fear in equal measure, but now she felt a new rush of strength coursing through
her. Getting to the hospital before dark would have been a fantasy without transport, but she had put her faith in these kids.
If they knew how to do anything, it was improvise.

She adjusted her grip on her corner of the blanket and
moved with the skids toward the front door. She had avoided
looking at Naira's face and now she glanced down, watching
the pain moving her mother's unconscious features, as if she
were asleep in the grip of some endless nightmare.

Then they were outside, the wind blasting the neighborhood's stink—a familiar odor of rust and sewage and cooking
grease—full in her face. Far off, a siren blared, but she knew
it wasn't coming toward them. It would be too much to hope
that someone in authority would come to their aid. As dusk
neared, even the police went into lockdown. The Cloaks didn't
care much about badges.

"Where the hell is—" Delmar started.

A horn blared, and they all turned to see the battered,
filthy white delivery truck that sat half on the curb and half
in the street. The big door at the back had been rolled up,
and Tynan stood behind it with a case of whiskey in his
arms. He hurled the case to one side to make space in the
truck, and Kayah heard bottles shatter. There were other
cases there, dozens of them, and as the wind shifted she
smelled the sweet, powerful aroma of alcohol. It ran in the

gutter, sluicing into an ancient, cracked sewer grating.

"Let's go!" Tynan said. "Almost ready."

Kayah, Quinney, Delmar, and Stavros practically ran toward the rear of the liquor truck, despite their burden. Naira had ceased to cry out in pain, unconscious but still breathing for the moment.

A tall cinnamon girl called Song stood in the back of the truck. One by one, she chucked cases of vodka and rum and whiskey down to Tynan, who tossed them aside.

"That's it!" Tynan said. "There's enough room."

Swift and careful, Kayah and the boys slid her mother into the truck. Naira's face was bathed in sweat and her breath came in shuddering little gasps.

"Stop . . ." a voice groaned from around the other side of the truck. "You can't . . ."

Kayah tore herself out of the cloud of her anguish long enough to glance around the corner of the truck. The last of Quinney's little tribe—a wiry, cruel eyed, blond girl named Hope—had the heel of her boot pressed down on the skull of a bearded man in stained work clothes who could only have been the truck driver.

When the driver saw Kayah, his eyes lit up, as if he had mistaken her for someone who might rescue him. And another day he might not have been mistaken. She would have stepped in, driven the others away.

"He wouldn't let us take the truck," Hope explained.

"You can't . . . ," the driver said. "It's gonna be dark—"

Hope kicked him in the back of the head. "So go inside. No one's stopping you."

The man cried out and curled himself into a protective ball. Kayah noticed that one side of his face had begun to swell, and his mouth was smeared with blood from the beating he'd already received. But her mother would die without transport, so sympathy and regret would have to wait for another day. And Hope was right—if he banged on doors, somebody would let him in . . . as long as there was still some light in the sky.

"Kayah!" Quinney called.

Delmar ran for the front of the truck as Quinney, Priya, and Tynan climbed into the back. Quinney and Tynan reached down and each took one of Kayah's hands, hauling her up after them. Stavros stood in the road with Song, watching them as the truck's engine growled to life. Hope had already begun going through the cast aside liquor cases, sorting through shattered glass to find the bottles that were unbroken. The three skids that were staying behind would go back inside, lock the building up, and have themselves a party.

With a final glance outside, Kayah felt hopelessness descend. The sky overhead bled indigo and the sun had already touched the western horizon. They would never make it. She thanked whatever god might be listening that the skids were crazy enough to try, as if running the gauntlet of dusk was an adventure that had always been waiting for them. All it had needed was the trigger, the dare that had come in the form of Naira Fallon's heart attack.

"Stand back," Kayah said, grasping the handle over her head and dragging the door down, even as the truck lurched into gear.

The door bounced upward a few inches, but Kayah forced it down again, and this time the latch clanked into place. She thought of Joli, back at Mimi's place, and was just happy that her little sister had someone to look after her from now on.

They rode in near darkness, listening to her mother's ragged, shallow breathing and soft moans of agony. Five people, jammed in among stacked cases of wine and liquor, forced into a closeness Kayah had never shared with anyone. Touching their skin. Breathing their air. Smelling their scents. Physical intimacy, yes, but something more. Mortal intimacy. The knowledge that death waited just a breath away.

She'd never been so close to anyone, and she had never felt so alone.

Kayah held her mother's hand, searching Naira's face for signs of consciousness. The truck swayed back and forth, and when Delmar took a hard turn they all had to brace themselves. Naira lay atop a rumpled mess of unfolded blanket, unmoving except when Delmar's driving made her head loll to one side or the other, her face pale in the sliver of light that came through the small gap beneath the door.

"Is she still breathing?" Quinney asked, his voice gentler than Kayah had ever heard it.

Kayah gave a single, curt nod, but her mother's breathing was so shallow that she held on to Naira's wrist, feeling for a pulse. It was there, but faint.

"I wouldn't take any bets," Priya muttered.

Quinney hissed at her to be silent, but Kayah paid her no attention. Quinney and his crew watched one another's backs because none of them—not a one—had anyone else to look out for them. Tynan and Quinney had no parents, while Priya had parents who didn't give a shit. Delmar lived with his junkie older sister. Kayah had always felt sorry for the skids. Though she and Naira fought plenty, she knew how fortunate she was to have a mother to go home to, someone who would never shut her out and who would love her no matter what mistakes she made. The rest of them might envy her that love, but they could never understand how much Kayah truly cherished it, or how much she feared losing it.

Tires screeched as Delmar took another sharp turn, and the truck canted dangerously to one side.

Tynan banged on the wall, screaming for Delmar to be more careful. "Getting us to the Emergency's no good if you kill us on the way!"

"You want us to slow down?" Priya asked. "You saw the skyline."

"Dead's dead either way," Tynan said. He drew back his jacket to display the gun tucked into the waistband of his jeans. "We get caught outside, we got a chance, but he plows us into a storefront, we don't live to see the sun come up."

Kayah caught his eye, and he grinned at her. Tynan had a skittish, manic energy and a talent for saying the wrong thing, but she knew he meant well. She mustered a wan smile, then focused again on her mother. Kayah pushed Naira's hair out of her face. Her clammy skin had turned cool and seemed even paler now, though that could have been Kayah's imagination.

The stink of gas and chemicals filled the back of the truck, overcoming the stale, sweet smell of old whiskey that had soaked into the floor and the crates. Kayah pulled up her shirt to cover her mouth, but kept her other hand firmly on her mother's wrist, feeling the thready flutter of her pulse.

"God, the smell," Tynan groaned.

"Gotta be the refinery," Quinney said. "Means we're only a few blocks from the Emergency."

He glanced at Kayah as he said this last bit, trying to reassure her. But she barely saw him, staring instead at the narrow gap at the bottom of the truck's rear door. There had been a hint of light there before—but now there was only darkness.

Nightfall.

Kayah slumped back against liquor boxes. Hollow, utterly empty inside, she glanced up at Quinney as if this pale, rough-hewn, ginger boy might be able to remake the world, to spin it backward to a time before darkness meant death.

The truck rocked to one side, the engine roared as Delmar gunned it, and then just as abruptly they came to a juddering halt. Quinney ratcheted the latch back and hauled the door open. Tynan jumped out into the parking lot, shouting for help.

"Quiet, idiot!" Priya barked as she followed him out.

Into the dark.

Time had seemed to flicker past while they drove, but Kayah saw that long minutes had gone by, and a blue-gray filter had fallen across the city. In the parking lot, cars shone in the wan yellow light of the rising moon.

"Go," Quinney breathed.

The word snapped her back to reality. Kayah leaped out the back of the truck, dropped to the pavement, and turned to grab the edge of the blanket. Quinney and Priya slid her mother to the edge, and Kayah grabbed hold as Priya jumped down to help her. Naira's face had gone slack and her chest seemed to have stilled.

No, Kayah thought, feeling the night around them and fearing they had risked all of this for nothing.

The city air had gone still. Even the breath in her lungs seemed to stop moving as she and Hope held either side of the blanket and Quinney jumped down from the truck to take hold of the fabric with both hands, almost cradling Naira's head. Kayah's mother hung down like a child in a sling, but they had no choice now—no better way. Delmar stayed in the truck, behind the wheel, and Tynan ran for the emergency room doors, the soles of his shoes scuffing the pavement.

"Oh shit . . . ," Priya whispered.

Kayah had been hustling along, arms straight down, trying to glide her mother as smoothly through the parking lot as possible. Trying not to breathe even as she wondered if her mother had stopped. Now she whipped her head up and stared at Priya . . . saw where the other girl was looking, and felt herself deflate. Tears sprang to her eyes.

"No," she said.

Quinney shot her a glance meant to silence her.

Sorrow and anger boiled up inside her as the first tears slid down her face.

"No!" she repeated, louder now.

The emergency room entrance had already been shuttered. At dusk, metal doors and grates would be lowered into place on structures all over the city, but hospital emergency rooms were supposed to remain open at least thirty minutes after nightfall, with armed guards at the doors.

Not tonight. The plate glass windows that looked out on the parking lot were shielded, and the doors were closed up tight.

"Tynan," Quinney rasped, "see if you can get them to open up. Be quick, but be damn quiet."

He glanced up. Kayah didn't dare. They were like ghosts out there in the moonlight, all of them pale and unearthly and easily spotted from above.

Tynan slapped an open palm against the metal doors.

Kayah could hear him hissing quietly, talking low in hopes that whoever was on the other side would open up. She could barely make out the words, but the phrase "dying woman" floated out across the lot as though they had been spoken right into her ear. In the cab of the truck, Delmar swore. Kayah and Priya and Quinney shuffled toward the blocked ER entrance with Naira hammocked in the blanket between them, but there seemed little point.

"This is damn stupid," Delmar said in a low voice. "We're dead out here, man. Get in the truck."

Kayah shot him a murderous look. His eyes were wide with fear so complete he didn't even seem to see her. Something broke inside her.

"Quinney," she said as they reached the metal doors blocking the ER. "You guys should go."

Tynan jumped back from the doors, nodding with a kind of manic energy, his arms flailing in a kind of pantomime. "That's what I'm saying. We shouldn't be out here to begin with."

Kayah nodded to Priya. A chilly breeze whistled past them, rustling the bushes off to the right of the ER entrance as the two girls gently lowered the blanket to the ground. Quinney had no choice but to do the same or risk dumping Naira onto the ground.

Kayah crouched by her mother's side, afraid that all of this had been for nothing, but then she saw the shallow rise and fall of Naira's chest and knew they still had a chance. Kayah kissed her mother's cheek and then jumped up and turned toward the metal doors. She slapped a palm against them, the blow echoing across the parking lot and into the night.

"Don't do that," Tynan said.

Kayah put her mouth to the gap between the metal doors. "Please?" she begged. "My mother's had a heart attack. Please!"

"Damn it, shut your—" Tynan began.

"Go," she said. "Just go. I understand."

"We're not leaving you here," he said.

"Maybe *you're* not," Priya replied.

Quinney snapped his head around to stare at her.

Priya sighed, bouncing nervously from foot to foot. "We gotta go, Q. You know it."

"Not if the hospital lets us in."

Kayah touched his hand, and he froze at the contact. Lifted his gaze slowly and stared at her.

"Thank you," she said. "But they're right."

Quinney hesitated again. "We had a deal."

For half a second she didn't remember. Then she stared at him. "You're crazy."

He gave her a sad, hopeless sort of smile, and for the first time Kayah understood that Quinney had not come with her for a kiss or to save her mother or out of some manic courage. He had helped her because he had grown tired of being afraid all the time.

"Count to ten and decide if you want to put your mom back in the truck," he said. "We're leaving. You stay, it won't just be *her* heart that stops tonight."

He started to walk away.

"Quinney," Kayah said softly, and when he turned, she rushed over and kissed him softly on the cheek. Then she shoved him backward. "Go."

The others urged him on. Delmar started up the truck, and it growled loudly to life, the noise rumbling across the lot. Kayah pounded on the ER door four times in rapid succession and called out for someone to let her in.

Over the truck's engine she could barely hear the voice from inside telling her to go away.

"Not a chance!" she snapped. "Let me in or you're killing me and my mother both!"

Behind her, Priya called to Quinney.

Once. Then a second time, and the second time her voice was full of despair, almost a moan. Tynan swore and Quinney snapped at them all to get into the truck, hissed at Delmar to roll up the driver's window.

Kayah turned and saw them running for the back of the truck. Tynan had his gun out, and now she saw Priya flip up the back of her jacket and slip her own nine millimeter from a thin holster clipped to her belt. Quinney glanced up at the sky as he ran. A shadow passed through the moonlight, and then, even over the rumble of the truck's engine, Kayah heard the sound, like the unfurling of a heavy canvas flag.

She looked up.

The Cloaks circled above, leather wings outstretched and long necks extended. Kayah had seen them from inside, cruising the night skies as if flying itself was enough of a pleasure to keep them contented. They sailed in the moonlight, and for a moment the wind gusted and the updraft off the face of the hospital pushed them higher. But she knew they would not stay aloft.

She twisted around and lifted a hand, ready to pound on the metal doors. Her hand never fell. Whoever stood on the other side had not been willing to open the door before—they would never do it now that the Cloaks had arrived.

Kayah knelt by her mother's side again and took her hand. In the moonlight Naira's eyes were open and gleaming, staring up at her.

"Momma?" Kayah said.

Naira couldn't speak. Pale and sweating, brow furrowed with pain, she couldn't manage a word, but she was alive.

In her eyes, Kayah could see the reflection of the Cloaks circling overhead.

She saw the first one dive toward the ground.

Delmar put the truck into grinding gear, and it lurched and began to roar away. Kayah closed her eyes.

"Damn it, girl, fight!" Quinney shouted as he lunged past her and slammed into the metal barrier. He banged on the ER door once, twice, a third time.

The first of the Cloaks arced down toward them, leathery wings fluttering. Kayah covered her mother's body with her own. Quinney swore again, and she glanced up in time to see him turn, take aim with his gun, and shoot the Cloak in the head.

It screamed—the sound spiking through her brain—and crashed into the pavement only feet away. For several heart-beats it lay still, but then she heard the wet sounds of the crea-ture peeling itself from the ground, and it began to push itself up on hands and feet that were dry, black leather, but some-how almost human.

"They left you," Kayah said, numb inside. *You're in shock*, she thought. But still the idea that the others had let Quinney get out of the truck, let him fight to save her, astonished her.

"Or I left them," he said, stepping up and firing at the grounded Cloak again before he turned to her. "Now we're going."

Quinney grabbed her wrist and yanked her away from her mother. Her feet were moving before she even realized it. Thirty yards away, the truck bumped to a stop, and the back door rolled up. Tynan and Priya stood in the open back of the liquor truck, outlined in the moonlight, firing at the Cloaks that began to descend as if they had a hope in hell of doing anything but slowing the things down. Bullets weren't enough. They had to take the monster's heads and set them on fire.

Fire, she thought, a sliver of hope rising in her. The liquor would burn all too well. In that moment, she allowed herself to rush toward the truck with Quinney, who continued to yank her along as he fired at two Cloaks who slid down through the moonlight toward them, long hands out and mouths gaping, silver teeth gleaming.

They darted away, avoiding the gunfire, and in that moment Kayah realized her mistake.

"Shoot them!" she screamed, grabbing Quinney's gun hand and trying to force it around.

He did, but too late. Her hands opened and closed emptily and then she grabbed for his gun, tried to wrest it away from him so that she could do the shooting herself. So that she could do *something*.

The Cloaks alighted around her mother. One of them ripped the blanket away with those long, black talons, so like human fingers. Naira flipped onto the ground between them as a third Cloak landed next to the other two and grabbed hold of her mother.

"Come on!" Tynan shouted from the back of the truck.

Gunshots cracked the air, bullets slicing upward toward the Cloaks who dove at the truck. Tynan and Priya were protecting themselves. Kayah fought with Quinney over his gun, and finally he just let her take it.

She screamed as she marched toward the creatures crouched around her mother. Tears slid down her face as she pulled the trigger, emptying the magazine. Two of the Cloaks went down, but in the space between breaths they were stirring again.

Quinney shouted her name, but she figured he was running for the truck.

Like Kayah should have been.

Like her mother would have wanted her to.

The last Cloak turned to sneer at her.

A burst of blinding light made her cry out and shield her eyes. The Cloaks began to scream, and she heard the ripple of their leathery wings as they jerked backward. They turned their backs to the enormous battery of solar lamps that shone down from above the ER entrance, and smoke rose from their flesh. The Cloaks stood up straight, wings wrapped around them as they padded away, unable to fly as long as they needed the wings to shield them. Wings furled, they looked like darkly hooded men, sinister figures in cloaks, lurking in the dark corners of human nightmare.

Just beyond the reach of the lights, the Cloaks began to shriek at the nighttime sky and spread their wings once more, leaping up into the darkness.

Kayah aimed Quinney's gun at the moon, hoping to shoot them, before remembering that she had run out of bullets.

The truck began to roar in reverse, Delmar coming back for them. Or at least for Quinney.

With a loud clanking, the metal doors in front of the ER began to roll upward.

Kayah and Quinney spun to see a scowling, white haired man step out into the glare of the solar lamps with a pair of women in security uniforms behind him. The guards carried assault rifles and hustled out, trying to cover Kayah and Quinney and the rumbling truck and the perilous night sky all at the same time.

"Idiot kids," the scowling man said. "Get inside. You've got about thirty more seconds of this light. We don't have the power to keep the lamps on for longer—that's why the damn doors were closed!"

The skids were already running from the truck, lured by the promise of the open door. They would be safe in the hospital until morning came, and they could go back to their lives.

Quinney gave Kayah a push and she started moving too.

"My mother—" she began, and the two of them turned together. They would take Naira inside, and the doctors would see to her.

Except that her mother had begun to writhe on the ground. Smoke rose from her face and seeped out from inside her clothes. Kayah couldn't move. The breath froze in her lungs, and the tears dried on her cheeks.

Beside her, Quinney spoke her name, oh so gently. That made it worse. His tenderness made it real.

On the pavement between Kayah and Quinney and the open doors of the ER, Naira began to howl in anguish. The armed guards and the white haired man jerked backward, ducking back inside. Beyond them, in the darkened corridor of the ER, Delmar and Tynan reappeared, trying to get a glimpse of what transpired outside.

Naira's scream cut off.

She bucked against the ground, more smoke rising from her flesh, and then she began to crawl. Kayah moved then, reaching for her, whimpering a word that might have been "momma." Quinney slammed into her, wrapped his arms around her, and yanked her out of the way as Naira scrabbled and slithered past them, dragging herself out beyond the reach of the sunlamps.

The sunlamps, whose battery life was ticking down to nothing.

The doctor and the security guards shouted at them to get inside, but Kayah felt as if they spoke to her from some other world, from beyond the wall between day and night. Hollowed out inside, she watched her mother rise from the pavement, there in the shadows at the edge of the pool of light.

Naira rose, shuddering, and the sound was like tearing leather.

The wings ripped out of her back and spread wide, then wrapped around her in a healing cocoon. A shroud. A cloak.

Quinney grabbed her face, turned her toward him. "Kayah!"

She fought him off, watching as her mother took flight, slipping up into the night sky as if she had been born to the moonlight. Almost beautiful.

"Come on!" Quinney shouted in her ear.

Kayah looked at him, met his gaze, and saw his regret.

"They bled her," he said. "You did everything you could, but they're gonna come back, Kai. We've gotta go inside!"

Voices were shouting from the ER. She glanced over and realized that she had been hearing a grinding noise for several seconds—the sound of the metal barriers rattling back down in their frames. The sunlamps flickered and began to dim, leaving bright afterimages in her eyes.

"Come inside!" Quinney insisted.

Kayah breathed. She stared at him. "You know I can't."

"Kai—"

"You know where she's going."

Quinney swore. He pressed his eyes shut for a second and then turned to stare out at the black silhouettes of the city at night, the buildings in the distance and all the open space in between.

They both knew where Naira would be flying. When the Cloaks bled someone, when they reproduced like that, the newborn monstrosity rose into the dark with only one objective—to return home and kill everyone they found there.

Joli, Kayah thought.

"Quinney," she said, taking his face in her hands. Turning him toward her, just as he had done a moment ago. "She's all I have left."

The truck still idled, engine growling, not thirty yards away.

Kayah and Quinney stood face-to-face as the metal doors of the ER rattled all the way down and locked into place and the sunlamps flickered out, leaving them in darkness.

They began to run.

Christopher Golden is the *New York Times* bestselling author of *Snowblind*, *Dead Ringers*, *Tin Men*, and many other novels for adults and teens. With Mike Mignola, he cocreated the comic book series Baltimore and Joe Golem: Occult Detective. His books are available in more than fourteen languages around the world. Golden was born and raised in Massachusetts, where he still lives with his family.

Website: christophergolden.com
Twitter: @ChristopherGolden
Facebook: facebook.com/christophergoldenauthor

Chlorine-Damaged Hair, and Other Pool Hazards

KENDARE BLAKE

He'd called her a mermaid, but he was the only one who did. She moved through water like she was made for it, he said. Like she had fins. Gills. She supposed it was a strange compliment. But it was nicer than the things that other people said. Things like Darla the Doberman. Darla the Dog. They barked at her when she took her mark. They barked again when she won her race. Even her teammates—and over time the insult had become almost a cheer, as if she really were Darla the Dog, their amazing swimming mascot, who jumped in to fetch floating balls and shook herself dry upon leaving the pool.

Darla never grew to like the names. She never accepted the role they cast her in, though sometimes it was hard. People liked dogs, after all, and after she won her breaststroke event they liked her plenty. They rubbed her head, and she almost let them. Being the Dog was degrading, but it was still an improvement over the things she'd been called before she made the swim team. Ugly Darla. Fugly Darla. Butterface. As in, sure, she's got a nice body . . . but HER FACE!

And then Jason Fahle called her the Mermaid. Right out in the open. Right in front of everybody. And what Jason Fahle said, nobody thought to question.

Darla sat at a table near the windows of Tom's Anchor and looked out at the quiet docks of the marina after sundown. No one out there now besides a few hunched fishermen, working under swinging lamps. The rich folks had gone home to their stationary houses on green hills, and their boats and daysailers would float quietly, untouched until the weekend. Darla liked the ocean at night. The ocean in the day was a bimbo with a broad smile, distracted and dumb. But at night what waves there were lapped restlessly at the sand and the wood, as if trying to puzzle them out. At night the ocean cared more about watching than being watched, and staring into the dark water felt to Darla almost like company.

She often came to Tom's Anchor at night, after her shift ended down the street at the Bay Club, the fancy restaurant where she'd worked for the last year, part-time during school and full-time in the summer. The manager who hired her had said she'd be out of the kitchen and waiting tables in three months. Almost a year later she was still in the back, washing dishes. They only let her out to bus after closing. A face like hers didn't belong around people trying to eat a meal. No one had said so to her directly, of course, but she knew what they were thinking.

Darla sighed and propped her feet up on the chair opposite. Her feet always hurt after she worked or stood for too long. It didn't matter how many supportive insoles she bought. Her feet were useless things, unable to bear weight. She looked out the window back at the waves until her eyes lost focus. The corners of the windowpanes at Tom's were dirty and speckled with fly dirt. Enough to be visible even during the late hours, when the only light inside was from the dusty lamps and equally dusty and cockeyed wall sconces. She thought how she ought to stop holding out hope of fattening her wallet on rich people's tips, and come to work here. Here, they'd let her out front. She could bust the fishermen's chops when they lost their sea legs on beer. She could get a better nickname. But there were so many rich people. And so many tips.

Jobs, she thought, and kicked her heel against her schoolbag, where it sat like a loyal pet. Green canvas with frayed edges and a brown leather buckle. It looked old, and a little filthy. No one ever bothered it or asked to see inside. That was a lucky thing, tonight.

"Here you go, hon. No tomato, and steak fries doused with sea salt and vinegar, just as you like."

Rose set down a platter of cheeseburger and fries, and a refill on Darla's Diet Pepsi. She had stuck her thumb into Darla's ketchup, and wiped it dry on her red apron.

"You okay, sweetie?" Rose asked. "You've seemed a bit down, these last few weeks."

"Just tired," Darla replied.

Rose eyed her skeptically, but said, "All right," and walked away, her ample hips and long blond hair swaying. Rose was a kind woman, if not terribly bright, and if anyone cared that she sometimes spilled a drink on you or put her fingers in your ketchup, then no one dared to say so out loud. It was common knowledge at Tom's Anchor that Tom's anchor was Rose, the only woman pretty enough to keep him on dry land after fifteen years of working the boats. Fifteen years on the boats, and another fifteen behind the Anchor's bar, and these days neither Tom nor Rose had much of whatever prettiness had drawn them together. But Tom still smacked Rose's backside whenever she passed him through the kitchen, and Rose winked more often than she brushed his hand away.

It was nice, love like that. It was true. It wasn't meant for Darla, with her hound's face and trash name. Darla. A name for bottle blondes. One day maybe she'd do it, if she could manage to grow her thin, mousy brown mop long enough to bother.

She eyed her fries, and after some staring, ate two. Before she knew it, the platter was empty aside from the garnish of iceberg lettuce. She hadn't figured on eating so fast. Hadn't figured on having much of an appetite at all. But that was all right. Judging by the good-time girl wall clock with the swinging, gartered leg, Jason would already be at the pool, waiting.

The first day he spoke to her was after practice. He came over like it was nothing, towel draped around his neck, T-shirt wet and clinging to every indentation of his chest, and she could say she hadn't blushed, but she'd be a bald-faced liar. Faces reddened routinely when Jason Fahle spoke. He was a man among boys, the kind that, had they been down south, would have been said to give girls the vapors. He had just broken up with Miranda Halverston, a rough, loud, soapy breakup that would have been humiliating for anyone else. But Jason walked the halls half smiling. Eyes front, he stayed in his lane. Darla had noticed that about him. Maybe he had noticed her noticing.

"That was good," he said.

She sat on the edge of the pool, the tiles sloppy with splashed water. She was still in her cap.

"You shaved off a second, I think."

She hadn't. She hadn't even swum particularly well. Darla was a competition swimmer. It was the challenge of unknown rivals that pumped her blood, not the tick of Coach Mathis's stopwatch.

"What are you still doing here?" she asked.

"Hot tub," he replied. "I think I strained something in my shoulder. Maybe I'm overextending."

"Didn't look like it to me. You looked fine. I got here early." She bit down on her tongue before she could explain further. She was on the girls' team. They had practice. She could be at the pool whenever she liked.

"I can tell that about you," he said. "You pay attention. You're focused. Outside of the water, that is."

"I'm focused in the water," she said, her voice low.

"You're driven in the water. There's technique but there's no precision. It's not an insult. You know you're the best on the team."

He leaned down, so close she could count the droplets on his biceps without it seeming like staring.

"You're like a mermaid, Darla," he said. "You swim on instinct."

Darla sat in the alcove of shiny red lockers inside the girls' swim room. The place was tidy as always, with stacks of white towels folded and ready to use and the showerheads sparkling. The school wasn't rich, but what money it did have it threw at sports, swimming first and foremost after the program spat up a string of state champions in the 1990s. Since then the trophy case had continued to grow, with Jason Fahle and Darla the Dog set to bring home another pair of golds.

Darla took a deep breath and wrinkled her nose. The swim room still smelled like chlorine—of course it always would, but the smell of chlorine had never bothered her. Chlorine was her world. It smelled like home and tasted like candy. But chlorine wasn't the only smell. There was something else. Something different, and sinister. Once, when she'd been beachcombing as a child, she'd come across a dead shark. Not a freshly dead shark, but one that had been dead for quite some time, dead and worked on by the ocean as a dog worked down a rawhide bone. It had been covered over by a wave until she looked up, and then the sea rolled back, as if to show her what it had. That shark, with the rotted, pockmarked, sandblasted skin, bits of itself drifting around like it was growing ragged seaweeds, had smelled a little like this. But not quite. That shark hadn't smelled so goddamn thick, so goddamn *heavy*, that it filled her head and made her legs go slack.

For a moment the stench of it almost made Darla change her mind. Only Darla wasn't the kind of person who changed her mind once it was good and made up. And besides, some small part of her had begun to suspect that she couldn't have changed course, even if she'd wanted to.

She slipped out of her backpack and shivered a little despite the humid heat. Her suit was hanging in her locker, probably still damp from practice. But she'd have to put it on. While she changed, the backpack sat on the bench, pulsing slightly.

Sometimes the sea sang. Sirens songs, the fishermen said, to soothe you on a hastened journey home or to lull you to sleep as you were drowning. The night that Jason told Darla where they stood, when she'd waded in up to her waist and felt her clothes moving against her in the black waves, the sea sang only to Darla.

It was cold that night, and the current pulled at her legs. It was strong enough to take her far out to drown if only she would sink, and she regretted she hadn't had the foresight to sew stones into her pants legs and pockets. But when she walked into the sea, she hadn't had any thought aside from the comfort she always felt in the water, the feeling of calm suspension, and sudden muted sounds when she went under. Darla felt that way every time she dove into the pool. She was happiest when her head was down. The roaring of the crowd when she surfaced only drove her back under again, faster. Jason had been right. She moved through the water like she belonged in it. So did he. That's why they made sense, despite their differences. Despite the fact that he was a tanned god and she was the dog-faced girl. In the water they were the same.

Darla let the ocean rock her back and forth that night. She listened to it sing and pull at her clothes as Jason's words ran through her head.

He'd brought her to the pool, the place where they always met. It was where they'd first swum together, and where he'd first kissed her. Where she'd let him take her as far as a girl could go.

"There isn't any way to say this that isn't going to sound shitty. It's Miranda. She wants to get back together. And I still have feelings for her, Darla. I still have feelings for you, too. I mean, I don't want to stop seeing you."

He didn't look sorry. He looked like he meant to look sorry. He looked sly as a tomcat with a live mouse asking to be let in the door.

He talked a lot about Miranda. What their problems were and how they'd fix them, as if Darla cared. Maybe he really thought she did. Maybe he thought she was just that big of a person, just that kind. Then he ran his hands through his hair, like he was suffering, and talked about how he didn't want to give up what he and Darla had. He said their connection was a different kind. That it was on another level. It wasn't a connection for the daylight. He looked at her body as he said those things, the way he always did. Jason hardly ever looked at her face.

He put his hands on her afterward, and she'd let him. She remembered his touch with bile in her throat, and in the sea the waves splashed against her chest and pushed her back. *Stupid girl, stupid girl*, it scolded as it cradled. As it sang.

She was in the ocean for a long time. She didn't know how long. She never felt cold and never shivered. But when she walked home, she caught a glimpse of herself in a silver inlaid sign near the docks, and saw that her lips had turned a strange shade of purple.

By the time Darla changed into her navy blue suit, the swim room was thick with the scent of the thing in her backpack, the thing that smelled like decayed shark and deep waves and nothing like those things at all. Whoever came in first the next morning would run back out immediately with their hand over their mouth and nose. They would report to the main office that something had died in there, perhaps a rat, or a dozen rats, softening in one of the walls.

Darla took a deep breath and scooped her backpack up off the bench.

When she walked out, onto the turquoise and white tile,

Jason wasn't swimming. That's usually how she found him when she was late. She'd walk out of the swim room and into the pool, and he would be lapping around lazily, turning and playing, lounging like an otter on its back.

"You're not in your suit," she said. She didn't need him in his suit, but a suit would make it easier.

"I wasn't sure if I should," he said. "I didn't want to assume things would be just like they were. I saw you, in the hallway. When I was with Miranda."

"And I saw you."

She'd seen him, all right, with his arms snaked around Miranda, one hand stuffed into her shiny, chestnut, society hair, and the other creeping onto her pert, straight A student ass. Creeping, but not quite there. Miranda wasn't Darla. Miranda was a prize. She wouldn't let Jason do the things that a dog would allow him to do.

"I should really go change, then?" he asked, and grinned when she nodded.

That grin. It was so boyish, so guileless. It would ensure that for the rest of Jason's life, he would get whatever he wanted. For some people it was that easy. One empty smile, and here, have the world. But even as Darla resented that, the part of her that had wished for stones in her pockets loved it, and smiled quietly back.

She put her backpack down by the edge of the pool. The scalpels inside made silvery sounds.

Jason came back fast. He must've shimmied out of his clothes like a snake from its skin and left them on the floor. Maybe he even had his suit on underneath. He didn't waste time.

"What's your hurry?" Darla asked. She looked down at his hand on her chest.

"Nothing," he said, and drew it back. "No hurry."

"You have a date or something, after this?"

"No," he said. He grinned that grin. She would never know whether he was telling the truth.

"Good. Then I want to swim first."

Jason dove in. Graceful. He never goofed around in the water. He'd laugh while the rest of the team splashed and dunked and did cannonballs off the board, but he never joined in. Darla had always liked that about him. He respected the water, even if it was sanitized and chlorinated, and tiled in place.

He swam around her in circles for a while. Flirting. Making amends. But then he forgot, and swam off on his own. She waited until he went under for a good, long kick before drifting to the corner and taking the loaded syringe out of her bag.

It was easier to take him down than she thought. She kissed him in the shallow end and bit his ear as she injected him underwater. The hard part came next, when she had to roll him up and out, but Darla was strong, wiry strong, and she got it done.

She pushed out of the water and slid her butt across the wet tiles. When she stood, the bottoms of her feet slapped down loud in the puddles, and she started to worry. Suppose someone found them? No one ever had before, but it only needed to happen once. She reached down for her bag, and in the corner of her eye, saw Jason roll over. Darla spun.

He hadn't moved. He lay on his back, beside the 4FT marker, just where she'd put him.

She didn't think it would feel this way. Nerves and jumps and a cold ball in the middle of her stomach. The waves had made it sound so easy. She took her bag back to where Jason lay and sat down beside him. She let her leg trail into the pool, and that was better. Water always made it better. Soon it would be better for Jason, too.

He started to come around after only twenty minutes, far sooner than Darla expected. Despite the newfound steadiness in her hands, she'd managed to make only the first cuts.

"Darla?"

"Yes, it's me."

"What happened? Did I hit my head?"

She felt him try to move his arms. A good thing she'd restrained him, just in case. The syringes she'd found on the Marine and Wildlife boat had been preloaded, and she had no way of knowing with what dose. It could have been enough to knock out a bull sea lion, or it could have been loaded to take down a muskrat. Judging by the scant time Jason was under, it had been closer to the latter.

"No, you didn't hit your head," she said, kneeling by his legs, still working.

Jason flexed his arms.

"Why am I tied? What's going on? Dar?"

She smiled. He never called her Dar. That was the drugs. Their relationship wasn't one of pet names and sweet whispers. It was swimming and it was sex. Base needs. Instincts. Survival.

"Did you give me something?" Jason asked. "What did you give me?"

"Fentanyl-diazepam. I got it from Marine and Wildlife." And it had been easy. She was on the docks so often that people looked right through her. She could have done it at high noon.

"Why?" Jason asked.

He looked down at himself and started to scream.

Darla held up the reddened scalpel, and he stopped. But she would have to gag him anyway. He was tranquilized, but not exactly anesthetized. Asking for quiet was asking for a lot. She reached across his torso and tore off more duct tape.

"Darla, this isn't funny. I'm not kidding around. I'm serious, goddamn it!"

"You shouldn't have used me, Jason."

"I didn't use you! We're friends. Aren't we, Darla? Aren't we friends?"

She raised her arm. The water in the pool reflected prettily in the silver of the blade.

"Darla, come on. Please. I never, never treated you like a dog."

"No, you didn't. People love dogs."

"Darla."

She slashed once, as a warning, to shut him up so she could stick the tape over his mouth. Talking was getting them nowhere. And they had so much work to do.

It was a gift, was what she thought when it surfaced. The sea gave gifts sometimes, fresh, white fleshed fish, or large perfect pearls, or a slick backed dolphin to lead a boat to harbor. Of course the sea took many things away as well; many, many drowned bodies sucked down and covered over with silt.

Darla stared into the water at the small, dark rectangle. It had lines of ridges running lengthwise on its greenish sides. It drifted in front of her waist, suspended and rocking in the current. She could see it very well, despite the dark and the utter blackness of the water. She couldn't see her jeans more than two inches below the surface, but the edges of the rectangle seemed to shine slightly, almost phosphorescent. It looked like a piece of seaweed, or a seedpod, but it wasn't. It was a—

"Mermaid's purse," she whispered.

She'd seen them before, washed up on the beach. Several different shapes and sizes, different textures. Some ridged like this one and others smooth. Some light, puke green like old canned string beans, others rich as emeralds, yellow or black.

Once she'd seen a fisherman cut a few out of a mother shark's belly. But she'd never seen one like this.

It glowed and twitched and pulsed with the excitement of whatever was inside, and she thought of those beans with larva in them, jumping and popping and waiting to get out.

Around her the wind howled above the sea's song, and the waves were choppy, but she didn't know when that had happened. All had been calm when she'd waded in. Her hair whipped into her eyes, and, above, a long vein of lightning illuminated the water. It was only a flash, but in that instant she saw something a few feet farther out, something black, and twisting, like a tail.

Darla smiled. She reached forward under the waves and grasped the mermaid's purse in her fist.

Darla knew just what to do. She knew just what it wanted. There was something comforting about that, like having it there to guide her through every cut of the scalpel. It felt as sure and natural as when she stroked laps in the pool.

"Can't you hear it?" she asked. "Can't you feel it?"

But it was obvious that Jason couldn't. With his eyes bugged out like they were, moaning and sweating through his gag of tape, it was obvious that he had no confidence in her whatsoever.

She'd started at his ankles, which perhaps she shouldn't have. They were bony and needed to be bound and re-bound together to make sure the cuts would line up right. But it wasn't as if she'd made a butchery of things. The cuts were clean, and straight, which was quite a feat, considering Jason had come fully awake and squirmed and kicked something fierce. In the end she had to lean down and lie across his knees to get it done, and even then he flopped. His heels splashed in the red water welled into the pool tile until she lost her temper and snapped at him. But that wasn't fair. The chlorine had to sting.

"I know, I know," she said as she pulled up the skin of his calf. It made an ugly sound coming away from the muscle, and she grimaced. She had to be careful not to pull up too much. It was surprising, how easy it was. She thought it would be more like slicing meat, feared that it would be tough, like leather or steak, something ragged and in danger of tearing. But the scalpel was sharp. She pressed and skin parted. Like butter.

Jason died from the blood loss. There was nothing she could do about that. She was no surgeon. He cried a little, and she supposed it had been bad. Painful. But it was really so much easier after he stopped struggling, and twitching.

Darla wiped sweat from her face. She glanced up at the clock on the wall, kept up by its metal cage. It had taken a while. Jason was tall. He had a lot of leg. She leaned over and took a breath and rinsed her red hands in the cool water of the pool. Then she wiped her forehead again and adjusted the way she sat before reaching into her backpack for the needle.

• • •

The first time they swam together was a Wednesday night. The pool was quiet. The whole school was quiet, except for the church group of twenty-five or so that gathered in the forum on the other side of the gym. Jason was already swimming when she came in. She watched him for two laps before he paused to check the door and saw her standing there. He grinned wide.

"Great," he said, hanging off the edge. "I wasn't sure if you'd come. Aren't you going to swim?"

Darla looked down at her clothes. She'd wanted to make sure he hadn't stood her up before she changed.

"Yeah. I just wanted to watch a bit, as long as you were already in."

"And? Like what you see?"

"You're dropping your left elbow in the catch," she said.

Jason's smile faded only slightly as he nodded. He could take criticism. He wasn't used to it, but he could take it.

"I'll work on it while you change," he said.

Once she was in her suit, Darla waited until Jason pushed off, and then dove in beside him. He was a freestyler, so that's what she swam. It wasn't her favorite, but she could do it all. They touched their lap dead even, and if he was upset by that, he hid it well.

"You're incredible," he said. "Better than me."

"No one else on the boys' team would admit that," she said.

"Well," said Jason, "I'm not anyone else."

They met again on Thursday night and again the week after that. Jason's times got better. He was easier to talk to than she thought he would be. By the fourth time they swam, she realized she had a crush on him. She probably always had.

The stitches weren't even. They zigged and zagged through the insides of Jason's pale, hairless legs like broken up railroad tracks. Darla hoped they would hold. In the center part of his thigh was a bulge. Inside it was the strange little mermaid's purse, under the skin and pulsing its wrong-placed heartbeat. She'd put the needle away, and the scalpel, after rinsing them clean in the pool. Her bag she set up on the bench even though it was probably ruined, wet and stained eternally red.

"I've got to clean this up," Darla said. "Underneath you."

She took a deep breath and slid both hands under Jason's back and hips, then rolled him up and over, back into the pool with a splash. She tried to ignore the limp way his arm slid across his stomach, and how cold he was. He drifted fast down to the bottom, his lower half trailing blood in a dark crimson cloud. She watched for a minute, just until the red started to fade, and he settled. Then she started to scoop the mess over the edge after him. There was so much blood that it was blood tinged with pool water rather than the other way around, but the pool would clear it all away. She scooped and scooped, pushed redness to the side with her hand flat, like a bulldozer. She splashed and diluted and spread it around until it disappeared.

"Okay," she said, and wiped her hands on a towel. She was exhausted. She wished she'd eaten more at the Anchor than just a quarter pound cheeseburger and salted fries.

"I should have ordered two," she said, and leaned over the side.

Jason was gone. For a mad second she looked up and all around the bleachers, like she'd somehow missed him. But then she relaxed. There he was, curling around the deep end of the diving well. He twisted and darted into the corners. He kicked hard, and Darla smiled. The stitches held.

In the pool, Jason turned his head and looked at her. He seemed unsure at first, but then he swam up fast and launched himself up and out of the water.

His eyes didn't look quite the same without lids, but they were still his, deep blue, and friendly. He pulled his lips back in his signature Jason grin. That didn't look quite the same either, with so many new rows of teeth, but she would get used to that.

He dragged himself eagerly forward, and Darla held her hand out.

"You know, Miranda Halverston has never swum a day in her life," she said.

Kendare Blake binge-watches *The X-Files* every couple of years. Her favorite episode is the one where the virtual reality game starts to really kill people, because she likes to hear Scully say that Mulder is getting his ya-yas out. She's also the author of six novels, including *Anna Dressed in Blood, Antigoddess,* and *Ungodly.*

Website: kendareblake.com

Twitter: @KendareBlake

Facebook: facebook.com/kendare.blake

The Old Radio

R. L. STINE

I'm in Full Panic Mode," Ziggy said. I saw drops of sweat on his forehead, and he was tapping both hands on the table the way he always does when he's stressed.

"Too soon," I said. "Let's give it one more try before we both go into fatal error shutdown." I stared at the pieces of laptop in front of me on the table until they blurred into a solid mass of metal and plastic.

"Connor, why did we do this?" Ziggy said. He brushed back his wavy blond hair. His chin quivered, another sure sign he was about to freak. "Why? What made us think we could do this?"

I blinked hard, making the electronic pieces on the table come back into focus. "We took it apart," I said. "We can put it back together." I kept my voice low and steady. I needed to keep Ziggy calm. I didn't need the big guy to go all berserk on me.

Ziggy and I have been good friends since ninth grade, mainly because we're both tech nerds who think we can build anything, program anything, and figure out what makes everything in the world work. We're friends because we both want to be the next famous computer geniuses, not because our personalities are the least bit alike.

Actually, we're not alike in any way. He's big and flabby and blond and red faced and sweats a lot and wears horrible bad-taste T-shirts with lots of unfunny sayings on the front, usually stained and smelly because he'll wear the same shirt for a week. He's heavy into trap and EDM, I guess because his name is Ziggy, and he knows how to deprogram his PlayStation games and turn them into new games he invents, and even though he's sixteen, same as me, I don't think he's ever had a girlfriend.

On the other hand, I'd be one of the cool kids if I didn't have to wear inch thick glasses and if I cared at all, which I don't. If I keep my mouth shut and you can't see my braces, I'm not a bad-looking guy. I have straight, long brown hair, which I use to hide my ears because they're way too big. I'm almost six feet tall, thin, and lanky. I'm not into sports, but I look like I could be.

I'm the calm one. I'm the one who keeps it together. If Ziggy is fire, I'm ice.

My dream is to invent the next Facebook. I mean, someone has to invent what comes next, right? I don't have any ideas yet. But when I do, I'll be ready, because I'm learning as much as I can.

Which, of course, is why Ziggy and I took apart my mom's

laptop. We wanted to get our minds around every circuit, every chip, every drive, every megabyte, every tiny piece of the hardware. We wanted to know it, to see it, to *absorb* it all.

That's what we do. We take things apart to study them. Then we put them back together. Only, this afternoon we couldn't get the laptop back together. We had it all back in place, except for three printed circuit pieces, which looked kind of important. "Mom is going to be a little angry with me," I murmured.

"Forget your mom. Harry is going to kill you," Ziggy said. His whole face was drenched in glistening sweat now.

Harry is my stepfather, and he has a temper. Although you have to really know him to tell when he's angry. Because Harry never yells. He never raises his voice when he's angry. He's one of these guys who kind of implodes. He gets totally quiet. It's like he only inhales. His eyes get real big and his lips go white. You wait for steam to shoot out of his ears. But he never says a word.

Harry is manager of one of those storage unit places where people stash the stuff they don't have room for. He's always bringing home weird things that people leave behind when they empty out their units.

"You're right," I told Ziggy, shaking my head. "Mom understands that you and I have to experiment. But . . . this is the kind of thing that makes Harry's eyes pop. Like the time we took apart my iPhone to replace the battery."

"That was a major fail," Ziggy murmured.

We both stared down at the computer parts on our work-table. Ziggy tapped his fingers on the wooden tabletop. I picked up a memory chip and tried to slide it into a slot. *"Yes!"*

Outside the window, the afternoon sun was sinking behind the trees. The sky darkened to evening. Ziggy and I were in our workshop. It's the front room of the little two-room guest cottage behind my house. The cottage was sitting empty, just falling apart. So Harry said I could use it as a workshop if I promised to keep it neat.

Right now, it was very neat. Except for the two computer pieces that sat on the worktable, refusing to fit into the laptop. "Let's start the laptop," Ziggy said. "Maybe it'll work without these pieces."

"Fat chance," I muttered.

Ziggy and I nearly jumped off our tall wooden stools when we heard a hard knock on the door behind us.

"It's either Mom or Harry," I said. "We're doomed." My hand trembled as I frantically shoved the two loose computer pieces out of sight. I took a deep breath. Could we fake our way out of trouble?

The door swung open. Harry walked in wearing his blue uniform with his name badge on the shirt pocket. He carried a large wooden object in both hands. It looked heavy. It made a loud *thud* as he set it down on the edge of the worktable.

"This is for you guys," he said, mopping his forehead with

his sleeve. He patted the top of the boxlike thing. "Do you believe someone left this valuable antique in a storage unit?"

I squinted at it. "What is it, Harry?"

His mouth dropped open. "You don't recognize it? It's an old radio. See the dial? The knobs for changing the station?"

"That's what radios looked like?" Ziggy said. He stepped up to it and twisted both knobs in his hands. "Where do the earphones go?"

"Very funny," Harry said, rolling his eyes. "The sound comes out of this speaker." He tapped a rectangle above the round glass dial. It had some kind of brown cloth cover.

"Only one speaker," I said. "No stereo."

Harry shook his head. "What's wrong with you guys? This thing is seriously valuable. It's probably seventy years old. I thought you guys would love it."

I smoothed my hand over the dark polished wood. The radio was in very good shape. Only a couple of thin scratches on one side. "Does it work?" I asked.

Harry shrugged. "Beats me. Plug it in and see. I thought you two would have fun taking it apart and fiddling around with it."

"It's cool," I said. "Thanks, Harry."

He turned to leave, but then stopped. "Hey, is that your mom's laptop?" he asked. "What's it doing here?"

"We're fixing it," I said.

• • •

I slid Mom's laptop to the end of the table and moved the old radio in front of our stools. I clicked the knob on the left a few times. It was obviously the on/off switch. The other knob moved the pointer in the round dial.

Ziggy turned the radio around, and we peered into the back. Several dust covered glass tubes were plugged into a metal chassis. They looked like slender lightbulbs.

"They didn't have chips or circuit boards then," I said. "I read about this. These are called vacuum tubes."

"Weird," Ziggy murmured. He uncoiled the thick brown cord from inside the back. It was a little frayed, but the two-pronged plastic plug was tightly attached. "Let's plug it in. Maybe we can hear some old radio programs."

I laughed. "Wouldn't that be awesome? What if it's some kind of time-warp machine, and it only plays music and stuff from seventy years ago?"

"I think I saw that on a *Twilight Zone,*" Ziggy said.

He plugged the cord in. I clicked the on/off knob. The dial lit up with an orange-yellow glow, but no sound came out. "Not looking good," I said.

But then a crackling sound came out of the speaker. I turned the knob and the crackling grew louder. "Static," I said. "Let's see if we get any stations."

I turned the other knob slowly. The static became a shrill whistle. Then more static. There were numbers printed on the dial. They went from 55 to 160. I moved the pointer a tiny bit at a time. Static and more static. "No stations," I murmured.

"It's broken," Ziggy said. He hopped down from the stool. "Gotta go. Almost dinnertime."

I kept my ear close to the speaker. I moved the dial as slowly as I could. Static. Crackling. Whistling. No voices. No music. "Maybe we can fix it," I said.

Ziggy turned at the door. "Of course we can. We're geniuses, right?"

I stared at the two unattached laptop pieces on the table. "Right," I said.

After dinner I played with Nicky, my four-year-old brother, for a while. We like to have wrestling matches on the living room floor most nights. Nicky likes them because I always let him beat me up.

When Mom took him off to bed, I did some homework. Then I went online and read some things about old radios. At nine o'clock, Mom and Harry were in the den watching a *Law & Order*. They watch that show whenever it's on, which is *always*. I don't think they heard me when I told them I was heading out to my workshop.

A light rain had started to fall. I ducked my head and ran over the wet grass to the front door of the guesthouse. Shaking rainwater from my hair, I clicked on the lights. The old radio glowed darkly on the worktable.

I climbed onto a tall stool and slid the radio around. I

knew why it wasn't working. I peered into the back, fumbled around, and pulled out a slender wire. The antenna. I'd read on a website that old radios needed antennas to work.

The antenna was connected inside the back of the radio. I stretched it out along the edge of the table. It was about three feet long. I turned the radio to face me and clicked it on. Once again, the dial lit up instantly. About fifteen or twenty seconds later, the speaker began to crackle with static.

I circled my fingers around the knob and slowly began to move from number to number. Static. Still nothing but whistling and static. Until the dial landed on number 70.

I nearly fell from the stool when a man's voice came from the speaker. "What do you expect me to do?" he said. As clear as if he were in the room with me.

I froze with my fingers around the dial. And listened.

"Just forget about it for once," a woman said. "Cut me some slack for once in your life."

"She's right, Nate." Another man's voice.

"You shut up! Shut up, Mike!" Nate screamed angrily. "Do I need your face in my business?"

"Nate, I'm not going to apologize," the woman said. Her voice trembled.

This is some kind of drama, I thought. *Maybe a play. Or a crime story.*

Do they still have crime stories on the radio?

"You embarrassed me in front of my whole family," Nate

said. "You humiliated me in front of my brother, Mike. Tell her, Mike."

"Leave me out of it," the brother said. "I don't like the way this is going, Nate. You need to get control of yourself. Before—"

"Shut up!" Nate screamed again. "Nothing is good enough for you, Anna. You wanted to move to Glen Mills so we moved to Glen Mills. You wanted a house on Clement Street. I bought you a house on Clement Street."

"Do you want an award, Nate?" Anna shouted. "Do you want the Nobel Prize because you bought us a decent house?"

Whoa.

I jumped to my feet.

I live on Clement Street. I live on Clement Street in Glen Mills.

This isn't a radio play, I realized. *These people live on my street? This is really happening?*

No way!

I forced myself to breathe. My mouth was suddenly dry as cotton. Was I listening in to someone's conversation? Someone in my neighborhood?

"Put that down, Nate!" the woman shrieked. "Control yourself. Put that down. I'm begging you."

"Nate—don't do it," the brother warned. "It isn't worth it. Is it? Is it worth years in jail?"

"Nate, please—" The woman was begging now.

I jumped as I heard a loud crash. And then the woman's

scream of horror rang out, making the radio speaker vibrate. "Stop! You're killing me! Stop! Get *off* me! *Stop!*"

The woman screamed again. But the scream cut off suddenly. And then . . . silence.

My heart pounded in my chest as I listened with my ear to the speaker.

Then the sound of footsteps came through the old radio. Running footsteps and heavy breathing. "I'm outta here," Nate said in a whisper. "Mike, you coming with me?"

Gasping for breath, I clicked the radio off. I stood there, watching the dial light slowly fade. The woman's shrill scream still rang in my ears. "That wasn't real," I said out loud. "That couldn't be real."

I started to the door, but it swung open before I reached it. "Harry!" I cried.

He stood in the rain, squinting at me. "Your mom and I didn't know where you were, Connor. What were you doing?"

"Listening to the radio," I said.

The next morning Harry had already left for work when I came down to breakfast. His plate with a few uneaten scrambled egg clumps was in the sink. Mom was on the phone. She stood at the counter with her back turned, twisting the phone cord in her fingers. (Yes, we still have a landline.)

I crossed the room and poured some corn flakes into a bowl. Mom hung up the phone and turned to me, a troubled frown on her face. She stared past me, as if she didn't see me standing there.

"Mom, what's wrong?" I asked.

She shook herself, as if trying to clear her head. "I just heard the most shocking, dreadful thing," she said, still avoiding my eyes.

I set down the milk carton. "What? What is it?"

"That was Carol across the street. She just told me the most awful news. Anna Perrin. You know. The Perrins, who live on the corner across Park Drive? Anna Perrin was found murdered this morning. And her husband and his brother are both missing."

My mouth dropped open and a squeak escaped my throat. I couldn't breathe. I couldn't speak.

Mom shook her head. "Such a terrible thing. And just a few houses down from us."

"Mom—" I finally found my voice. "Mom—I heard it. I-I heard the whole thing," I stammered.

Mom made a gulping sound. She narrowed her eyes at me. "Oh, Connor, no. Is that true? You heard the murder from your bedroom?"

"No," I said, my voice trembling. "I heard it on the radio."

She pressed both hands against the kitchen counter, as if keeping herself from collapsing. "That isn't funny," she said softly. "A nice woman we all knew was killed last night. Why would you make a dumb joke like that?"

"It . . . isn't a joke," I choked out. "Harry gave me an old radio and—and—" My heart was pounding like crazy. I heard the men's angry voices again and the woman's horrifying scream cut short so suddenly.

"Mom, I was trying to find stations on the old radio Harry gave me, and I heard the murder. I'm not making this up. I heard Mrs. Perrin's husband. He . . . he threatened her. And I heard her scream. And . . ."

Mom crossed the room. She placed both hands on my shoulders. "I can see you're in shock about the murder," Mom said. "Perhaps I shouldn't have told you about it first thing in the morning when you're just waking up. Do you want to see a counselor? I can call Dr. Ackerman this morning. It will help if you talk to someone, Connor."

I took a deep, shuddering breath. I desperately wanted Mom to believe me. But as she stood there studying me, holding me by the shoulders, trying to calm me down, I realized it was impossible. Of *course* Mom wasn't going to believe that I heard Anna Perrin's murder on my radio. Why would *anyone* believe it?

I heard a noise at the kitchen table. I turned and saw Nicky sitting there. I didn't even realize he was in the kitchen. He had oatmeal smeared all over his face. He even had some clumps in his hair. "I spilled a little," he said.

Mom grabbed a bunch of paper towels and hurried to clean him up.

"Hey, listen. I'm okay," I told her. "I'm going to school. Don't worry about me, Mom. Take care of yourself, okay?"

She was bent over Nicky, trying to get him to hold still so

she could wipe his face. "Connor? No more crazy radio talk?"

I nodded. "No more crazy radio talk."

As soon as I got to school, I pulled Ziggy out of homeroom, dragged him to an empty science lab at the end of the hall, and blurted out the whole story.

Ziggy laughed. He didn't believe me either.

I raised my right hand and swore I was telling the truth. He just stood there staring at me with this amused look on his pudgy face.

"Ziggy, the woman really was murdered. Why would I make up a crazy story about it?" I demanded.

He scrunched up his face. "Because you're weird?"

"Come to the workshop after school," I said. "Maybe we can hear something else on the old radio. Something from real life. Then maybe you'll believe me."

He shook his head. "Can't. No way. My cousin Ivy is sick and Mom is taking me to her house to entertain her."

I squinted at him. "Entertain her? How are you going to entertain her?"

Ziggy shrugged. "Beats me."

I thought about the radio all day. I knew I hadn't imagined those voices. I had listened in on an actual murder. The thought gave me the shivers and made my stomach feel as if it were turning somersaults.

I hurried home after school. Harry was still at work. Mom left a note on the fridge saying she had taken Nicky to his toddler playgroup.

I darted into the workshop, clicked on all the lights, hoisted myself onto a tall stool at the table, and hunched over the radio, leaning into the yellow-orange glow of the tuning dial. I turned the dial slowly, moving to one end, then the other. Static . . . nothing but whistling and static.

One more try. I moved the dial slowly, my face close to the speaker.

I let out a startled cry when a man's voice erupted in my ear. My hand shot off the dial. I stared at the radio.

"I think we have a problem," the man said. I held my breath. I recognized his voice. From last night. Nate Perrin.

"What kind of problem?" I recognized that voice, too. Nate's brother Mike.

"I think we weren't alone last night," Nate said, his voice hushed, just above a whisper. "I think someone heard us."

His words sent a tight shiver to the back of my neck. I gripped the tabletop. My hands were suddenly cold and wet.

"Don't be crazy," Mike told his brother. "We were alone. There wasn't anyone in the house. And when we got out of there, there was no one on the street."

"Someone heard," Nate insisted. "There's a witness. I know it."

"Oh wow," I murmured. Another shiver rolled down my

body. I realized I was trembling in fright. *This isn't happening.*

"You're being paranoid, Nate. Get over yourself. We've got real worries," Mike said. "How long before the police figure out where to find us?"

"Someone heard everything," Nate said, ignoring his brother. "That's a problem we have to take care of. We can't have a witness, Mike. No way we can have a witness out there."

I realized I was still holding my breath. I let it out in a long whoosh. *They can't know about me—can they? They can't know I was listening. That's impossible.*

"I think I know how we can find this person," Nate said. "I think I can track him down. We have to take care of him, Mike. We have to take him out. You know I'm right."

"I *don't* know you're right. I think you're talking crazy, Nate. I say we get the plane tickets and get out of here while we have the chance."

"I want to see if I can trace who was listening," Nate said. "Meet me here at eight, okay? Be here at eight sharp. Then you and I can decide what to do."

"Okay. Eight sharp. But don't do anything on your own. Don't do anything till we decide."

"Okay, Mike. No problem. See you here at eight o'clock."

The radio went silent. I stood there, staring at the glowing dial, my arms crossed tight in front of me, trying to stop the shudders that shook my body.

Eight o'clock. I've got to be back here at eight. I have to listen to what they decide to do.

My brain did flip-flops in my head. I kept hearing their voices. Replaying what they said, a jumble of frightening words repeating and repeating in my mind.

"I have to get help," I said out loud.

I clicked off the radio, turned off the lights, and staggered out of the guesthouse, my legs as shaky as Jell-O. Mom's car was just pulling up the drive. I ran over to it, waving my arms and screaming. "Mom! I've got to talk to you! Mom!"

She rolled down her window. "Connor, take Nicky into the house. I can't stay. I have to go meet Harry right away. You'll have to babysit for him."

"But, Mom—"

"Dinner is in the fridge. Just nuke it for three minutes. We'll be home pretty late. Take care of Nicky, okay?"

"But Mom, I have to tell you something. About the radio. I just heard—"

She sighed. "You promised. No crazy radio talk. Remember? I don't have time now. Get Nicky into the house. I'm already late."

My head spinning, I pulled Nicky from the car and led him into the house. I saw Mom back down the drive and roar away.

I'll call the police. The words flashed into my mind. *I have no choice. I'll call the police.*

"Can we wrestle now?" Nicky said, wrapping his arms around my leg and trying to pull me down to the floor.

"No. Not now. Give me a break." I pried him off me.

"I'm hungry."

"I'll make dinner in a minute," I said. I handed him Harry's iPad. "Here. Play with this." Harry hated for anyone to touch his iPad. But I was desperate.

Nicky carried it to the couch, plopped down, and started poking things with his finger. I crept to the kitchen, closed the door so he wouldn't hear, and dialed 911.

The call didn't go well.

The receptionist put me on the line with a gravelly voiced police officer. As soon as I told him I heard the murder last night on the radio, he started shouting. "Is this a school psych experiment?" he demanded. "Or is it just your idea of a funny prank? Did you know there's a very strict penalty for interfering with a police investigation?"

I apologized and hung up. I hugged myself to stop the trembling. *You weren't thinking clearly, Connor,* I told myself. *What made you think any police officer would believe you?*

I had no choice. I had to be in front of that radio at eight o'clock. Then I would hear my fate. Then I would hear if I really was in serious danger. *Maybe Nate and Mike will decide I'm not worth bothering about. Maybe they'll go to the airport instead and make their escape.*

Eight o'clock. I had to be at that radio at eight.

I gave Nicky dinner. I picked at my food a little, but I couldn't eat. My stomach was doing somersaults again. I tried to act normal. I wrestled with the kid for a while after dinner, but I kept my eye on the clock the whole time.

He wasn't into it, either. He was cranky and tired from his playgroup. He went a little berserk, punching me as hard as he could in the stomach with both fists. I tucked him into bed a little after seven thirty, and he barely protested.

A few minutes later the little guy was sound asleep. Not a care in the world. I checked the kitchen clock. Ten till eight. I crept out the kitchen door.

It was a windy night. The trees were shivering and shaking, making whispery sounds like in one of those cornball horror movies. The swirling gusts made the lawn tilt one way, then the other.

I was halfway across the backyard when I realized the lights were on in the guesthouse.

I froze. I could feel my heart leap to my throat.

Nate and Mike are already there. Waiting for me. They didn't wait till eight o'clock.

The wind blew a string of scratchy dry leaves around my ankles. The trees suddenly stopped whispering. I squinted into the front window. A shadow moved inside the workshop.

"Waiting for me," I murmured.

I turned back to the house. Should I make a run for it? What about Nicky? I couldn't leave him alone. And . . . I couldn't call the police. I'd already blown my chances with them.

Nate and Mike tracked me down. They know I heard them. They know I heard the whole thing. And now they're here waiting for me.

I stood frozen, my brain spinning, unable to think straight, unable to move. Then, without realizing it, I took a trembling step toward the guesthouse. My eyes gazing into the yellow light of the front window, I took another step.

The door swung open.

And I screamed.

"Connor? What's your problem?" Ziggy shouted.

He stood in the light from the workshop, his big body nearly filling the doorway.

"Ziggy? You're here?" My voice came out tiny and shrill, like a baby's cry.

"I got home from Ivy's house and came right over," he said. "Been waiting for you. Didn't you get my text?"

"Uh . . . no."

My heart refused to stop pounding. My legs felt rubbery and weak, but I managed to cross the lawn to the doorway. Of course, I was relieved to see Ziggy. But I knew my problems weren't over. "Is it eight o'clock yet?" I asked. "Is it?"

Ziggy nodded. "Almost." He pulled out his phone and glanced at it. "Yes. Almost eight."

"The radio—" I murmured. I could barely form words. "Eight o'clock. The radio."

I pushed past him into the workshop. He followed close behind me. "I thought I'd get a head start," he said. He motioned to the worktable.

It took my eyes a few seconds to focus in the bright light. And then I started to choke. "You—you—you *didn't*!"

"I took the old radio apart," Ziggy said. "So now we can put it back together. Do you *believe* all these glass tubes and weird wires?"

I stared at the radio parts scattered over the table. My legs started to fold. I sank onto the stool next to him. I could feel the blood throbbing at my temples. The whole room spun in front of me.

"Hey—what's wrong with you, Connor?" Ziggy asked. "Why do you look so weird?"

I didn't have a chance to answer.

I heard the soft scrape of footsteps outside. And then a pounding *knock knock knock* on the guesthouse door.

"Who's *that*?" Ziggy asked.

R. L. Stine is one of the bestselling children's authors in history. His Goosebumps and Fear Street series have sold more than 400 million copies around the world. He has had several TV series based on his work, and the *Goosebumps* movie stars Jack Black as R. L. Stine himself. Bob lives in New York City with his wife, Jane, an editor and publisher.

Website: rlstine.com

Twitter: @RL_Stine

Facebook: facebook.com/rlstine

Rites of Passage

JADE SHAMES

Sparrow

"Yesterday," said Kelsey, "I saw a sparrow fly around the
living room."
I was fourteen, but even then I knew
there was no sparrow.

At a sleepover in the dark,
I listened to the way her body hushed,
and she told me a secret—
that she could see the colors in music.

She put on "Hey Jupiter."
It was this song
that really hit her hard.
The twisting, unpredictable piano,
a witchy female voice sang in delirium.

I should have known these were the warning signs

of some form of psychosis.

But I was just a boy,

and she was my friend,

a little older,

telling me about things to expect,

and introducing me to new music.

After losing touch with her for many years,

I bumped into a friend who told me she had died

of a drug overdose after a long battle with insanity.

My immediate instinct was to act,

but I probably won't.

I won't petition

or picket for anything,

or build a foundation,

raise awareness,

start a war.

But what's weird is this daydream I keep having

where I fly into her living room,

and even though this is in the past,

I'm not a boy anymore,

and there is Kelsey, picking apart her furniture,

and I place my hand on her head,

and lean in and whisper something I can't quite hear

but I know it's absolutely the most perfect thing—
my whispering acting like water on the fire pit of her mind
she breaks apart into a flock of wild birds,
and the rustling of feathers is like applause,
and each bird flutters out the open windows,
and falls upward
all the way to Jupiter.

Thinking of Kelsey, and how she went to high school one
year before I did and said that it was horrible, and how many
years later she overdosed on Benadryl in a bathroom because
she believed werewolves were waiting for her outside, but
really it was a schizophrenic relapse.

Somehow
this is what I can't
wrap my head around:

She was older
than me. And now,
I am the one
who is older.

Trench Coats

It was the five of us loitering in my friend's backyard,
which was less a yard

and more of a concrete pit and a compost heap.

There was a view of a bank and a used car lot
and smoke.

This was northeast Philadelphia, where I got an accent
that I slip into when I go back there, but I rarely do.

We all knew
about the Jardel gang—named after the nearby community
recreation center where they played basketball.

I still remember being at the neighborhood carnival when
there were gunshots
and young men chanting its name.

But Jardel was where the courts were.

This was back when I was fourteen
and still walked around in a black trench coat despite
Columbine.

While looking at mine,
Jay remembered that he had just gotten a long black coat
for his birthday,
and his cousin also had one inside,
and Nicky dug his father's out of storage, and Lance, well, he

just looked the part despite his dark windbreaker.

All five of us walking at one in the morning, like a mafia,

with this attitude

of absolute certainty, that to this day,

I don't know

if I was the only one who was terrified.

There was one light still lit

over the half-court,

and part of a chain-link net dangling off the hoop,

and we played

like we were dancing

on hot coals.

War Paint

I want to remember this,

my dad and I together in war paint,

in the desert outside of San Diego.

A photographer dressed us.

He had his glasses off and I had not yet gotten them.

We looked serious for the camera,

I had more red around my eyes

and he had green,

but we both had dark blue battle lines on our cheeks.

The powdered paint covered our faces and bare chests,
my dad said something about me being an Indian
The warrior
like him.

I want to remember this,
I want to quit my job
and run over to my dad's house—
down into the basement
and pull him off the couch,
away from the TV
and tell him that I remember that power again
and we would track down that photographer back in San
Diego

We would take our glasses off
We would demand that she get her powdered paints
We would tell her to dress us again
In the warrior colors.
But this time
there would be no camera.

Jade Shames is a screenwriter, fiction writer, and poet living in Brooklyn. He is the grand prize winner of the 2013–2014 Fresh Voices screenplay competition and the recipient of a creative writing scholarship from The New School's MFA program for poetry. His work has appeared in a variety of publications, including The Best American Poetry blog, *H.O.W. An Art and Literary Journal*, and *LA Weekly*.

Website: jadeshames.com
Twitter: @JadeShames

Corazón Oscuro

RACHEL CAINE

There were probably lots of things worse than a road trip with Mom through a no-cell-signal West Texas desert in the middle of the night, but honestly, Zen couldn't think of any. It was too dark to read the book she'd brought; she tried to use the flashlight, and her mother snapped at her to turn it off—it was messing with her night vision.

"You have headlights," Zenobia said without looking up. "Why does it bother you?"

"Headlights are out there, you're in here—*turn it off.*" Her mom sounded really tense, which wasn't a surprise. They were both exhausted and cranky, and that fifth cup of coffee for her mother had obviously been a super bad choice. "Check the map. How much farther to Pecos is it, anyway?"

"A billion miles."

"Zenobia, *por el amor de Dios*, just tell me!"

"Do you have to pee? Because I'm pretty sure the last gas station was back in Monahell."

"Monahans."

"Did you see it? God. My name is so much better." She
hated this. Hated leaving El Paso and her school and her best
friends. Hated leaving the boy that *might* have been the love
of her life, if he'd ever asked her out, and she knew he'd been
about to do that, she *knew it.*

This was ruining her life. It wasn't her mother's fault, but
she couldn't help but blame her too. *Blame Dad, because he's
the one who made this happen.* That was true too, and she knew
he was the bad guy, the one who'd screwed around, the one
who had leaped at the chance for a divorce, who'd left them
with nothing.

And her mom was brave for starting over. *She knew.* She
just hated it, all of it, and she wanted to get lost in a dark, dys-
topian world where at least you could fix the things that were
screwing up your life.

She'd only gotten a paragraph in when her mom sighed
and said, "I'm not going to tell you again. Turn the light off!"

Zenobia sighed and clicked the flashlight off. Obviously,
her third reading of the battered copy of *The Forest of Hands
and Teeth* was going to have to wait until when her mother
wasn't on too much caffeine. "It's another hour to Pecos, okay?
Happy now?" She didn't wait for her mom to tell her how much
she wasn't. She grabbed the side handle on the seat and pulled
up, and her seat leaned backward, faster and harder than she'd
imagined it would. Her mother let out a little yelp of fright
and frustration and sent her a glare that, by the light of the old

dashboard's red glow, looked more than a little demonic.

Her seat slammed into a box about eight inches back, and she heard something shift inside. She hoped that wasn't one of Mom's precious ceramic angels. If something broke, she'd catch hell for sure.

Life sucks enough already. She was stuck in the desert with her entire life stuffed into the back of an ancient old station wagon with the fake wood paneling peeling off the sides, and there was no cell reception. Which meant no social media. No texts. No music. *Nothing.* And nothing to see, because out here in the desert was like being in outer space, all hard black sky and bright cold stars, and the road only an illusion vanishing just past the headlights. Like floating in a big bowl of darkness. *Maybe we're not really going anywhere. Maybe we're trapped going around in a circle. With no GPS, how can we tell?*

She already knew what her mom would say to that, in that aggravated, superior way old people had. *In my day we could use maps. It wasn't that hard.* And phones had dials, games had boards, blah blah blah. She could recite all of the anti-new-stuff rants from memory.

Three more years until she could move out on her own, and she could not *wait.* She'd get her own apartment. Something tiny and cute, with a big chair. And a dog. She wanted a dog. They hadn't had one since Alfonse, the greyhound rescue that her dad had brought home one day. Alfonse had been shy and skittish, and limped a lot, but she'd loved that dog. She'd cried for days when he'd died. In fact she felt her throat clench up just at the thought of his sad eyes, that velvety gray coat, the fast, scared beat of his heart when she'd held him for the last time.

She shut her eyes. Her mom punched buttons on the ancient stereo, trying to find some station out here in space. *Never happen. Give it up.* And even if they'd thought to bring the old CDs (which her mom still had), the wagon didn't even have a CD player.

Dark Ages. No wonder her uncle had sold it to them for five hundred bucks.

"Are you warm enough, Zen?"

"Sure." She wasn't, really, but she knew the heater was already up as high as it would go. The desert got hot, but at night, the temperature plunged. It was so cold out there she felt it breathing through the leaky edges around the passenger door. "I'm going to sleep."

"Okay." Her mom gave up the hunt for music with a sigh, turned off the static, and put a thin hand on Zenobia's leg, a silent affectionate pat of apology. Zen struggled to turn over on her side, but the seat was more spring than padding. She compromised somewhere in the middle, an awkward lean more than anything else, and wished like hell she didn't have all her music in the cloud, because she wanted to put her headphones in and drift away, just drift. . . .

"*¡Mierda!*"

Zenobia had just started to relax when her mother spat

the curse out and wrenched the wheel, and Zen lurched hard against the straps and bumped her elbow hard enough to see spots. *Ow.* The station wagon's tires screeched as it skidded, and the back end tried to fishtail, but somehow her mom got it under control as she applied the brakes, hard. Zenobia slid forward, yelped, and braced herself with her feet in the passenger well. No air bags in this clunker. They'd better not crash.

They didn't. Her mom brought the car safely to a stop, and the engine began making a strange, gargling sound, shaking like it was afraid. Zenobia struggled to sit up, but the belts and her reclined seat were holding her back. She fumbled for the lever and slammed the seat up, which only made the straps tighten more over her chest, and for a second she genuinely thought this stupid old car was going to kill her. She yanked on the shoulder strap and got it loosened enough to let her catch her breath.

"Stay here," her mother said in a tense, focused voice. "I mean it, Zen. Stay here. Do *not* get out of the car."

There was a wreck up ahead. They'd come up on it in the dark, and it had been amazing her mother had been able to stop in time; the car was on its side, undercarriage showing like the bottom of a dead turtle, and it looked crumpled and bashed all over. Must have rolled, Zenobia thought. There was no way to tell how long ago it had happened, but this wasn't Interstate 10, with steady traffic; they were on the so-called *scenic route*, which mainly meant lots and lots of desert and nobody else in sight. According to the map, they were on Highway 18, heading for Highway 302, if they were going the right way, which was impossible to tell, and *oh God* there was somebody lying on the ground next to that car.

"Mom?" Zenobia hardly recognized her voice. It sounded like she was ten years old again. "Mom?" She pointed over the dash at the legs sticking out in the wash of the headlights. Blue jeans and sneakers. "Oh God, Mom—"

"*Stay here.*" Her mother got out of the station wagon, went to the back, and opened it up. She grabbed a backpack and slammed the station wagon's door with enough force to make the whole car shudder.

How long had this wreck been here? It had no lights, no headlights or taillights or anything. Was that person a woman? A dead woman?

Zenobia didn't get out of the car, but she rolled down her window so she could hear her mother. In case she needed anything.

"Ma'am?" her mom was saying as she knelt down next to the body. "Ma'am, can you hear me? My name is Dr. Mariana Gomez, and I'm going to help you, all right? Ma'am?"

That was her mother's calm, smooth, professional voice, and Zenobia watched as she bent down and did all the things that doctors did to check for life. She must not have found it, because she stopped talking, sat back, and looked over her shoulder at Zenobia. There was an unreadable look on her face.

"I'm going to check for any other passengers!" she called back, and Zen had to resist the urge to tell her *No, no, let's just go, let's get out of here*, because first of all it would be wrong, and second of all there was no way her mom would listen anyway.

Zenobia checked her phone for the millionth time. Still no signal. Where were they, on the fricking *moon*? "Come on!" she whispered, and shook it. That didn't help, but it made her feel better. Her mother was up and walking around the overturned car. "Come *on*!" She held it at arm's length out the window, and the glowing screen finally showed one tiny, faltering bar. "Mom! I've got a signal! I'm calling 911!"

She popped her door and got out of the car, because even though her mom had been very specific, surely she didn't mean *Don't call the cops*, because this needed calling in, and it was just a couple of steps, anyway.

God, it was dark out here, with just the stars and dim headlights; their glow looked fragile in all this darkness, and the silence seemed so big around the unsteady, shuddering idle of the car.

She dialed the emergency number and watched the bar anxiously. It flickered, strengthened to two, then dropped back to one again.

But the call went through.

"Yes?" The relief at hearing someone's voice was so intense that Zenobia gasped and felt a sting of tears in her eyes. Sure, the voice was young, and weirdly enough sounded like she'd been laughing, but that didn't matter.

"Um, there's a car wreck, and somebody's hurt. We need help here." She was lying, she realized—somebody wasn't hurt. Somebody was *dead*. "We're on Highway 18, I guess, between I-20 and 302?" She didn't hear any response. "Hello? Can you hear me?" She checked the bar. Still solid. She could hear the faint hiss of an open connection. It didn't feel right, though. Not right at all. "Hello?"

There was a strange metallic sound, like a scrape, and then a voice said, "Help. Help." The drawn out words had a weird electronic sound to them, like Auto-Tune. It sounded like a girl, but somehow, it also didn't sound like a *person*.

Zenobia hung up the call and ran forward, around the front of the car. Her shadow, reflected on the undercarriage of the wreck, looked twisted and weird, and for the first time she saw the woman who was in the road—really *saw* her, and all the blood sprayed around her body.

The woman had been thrown out of the car, and there was no way she was alive. She hardly even looked human anymore. The car must have rolled over her.

"Mom!" That came out as a scream, a full, uncontrolled scream of terror, and she pressed her hands to her chest because her heart hurt with the slamming impact of the world going sick and wrong. Zenobia backed away from the dead woman—she was old, a white woman, with cloudy blue open eyes—and ran around the front of the wrecked car. It was dark beyond the glow of the car headlights, and she fumbled with her phone and turned on the flashlight app. It wasn't very bright, but she saw her mom crouched down next to another body.

"Zen," she said, and beckoned to her. She'd gloved up from her emergency kit, and her face looked tense and stark in the bluish flare. "Bring the light over here."

"Mom, that woman—"

"Zenobia, I need you to focus, okay? Just stand there and hold the light." Her mother got like this under pressure, focused and sharp and commanding, and Zen realized that she was kneeling next to another body. A man. He was still breathing, but she didn't think he would be doing that for long; he was all busted up, trickling blood onto the dark road, and he was breathing in slow, convulsive gasps. "Did you get the ambulance?"

"I—I tried. Mom. *Mom.* We need to go."

"I can't leave him until an ambulance gets here, sweetheart. He needs a hospital if he's going to survive. Honey, if you're scared, reach in the bag, in the outside pocket, and get out the gun."

"What?"

"There's a pistol in the outside pocket. I brought it for the trip. I want you to get it out and hold on to it. You know how to shoot. Your dad told me how good you were at the range."

"You have a *gun*?" Of course she did, she'd just said that, and Zenobia held the phone out to keep the light shining as she fumbled in her mom's bag with her other hand, unzipping the outer pocket. There it was, a black automatic. "Is it loaded?"

"Yes. Safety's on."

Zenobia thought she should have felt safer, holding the gun, but she didn't. Her hand was shaking. She felt like she'd forgotten everything she'd ever known, out here in the dark, and she didn't know how her mom was acting so *calm*.

"Zenobia." Her mom was watching her as she put pressure on the worst of the man's wounds, and incredibly, she *smiled*. "You've got this, *querida*. It's just for safety. We're fine. Everything's fine. The ambulance is coming. All right?"

"I don't think it is," Zenobia said in a small voice.

"What?"

"I think—" She remembered the lazy pleasure in that voice on the phone, and shivered. Her fingers tingled from the chill. "I think I got somebody else."

"That's not possible. You called 911, right?"

"Yeah. But—but it was wrong, Mom. Something's really wrong here. We should just *go*. This wasn't just a wreck, somebody . . . somebody *did this*. What if they're still here?"

Her mother started to answer, and as she drew in breath, the man whose chest she was tending made a sound like a wet, strangling cough, only it lasted longer than it should have, horribly longer, and then he stopped breathing.

"Damn." Her mom checked the man's pulse and put her ear to his chest. She used her hand over his gaping mouth to check for breath. "He's gone. I can't do chest compressions— he had a wound too close to the heart. . . ."

"Mom! We need to *go*!" Zenobia was jittering back and forth, foot to foot, and the light from her phone was dancing all over the scene.

It caught on a pair of reflective eyes, and for a second she thought *coyote*, but it was taller.

It was on a level with her own height.

Her mother, stripping off her bloody gloves, said, "Zenobia, we're going to be fine, really. I know this is shocking for you but—"

Zenobia wasn't even breathing now. She watched those reflective eyes blink. She couldn't see the actual *person*, other than as a shadow, and she knew that people, *real* people, didn't have those kinds of eyes.

"Stay down, Mom," she said. All her fear left, just drained out of her, and what was left was a warm, steady sense of concentration. Maybe she got it from her mother.

Focus.

She brought the gun up. Her dad had taught her proper shooting stance, and she slid her feet into place, braced her arm for the recoil, and aimed at the reflective eyes.

They blinked, and disappeared.

Her phone rang.

Her concentration broke, and as she fumbled for it, she almost dropped the device. Thank God her dad had also taught her proper trigger discipline, and she automatically took her index finger away as she lowered the gun, or she might have shot her own mother. Or herself. The screen caller ID said *911*. Zenobia pressed the button and raised the phone to her ear. "Hello?"

Just electronic hiss and then, softly, that same eerie electronic voice said, "Don't leave meeeeeee. . . ."

Zen shut off the call and shoved the phone in her pocket. "Mom, *come on*. We have to get out of here."

Her mother didn't argue. She grabbed her bag, and the two of them moved around the wrecked car, back into the glow of the station wagon's headlights. . . .

And the car died before they got there, with a soft, apologetic cough and shudder. The lights faded out, leaving them in the cold glow of stars.

"Stop," Zen said as her mom made a move for the car. "It didn't shut off all by itself."

The phone rang again. Zenobia ignored it this time and concentrated on the dark around them. When the phone fell silent, she heard a whisper of blown dust hissing over the road, and then a profound silence.

"I know you're out there," Zen said. "Come out." She pulled her mom away from both cars, out to the center of the starlit road where she could see someone, *something*, coming.

Her mother was breathing fast now, and shaking, but she had gotten into her medical bag and was holding a scalpel now. "Come out! Are you scared?"

There was a rustle from the other side of the wrecked car, where the shadows were deepest, and she saw a flash of eyes. Lower to the ground this time, as if it was crouching, whatever it was.

"Don't leave me," it whispered, and it was the same voice, weirdly processed, artificial, inhuman.

Zenobia aimed and fired, three tightly grouped shots right where the eyes were, but they were gone, and she didn't think she'd hit it. Whatever it was, it moved fast. And silently.

The roar of the shots seemed both enormous and oddly flat out here in this vast, empty place. She'd hit the wrecked car, for sure; she heard the falling tinkle of broken glass, probably from the windshield. But nothing else.

"We need to make it to the car," her mother said. "Zen—"

Something flew out of the shadows by the wrecked car and rolled unevenly to a stop by Zen's boots. A faded red heart that her mother kept on the keychain.

It had taken the car keys.

What do we do? Getting in the car was useless. It hadn't protected the two dead people on the road. Something out here in the dark had rolled their car into scrap metal until they came out.

Come on, come on, someone help us. . . .

There was a flickering light on the horizon. Moving toward them.

It was a car.

"Mom! Run toward it! Stop it!"

"I can't leave you!"

"Just go!" Zen brought the gun up. She'd fired five shots, she thought. She didn't know how big the clip was, and she didn't dare check. *Save the bullets. Save it till you see it.* She began walking backward, focused on the shadows near the bodies, where the creature liked to hide. She heard her mother's running footsteps behind her slapping on the still-warm surface of the road, and Zen took step after step, steadily backward.

The growl of an engine got louder and louder, and now the lights were splashing bright over the road's surface, throwing Zenobia's shadow into a long, thin pointer toward the silent station wagon. It lit up the overturned car, too, and just for an instant she thought she saw . . . *something.* Something black and tangled and angular and only vaguely human, with eyes that flared like cold moons before it was gone.

Her mother was yelling something, probably to the driver, but Zenobia didn't dare look back. She had to keep her attention out *there*, in the black beyond the headlights, because that was where the danger waited.

She could hear it making that awful, atonal crying sound. It was like sheets of metal scraping together.

Zen backed up until she was even with the bumper of the vehicle—it was a pickup truck, a big one—before she risked a look at it. The driver had his door open, and he was stepping down. Her mother was giving him the highlights, talking fast, the way she'd update other doctors in the ER.

He was young—eighteen, if that. Tall and thin, dressed in jeans and a checked shirt and cowboy boots. He was carrying a shotgun.

"Get in the truck," he said, and racked the shotgun like he knew what he was doing. Her mother scrambled in and waved to Zenobia.

Zen shut the door on her and turned to face the boy. "What is it?" she asked him, because she could see it in his face. He knew. He hadn't been out here by accident, cruising around with a shotgun. There was no surprise on his face, looking at the scene in front of them. "What is this thing?"

Her phone rang. Without looking away from the road, he said, "Don't answer it."

"I called 911. It answered!"

"Yeah, it does that," he said. "I'm Mateo. You?"

"Zen. Zenobia." She laughed, because it was crazy, really. "We're stranded in the middle of nowhere with a monster, and you're introducing yourself?"

"Seemed polite," Mateo said. "So, Zenobia, how are you with that pistol?"

"Not bad. You didn't answer me. What is that thing?"

"I call her Corazón Oscuro," he said. "Dark Heart." He aimed the shotgun suddenly at a patch of darkness. "Get in the truck. We're leaving."

"But—"

"Okay, let me say it different. The truck is leaving. Stay if you want."

She gave him a fast glare, but didn't argue. She dashed around to the other side of the truck and got in as Mateo did in the driver's seat, with her mother wedged in between them. He put the truck in gear and whipped it in a fast turn; it went off the road and into the crunchy shoulder, then into sand, but the big tires kept them moving, and he slammed his foot down as something darted out of the cover of the shadows. She saw it in the rearview mirror, lit red by the taillights, and this time, it was clear.

It was a girl. One no older than Zenobia, but covered in moving black shapes that had claws, arching tails, barbs. *Covered in scorpions.*

Her eyes reflected the taillights like doorways to hell.

Her phone rang. She exchanged a look with Mateo, and this time, he nodded. She took it out and answered it on speaker. *"Diga me."*

Static, and then a scream, inhuman and metallic and shockingly loud, and without thinking, she hung up on it.

"What in the name of God is going on?" her mother asked. She sounded uncertain, for the first time. Lost. Adrift, the same way that Zenobia felt. "We left our car. We can't leave our car—it's got everything we own inside—"

"You can't go back until morning," Mateo said. "I'll take you at first light, and you can be on your way. For now, I'm taking you to my house. You can wait there while I'm gone."

"Gone?" Zenobia leaned over to look at him. "Gone where?" He didn't answer, but she saw his jaw was set and the sweat trickling down from his hair on the side of his face. "You didn't find us by accident. You were looking for it."

He didn't confirm that, but she already knew.

Her mother reached over and grabbed Zen's hand and held it tight. She still had the scalpel in her left hand, and Zenobia's right held the pistol. The shotgun was on the rack behind them. And the truck sped on through the empty night, with the stars looking down in terrible, distant pity.

Mateo's house was just a tiny place, a faded old ranch style house that had been plain when it had been built, probably forty years back; now, the desert sun and sand had blasted the paint away, and the whole place had a half-abandoned feel. Someone had loved it, though. Zen could see spots out in the fenced yard that had once held a garden, or flowers; all that was left now were a few cacti and some old, brittle corpses of plants long dead. There was a small stone alcove with a statue of the Virgin Mary in it, and a faded photo in a frame with some plastic flowers in a pretty vase.

Mateo pulled the truck to a stop and said, "I'm going to go open the door. Wait here."

It felt safe in the truck—safe and warm, and he locked it up with them inside as he headed for the low front steps. Zen looked at her mother, who was staring straight ahead now, and she looked frozen and pale and very odd. "Mom? Are you okay?"

"No. I am not even a little okay. What—what was—"

"I don't know, okay. Let's not think about that right now. Just . . . breathe."

Her mother nodded and reached for Zenobia's hand, and the two of them sat in silence, waiting while some stranger opened the door of a house they'd never seen before, and how was it possible that this was the *best alternative*?

Strange, possible creepy killer guy, or the obviously *not right* dead girl with scorpions all over her . . . Yes. It was the best possible alternative.

The door of the ranch house opened, spilling a warm yellow stripe of light out onto the porch and casting Mateo into silhouette. She saw him beckon to them, and nudged her mother. "Mom. Let's go."

"I should—we should call someone first." Her mother felt around her pockets and seemed surprised. "I left my phone. Oh God, I left my phone in the car."

"It's okay. I have mine." Zen flicked it on and checked; the familiar glow of the screen, with its background of her making stupid faces with her best friend, Gloria, was still the same. Normal world, when nothing was normal anymore. She checked the signal. "There's still no signal, Mom. Maybe Mateo has a phone inside."

She nodded silently, and Zen could see her gathering mental strength before she reached out and unlocked the door. "Wait," her mother said. "Give me the gun. I'll hang on to it." She didn't trust Mateo. That seemed crazy, since he'd just rescued them, but Zen handed the gun over, and her mother checked the clip. There were still bullets left; how many, Zen couldn't tell. "If anything happens, Zen, you stay down," she said.

"Mom, be careful with that!"

"Safety's on," her mom said, and tucked the weapon in the back of her jeans, under her shirt.

It wasn't far to the house, maybe five or six steps, but it felt like an eternity between the safe space of the truck and the beginning of that square of light from the open door. Mateo rushed them inside and slammed the door; there were a lot of locks on it, and those dead bolts looked pretty new. He didn't relax, even then, and went from window to window, pulling back dusty curtains and checking each. "Stay here," he said, and disappeared into the rest of the house. Zenobia sat down on the edge of a sofa that had seen way better days, and felt the delayed shakes start to hit. Her mother didn't sit—she paced, as if she couldn't relax enough to let her guard down even for a moment.

The house looked like a typical family home, with pictures of kids on the walls and on top of the old-fashioned TV set that had to date back to the '90s, at least. There was a fine reddish sift of dirt on top of almost everything. The house smelled oddly lifeless. No odors of food or laundry. Just stale air and dust.

Mateo came back after a few moments, and he seemed slightly less tense. "We're secure," he said. "For now. You need to hold out until first light, then I can get you back to your car." He paused, then said, a little awkwardly, as if he weren't used to asking, "You need something? Coffee, maybe?"

"Bathroom," Zenobia's mother said. He nodded and pointed down the hall, and she headed that way.

Mateo looked at Zen, clearly asking the same question, and she shook her head. She needed answers more than hospitality. "What is that thing out there?"

"Not your business. You can be in your car and on the road tomorrow morning. You figure out whatever story you want to tell and stick to it."

"What are you going to say?"

He shrugged. "Depends on which cops show up. If it's somebody I don't know, I'll say I was passing and I picked you up, and you were too scared to go back. It's true, anyway."

"Won't they think you . . ."

"You're my alibi. I couldn't have done it if I came along later, right?"

"You could have circled back."

It seemed like he hadn't thought of that, and she wished she hadn't said it, because he looked genuinely worried now. Maybe he wouldn't take them back after all. Whatever they'd seen back there (*that girl, buried in scorpions*), maybe it was just panic and shadows, and they'd really hitched a ride with the boy who'd just killed two people.

To cover her sudden unease, Zen got up and walked over to look at the photos. They were faded from sun and time, and in the earliest ones the colors had gone shabby and beige tinged, with only a little blue and red still standing out. It was a Hispanic family, and the photos showed new additions . . . first a boy, then another boy, then a girl. Then, in the later photos, just the two boys and no girl. Then the mother was missing, and there was something about the strained smiles on the faces of the boys, the haunting look in their eyes, that made her feel even more afraid.

That, and the fact that neither one of the boys was Mateo, who was restlessly still flicking the keys around his finger.

"Those are my cousins," he said. "My uncle. You wanted to know about Corazón? Here she is." He put his finger on the last photo that held the girl. In it, she was a fresh faced teen about Zenobia's age. Pretty, hopeful, smiling. What was unsettling was that she was the *only* one smiling. The mother looked pale and wan; the two boys were trying to smile but not making it. And the father was looking right into the camera with so much

intensity that Zenobia took a step back when she met that captured stare. "She went missing a few months later."

"Missing?"

"My uncle said she ran away. I don't know, I wasn't here,
but then his wife, Marta, killed herself. Then it was just my
uncle Nando and the two boys."

"Where are they now?"

"My cousins are dead," Mateo said. "Nando's on death row
in Huntsville. They found five girls buried in the desert out
behind this house. They say he killed the boys, too, when the
cops came. They found all three of them on the ground outside, shot, but Nando lived. Guess he wasn't much good at suicide." There was no emotion in what he was saying, just a simple
statement of fact, though she thought she saw something burning deep in his dark eyes. "The house has been mostly empty. I
came here when the reports about Corazón started."

"What kind of reports?"

"People saw her standing on the side of the road in their
headlights, trying to get help. Most didn't stop. Some did,
maybe tried to help, I don't know." He looked away. "She wants
somebody to find her, I guess. I've been trying, but I don't
know where to look."

"Does she always show up at the same place on the road?"

He shrugged. "As far as I can tell, yeah. But I've looked all
around there. I couldn't find her. It's a big desert, Zenobia."

Zen stared at the picture of smiling young Corazón, with

her whole life ahead of her, and asked, "Do you have scorpions out here?"

"It's the desert. Of course we do."

"We used to have them around my house in El Paso," she said. "We used black lights to look for them. They show up real well."

He nodded, though he looked a little lost, until he finally put it together. "You . . . think the scorpions might lead us to her."

"They might," Zenobia said. "If all she wants is to be found."

He smiled bitterly. "Don't suppose you have a black light, do you?"

"How do you think I found them in El Paso?" Zen asked. "I have an app for that."

"This is crazy," her mom said for the thousandth time as Mateo edged the truck to a quiet stop on the side of the road. He'd taken some time to put together a kit, though what was in it, Zenobia didn't know . . . more shotgun shells, she hoped. Ahead, the station wagon sat silently where they'd left it. Both doors were shut now, which seemed weird. The wrecked car was still on its side, and although Zen couldn't see the bodies, she knew they'd still be there too. "We should drive straight to the nearest town and call the police. It's the only thing to do."

"She wants help," Zen said. "Until she gets it, she'll keep stopping people. Mateo, has she killed before?"

"No," he said. "Never. I think this was probably an accident. She must have tried to get them to stop, and they panicked and flipped the car. She tries to talk to people on their phones—maybe that freaked them out."

"It freaks *me* out," Zen's mom said. "Are we talking about a *ghost*? Really?"

Mateo shrugged. He switched off the headlights, and the night seemed incredibly black now. "Stay close. I'm not sure what we're going to find, if we find anything at all." He got out of the truck and grabbed his pack from behind the seat, then the shotgun.

Zenobia started to get out, but her mother grabbed her and held her back. "Zen. Wait. This is crazy. You know that."

"I *saw* her," Zenobia said. "So did you. Crazy or not, this is what we need to do."

"I don't believe in monsters." But out here, in the vast, empty desert, that sounded like a lie.

Zen silently broke free and got out of the truck, and her mother followed.

"So what are we looking for?" Mateo asked her.

"If Corazón wants to be found, then she's going to try to lead us to her," she said. "Right?"

"Right."

"So, look for scorpions," she said. "Here. Use the black light."

It probably didn't even qualify as a long shot, but it was all

Zen could think of, and when Mateo activated the app, a sick purple glow bathed the ground by the side of the road.

A scorpion lit up like a neon sign. It was the size of Zenobia's hand, pale, and it arched its tail and scuttled quickly off.

"Could be nothing at all," said her mom. "It's the desert. Scorpions live all over the place."

"It's worth a try," Mateo said, and followed the scorpion's trail.

It didn't seem to mind being followed, which seemed weird; it kept a steady pace and ignored them as it scuttled along over a sand dune and down the other side around a spiky explosion of mesquite bush. As Zenobia looked around, though, she caught more faint glows around them—more moving shapes, pincers, and barbed tails. It was like a . . . migration. Did scorpions migrate? She didn't know.

They kept walking, dodging around bushes and rusty pieces of junk left out in the wilderness; one piece was the remains of a classic car abandoned at least fifty years ago, all the fabric and rubber long rotted away. Snakes slithered away as they passed, and Zenobia realized she hadn't even thought of the danger of walking around out here. What if they got bitten by rattlesnakes? What if . . .

"Hold up," Mateo said. He sounded shaken and tense. "Man, there are a *lot* of them. See?"

Zenobia looked over his shoulder. Down in the sandy hollow below, the whole ground *moved*, and where the black light bathed the sand, it showed scorpions crawling over each other, so many of them they tangled and squirmed like a poisonous blanket.

"That isn't normal," he said. "Right?"

It didn't feel normal. Not at all.

And then Mateo's phone rang, a loud musical jangle that made all three of them flinch. The scorpions below didn't react at all.

Mateo pushed the button to accept the call and said, "*Diga me.*"

Just a static hiss at first, and then a whisper. Slow and weirdly metallic. "*Heeeeeeeerrrrrrre.*"

It was like a long, electronic sigh, and then the call ended. The black light app kicked on again, bathing the scorpions in the weird neon glow.

"Oh sweet Lord, she's under there," Zenobia's mother said. "That girl's *underneath.*"

"So what do we do?" Zen asked. She was asking Mateo, but he wasn't answering. He just stared down at the hollow, with its carpet of scorpions, without moving.

Zenobia's mother said, "Give me your phone."

Mateo handed it to her, and she stepped past him, down the slope toward the crawling nightmare below.

"Wait, Mom! What are you *doing*?"

"If she wants us to find her, then the things won't stop me." And her mother, Dr. Mariana Gomez, pushed her foot into the nest of scorpions, and nudged the first of them aside.

It was as if she'd sent some signal, and they began to scatter in all directions, a scuttling wave that streamed straight up the sides of the hollow. Mother scorpions loaded with crawling babies scrambled past Zenobia, who gagged and found herself pressed tight against Mateo's side. "Don't move," he told her. The scorpions weren't coming at them, just near them, and none of them made any move to strike.

Her mom crouched down in the sand as the last of the scorpions withdrew, and began to brush the dirt away.

She exposed fabric underneath. Tattered, bleached by time.

There wasn't much of Corazón left except bones, shoes, and the clothes she'd worn when she'd died, but she was still there, and there was compassion in the way Zenobia's mother brushed the sand from the white skull. More scorpions writhed free of the rotting shirt and fought their way clear from the old, stiff blue jeans.

They'd made a nest here. A nest in her body.

"She's dead," Mateo said. He sounded weirdly relieved. "Now she can rest."

"She was stabbed," Zen's mother said. "There's one wound through her shirt, but the whole shirt is soaked with blood, so she was alive for a while. How far are we from the house?"

"Why?" he asked.

"Maybe a mile," Zen said. "I mean, in a straight line. On the road, maybe two?"

Her mother sat back on her heels and looked at Mateo. "The other girls—you said they were buried behind the house. No one buried her—this is just drifting sand. I think she ran away and died out here, all alone."

Mateo kept staring at the body. He didn't seem relieved anymore. He seemed angry.

Zenobia's phone rang. Caller ID said it was 911, and she lifted it to her ear. She had three bars now, remarkably, and this time, the voice came through as clearly as if the girl were standing right beside her.

"My cousin's going to kill you," she said. "I'm sorry. But at least I won't be alone anymore."

Zen pulled in her breath in a gasp, and Mateo turned to look at her. In the strange purple glow of the black light, his eyes looked darker than the night. She saw him realize that she knew.

And she realized that he had the shotgun.

He raised it, but not at her. At her mother, who was still bent over the corpse of Corazón.

"No!" Zen screamed. She didn't have the handgun, her mom had it, and her mom's back was turned, so she did the only thing she could; she lunged hard at Mateo and knocked him off balance. The shotgun blast ripped into the sand two feet away from her mother, who threw herself to one side and clawed for the gun in the back of her pants, but Zen barely registered that because she was slamming into Mateo again, harder, and this time, he lost his footing and tumbled into the sand.

He raised the shotgun and pointed it right at her face, and behind it she saw his eyes, crazy eyes, *deadly* eyes, and she knew she didn't have time to dodge.

Her mother fired first. She didn't kill him, but she caught him in the arm, and he fumbled the shotgun. It went off and blew part of his foot away, and Zenobia lunged forward and grabbed the searing hot barrel, yanked it free of his hands, and turned it back on him. She backed away, and her mother rushed up the sandy hill to stand beside her.

Mateo was screaming and flailing, and blood was pumping out of what remained of his boot, but the desert greedily soaked it up.

"Try again," her mother said, with remarkable calm once again. "Call 911."

This time the call went through, and the response was reassuringly normal. "Nine one one. What is your emergency?"

"Uh, there's a wreck on Highway 18, between I-20 and 302," Zenobia said. She felt weirdly disconnected now, and Mateo was yelling and cursing at them and flailing around in the sand, and she was afraid he was going to get up. "There are a couple of people dead. Please send the police."

The operator assured her that help was on the way. Zenobia hung up the call.

"I'm going to kill you, bitches!" Mateo screamed.

"Like you did Corazón? And all those other girls? You

were living with them, weren't you, with your uncle and his family. He didn't kill anybody. *You* did. And he took the blame for it. What happened, Mateo? You thought Corazón was dead, but she wasn't? She got away and you couldn't find her?" Zenobia had somehow taken on her mother's calm now, and it felt good. It felt powerful. So did the shotgun in her hands. "The one that got away. And she kept coming back, trying to get help. Haunting you."

"I'm going to *gut you!*"

"No you won't," Zen said. "Because she's coming for you." She lowered the shotgun and stepped back, because something was coming out of the darkness behind Mateo now, a hiss of bodies over sand, a neon bright wave in the fallen black light of claws and joined tails and barbs.

She grabbed her mother and pulled her back as the scorpions reached Mateo.

He didn't scream for long, not because he didn't want to, but because they went in his open mouth and choked him silent. Covered him in a moving blanket of black, and their tails rose and fell, poison drops on their barbs. Thousands of scorpions, clinging to him with their pincers as they mercilessly stung him to death.

Zenobia's phone rang again. It was the 911 operator, assuring her that everything would be all right. She heard the distant wails of the police car, still far away.

"We should go," Zenobia said to her mother, and put down

the shotgun. She pulled the pack that Mateo had brought with him over and checked inside.

Knives. Rope. Duct tape. A video camera. His killing supplies.

He'd meant to bury them out here with Corazón, after all. She left it all with him.

They went back to the road, and the police came. Zenobia and her mother told the officer about Mateo and the dead girl in the desert, and just before dawn, as more and more police arrived to crowd the empty road, Zenobia's phone rang one last time.

She looked at the screen, and this time she didn't answer it. She just let it ring and ring and ring.

Because sometimes, it was just better not to know who was on the other end.

"We're all right," her mother said, and hugged her close. "We're going to be all right, Zenobia. From now on."

They were. But sometimes—just sometimes—when her phone rang, something told Zenobia not to answer it.

Dark hearts never died.

Rachel Caine is the *New York Times* bestselling author of almost fifty novels and even more short stories. Her most recent releases include *Dark Secrets: A Paranormal Noir Anthology*, the Morganville Vampires short story collection *Midnight Bites*, and *Paper and Fire*, the second book of her Great Library series.

Website: rachelcaine.com

Twitter: @rachelcaine

Facebook: facebook.com/rachelcainefanpage

The Boyfriend

STEVE RASNIC TEM

Aria's mother was about to have her third baby, fourth if you counted the miscarriage. Aria loved babies, even when they screamed and were impossible, which was a lot of the time. She'd been a good babysitter for her little brother, and even now when he was older and not as much fun, she loved him so fiercely that sometimes it was almost scary. She couldn't help it—when you spent a lot of time taking care of a baby, you just naturally became superprotective. It was like a Law of Nature or something. She would never let anyone hurt her brother. That just could not happen, as far as she was concerned. Aria was ready to do whatever had to be done to protect that kid. It didn't matter what it was.

Aria had been Mom's first baby—she was born long before Joey. Because her dad was never in the picture, she had Mom pretty much all to herself for years, and that made her Mom's most important person in the world. Even when Mom had a boyfriend, and there were a lot of boyfriends, Aria had always come first. Aria didn't care what anybody said—as far as she was concerned, that was proof Mom was a good mother.

"Aria, make me a sandwich?"

Joey was yanking on her jeans. He was only five. "What are you supposed to say, Joey, when you want something?"

He looked at her like he couldn't understand English anymore. Then suddenly his face got bright. "Please!" he shouted.

"Good job!" she said. "Go sit at the table and I'll bring it to you." She felt a little silly, always telling him "Good job!" as if he'd just done the greatest thing in the world, but when you took care of little kids, sometimes goofiness was required.

He was adorable sitting there trying to be patient, waiting for his sandwich. (Peanut butter and jelly—that's what "sandwich" meant to Joey.) Kids could be cute without even trying—that was probably the best thing about them. That's why you wanted to love and protect them. She'd read somewhere that "cuteness" was part of evolution—if humans and animals had ugly kids they might not try so hard to keep them safe. That seemed pretty harsh, pretty judgmental, but the world was a harsh place. Mom used to say that a lot to Aria when she was growing up, and now that Aria was a teenager she said it even more. "It's a harsh, harsh place, and you have to be ready for it!" Sometimes, when you were a kid, you forgot that—you expected everything to turn out okay like it did in the storybooks. Now Aria was old enough to understand that was rarely true.

She put his plate down in front of him. Joey started eating

his sandwich, really going at it, tearing it apart like he was some kind of wild animal. It was pretty amazing, actually. Aria should have stopped him and made him eat it right, teach him some good manners, but it was too much fun watching him. That's when the clown came in.

That's what Aria called the new boyfriend. She wasn't being disrespectful, not really, because that's what the boyfriend did for a living, part-time at least. The rest of the time he didn't do much of anything, as far as she knew. He dressed up like a clown for kids' parties, acting all crazy and performing stupid magic tricks. Clown stuff. She guessed he was good at being goofy, and the kids all seemed to like him, but it creeped her out. Clowns creeped her out. She couldn't believe her mother was dating a stupid clown when she knew how much Aria hated them.

They *lied* for a living—that's what they did. They pretended to be happy when they weren't. They pretended everything was a joke, but some things were too sad and scary to joke about.

The boyfriend had just gotten out of bed, and he still had some of his clown face on. That was typical. Sometimes after a clowning job he'd drink, and he'd rub his face with a towel, not enough to remove all the makeup, just smear it around some, and then he'd just flop down in bed and get his face paint all over Mom's pillows, so it looked like his face had melted, or maybe he was a person magically turning into a clown, or maybe he was a clown trying to turn into a person. Aria had no idea. But either way he never finished his transformation, so he just looked like this trashy thing that was all dirt and grease and a big, scary mouth.

"What are you looking at?" he was saying to Joey, growling like he was some kind of bear.

"Noth . . . nothing," Joey said, looking away.

"Don't lie to my face!" the angry clown shouted.

"Don't yell at him!" Aria pulled Joey out of his chair and sent him and his sandwich off into his bedroom. Joey ate in his bedroom a lot when the clown was around.

The clown watched Joey go into the bedroom and close the door. Then he turned to look at Aria. Except it wasn't like he turned his head in any normal way. His painted features just slid around his head so that his bruised clown nose and his big, ugly clown mouth were just below his ear, and his eyes were peeking out of the side of his head. And the right eye was almost swallowed up by his long, greasy hair.

Then, as if he'd just realized he'd done something wrong, he moved his head around so that his real eyes and nose and mouth and his clown eyes and nose and mouth all matched. Or almost. His clown mouth wriggled a little below his real mouth, like he was fighting between a smile and a frown.

"Don't . . . ever . . . do . . . that . . . again!" his struggling mouths growled. "You . . . don't know . . . what I . . . what I . . . can do."

But Aria *could* imagine. She could imagine very well what that angry clown could do. And then Mom's boyfriend's face settled down, and he was just this sleepy, lazy guy, slurring his words. "It's my house. You're living in my house now."

Which wasn't even true, because Aria's mom was paying most of the rent. But she didn't bring it up because it wouldn't matter anyway. She went into her room and locked the door.

Most days the boyfriend spent the morning in bed, coming out of the room he shared with Mom around noon. So at least Aria didn't have to see him at breakfast or before she went off to school each day. The clown was just this *thing* living in their apartment that came out every now and then to annoy and frighten them. Aria worked hard not to resent Mom for it. Her mother was a smart lady, in everything but this one area. She just had this weird thing about men. She was always picking out the broken ones, the ones that women with good sense didn't want. Aria kind of understood this. When she was little, her favorite dolls were the messed up ones, and who didn't like an ugly puppy? But those were things that were just broken in their looks. And nobody was perfect in their looks. What Mom didn't seem to understand was that not everyone was good on the inside. Sometimes a guy who was all weird on the outside was even weirder on the inside.

Every afternoon Aria would meet Joey at his school and they would walk home together. Joey was always a little sillier the closer they got to their apartment building. It annoyed her, maybe because it reminded her too much of the clown. But Joey couldn't help himself—they never knew what they'd find when they got home. The boyfriend might be up, playing video games, or in some crazy mood. Mom wouldn't be home from work for at least a couple of hours.

"Black Hawk down!" Right when they got in the door. A black remote control helicopter buzzed right by their faces. She saw Joey's hair move—the idiot flew his toy *that* close to her little brother's face! The first time it happened, Aria had freaked, thinking it was a giant insect or a bird or a bat or something. At least now that it happened all the time, she knew what it was. The boyfriend had these remote control toy helicopters, three of them, and he liked to fly them at you. Just never when Mom was around. So when Aria complained about it, he could always say she was just making stuff up, or exaggerating. She could tell her mother was suspicious, but Mom seemed to believe the boyfriend anyway, or at least pretended to. Aria understood that, even though she didn't like it. If you had a boyfriend, you took his side if you wanted to keep him. So maybe she'd never have a boyfriend. She never wanted to do that. She thought it was a crazy thing to do, actually, but she would never call her mother crazy.

"Kaboom!" the boyfriend shouted. The helicopter crash-landed on the coffee table in front of Joey. Joey screamed with laughter. He couldn't help himself. Aria could see that it was a growing problem—Joey was a kid, and boys especially could like things and be scared of them at the same time. It was exciting for them. They were mixed up like that. But you tried to help them get un—mixed up.

"Here. You try it, Joey!" The boyfriend hunkered over and shoved the remote control into Joey's hands. Joey cheered with pleasure. Aria walked toward her room, but before she got there, Joey flew the helicopter into the back of her head, with some steering help from the boyfriend. Joey howled with laughter and the boyfriend hooted like a loon. She turned around angrily and stared at the helicopter lying there on the floor. She wanted to stomp on it. But who knew what might happen if she did that?

Inside her bedroom Aria tried to do her homework while listening on her headphones, but sometimes she'd slip them off to get some sense of what was going on in the rest of the apartment. Of course it was a madhouse, Joey and the boyfriend running around and making noise. She should be out there, watching Joey, but the boyfriend was out there too, and she just couldn't deal with him. She was afraid. She'd feel terrible if anything ever happened to Joey, but she just couldn't be out there. She guessed she was just some terrible coward.

"Kaboom! Kaboom! Rat-a-tat-tat-tat!" That wasn't Joey—that was the boyfriend. What was he, five? She thought about the creepy clown face, and what she had seen it do. Maybe her nerves were just getting to her. The boyfriend was crazy. That was certainly bad enough, but that was all there was to it. Sometimes your nerves made you see things, incorrectly.

The situation always calmed down a few minutes before Mom got home. The boyfriend was pretty careful about that— he seemed to have a special sense for when Mom was going to walk through the door. Suddenly he would stop what he was doing and start straightening things up, picking up all of Joey's toys and his own toys and getting the dirty dishes into the dishwasher. Sometimes Joey and the boyfriend would be sitting together there on the couch watching television when Mom got home, even when they had been yelling at each other just minutes before. Even when Joey didn't want to be sitting on the couch. Aria would come out of her room and say hello to Mom, and Joey would look at her like he was begging her to do something, but neither of them ever said a word. What was there to say? The boyfriend looked at her too, not saying anything, but daring her with his eyes as he put his big arm across Joey's little shoulders.

Tonight was no different. Joey and the boyfriend played like crazy until Mom got home, and everybody said hello as if nothing were going on. Then they went their separate ways. Aria and Joey always had homework to do, and the boyfriend would sit out in the living room with Mom, and she would talk about her day and he would lie about his.

But then later that night, when Mom called them all to din- ner, Joey and the boyfriend both showed up in clown makeup.

They were a mess. Obviously, the boyfriend had painted

on both of their clown faces. She guessed they were meant to be identical, but that just meant the boyfriend had smeared greasepaint on approximately the same places on Joey's face. Mom stared at the two of them for a minute or two when they sat down. Aria was sure Mom would yell at the boyfriend for this one, but she looked so tired, and her belly so huge, about to burst, that it didn't really surprise Aria when her mother said, "He's kind of cute. What, is he your little twin clown, your little buddy?"

"I'm thinking I might add him to the act," the boyfriend said. Aria shuddered to hear this.

"I'm Boo Boo the clown," Joey said, and giggled. But it was a tired, sleepy giggle.

Mom turned to the boyfriend then. "So does that just make you Boo? Or Big Boo?"

The boyfriend frowned, looking like he wasn't sure if he was being insulted or not. "Boo," he said. "Just Boo." He looked ready to be angry, but he looked that way most of the time, just waiting for somebody to say the wrong thing. "Just trying to teach him a few things about work, about being a guy. Trying to spend some quality time with the little fellow."

The idea of the boyfriend teaching her little brother anything made Aria feel cold inside. Mom stared, looking as if she was trying to decide something. "I'm glad you're spending time with him, but maybe he shouldn't dress like that for dinner."

"He's fine. I'm dressed like that." Using his spoon, the boyfriend started shoveling mac and cheese into his greasy mouth.

Mom looked irritated then, but didn't say anything, so Aria didn't think she could make a fuss about it either. Mom kept stretching out her hand and holding it under her belly like she was trying to hold the baby in, like maybe the baby wanted to come out right then, and Mom was trying to tell it that now wasn't exactly the most convenient time. Aria kept watching her face, and sometimes Mom would wince a little, then she made this awkward smile like she was trying to cover it up. Of course the boyfriend didn't notice a thing—he was too busy feeding his face.

His clown makeup looked creepier than usual. The black grease around his eyes made his head look like a skull, the pale white eyes just flopping around inside the big, deep holes. And the purple spots on his nose made it look like there were pieces missing out of it. And the red smeared and runny around his mouth made it look as if he were eating himself alive.

Aria tried not to watch the boyfriend's mouth, but it was like seeing a train wreck—she just couldn't turn away. He was eating just plain old mac and cheese, but every once in awhile something odd would pop up between his lips: a fish head or the tail of one of those plastic ducks from the bathtub, or a skinny bird's leg, claws and all. It made her put her fork down. She was unable to eat.

So she started watching Joey, and Joey looked all wrong under that nasty clown makeup. He looked worn out, and too old, and like he hadn't slept for about a thousand years. He had red smeared around his eyes, and it looked like some of the red had spread onto the whites of his eyes. And the way his hair was pulled up on top and dyed orange. An old, old man hiding inside a little boy's body.

A huge bug appeared between Joey's lips, its legs claw claw clawing at Joey's mouth, trying to get out.

"Can I be excused!" she said too loudly, and jumped to her feet. Joey and the boyfriend stopped eating and stared at her. The bug leg disappeared back into Joey's mouth.

Mom looked up at her. "What's wrong, sweetheart?"

"I think I'm going to be sick," she mumbled, not sure if it was actually a lie or not.

"Oh, honey, maybe you should go lie down." Mom reached up and touched her on the back, and Aria felt a little shiver. She couldn't remember the last time her mother had touched her like that.

"Maybe I will," she said, leaving the table. The boyfriend watched her with cold lizard eyes. Joey was busy eating again. The clown makeup was leaking away from his mouth, getting all over his tongue, all over his food.

Aria lay down on her bed with her music, not really wanting to rest or sleep, just needing to hide. And not knowing what to do with herself while she was hiding. If it had been a few years ago, she knew Mom would be coming in and check-ing on her from time to time, but that kind of thing didn't happen anymore. Maybe that was okay—maybe she was get-ting too old for that anyway. Getting older sucked sometimes. Little kids could be dumb and happy. As you got older, you suddenly understood too much about things you couldn't do anything about.

Every few minutes she'd slip her earphones off and try to listen to whatever was going on in the rest of the apartment. They had music playing too—that weird South American stuff the boyfriend liked to listen to. Usually, Mom didn't let him play it when she was at home—it made her nervous. Aria hoped Mom wasn't getting too agitated—it was bad for the baby.

The parking lot outside the apartment complex seemed unusually busy tonight. Headlights kept burning through her curtains, washing across her walls. It made her room look cheap and bare. She should put up some posters, but she never could make up her mind about what to put up. She never seemed to like anything for very long anymore.

Then she heard her mother laughing and the boyfriend making those stupid ape sounds he liked to make sometimes. Mom's voice went high all of a sudden, like she was in pain. Aria got out of bed and went to the door, cracked it open.

They had most of the lights out except for that little pole lamp by the couch. Mom and the boyfriend were sitting there, and Joey was on the floor in front of them, dancing to that ridiculous bongo and guitar and flute music. At least she guessed it was supposed to be dancing. Joey didn't know how—he must have just been imitating something he saw on TV. He was twisting his body around and around, and kicking his legs up, and wiggling his head. Maybe it was his little clown dance—it looked like he was suffering from some kind of tragic nervous condition. It was hard to watch for long—it made Aria's head hurt.

Whatever it was supposed to be, Mom and the boyfriend were howling with laughter, the boyfriend making that hooting sound, his arm around Mom, rubbing her shoulders. It was upsetting to see. Aria studied her mother—was she really having a good time, or was she nervous, or maybe even scared? Aria couldn't tell. Mom's pregnant belly looked a lot bigger than it had at dinner—it hung so low, like the weight of it might drag her right off the couch and onto the floor.

Aria tried to focus on Mom's belly, the way it moved. Was that just the laughter shaking it, or was the baby doing a clown dance? She shut the door carefully and sat back down on her bed, put the earphones on, and took them right off again. She was too nervous to do anything, to even know what she *should* be doing. She sat that way for hours.

Eventually, things got quiet again. She heard Mom put Joey to bed and then Mom and the boyfriend go into their bedroom. There was still laughter sometimes, but eventually the apartment grew silent. Aria still waited. Finally Mom's bedroom door opened again. That's what Aria had been waiting for. She walked carefully to her door, opened it, and peeked out. The boyfriend went out almost every night. She'd heard him many, many times before. And there he was, standing in the living room rubbing more greasepaint into his face. But this time he bent down, and when he bent down, she could see that Joey was standing there with him. The boyfriend was putting more paint on Joey as well.

Then the boyfriend and her little brother left the apartment together. She should tell Mom, but wouldn't that just put Mom and the baby in danger? She didn't want to, she was terrified to, but Aria waited a few minutes and then followed them outside.

Joey and the boyfriend moved swiftly over the empty field behind the apartment complex, their dark shapes cutting through the tall grass, the moon making the tops of their heads glow silver. It might have been beautiful if it hadn't been so frightening. They almost looked as if they were flying, and Aria's chest pounded and her legs ached trying to keep up. Finally, they paused at the far edge of the field, and the boyfriend looked around. Aria crouched down so he wouldn't see her. His white greasepaint made him look zombielike, and when he opened his mouth, it looked like he had the largest, reddest tongue she'd ever seen on a human being. Suddenly, he reached down into the tall grass and came up with a furry, struggling thing. Was that a rabbit? He thrust it into his mouth, and the struggling stopped.

Aria leaned her face into the grass and started crying. She desperately wanted to run back to Mom, but how could she leave Joey out here?

She raised her head a bit and peeked. The clown was shaking his head back and forth, blood and bits of fur flying everywhere. Then he spit it all out with a great *ptui!* sound. Then he laughed. Worse, there was a smaller laugh rising up beside him.

They were moving again, and Aria was moving with them. They got to the little kids' playground on the edge of the field, and the clown leapt on top of the jungle gym. He jumped from one bar to the next, not holding on to anything. Then he reached down and pulled Joey up there with him. Aria gasped and started leaking tears again, she was so afraid. *Stop it! Just stop it!* She made herself calm down. She wasn't helping Joey any by crying.

When they leapt off together, it was like two apes, or maybe two fierce cats. If she hadn't already known, she would never have guessed that the smaller shape was a little boy's. It looked like something wild and brutal.

At least playing around the jungle gym had slowed their forward progress some, and Aria was close enough to see their faces as they ran into the busy street below. There was a crowd of shabby, swollen-looking men there, and some of them seemed to know the clown, because they laughed out loud, and shouted his name, and slapped him on the back. And the clown shouted back, and he made little Joey perform for them, and when Joey did his silly clown dance they laughed even louder, and a couple of them tried to pick Joey up, but they dropped him. Aria just wanted to yell at them, but she was so terrified, and knew she shouldn't show herself yet. Joey turned on them with a red face, and jumped up on them, and they screamed. They were actually screaming because of something her little brother was doing to them.

The clown grabbed Joey by the arms and pulled him away. Some of the men were lying on the ground. Joey and the clown ran down the sidewalk toward the highway overpass, jumping, celebrating, shouting as if they'd scored the winning goal.

Aria ran through the group of men, trying to pretend they weren't there, that she hadn't noticed them. A few of them said things, but she wouldn't let their words inside her. Ahead of her Joey and the clown were going onto the bridge that crossed over the interstate highway. Even at this time of night the asphalt below ran swiftly with a glowing stream of light. As she got to the beginning of the bridge, she saw the clown leap up onto the short barrier wall. He was dancing and jumping up and down. He was clowning around.

They didn't see her approach. The boyfriend was shouting at the traffic below. Suddenly, he turned around and his red rimmed mouth was large enough to swallow a basketball with ease. But she didn't think he noticed her, even though she was getting very close. He was far too crazy to notice much of anything.

He reached down and tried to grab Joey's hands to pull her little brother up there with him. And Joey wanted to be up there. He didn't seem the least bit afraid. But he was so agitated, so excited, that their two sets of hands wouldn't quite connect.

Aria ran forward to get between them, or to pull her little brother away from the barrier. Surely, even now he wouldn't try to hurt her? But he was kicking out at her, trying to kick her away. And the clown had one of Joey's hands firmly in his grip.

They were howling. Both of them were howling like wolves. It was like the sound they were making was about to swallow up her mind.

She reached up onto the barrier and grabbed the dancing clown by the ankles. He was so surprised. She would always wonder if he fell because she'd surprised him, or if the small push of her hands had been enough to send him over. Either way he had let go of Joey. She would always understand that it might not have turned out that way. The clown might have still held on, and there would have been nothing she could have done.

They didn't stay. She grabbed Joey by the hand and led him away, and she wasn't about to let go.

He said nothing for a while. Tears and sweat had cleared the center of his face, leaving the rest of his head a mess of colored shadow. Then he said, "Don't tell."

"Joey—"

"Don't ever tell."

"Joey, a human being died out here. We can't just—"

"No, no, he wasn't. Don't tell." She knew it would cost her, but she never did.

A couple of weeks later they had a new baby brother. For the longest time Aria would dread his smile.

Steve Rasnic Tem is a past winner of the World Fantasy, British Fantasy, and Bram Stoker awards. His novels include *Deadfall Hotel* and *Blood Kin* and, most recently, *UBO*, a dark blend of science fiction and horror.

Website: m-s-tem.com

Twitter: @Rasnictem

Facebook: facebook.com/steve.tem

Bearwalker

ILSA J. BICK

Wow." Bethie uncorks her mouth, her right thumb wrinkly as a prune. (Her sucking's way worse since the police came for Dad, though that wasn't on account of Ms. Avery up and disappearing. Mom had filed a restraining order and served papers. Bethie thought Mom fed their dad notebooks for dinner, but what did you expect; her sister was only five. On the other hand, *she* was twice as old, and that was Sarah's first thought too. *Like . . .* Mom, *seriously*? If she'd been Dad, she might've gotten kind of hot, though she wouldn't have axed the bay window.) Bending over Hank's front counter, Bethie studies a fringed leather pouch covered with wiry black hair. (Honestly, to Sarah, it looks like a scalp.) "So that's really *Indian*?" Bethie asks.

"Native American," Sarah says, but it's automatic. God, when will Mom be done? Snatching a glance out the gas station's window, she sees Mom still chain-smoking and yak-yak-yakking on the pay phone because the phone company cut their landline. They live in the sticks where cells don't work. Even if they *did*, there's no money. (Well, unless

Mom quits sucking cancer sticks and chugging Four Roses.)

Please please please, Mom, can't you just shut up so we can leave? Normally, she likes Hank's because of all the good smells: yeasty Krispy Kremes, brewed coffee, juicy brats turning on those little metal rollers. But she's dying here. Partly, this is because the station's so superhot, sweat oozes from every pore. She wants to strip and run screaming into the frigid winter air, maybe make a naked snow angel.

Sick. Skimming her tongue along her upper lip, she grimaces against the taste of dank salt. *Maybe the flu.*

Or a guilty conscience, sugar? It's Ms. Avery, staring out from a mirror mounted on the wall behind the front counter. Her face isn't smooth and pretty anymore but darkly marbled with green veins like steak starting to turn. She probably smells. *Maybe something festering in your innards?*

She's not real. Sarah thumbs stinging sweat from her eyes. Ms. Avery's aren't like nice chocolate anymore but as glittery and red as coals. *There's no such thing as ghosts.*

Except this one, sugar. Ms. Avery's voice flowers in a black rose right behind Sarah's eyeballs. *Except the ghost you deserve.*

"Actually, it's Ojibwe," says Hank.

"What?" Jerking her gaze to the old man, Sarah almost blurts, *I didn't know Ms. Avery was Native American.* "You're . . . uh . . . you're Native American?"

"No way," Bethie says. "Your last name's McDonald."

"What, you were expecting White Feather? Cut Nose?"

Hank kicks his wizened features into a lopsided smile that shows uneven teeth yellowed by nicotine and years of strong coffee. "My great-granddad was Scottish, come over for the fur trade after the Civil War. Met and married my great-gran, who was from a tribe in Ontario, way up around Michipicoten Island. She was a *midé*, an Ojibwe healer, and this"—Hank gives the mound of black fur splayed on his counter a pat— "was her medicine bag, a *midé wayan.*"

"How's that different from, like, a *bag* bag?" She's grateful to have something else to focus on instead of a very probably dead woman. Then she wants to kick herself: *Stop it. You don't know anything for sure.* The last she'd seen of Ms. Avery, the social worker was striding past the nailed-on boards that scale an old oak to Sarah's tree house and heading for the immense tamarack bog where her dad was laying his muskrat traps way out in the deeper channels. (He'd explained it to Sarah once: *Whatcha do is you lay your line where the rats gotta swim to get to their houses. They take the bait and bam! And what's sweet?* Her dad's lips peeled from pointy incisors in a grin. *Rat saves you the trouble by drowning hisself.*)

Ms. Avery, of course, is not a muskrat or rabbit or any of the critters her dad traps for skins and food. That doesn't make her any less dead, though. Maybe.

Uh-huh. Ms. Avery's tone is dry. *Tell me another.*

But you knew Dad might be mad. I told you so. Sarah sneaks a finger to an aching temple. She's so sweaty she can smell herself. Step outside and she'll steam. *Get accused of abusing kids, and see how* you *feel. I told you: Falling downstairs was an accident.* Even though it's out of the cast now, Sarah's right wrist still tingles with the memory. *It's what I told the doctor, I*

(Get the hell out of my way.)

tripped over my own feet.

(Christ, I barely touched her! Is it my fault she's so clumsy?)

So this isn't my fault, she thinks to the ghost in the mirror. *I didn't* do *anything.*

And that's the trouble. The words *bong* like doom in the middle of Sarah's brain. *You need to tell the police the truth.*

She doesn't know what that is. That afternoon, when her dad dragged twenty rats and five rabbits back, he only looked blank when she asked about Ms. Avery. *Never showed,* he grunted, then flung the rabbits onto planks set up on sawhorses by the fire barrel. *Strip out those muskrats first, then get a pot going and do the rabbits. Got my mouth set on bunny stew.*

When the police came three weeks later, Dad told them pretty much the same thing. *Never saw her.* Her dad's a stocky, ex–football jock with the neck and shoulders of an ox, so much kinky black hair on his arms and knuckles his buddies say his mom musta married Bigfoot, and a flat face that he knows how to rearrange. *It's real easy to get turned around out here,* Dad said, showing the detectives how the path forks after a quarter mile before both feeder trails peter out and the trees close in. Deep enough for a lake in places, the bog stretches five miles east and north. Why, you could yell yourself silly, and no one would hear. If Ms. Avery had a gun and fired off a couple rounds, sure, her dad would've heard. But there'd been no shots that afternoon. Sarah told the police that too. Her dad's nasty-looking Glock, as well as his shotgun and .22, were still in the shed where he kept spare traps, and that was the truth. (Now, the fact that no one bothered wondering why she might be *concerned* if one of those guns had developed legs . . . well, that was the truth, too.)

But—Ms. Avery's tone is stern—*that's not the* only *truth. Is it, sugar?*

I don't know what you mean. The ache in her temple is a steady throb keeping time with her heart. The pain's so bad her brain's going to run out of her ears any second.

"So," she chirps, as bright and *OH WOW!* as the guys on her mom's infomercials, the ones that promise tight glutes and rock-solid abs, "what's a *midé*"—her tongue works the unfamiliar words—"*wayan*, Hank?"

"Special kind of medicine bag. This one's a big old black bear paw." Hank's face folds in a frown. "Odd that a museum had it. A *midé*'s bag is supposed to be buried with its owner. Of course there's another reason why the museum people mighta wanted to get rid of it." Hank digs his nails into his knobby Adam's apple for a lazy scratch. "If my great-gran really *was* a sorcerer, that is."

"A sorcerer?" Bethie's mouth is as round as her eyes now. "Like a *witch*?"

"Yup. If the old stories are true?" Hank gives a grave nod. "This bag is cursed, inhabited by a restless spirit hungry for the guilty and sick of heart."

Of course, Ms. Avery *would* chime in.

Wellll, sugar, the ghost drawls, *I coulda told you that.*

"Here." Hank's pulled out an old book: *Ojibwe Religion and the Midewiwin*. "Says there were sorcerers who knew poisons, black magic, omens."

"How would you tell?" Sarah asks. "If this is a sorcerer's bag, I mean?"

Hellooo, Ms. Avery says. *Rotting ghost in the mirror?*

I'm not asking *you*. "Is it because it's a bear paw?" she says.

"Not necessarily. Bags are made from the skin of whatever spirit animal the healer meets in a vision quest. You know, where the initiates fast . . . means they don't eat," Hank adds in an aside for Bethie, "and then take themselves to a sweat lodge. Everything that's unclean comes out with the sweat, and I guess how long you sweat depended on how contaminated you are. Thing is, there are different degrees of *midé*. Like karate, you know? Different levels? A bear bag means you've had a lot of training."

"Is there stuff inside?" Bethie asks.

"Oh yeah. I'm sure there was more that's gotten lost or

stolen or just plain rotted over the years." Hank gently withdraws items that he lines up on the counter. "But these are pretty interesting."

"Rocks?" There are three pretty blah stones as well as a small string of glassy red beads and a black-tipped white feather with a rust-colored splotch. The only *really* cool item that snags her attention is a tiny bird's skull, with a black beak and a leather cord running through over-large sockets. Blotting sweat from her cheeks, Sarah says, irritably, "They're just *stones.*"

"*Wellll.*" Hank fingers a baggy wattle of skin under his chin. "Ojibwes believe everything's got a spirit, including trees, the earth, water . . . even rocks and crystals." He fingers the string of beads. "Like these amethysts."

"Amethyst is purple." Without realizing it, she's stroking the skull. The feel of pits and ridges where veins and arteries and nerves ran fills her with a shivery thrill.

"Not when it's got a lot of hematite like these. Then amethyst turns bloodred, a powerful color. And that eagle feather? Red spot means the owner killed someone."

"What about the skull?" The bone is so cool, she wants to hold it to her fevered skin like a wet compress.

"Screech owl. Eyes face forward, you know, and a screech is tiny, about"—Hank pinches off eight inches of air—"yay big."

"What's it for?"

"Well, for the Ojibwe, owls are bad omens. You hear or see one, death isn't far behind."

Whoooo. At the sound, Sarah snatches her hand from the skull as if it's gone white-hot. *Hoo-hoo,* Ms. Avery says.

Stop that. Sarah's jaw thrusts in a stubborn jut. *I can't help you.*

What makes you think that's why I've come, sugar?

"You know, now that I think about it"—Hank's lips pucker to a rosebud—"this bag holds nothing *but* death."

It pops out before Sarah can think about it. "Maybe that was your grandmother's special power. Maybe *that's* the curse."

"Bringer of Death?" The way Hank fingers that wattle, Sarah thinks he really does look like an old turkey vulture. "It would fit with the beads. This design?" Hank touches a cracked fingernail to the primitive outline of a bird. "That's a thunderbird. Means the bag has a lot of power. But," he says, turning over the pouch, "these two designs are the ones give me the willies."

One symbol's a gimme: two-legged, clawed, a head like Smokey's. Horns are weird, but . . . "A bear?" she says.

"Almost. Ever hear of skinwalkers?"

"Like mummies?" Bethie says.

Worse. Ms. Avery's left eyebrow tents, and that is when the skin tears free from her nose to reveal decaying muscle the color of mud on yellowish bone.

Oh! Sarah muscles back a shout as green ooze dribbles down Ms. Avery's cheek in a sludgy tear. Her stomach churns. *Stop that.*

I can't, the ghost says. *I won't.*

"Oh, much worse than mummies," Hank echoes as if he's channeling Ms. Avery too. "They're Navajo black witches, who use charms or shapeshift into any animal they choose, then stalk and murder their enemies."

"Sounds like voodoo," Sarah says. "Or like a werewolf." Or her dad, come to think of it, when he's had one too many or a couple pipes, which is most of the time. Then he's this raging, raw-eyed maniac. Not that Mom's much better. Two of them go at it? Spitting, hitting, punching, biting . . . like feral cats in a burlap sack.

"Every culture has its bogeymen. The thing about the dark path is that evil always returns full force to the place where it was born. That's why the *midés* don't talk about sorcery. Doesn't mean it's not practiced, though. I think that *this*"—he taps the beaded bear again—"represents the Ojibwe version of a skinwalker, only they call it a bearwalker."

"What about this?" Grimacing at the brush of thin, decrepit fur against her hand—it really *is* nasty, like rangy dead possum—Sarah fingers a weird beaded figure with horns and wings that sprout from naked ribs. "What's the flying skeleton about?"

"Maybe it's a black witch-angel or something," Bethie says.

Hank consults his book. "If I'm reading right, this is a *maji-aya`awish*, a real powerful, evil *manidoo* with skin so glassy you see its bones, and eyes that glow like fire."

No. Sarah meets Ms. Avery's gaze, which is red, steady, and hot. "What's its name?" she asks, not knowing why she *needs* to know. She palms sweat from her neck. "What do they call it?"

"Longfellow said it was Death in that old Hiawatha poem. The Ojibwe call it 'Baykok.' But me?" Hank bobs his head, that vulture's wattle wobbling. "I think *Murderer* 'bout sums it up."

There is a gush of icy air. "Kids." Their mother, face pinched, hangs in the open door. "Time to get going." She sucks a cancer stick, then jets twin streamers of blue smoke from her nose. "Got to hit the food pantry before it closes."

Normally, Sarah'd be embarrassed, but she's desperate to leave this stifling little station. For the first time, though, she wonders: Will Ms. Avery follow? Hang with her forever, like Hank said about hungry spirits? *Oh, don't be stupid. You're not Ojibwe, and she's a ghost.* She bets that bag is the only reason she can really *see* Ms. Avery so clearly. Leave the *midé wayan* behind, and she's home free.

You keep telling yourself that. But Ms. Avery doesn't sound angry or even amused. Just tired, like a teacher waiting for a slow student to finally catch on. *We're not quit yet, you and me.*

"Hold on there, kids." Hank's rummaging in a pocket. "Got a couple coins need a home."

"Hank, you shouldn't," Mom says.

"My shop, my rules." To Sarah and Bethie: "Go give that jawbreaker machine a workout, why don'tcha?"

Sarah has never felt less like having candy in her whole life. "Sure!" Plastering on a grin, she leads Bethie to a trio of old-fashioned candy dispensers full of M&M'S and gumballs. Behind, her mother begins: "Hank, about the bill . . ."

Hank: "Now, don't you fret, Jean. Let's go outside and . . ."

God. Slipping in a dime, Sarah cranks the jawbreaker handle hard. *Can you please just stop begging, Mom? Be a grown-up for once.*

"I don't like the white ones." Bethie gives her candy a forlorn stare. "I want cherry."

"Luck of the draw." There's a cruel lash to her tone that sounds a lot like Dad. But she's not a fan of the white ones either. They look like fish eyes. As Bethie's lower lip begins to quiver, she snarls, "Oh, fine, *fine!*" Snatching up the white jawbreaker from her sister, she deposits their second dime and gives the dispenser another vicious crank. Of *course*, what rattles out is red, which means cherry, and that's *way* better than the ooky, white, fish-eyeball variety, and what a *gyp*.

"*Here.*" Furious, she almost throws the candy at her sister. *Suck on it and choke, you little . . .*

"You don't have to be so mean." The jawbreaker is so huge Bethie looks like a chipmunk with a toothache. "Aren't you going to eat yours?"

"Yes." Sliding the white jawbreaker onto her tongue, Sarah wrinkles her nose. The candy's so ancient it tastes like an old chicken bone. Through the station's windows she can see Hank listening patiently as her mother talk talk talk talk *talks*. Sarah knows the litany by heart: bills for this, expenses for that, and kids these days, they grow so fast, always needing new clothes, new shoes and . . .

That's right. Blame us. Eyes stinging, she turns away, absently smearing sweat from her cheeks—and then she is standing over the *midé wayan*, her fingers tracing its beaded patterns, tangling in its long wiry fur that is not so unpleasant now but somehow softer.

"Baykok." She tries that out, lets its weight sit on her tongue. "Skinwalker." A good word. "*Bear*walker." That feels even better.

Bethie, at the door: "Are we going?"

"Yeah." *No.* She is sweat-slicked and very hot, but now she really doesn't want to leave. She is aware of Ms. Avery in the mirror and

(Murderer)

Baykok against her skin, and she thinks, *I want you.*

That's right. Those fiery eyes laser words into her brain. *We're meant for each other. We'll make a really good team.*

"I don't know what you mean," she says, around candy that doesn't taste right and feels . . . strange. "Team?"

"What?" Tonguing her jawbreaker to the opposite cheek, Bethie's doing the freezing little kid two-step. "Come on, Sarah, it's *cold*."

"Yeah, yeah, yeah." But, as she turns, she quickly sweeps

a hand over the counter and then into her pocket, the movement automatic, almost unconscious.

Or maybe she can't let herself really think what this means
just yet.

They are hauling open balky doors on rusting hinges when
Bethie asks, "Who were you talking to, Mommy?"

"My lawyer." With a weary sigh her mother backhands
hair from her forehead. "Your dad made bail."

"Wait." A butterfly that might be both dread and hope flutters in Sarah's throat. Things were never great, but with Dad
back, they'll have more money. If Sarah never sees another
food pantry box of Kraft macaroni and cheese, it'll be too soon.
There is Ms. Avery, of course, but she's only a bad memory, a
ghost in a gas station mirror. Of course . . . she dips a hand into
her pocket to caress something small, smooth, not quite like
stone . . . maybe some ghosts are like bad pennies and turn up
no matter what, even though you're old enough to know better
than to want them to stick around. "He's coming home?"

"He's not supposed to. That restraining order's still in
effect." Her mother socks a key into the ignition. "For all the
good it will . . ."

At that moment, the station's door bangs open, and there's
Hank. "Girls?"

Oh boy. That flutter is definitely dread now. The candy
in her mouth is odd, weird, strange. *He knows what I did.*

Shit—this is a word she's never let herself actually say—*shit, what's* wrong *with me?*

"Here you go." Trotting up, Hank proffers two foil-wrapped packets, each roughly the size and shape of a giant beef brat, and then a small paper bag. "Napkins, ketchup, relish, mustard. Now, *don't*." Waving her mother off. "I don't want to hear it, Jean. Those brats have been turning since July. They're probably rubber by now."

Bethie is beaming. "*Thanks*, Hank! I *love* brats!"

"And they love you, sugar." Hank's tousling Bethie's hair, but his eyes tick to Sarah. "Why, you're whiter'n a ghost, honey, and sweating to beat the band. You coming down with something?"

"Yeah . . . I mean, no." The words ride a breathless gasp. She needs a shower, and this jawbreaker is *awful*. She's going to spit out the stupid thing as soon as she can. "Thank you, Hank." Before he can respond, she practically dives into the car and slams the door. Reaching around for her belt, Sarah hauls it across her lap and—

And Ms. Avery is there.

In the *car.*

No. Sarah's eyes bug. *Nonono!*

Ms. Avery smells like the inside of a deer that Sarah's dad's just gutted, its liver and lungs and intestines and bulging blue colon mounded in a steaming, putrid mess that reeks of dying blood and new shit. Her eyes are fire.

Hey, sugar. When she smiles, Ms. Avery's mouth splits into a wide clown's grin. Mottled with decay and Coke-bottle green, the flesh from cheekbone to jaw peels away to hang in ragged flaps. Dead-white maggots squirm from Ms. Avery's ears and nostrils. *That brat smells so good. Can I have a bite?*

"No!" She doesn't know if she screams this out loud. Later, when she has time to think about it, probably she doesn't scream, because her mother keeps driving as Bethie munches a brat drippy with ketchup that squirts like blood from the bun. "Go away!"

Now? We're just getting started. Skimming a blue-black tongue, Ms. Avery flips maggots into her mouth, then grinds down until they burst in snotty, white spurts of maggot guts. *Mmm-MMM*, the ghost says.

Oh my God. Sarah suddenly remembers the jawbreaker, how odd it feels and tastes and . . . "Guh!" Spitting out the candy, she looks at the gluey orb in her palm . . .

And it is an eye.

Soft. Trembling. Milky white, with tiny green veins. Its iris is cloudy with death, but not so much that she can't tell that its color was once deep brown, like fine chocolate.

Oh jeez. Picking at her teeth, Ms. Avery sucks the remains of a maggot from a fingernail grown long as a talon. *I wondered where that got to.*

"Mommy? *Mommy?*" Bethie gives a sudden, shrill shout. "Sarah's being sick!"

• • •

Hours later:

She's burning up, sprawled in a tangle of sweat-soaked sheets. She's inched as far away as possible from her little sister, who shares with her in winter. Deeply asleep, Bethie lets out the occasional musical snore. From downstairs drifts the low mutter of the TV punctuated by the occasional, breathless *OH WOW TIGHT GLUTES* note. Infomercials mean Mom's probably finished off that bottle of cheap red wine she snagged on the way home. You'd think that Sarah puking her guts out might prompt a mom to, oh, take her sick kid home or at least climb out and hold her kid's forehead while she yorps, but *nooo*. (Instead, Ms. Avery did that, one skeletal hand, ooky with liquefying flesh, on her forehead and the other, equally as disgusting, holding back Sarah's hair.) After Sarah emptied her stomach and was down to dry heaves, her mother swung by Jake's Liquor, where her credit was still good.

It's not right. Sweat dribbles down her temples to soak her hair. Raw eyed and furious, Sarah stares at shadows swarming and bunching in the well of her ceiling. Her busy, busy fingers caress what she's stolen from Hank. *Mom says we have no money, but she can buy smokes and booze.*

Adults are such pricks. In a far corner Ms. Avery—or whatever the ghost's becoming—perches ghoulishly like a gigantic, malevolent parrot atop the rail of a straight-backed chair. When the ghost moves, it rustles like dry corn husks.

Yet her voice seeps from the tiny owl's skull Sarah holds. *But you're just as bad, you liar.*

I'm not a liar. She fingers the skull. She just didn't volunteer. Don't ask, don't tell. *He's my dad.*

Among other things.

"What does that mean?" And, oh, why isn't she surprised when the skull chooses not to answer? *Fine, keep secrets. Bitch.* (Another word she never says but which feels *good* and *right* nonetheless.) She shifts her gaze back to the ceiling. Those shadows creep her out, and after what she's seen today, that's saying something. She thinks they are faces. In fact, they're like those monster-angels from an Indiana Jones movie: first pretty and then raving skeletons. Heck, maybe that's Ms. Avery. Maybe Sarah's only getting the monster-angel she deserves.

A rustle from the corner: *Perhaps I am the angel you need.*

Sarah returns her gaze to the tiny skull's wise, eyeless sockets. "For what?"

Big surprise: no answer. *Bitch.* She clenches the owl skull, hard and then harder. Be easy to crush, grind to dust. Her dad does that. Says bone's good for the garden, so he dumps the skeletons of his kills into a fire barrel, gives it all a good, long squirt of lighter fluid, and *whump!* Then her dad stirs and stirs, like a witch at a cauldron, raising great black clouds that coat her nose and throat and turn her spit black.

He's inside you, the owl skull says. *You're infected with him, his crime.*

"No, I'm just a *kid.* Can I help it that you were so stupid you didn't stop to think that maybe he was *danger—*"

All of a sudden, a knife of bright yellow light slices her room, going from left to right as someone turns into their drive.

Uh-oh, the skull says.

Car. Her heart crams up against her teeth. Whoever this is, she can tell from the way the gauzy curtain has lit up that he/she/it is simply waiting, coming no closer but not going away either. Pulse thumping, she holds her breath and listens above the still-muttering TV. After a second she catches the slight *chug-chug-chug* of an idling engine. Who would come by this late at night?

Take a guess. In the corner the Ms. Avery–thing swells and stretches with a rustle. A limb moves into and then out of the light. The moment is brief, but Sarah can see how thin Ms. Avery's arm now is, the skin shiny and taut. *Skeletal.* Ms. Avery's like an X-ray come to life.

Forget me, the skull says as the light firing Sarah's curtains winks out. *You've got bigger problems.*

Slipping from bed, Sarah pads to the window, then carefully inserts a single finger into the slit between her curtains. High above the trees the moon is a thick, blue-white thumbnail. Lances of bright silver moonlight spear through trees and glimmer over a truck perched at the very mouth of the drive. Then, an orange flash from the truck's dome light as the driver pops his door, and Sarah gets the general impression of a stocky man with big shoulders, a bull neck. Unfolding from his seat, he stands, muscled arms loose by his sides. She doesn't need light to know that his hands are large, the knuckles sprouting black wiry corkscrews, the backs matted with so much hair his buddies tease that his mom musta married Bigfoot.

It still might be okay. Dread walks the knobs of her spine. *He's not coming any . . .* That thought stutters as he pulls something long and heavy from the truck.

You know, the skull says, *now would be a good time.*

"Bethie!" Whirling, she dashes to the bed. "Get up, Bethie, get up!" Then she's out the door, sprinting for the stairs. "Mom! *MOM!*"

The only light downstairs is the soft blue pulse of the still-muttering TV. On the screen some guy's spazzing about soap guaranteed to take away any stain, even blood. Sprawled on a lumpy couch, her mother's asleep, head flung back, her neck arched as a swan's. The air is fruity with cheap booze.

"Mom!" She gives her a violent shake. "Wake *up!*"

"Huh?" Her mother opens a single bleary eye. "Wuh?"

"Mom, get *up!*" Sarah throws a look toward the boarded-up bay window. She can't see out, but that also means her dad can't see in. *So, if we're quiet, move fast, we can get out of the house.* She lowers her voice to a whisper. "Mom, Dad's *here.*"

"Daddy?" Sarah can't tell if her sister is scared or excited. Maybe she's a bit of both. "He's outside?" Bethie asks.

"Wuh?" Moaning, her mom struggles to a sit. "Honey, go

back to bed." Propping her forehead in one hand, she yawns. "Your dad's not . . ."

"Mom, I *saw* him. His truck's blocking the driveway." When her mother doesn't respond, she gives her another impatient poke. "Mom, *please*."

"Sweetie," her mother says, thickly, "I don't think . . ."

And that's when the lights go out.

Oh no. Sarah stares at the ceiling as if this might make the suddenly dark fixture wink back to life. In the corner the TV screen is only a muddy, gray, quickly fading glow. "It's Dad," she says, her voice hoarse with urgency. "Mom, he cut the lights."

"But why?" Bethie asks. "Mommy, did you forget to pay the 'lectric bill?"

"No," her mother says, her voice still gluey, although Sarah can now hear a note of worry.

You're running out of time. The skull warms the hollow of her throat. Until this moment, Sarah hasn't realized that she slipped the cord around her neck. *Get out, now.*

The skull's right. "Mom." Sarah pulls at her arm. "We have to *go*!"

"Go?" her mother echoes.

"Go where?" Bethie says. "You mean, out . . ."

BANG! The sound is sharp, hard, an explosion. Crying out, Sarah wheels around as, from just beyond the front door, there comes a harsh bellow: "Jean?" Another *bang* as either

her dad's fist—or the club end of that bat or axe—connects with the front door. *"Jean?"*

"Oh!" There is a glassy *clink* as either her mother's knee or hand knocks a bottle or glass. Something topples, and then the stink of booze rises in a stinging cloud. "Oh, sweet Jesus," her mother says, but she's on her feet at least.

"Jean!"—and then there is a sound that is not a *bang* or *bap* but a hollow *chock*, and Sarah thinks, *Axe.* The cheap door bawls a high, grinding squeal that echoes Bethie's shrill screech. "Open the damn *door!*" her dad shouts.

"Mom!" Sarah finds her mother's wrist and hangs on. "What do we do?"

"I . . ." Her mother swallows. "Basement. Or your room. Lock the door and . . ."

"Against an *axe*?" Another hollow *chock.* The front door rattles in its frame, and something—a chunk of wood—*tocks* to the floor. Splinters of light seep through sudden cracks in wood. "Mom, we can't. He'll break through every door if he has to, and there's no way out of the basement!" Get trapped down there and they'll be like muskrats that save her dad the trouble. "What do we . . ."

Here. Craning, Sarah looks down the hall toward the kitchen. There, two red sparks hover in midair. *Back door. This way. Hurry.*

"We'll go out the kitchen." Sarah tugs harder at her mother's hand. "Mom, we have to leave!"

"Into the w-w-woods?" Hiccupping, Bethie's voice hitches. "It's d-d-dark!"

"No, not the woods." Sarah's thinking of the shed, her dad's nasty Glock, the rifle. If she can get to a *gun* . . .

And do what? From its place around her neck, the skull thrums. *The shotgun and pistol are too heavy. You might manage the rifle, but you've never shot a moving target, much less a person. No, Sarah, there's another way.*

"What other way?" Sarah shouts at the cinder-red eyes. "What are you talking about?"

"S-Sarah?" Bethie wails. And her mother: "Sarah, who are you talking to?"

Sarah pays them no mind. "*Tell* me!"

Do what I say. The skull is relentless, as remorseless as the tide. *This house is lost. Run, Sarah. Run NOW.*

"*BITCH!*" Sarah rages as, outside, her father bellows again—and they are, for that second, one voice eerily in sync. "This way!" Sarah yanks her sister toward the kitchen. "Mom, come on!"

"Wait, wait!" Bethie balks. "Sarah, the woods are scary. . . ."

"Scarier than Dad?" She isn't wild about the woods either. Where would they go? Her dad knows them. They're *his*. No, best to get to the shed, a gun . . .

No, Sarah. The owl has grown so hot that it is flame. *Do what I* . . .

"Jean?" Through a jagged gap in the front door, Sarah sees

her father. His face is thickly bearded as if his skin hasn't seen a razor in months. His long hair is a ratty tangle. He looks like a mountain man who's been hunkered in a cave. "Damn it, look what you made me do."

"What do you want, John?" Her mother's come to stand between them and her husband. Her tone is surprisingly steady. "You want to talk? Fine. But you have to stop this."

"Mom!" Sarah pitches her voice into a harsh whisper. "What are you *doing*?"

Giving you a chance. The Avery-thing is just to her right, above her shoulder. Sarah can't tell how large it is, but her hair riffles over her forehead from the force of its wings. *Run, Sarah.*

"Goddamn it, Jean, will you just open . . ." Another blast from the axe, and now there is blue light as moonbeams spill through wide splits.

Her mother doesn't budge, and now Sarah understands why her mother stands where she does: so their father can't see where they've gone. *No, I can't leave you, Mom. We can't . . .*

"Go." Her mother doesn't look, but her hand moves in a quick snap. "Get out, girls. Go now."

"But, Muh-muh-muh*mmeee!*" Bethie wails. "We c-can't . . ."

Yes, we can. We have to. And maybe it will be all right; maybe nothing bad will happen, and maybe pigs have wings, but at that moment, Sarah has never loved her mother more for giving them this one chance.

She's right. Go, the skull urges. *Don't make this be for nothing.*

"Come on, Bethie." Dashing to the back door, Sarah wrenches it open at the same instant that her father finally breaks through. She doesn't look around, but she hears her mother trying to soothe him. "John, take it easy. We can talk." Then: "John, I don't want to die."

"Yeah?" The word is rough, guttural, a growl. "You shoulda thought of that before."

Sarah doesn't wait for any more. She pulls her sister out the back door, and they plunge into the night.

The cold slaps. Icy fingers jab through her thin pj's to sting her arms, her legs. Stones and twigs bite her bare feet, and she stumbles as her toes fetch up on a rock. A bolt of pain shudders into her right ankle, and she gasps, her breath bluing in the moonlight.

"Ow, *ow!*" Beside her, Bethie staggers. "This *hurts!*"

"Too bad." They are a good fifty yards from the house now, out by the burn barrel with its oily reek. "We have to keep going. We can't—"

A scream, high and shrill and bloody, rips the night. Starting, Sarah whirls as another scream boils from the black maw of the open back door.

"Mom! She's *hurt!*" Bethie cries out. "Sarah, Mommy's . . ."

Mom's dead. "Come *on.*" Turning away, she pulls her

still-stumbling sister after. She is aware of a presence above and off her right shoulder, a rush of air. She risks a single glance, and it is so odd because, in the moonlight, there ought to be something: an outline, a form. Yet there are only those steady red eyes and a larger blackness looming in the dark surround. From far away, in the bog, comes the *hoo-hoo-hoo* of a horned owl, doleful as a foghorn.

"But wh-where?" Bethie is gasping. "Where are we going?"

The woods, the skull says. *The bog.*

No way. "Over here," Sarah says, veering not left but right toward a wink of glass.

"The shed?" Bethie asks. "Are we going to hide?"

If they are lucky, they won't have to. Grappling for the knob, Sarah heaves a relieved sigh as the cold metal turns, and the tongue snicks back. *All right.* But when she pushes, the door creaks only two inches before hitching up with a metallic clank. *No, God, that's not fair!* Her fingers spider over the rectangle of a hasp and staple secured with a chunky padlock. *No, when did he do that?*

Go into the woods. The skull's voice drills into the center of her brain. *Head left, for the bog.*

"No, are you *crazy*?" she hisses. "*Help* us!"

"Sarah?" Bethie sounds even more frightened. "Who . . ."

I am. I will. This comes not from the skull but her far left and high up. Sarah lifts her gaze to find the Avery-thing's eyes burning bright as beacons. *Bethie. Up here.*

"A tree?" Sarah says, and then realizes: *Wait . . .*

"What tree?" Bethie asks.

"My old tree house." She looks down at her sister. "You climb and hide . . ."

"Girls?" Jumping, they both wheel. The house is far enough distant now that their father is only a lumpish bear of a man on the back stoop. "Girls?" From the question and then the pause, it's clear he can't see them. *"Kids?"*

"Listen," Sarah murmurs to her sister. "When I say go, you head for the tree house. Stay there until it's safe, okay?"

Bethie's stricken. "You're *leaving*?"

"Just for a little while." She grabs her sister in a rough hug. "As soon as I move, you run, okay?"

Bethie presses her face into Sarah's middle. "Please, don't die."

"I won't," she says, not knowing if this is a lie. Then, before she can change her mind, she pivots and sprints for an open patch of ground splashed with moonlight.

"Hey!" her father shouts, and she knows she's been spotted. "Sarah, wait!"

"No!" The trees suddenly loom, and then she's in the woods. The air *hooshes* in a gush, or maybe those are wings beating at her back, speeding her on. The forest is alive, all greedy arms and whippy fingers and sharp talons snatching her hair. Something juts for an eye, and she gasps, jerking aside, feeling a branch draw a line of fire on her cheek. Over the thunder of her pulse she can hear him thrashing after, bull-ish and wild, hot on her trail.

He missed Bethie. Her breath tears in and out of her throat. *She's safe.* But maybe not for long. *If I can get to the bog* . . . Yet how will that help? She doesn't know, and neither the Avery-thing nor the skull will say.

"Sarah!" Her father bellows something formless, the bawl of a dragon, a gargoyle. A devil. Maybe, in these woods and at this moment, he is no more human than the Avery-thing. Maybe the animal in him is so immense he can't contain it any longer. *"SARAHHHH!"*

Ahead, the fork appears. Go right, and she can circle out of the woods and to the road. Instead, she veers left. Her lungs burn. Her heart thrashes the cage of her ribs. *Come on, come on.* Her feet are one bright blister of agony, and she is vaguely aware that the sudden slippery feeling on her soles must be blood. *How much farther* . . .

And then there it is, flashing to brilliance. Studded with tamaracks, as straight and true as ships' masts, the bog gleams like a vast mirror-ocean. Along the deepest channels to her left, muskrat houses rise in messy jackstraw islands.

Now what? What do I . . . Suddenly, the ground under her feet turns cold. Startled, she comes to a dead stop. *Ice.* No wonder the bog is so bright. *It's iced over.* Is it thick enough? At the thought her toes curl like frightened snails. *I can't walk on thin ice.*

You don't have a choice, the skull hisses. *Go.*

"Sarah!" It's her dad, coming on strong, blowing hard as a bull. "Sarah, don't make me have to punish you!"

Go! Turning, she sprints onto the ice, something she shouldn't be able to do but does. She is moving fast, nearly flying, racing over paths of glare ice. Yet, with every step, the bog shudders and groans and cracks. It ought to break apart but doesn't. *What am I doing, what's happening?* This bog and these channels go on for miles. It hits her then that she hasn't seen the Avery-thing's eyes in what seems like forever. There is no sense of anything at her shoulder. *It's gone?* The thought makes her stop. At a glance she can see that she's somehow made it to the middle of a broad expanse of ice, a span that is easily an acre, studded with only a few muskrats' houses poking up like dark anthills.

"Where are you? Ms. Avery?" No answer. Hauling out the tiny screech owl skull on its leather cord, she gives it a ferocious squeeze. "Don't leave me!"

"Believe me, sugar"—and at that, her heart fails because she knows, even before she turns: she's done for.

"I won't," her dad says.

"Come on now." His voice sounds like he hasn't used it in a century. Her father holds out a hand, and she can see a thick, oily stain slicking his palm that stinks of wet iron and which she knows is her mother's blood. Moonlight breaks over his head and shoulders, and if it is possible, he is hairier than ever, as shaggy as a beast.

And who, she wonders, is the bearwalker now?

"It's not safe out here," her father snarls in his new animal-voice. "This ice is too thin. Come with me now."

Go with him, and she's dead. Or she'll become what he is, which amounts to the same thing.

She slides back a step.

"Sarah." His face darkens. "What are you doing?"

Another step back, and then she sees what she hasn't noticed: that she's blundered onto the bog where the channels are deep and the trapping best.

"Sarah, damn it! Come . . ." Abruptly, he lunges. Gasping, she stumbles, her heels tangling, and then she's falling as he looms. *"DAMN IT!"* he roars. *"Look* what you've made me . . ."

There is an enormous *CRACK* louder than any blast from any weapon she has ever heard. Her father suddenly cries out, throwing up his arms in a wild windmilling semaphore, and for a second, she thinks, *He's shot, someone's—*

With a loud groan, the bone-white ice gives, opening wide as a mouth, as the jaws of a skull . . . and swallows her father whole.

A gurgle. A slosh. The *chik* of broken ice against ice, and the more distant echoes of her father's single cry. Close by, an owl hoots.

Silence.

For a shuddering instant Sarah can only pull in one ragged breath after the other. Her heart's booming. Spread before her, the open blight in the ice is black and still.

"Dad?" The word is tiny. High above, the wind sighs and makes the naked tree limbs clack. *Like bone.* She looks up. No fiery eyes stare back. "Ms. Avery?" Moving to a crouch, she creeps toward a ragged lip of ice. "Dad? *Daddy?*" The inky water is still. "Dad, can you hear . . ."

All of a sudden the water ruptures in an icy geyser. Breaching the surface, her father porpoises in a huge gush and draws in a shrieking breath. "S-S-Sarah! *H-honey!*" Spluttering, her father flails. His terrified eyes are wide and white as boiled eggs. It might be her imagination, but his face is clearer, not as hairy, the animal in him . . . less? Fading? "Sarah! I'm caught! My feet . . . the rats . . . I'm . . ." His body slides back now, his face submerging again before he bobs back, vomiting water. *"I'M TRAPPED!"*

Her father's voice from another time floats through her mind: *Rat saves you the trouble by drowning hisself.* His chin slides beneath the surface, and then his face. Choking, he surges up again. "H-help! Help me! I'm sinking, b-baby, I'm s-sinking"—his body slips down again, and now he's tipped his head so far back, he's shouting up at the sky and into the night—"S-Sarah, don't let me d-drown, d-don't . . ."

Dad. It's his voice now, his real voice. He killed her mother;

he must've murdered Ms. Avery. *He's sick. It's the drugs, his temper, the booze.* She might never forgive him, but she can't let him drown. Not now when, at least, he's a man again.

"Daddy!" She scurries forward on the ice, but awkwardly, aware that the ice is much more slippery, as if whatever dark magic has led her to this place is fast draining away too. As he begins to sink again, she flattens onto her belly and worms for the edge. She hears a tiny *tick* of the owl's skull, still on its leather cord around her neck, against the ice. Thrusting her hand out over the water, she shouts to her struggling father, "Grab it, Daddy! Grab onto me! I'll save you!"

"That's g-good, th-that's . . ." Lunging, her father grapples for her hand. Their fingers brush, but then he's falling back, coughing, spluttering, sliding away from her.

"NO!" Her chest hovers over black water; her naked toes dig into glare ice. "Daddy, Dad, take my *hand*!"

With a gigantic effort he thrashes up. His hands fall in an arc, grappling first in her hair, then slipping away before catching: his right digging into her shoulder—and the left knotting in the owl necklace around her throat.

"Get me *out*!" His teeth are set in a panicked rictus. *"Get me out of here!"*

"I c-cuh . . ." He's choking her. The leather cord cuts into her throat, and her air is gone. Bright orange spangles burst over her vision even as it is darkening, and she can feel herself being pulled, inexorably, to her death. He's got her; he's killing her. Maybe he knows this, maybe not. Maybe, regardless, he doesn't care. *D-Duh* . . . A hole opens in the center of her vision. She claws futilely at his hand that is tight and then tighter on the cord that is sawing through her skin, cutting off her air. Her blood pounds, and yet everything else is fading, even her father's shouts. Distantly, she feels her naked feet drumming solid ice, and now there is frigid water slopping against her face, her chest. *D-Daddy . . . p-please . . .*

Let me. An arm that is only bone suddenly emerges from the dark waters, and then the Avery-thing is rising from the bog like some prehistoric behemoth. *He's mine.*

Her father screams, a high keening wail. There is a jolt as the leather cord snaps. The pressure around Sarah's neck is suddenly gone. By all rights, she should swoon into the water, and yet she feels something—a hand? A *claw*?—shove and send her sprawling back onto solid ice.

In the water, above her father, the Avery-thing unfurls. Tipped with razor talons, its massive wings stretch to their full length. It is *huge*, awesome and beautiful and terrible all at once, something that lives only in a high-fever dream. For the first time, Sarah clearly sees the spirit as it now is: all bone and glass-skin and hot scarlet eyes so bright they ought to boil away her sight.

"SARAH!" Her father's face is a white mask of terror. The owl's skull still dangles from his left fist. *"SARAH, DON'T LET IT TAKE ME, DON'T LET IT . . ."*

• • •

Except for Hank, no one will believe her. They will make her see a psychiatrist who will decide that she was delirious with fever and fear and very lucky to escape, what with such thin ice. She and Bethie will bury their parents and, eventually, live with a distant cousin of their mom's.

When Sarah asks to go to Ms. Avery's funeral, the shrink thinks this will bring *closure*, a ridiculous shrink-word for *forgetting* (as if nightmares can be wrapped with a bow and slotted onto a high back shelf). The casket is shut on account of how long Ms. Avery, wrapped in the linked chain she'd been strangled with and then secured to weighted muskrat traps, had been submerged. Even though the deep water was frigid, the fish and muskrats were hungry. Instead, Ms. Avery will smile from a picture surrounded with red geraniums, and never once throw Sarah a wink.

But that is the future she doesn't know yet.

For now, this one instant, she still clings to hope the way a drowning man, like her father, clutches at a straw—or a tiny, fragile skull, in the belief that he still might cheat destiny.

"W-wait!" Eyes streaming, Sarah crouches, shivering like a small, frightened animal. She is so cold, as if the long fever of her guilt has finally broken, and she is fated to live after all. "Please! C-can't he . . . maybe I can . . ."

No. Some things are beyond repair. Let him go, Sarah. Wrapping its skeleton's arms tight, the Avery-thing—*Manidoo,*

Maji-aya`awish, Baykok, Murderer, whatever its true name—folds her screaming father close in a last, fatal embrace. *Let this evil go, and live.*

Then the Avery-thing slips beneath the bog's black surface, drawing her father away from the light and her life—down deep and into the dark.

Ilsa J. Bick is a child psychiatrist as well as a film scholar, surgeon wannabe, former Air Force major, and an award-winning, bestselling author of dozens of short stories and novels, including the critically acclaimed Ashes Trilogy, *Drowning Instinct*, and, most recently, her Dark Passages series: *White Space* (long-listed for the Stoker) and *The Dickens Mirror*. Currently she lives on a mountain in Alabama with several furry creatures and her husband. On occasion she even feeds them. Follow her, as well as the cats, the backyard, assorted wildlife, Friday's Cocktails, and Sunday's Cakes:

Website: ilsajbick.com

Twitter and Instagram: @ilsajbick

Facebook: facebook.com/ilsa.j.bick